SEE YOU IN BUDAPEST

(OPERATION BLACK SUN)

JO KAPLAN

Prime Seven Media
518 Landmann St.
Tomah City, WI 54660

Printed in the United States of America

TABLE OF CONTENTS

MAIN CHARACTERS

Mario Vaillante: son of Caterina Vassalli of Santa Tecla and Ervé Vaillante

Cynthia Uberti Stephenson Biographical daughter of William Uberti and adopted daughter of William Stephenson, founder of the OSS.

Walter Westerhaupt son of Karl Westerhaupt gunnery officer of the auxiliary cruiser Koenisberg and Freja Olesen

Horst Luderiz Westerhaupt Walter's half-brother grew up in German South West Africa in Walwis bay.

Count Carlo Vassalli of Santa Tecla grandfather of Mario Vaillante

Sabine Rinkweiser, daughter of a Swiss Foreign Ministry official Fabian Rinkweiser

Albert Einstein

Otto Hahn

Werner Hieisenberg

Hector Majorana

Anne Marie Lesser aka Madamoiselle Docteur

Caireen O'Mallei tutors Cynthia at Vassar College

1

THE PAST NEVER DIES

Hungarian-Austrian border, December 1956…

It had just snowed, the white blanket was thick and soft, it could have looked like a Christmas postcard, but the spirit of the group of people who were struggling forward in that frozen cream, had nothing to do with the most beautiful celebration of the year.

They were moving forward on a barely visible path between the fir trees, also covered with snow. It was night and terribly cold. Greta had wrapped her son in long strips of wool blanket that ran behind her back, keeping the child glued to her chest, protected inside the large padded military coat that the young woman had put on, along with a couple of wool sweaters, salvaged as best she could, from which the baby's head barely stuck out. The baby was sleeping. He had stopped coughing, fortunately. Greta checked at regular intervals that he was breathing, she was terrified at the idea that he might die suddenly, even though her maternal instinct made her feel that her creature would fight and win the battle against death.

They had fled Budapest, just in time before a raid by Russian military police descended on the old building where they had taken refuge, immediately after the end of the uprising. Who could have betrayed them? They were spoiled for choice. After the popular uprising in October, the Russians had played the moderation card, but things had not gone as planned. Hotheads and utopian hopes for freedom, international pressure, appeals from intellectuals... in short, the situation had gotten out of hand and the freezing winter of Soviet repression had arrived. Spies and traitors had sprung up like mushrooms, many of them were just victims, who had spoken out to save their lives and those of their families.

Walter stopped and looked around at the three people who were part of the group together with Greta, Hagen and little Loengrin. They looked at him in turn, as one looks at a messiah from whom one expects salvation:

"What's happening?" Greta asked, murmuring.

<<All this snow and darkness, I can't find my bearings. Then this damned forest helps even less... We should be close to the Austrian border, but those Russian bastards have removed every sign indicating the border, we could already be in Austria or we could still be in Hungary >>

Greta looked at Walter, at the other people who were with them, they all looked exhausted. They had been marching for hours, without eating or drinking. The child was starting to move, and Greta felt that he would wake up, keeping him quiet would be a problem. The forest seemed to be about to end, about a hundred meters away you could see a long valley free of trees. Walter checked the compass, the area where the trees ended was towards the south. There, somewhere there must be the Austrian border. The man signaled to stop and stay in the shelter of the mighty trunks. He approached the edge of the forest and saw something that filled his heart with joy. About two hundred meters away you could see a long row of lit up Christmas trees, from their position you could tell that they marked the border between Austria and Hungary. The only way to allow the fugitives to understand where their destination was, without creating diplomatic incidents with the uncomfortable Soviet neighbor.

Two hundred meters, only two hundred meters between freedom and death, Walter turned back.

<<Listen, we are very close to the border. Beyond those trees you can see an endless row of lit up Christmas trees, marking the border. You have to reach them ...- then he looked at Greta and Hagen- I will not follow you, I will stay here to cover you, I am sure that the Russians are lurking somewhere and in any case we cannot run the risk of moving all in the open>>

Greta looked at him with a stern and sad expression. She knew that it was not just what he was saying, she knew that he would go back and continue his work, according to the orders of the head of the West German secret service, Rehinardt Gehlen and therefore she knew that she would not see him again any time soon. Maybe she would never see him again.

Walter responded to her look: <<Greta, don't worry, it's a matter of time, I'll join you>> he lied, knowing that the girl now knew him and the world he moved in, too well to believe him.

He took the PPSh43 out of his backpack, opened the folding butt plate and cocked the bolt of the machine pistol. He looked around, then began to advance through the snow to the edge of the woods. He took a pair of binoculars from a haversack at his side and looked at the line of trees. Between the bushes on the other side of the bare strip he saw something that was glowing slightly in the light of one of the Christmas trees; they were the lenses of a telescope with which an agent of the Osterreichen Zollwachen, the Austrian border guard, was observing the Hungarian part of the camp. Walter signaled his group to come closer, then took another look around the horizon and saw them; to their right, a little more than three hundred meters ahead, crouched in the snow were three Russian soldiers, one with a Moisin Nagant rifle with a telescoping rifle, the other two were armed with Kalashnikovs, they were waiting for their prey.

Walter had everyone come closer, took out a piece of paper and a pencil and wrote in German "I'm moving away, when you hear shooting start running, towards the point I'll point out" and he signaled all four towards the bush where he had seen the Austrian gendarmes.

Then he looked at them and raised his thumb, staring at them with intent. He looked at them all one by one, he saw the child's head sticking out just a little from the collar of Greta's coat, he had a hard time looking away from that scene. Greta was staring at him with a firm expression, he came closer to her and murmured in her ear: <<We'll see each other soon... trust me>>. She struggled to swallow a sob, stopped a small tear with her only free hand, then signaled him to go. Walter looked at Hagen, who was also staring at him, he had a slightly lost and disappointed expression, he had recently found a father again and perhaps he was losing him forever.

Walter cautiously climbed up the edge of the woods, stood behind a tree, aimed his machine gun at the man with the rifle and the telescope, he was the most dangerous, he was the one who could stop the fugitives. He held his breath and briefly pulled the trigger. The burst of fire hit the soldier who fell to the ground in the snow, the others rolled to the side and began shooting a bit randomly.

Walter saw his group get up and run laboriously through the snow, he pointed his gun at their opponents again and fired again.

Greta felt the burst, got up and started running with all the strength she had in her body. The snow was hindering her, it was as tiring as having two hundred kilos of weight on her. She went a hundred meters, and fell, she managed to avoid crushing the child, one of the others helped her up, they heard two more bursts to their right, but there was no time to see where they came from and who was shooting at her.

They started running again, now the little one was screaming at the top of his lungs, Greta saw a bush from which the figure of a man in a white uniform, a snow camouflage, emerged as if from nowhere, who ran towards her and supported her up to the trees: <<Wie sollten wir frau [how are you, madam]?

<< Ich weiß nicht, wo wir sind [I don't know.. where are we] ?>>

<< Sie sind in Österreich sehr geehrte Frau , sie wurden gerettet [you are in Austria madam, you are safe]>>

Greta turned towards the place where the shots had come from, she couldn't see or hear anything, full of anguish she wondered when she would see Walter again.

Walter watched the group approaching the border, the Russian soldier he had shot was lying on the ground, his blood staining the snow, like grenadine on ice.

The second and third soldiers did not understand where the burst of gunfire had come from. They remained lying on the ground, looking around from that position. Walter, keeping them under fire, moved away towards the woods, he barely had time to disappear into the thicket when a series of shots seemed to chase him, hitting his footprints. With difficulty, with the snow reaching halfway up his thighs, he advanced into the forest until he reached a path. He came out of the woods and walked along it, he moved calmly, while the breath coming out of his mouth filled the air with steam, which immediately disappeared. He reached the main road, the soldiers suddenly emerged from the ditch and surrounded him, the *Starshina (sergeant major)* who commanded them pointed his short machine gun at him and said something to him in his own language. Walter dropped his *PPSH* (machine pistol) and raised his hands. They then handcuffed him: *"Idti vpered"* (go ahead, walk) the NCO said in a threatening tone, accompanying the phrase with an unmistakable gesture of the gun barrel. The circle of soldiers opened and Walter, with his hands raised, walked in the direction indicated by the sergeant. There was a BTR40 armored car stopped in the middle of the road. The sergeant handcuffed Walter, with his hands behind his back, then made him get into the vehicle, pushing him brutally. He ordered him to lie down on the floor, face down, then signaled him with his finger in front of his mouth to be quiet and showed him the bayonet in an unmistakable manner. The floor was cold and wet, and his face rubbed against it, Walter could smell the metal and oil rising from the bottom of the vehicle, his nose a few centimeters from the snow-covered boots of the soldiers. That smell reminded him of another one, the one in U-boats. Someone put the butt of the rifle on his back. The BTR started off, jolting along the bumpy road, causing the man lying on the floor to painfully hit the steel of the floor. After about an hour it stopped. They made him get out; they were near a crossroads, on one side the road seemed to plunge into the woods, on the other, as a slightly crooked sign indicated, it headed toward Budapest.

The East German VOPOS (Volks Polizei) officer was standing, his collar turned up and his peaked cap perched on his hips, "like the SS used to wear," Walter thought, and a pair of sunglasses. There was a Wyllis-type Jeep with Russian markings up ahead. The engine was running, blowing a thin, whitish vapor into the air. Walter looked around, the VOPOS officer came up to him, took him over, and asked him to give him the keys to the handcuffs. He thanked the Russian soldiers in their own language; he accompanied him to the jeep, had him climb into the passenger seat, took the driver's seat and drove off, kicking up a spray of snow. After the first bend, the jeep stopped. The officer got out of the vehicle, signaled Walter to get out too, then took out the Makarov pistol he was carrying at his side, pointed it...upwards, fired a first shot...waited a few seconds and fired a second. Then he turned behind Walter. He freed him from the handcuffs and signaled him to get back on the vehicle. They remained in silence for a few kilometers, then the VOPOS officer, suddenly, as if he had noticed Walter's presence at that moment, exclaimed: "Welcome beyond the Iron Curtain!". Walter turned, looked at the officer's profile for a moment. He couldn't help but feel a strange sensation every time he looked at that man's face, a kind of vertigo, the same one he had felt many years before. Meeting him for the first time. "Thank you.." he replied after a few seconds of silence.

The officer continued: "In a few kilometers we will reach a village, it is called Sarbogard, there we will split up and reach Budapest separately..." he looked at Walter sideways "I don't think I need to explain to you how to get to the capital..." Walter made a small grimace and a vague wave of his hand.

"Well," concluded VOPOS, "as if to say: See you in Budapest!" And he half laughed.

Walter shook his head, that sentence coming from Horst's mouth reminded him of a past that was anything but funny, but that man's humor had always been rather chilling. Walter turned to the window, outside the snow was very white, the landscape seemed like a huge, boundless, white desert, which met the lead-gray sky, in a remote place on the horizon. That light had a hypnotic effect on him, his mind began to go back, a slow and soft flashback. Now, in this muffled and bizarre present, he was traveling with Horst towards that unknown country in the Hungarian countryside, but they had arrived at this present through a series of complicated events that found their remote origin many years ago and far away from there...

2

THE PLOT OF THE "STORY"

2.1 Marblehead Massachusetts....July 1919:
The Puppet Master

WB looked out to sea, in the little port in front of his house, moored to the pier was a launch, in reality a motorboat of considerable power with classic lines and certainly not aerodynamic. It looked a lot like one of those boats used by the Doges of Venice or the monarchs, a small and rare indulgence to his vanity.

And yet he would have had good reason to flaunt his vanity: his power was far superior to that of the Doges and even of the monarchs, he was the Grand Master of the Order, the most powerful secret society in the world, the secret society of secret societies. Those who had created and destroyed empires, who had supported Kings, feudal lords, ministers and heads of state, who had founded colonies, like the thirteen original American colonies, financial potentates, like the East India Company, great universities like Cambridge and Princeton; who had supported the defeat of Napoleon with money from everywhere; all the wars to prevent the creation of a hegemonic power in Europe, which would disturb the country where the mother house of the Order itself was located: England, or better still the state within the state that was the City of London. They had used all means from corruption to dissuasion, from esoteric sects to conservative and revolutionary parties depending on the need. Any means to allow the group of powerful families, twelve in all, who represented the heart of the order, to continue to control the world. They directed it in a Secret Council, and expressed in turn a grand master, who was renewed periodically, when the Secret Council decided that the time had come.

In reality, what bound this powerful association was a set of ancient personal relationships. Of marriages, of common acquaintances, of courtyards of the same schools where they had learned what power was and how to manage it, of halls of great mansions, where they met since they were children, speaking different languages and always understanding each other. Because there was something between them that went beyond the language and the land where they were born, which often belonged to them personally.

It was precisely for this reason that WB indulged very little in vanity; a thing for frustrated half-wits, what was the point of showing off a power, which one did not have, through external signs that only affected those who counted for nothing. Order, on the other hand, was the great weaver of the plot of history, it wove the threads like a carpet, whose design was visible only from above... but you had to be very high up.

Soon he would be down at the dock, to climb on that bizarre, out-of-time launch, to reach his cutter, which would take him to a place not far from there, to take care of something that concerned a distant country that was key to the European balance. That balance that only a few years before had been thrown off, also thanks to a discreet intervention by the Order, which had decided that a change was necessary to the now dormant and near-end system of European imperialism.....

2.2 *Kennebunck Port, Maine, July 1919 … the puppet theater*

The delegate was sitting in the back seat of the black Ford T that was slowly driving along Ocean Road. It was a beautiful day and it was quite hot, the view of the ocean and the beaches of that enchanted corner of Maine seemed not to interest the man. His gaze was lost in space, he seemed worried, but in reality he was only haughtily annoyed by the idea of traveling in that contraption, on the country roads of that town in the American province. The ones who forced him to travel in that way were his "American friends" Hariman and Walker, who had organized a meeting for him with a powerful and mysterious character. They said he was the president of a foundation: the "Russel Trust Association", which according to Walker and Hariman was able to help him solve his problems. The two had asked him to meet this character in Herbert Walker's cottage, to avoid prying eyes seeing the mysterious Mr. WB together with that former official of the German embassy who a few years earlier had been expelled from the United States, at the request of President Wilson himself.

They reached the entrance to the villa, there was only a low fence, and the gate was opened by a man wearing ordinary civilian clothes, but carrying a revolver at his side. The caretaker, however, did not seem particularly concerned. He did not even look at the man sitting in the back and slowly closed the large gate, while the car entered the courtyard of the cottage.

The delegate waited for the driver to open the car door for him and got out. A tall, light-eyed, sporty-looking young man approached him. He held out his hand to the delegate, in a detached manner and said: "Pleased to meet you, I am Prescot Sheldon Bush, I will accompany you to your house, Mr. WB is waiting for you along with Mr. Walker and Mr. Hariman".

"Pleased to meet you, I am Von Papen," replied the delegate.

The three men were waiting for them in the drawing room, soberly furnished in Edwardian style. They were standing, one of them was noticeably shorter than the others, he had a small head completely bald, and a short pointed nose, he wore no moustache, no beard and he had eyes that seemed to eat his face, dark and glittering like burning coals.

He held a cup in his hand and immediately looked straight into the eyes of the entering guest.

A penetrating gaze to the point of almost giving a physical sensation of discomfort.

He got straight to the point without preamble:

"So, Herr Von Papen, my friends tell me that the situation in your country is very..." the man paused, looking at Hariman, "dramatic."

Von Papen sighed: "The definition of dramatic, my lord, is a pure euphemism. The Treaty of Versailles has humiliated Germany. The republic is fragile and there is the threat of new revolutions. The position of the Junkers has been greatly weakened. Germany is in the hands of small bourgeois Jews, who think only of enriching themselves and making agreements with the Social Democrats. Of course, the Freikorps have up to now ensured that the revolutionary follies did not prevail, but the government is not very effective and there is always the risk that the Bolsheviks will take power, taking advantage of the economic crisis caused by the reparations provided for by the treaty. Germany will never be able to repay 132 billion marks, it is an absurd figure, conceived only to prevent a great nation from regaining its rightful place among the great nations of the world..."

Von Papen paused, took a sip from the cup of tea in front of him. His interlocutors looked at him: Hariman and Walker had worried and sympathetic expressions, while WB was impenetrable.

Von Papen continued: "It is necessary to reinstate an authoritarian government in my country: Germany is not made for democracy and democracy is not made for Germany. We need a strong government, which can keep the Bolsheviks and the Jews under control. A government that is firmly in the hands of those who alone can prevent the most powerful nation on European soil from falling into the hands of revolutionaries: that is, the Prussian Junkers. Only they can ensure the country the authoritarian government it needs.

If Germany were to fall into the hands of the Reds, nothing could stop the advent of socialism throughout the European continent. And that would give rise to a world revolution, and I think it is useless to describe the consequences of that to you here in the United States.

The German fell silent, took a last sip of tea, and put the cup down. Then he looked at everyone present, with the expression of someone who felt he had made irrefutable statements and expected broad consensus from those present.

WB remained impassive. "I realize... but what are you asking of us at the end of the day?"

Von Papen seemed slightly surprised by the question.

"Your Excellency, perhaps my friends here have not explained to you who I represent..."

"Vaguely..." WB said

Von Papen's expression became even more surprised: "How did I think that gentlemen..."

WB seemed to suddenly become animated: "Mr. Von Papen, I cannot be satisfied with what I am told by other people, on such an important subject as an action to influence the internal politics of a country thousands of miles away from here and with which we have just fought a war. Your remarks about the weight of Germany in Europe and the risk of a revolution in your country are certainly true, but who guarantees me that you are not an agent of the Bolsheviks. Who guarantees me that I and my brothers will not finance the revolution in Germany instead of the other way around?"

Von Papen seemed struck, he remained silent for a couple of minutes, there was a deafening silence in the living room, it seemed as if even the breathing of those present had stopped.

The German looked resigned.

"You are right, the Bolsheviks are very good at espionage and subversion. However, I can prove to you that I represent very powerful German institutions. I have letters of introduction from the main shareholders of all the most important German industries."

Well hidden under his jacket Von Papen had a briefcase, which he had to remove, for which he apologized ceremoniously. The briefcase was tied to his back with two straps that passed around his shoulders and tied to his trouser belt.

Von Papen freed himself from the complicated harness with some difficulty, under WB's impassive gaze, opened the folder and took out a bundle of letters which he handed to his interlocutor.

WB opened them one by one. Each letter was written on letterhead, and the letterheads were those of major German companies: Thyssen, Siemens, IG Farben, Krupp, Junker, Bayerische Flugzeugwerke AG (BFW). Then he turned to Mr. Walker.

"Mr Walker, would you please send the message I am now going to write to you by your private telegraph to the telex addresses you find on these letters?"

WB handed the letters to the host, then took out a pencil from a silver pencil holder, took a thin notebook from the same pocket and wrote a short sentence on a piece of paper.

Walker read:" *wie sie genannt wird die Wanderer* " (what is the name of the wanderer).

WB stared intently at Walker.

"Within two hours you will receive a reply from each of the recipients, the replies must all be the same in German and will be: *"der Nachkomme Peter"* (the descendant of Peter). If this is not the case, this gentleman is an impostor," he said, with a slightly disturbing smile.

Walker disappeared from the living room, using a door at the end of the room.

Almost simultaneously, someone knocked lightly at the other entrance.

"Go ahead," said WB.

A butler opened the door and said, "Gentlemen, breakfast is ready in the dining room.

"Well," WB exclaimed, "we have some time, shall we take advantage of it to feed us?"

The three of them left the room and moved to the dining room, where a classic American breakfast of eggs, bacon, white bread and coffee had been prepared.

After exactly two hours the confirmation telegrams arrived.

"Well," WB exclaimed, after reading them one by one, "let's go back to the living room."

It was clear that the man, although he was not the master of the house, had a clear position of superiority over both the guest and Mr. Harimann.

They each sat back down in their previous places.

WB looked at Von Papen: "Well, Mr. Von Papen, we don't have much time. If the new constitution of the Weimar Republic is approved, there will be new elections in Germany in June. It is clear that we don't have time to influence them enough to determine the winner. We have to take more time, but the work must begin immediately."

WB was silent for a moment, thinking, then continued. "The fact is that what you said is true, but my recent information is even worse."

We must find a political entity suitable for our purposes, an entity that is able to take firm control of the country and can act as a barrier against the spread of Bolshevism, this is the real enemy. The Junkers are not able to do it directly. They demonstrated this with the last war, something different is needed. When this Government has taken control of the country we will help them financially. A powerful Germany is certainly a very good deal for us..."

Harriman had a puzzled expression, WB saw him: "any observations mister Harrimann?"

"Now," said the man, "an authoritarian government and a powerful Germany would never be accepted by the English and the French. Perhaps at first the idea of standing up to the Bolsheviks might work, but the English won't buy it for long..."

WB smiled slyly: "The English have other problems, in their colonies around the world. The empire is crumbling, as for the French, they are also reduced to a thread: all of Europe is in debt to us for the next hundred years... And then even if they had the bizarre idea of unleashing a new war on the continent... when has a war ever been a bad deal?"

Hrrimann looked at him again perplexed, he seemed speechless, after a long pause, almost as if he was struggling to express himself he said: "...But Germany is not South America, we cannot think of installing a government under our control, out of nowhere..."

WB's gaze became even more lively, his eyes seemed to be laughing: "Well, first of all I do not pretend to control Germany as we do with the countries of South America. I mean a government that we will influence, with the means by which governments are influenced, from the supply of strategic materials, to suggestions, to the financing of political campaigns.

Dear friends, we will inaugurate a new way of doing politics, and a new way of conquering power, which is always the old one, using new means.

Europe today is the right place to experiment with my project, Germany is the ideal country for our experiment."

They were all looking at him with astonished expressions.

"You see, in Europe the war has shaken the power. The monarchies, except the English one, which won the war, are finished. All the nobility have ended up in nothingness. Thanks to their incompetence, a conflict has been unleashed that has gone far beyond their expectations and has disintegrated the political structures of European societies, leaving room for the revolutionary Bolshevik parties, who are eager to seize power. The place where this game began is Germany. Do you know why...?"

He looked around in a circular fashion, but no one wanted to answer:

"Because Germany is the most powerful nation in Europe, with the most important industrial system in Europe, a strategic position in the center of Europe, the richest in natural resources in Europe. If it falls into the hands of the Reds, about this Mr. Von Papen is right, the whole continent will become socialist, for us and for many of our friends in Europe it would be a colossal disaster.

At this moment, power in Germany is in not weak, but very weak hands. The Bolsheviks, who are very well organized, would need nothing to seize it. Colonel Bourdon of the Deuxieme Bureau has just sent a report to his superiors that has disturbing contents. I have it in my possession. It shows that the German Social Democrats are establishing relations with the Russian Bolsheviks in the field of industrial production.

The capacity of German industry, combined with the propaganda power of the Soviets and the size of Russia, would be a terrifying threat to capitalism, and would spread throughout Europe, risking the creation of a military, political and industrial colossus that would put Great Britain out of the game and stop forever our project to conquer European markets.

So it is necessary to organize a political force that opposes him to do so, then we will have to make sure that this political force wins the elections. At this moment there is no one who can be credible at the head of a political movement. Of course there are heroes like Ludendorf or Hindenburg, but they would not be able to govern a modern nation like Germany, and then they would not be controllable by us and our friends. No, we will find a man who has great apparent charisma, a great actor, and behind him we will build a movement"

Harimann looked uncertain: "But how will we get the German people to investiture him?"

"With the show dear Harimann... we will build a party that has an ideology that plays on all the fears and hopes of the Germans. We will unleash their frustrations for the defeat, and we will look for all the most suitable scapegoats. We will go and get all those nationalist and xenophobic authors who were so successful in Germany before the war and with their ideas we will build the ideological apparatus of this new movement. We will use the love that the Germans have for great celebrations and for heroes, think of Wagner, the Nibelungs.

The man we choose will have to be its high priest, or rather its messiah, because we will make it a kind of religion. A religion specially packaged for the Germans, he will be a man with great authority, because the Germans love authority. We will use communication, new means such as the radio, and old ones such as newspapers. We will also deploy astrologers and prophets, when we speak to the emotions as in our case, the use of the metaphysical is fundamental.

"Dear Von Papen, what do you think about it?"

The German delegate seemed very perplexed: "Well, I mean... is it really necessary to do this?"

"It's the only way, otherwise Germany will fall into the hands of the Communists... we'll take care of it, you just have to help us find allies for our movement..."

3

THE ACTORS.....
THE STAGE

3.1 Mario Vaillante…. Piacenza, spring 1919…..the island not found

*"But most beautiful of all is the Non-Found Island:
the one that the King of Spain received from his cousin the King of
Portugal with a sealed signature and bull of the Pope in Gothic Latin."*

Maestro Guzzetti had an extraordinary voice, deep and mellow, it seemed made on purpose for telling stories and reciting poems, more than a professor of literature, Guzzetti seemed like a fine orator.

Mario was listening to him, enchanted: he felt like he was on the bridge of one of those ships of the King of Spain, together with Amedeo, his friend and companion in adventures.

Actually, it was a pirate galleon, like the one of the Black Corsair.

They were on the stern castle, leaning on the inlaid wooden railing and scanning the sea with two long brass telescopes covered with leather. Behind them a powerful black sailor, dressed in a pair of wide Turkish trousers, held by a multicolored sash, held the wheel, with a proud and menacing look.

He seemed to see the green edge of a forest that ended at the edge of a very white beach, on whose shoreline the waves of a crystalline sea like emerald lapped.

From the island came a light wind full of aromas, seductive and unknown. Mysterious perfumes, that wrapped him like a silk cloak, and that stunned and inebriated like the fumes of incense and sandalwood.

He felt a sort of arcane nostalgia for that land he had never visited, a soft languor, like velvet, a poignant sensation of joy and melancholy at the same time.

announces itself with its perfume, like a courtesan
... But, if the pilot advances, it quickly vanishes like a vain semblance,
and is tinged with the blue color of distance...

The poem ended, there was silence in the classroom, Mario hadn't noticed that two big tears were slowly falling from his eyes.

He felt someone touching his arm, it was Amedeo: "What are you doing, crying...? Are you an idiot, what are you whining about?"

Mario tried to explain himself. To explain those feelings to his friend Amedeo Guillet, but he couldn't. Finally the boy gave him a mocking smile: "Are you becoming a sissy...? Look, we're soldiers, you and I, not two romantic wimps... Oh, don't you remember?"

Mario was ashamed, how could that thing have happened, damn it, of course they were two soldiers, he and Amedeo, like their fathers, Guillet's, an officer of the royal carabinieri, wounded on Podgora, and his; captain of the Alpine troops and guide from the Aosta Valley, who died fighting on Adamello.

And then he also thought of his very strict grandfather, an engineer. A gentleman from Varese, with an irrepressible passion for flight, who had agreed to work, like any designer at Caproni, first in Taliedo and then in Vizzola Ticino.

The lesson ended and with all the commitments that the rigid rules of the college imposed, Mario forgot about the strange spell that had taken over him. They played football and he was kicked twice by the fullback of the other team, but he managed to score a goal. But when night came the dream had its revenge

Now he was on the beach, he felt the heat of the sun on his limbs, inside he had a feeling of dizziness, a dizziness of joy, like a prisoner who had just regained his freedom. He felt the cool kiss of the sea waves on his feet, the sun did not dazzle him even though it shone in a sky of a deep and dazzling blue.

He was hit by an inebriating scent: it was the smell of bread... No, the smell of flowers, those of his grandfather's garden in Vizzola... No it was his mother's scent when she came to wake him up in the morning when he was little, or maybe not even that, he didn't understand what the scent was, but he saw where it came from: a girl was coming towards him along the beach. She was carrying a basket on her head, full of white flowers and she was moving sinuously like a belly dancer, to the rhythm of a music that had suddenly entered Mario's ears, a music of flutes and drums. The girl was close to him, she had amber skin, two shining eyes shone with an emerald fire. She had hair as black as the night, which seemed to have blue reflections, her body wrapped in silk veils was perfect. She was smiling, with pearl teeth and a full mouth, which promised an unimaginable softness.

Mario felt that vertigo growing enormously, he couldn't resist and stretched out his hand to touch her, and she vanished like a mirage, but slowly "tinging herself with blue... the color of distance...", suddenly leaving him with the sensation of being the loneliest child in the world.

He woke up panting, his pajamas were soaked in a warm, sticky liquid. He remained still for a moment, his breath caught like when you fall into the void. He decided to wait until morning to change. He didn't know what the hell that stuff was that was filling his underwear, but something told him that it was better to keep all those sensations and that invasion of his intimate self to himself, he was sure that if a prefect of the college caught him he would get him into some trouble!

It was summer and Mario had returned to his grandfather's house like every year for the holidays.

As the diligent boy he was, he studied a little every day. His grandfather watched him with his stern eyes and a satisfied expression. Then he made a gesture with his right hand, twisting his mustache, and walked away.

One day when he had finished studying he had gone out into the garden, idle, playing with the house cat, a Chartreux they called Svetonio. At a certain point the cat decided to run away into the house and Mario followed him, to prevent him from causing disasters in some other room, or worse in the living room furnished with antique furniture, full of trinkets and various objects, which had been particularly dear to his grandmother, who had died a few years earlier of a heart disease. But the cat, instead of slipping into the living area on the ground floor, quickly headed up the stairs, then continued to climb, disappearing into the half-open trap door in the attic.

Mario followed him, threw open the wooden door and, as if emerging from a hatch, found himself in a mysterious place, immersed in the shadows. The place was kept in meticulous order, but there was a light veil of dust over everything, which gave the impression of a place abandoned for a long time, a sort of archaeological site, never violated for centuries. There were also some cobwebs, illuminated by the sun that penetrated from the skylight.

There were a series of shelves, with long rows of books lined up, bound in green cloth, with a progressive number, engraved in gold, and often faded, starting from 1898. Probably, Mario thought, they were numbers of years. He took one at random, and opened it. They were diaries, on the first page of the one he had taken out, it was written: "1915, diary".

He began to leaf through them; they were filled with impetuous but precise writing, a little rambling and very legible.

He stopped at a page dated June of that first year of the war.

Mario began to read: "*I was summoned by a certain Colonel Poggi, a friend of Caterina's father...*"

Mario reread several times. Who could be the author of that diary? Caterina's father could only be his grandfather. So he was not the author. He looked at the other volumes. They had dates prior to 1915 and told episodes of daily life in Italy during the Belle Epoque. Mario did not find them particularly interesting, so he took the 1915 volume again. He opened it at random and read:

"The die is cast, I have decided to enlist as a volunteer... With my experience as a guide it is certain that they will put me in the Alpine troops so that I will immediately be in the centre of the conflict, at the furthest borders of the homeland among ice and snow, to face the foreigner, where he is best prepared, but where we too can give a great demonstration of our value.."

The date was January 13, but who could have been the one who had volunteered at the beginning of that fateful year?

Mario felt like his heart sank; it seemed as if his stomach had contracted until it sucked itself in. Perhaps the person writing was his father? The man who on a distant day in 1915 had left for the war and who, after sending a few letters to Mario's mother, one day had disappeared into thin air, without ever giving any news of himself. They had told him that he was missing. Never returned from an attack, never found his body. His mother Caterina had suffered for a long time from that disappearance, to the point of going mad and being hospitalized in a clinic in Varese, where she died in 1917, without regaining her sanity.

Mario wondered if those diaries would reveal some secret to him, about that father he had missed so much and of whom he had only vague memories. He returned to the page he had read first.

"I have been summoned by a certain Colonel Poggi, a friend of Caterina's father... it is a telegram that orders me to present myself in Milan, at the Magenta barracks, in via Mascheroni..."

The diary continued a few days later.

"That Colonel Poggi is the head of Office I, created by the General Staff. An intelligence service that should include a foreign spy network. He said that my knowledge of German is useful to the new service. He told me verbatim: <<we have plenty of cannon fodder, we need someone who speaks German. The Austrians of the Evidenz Bureau have set up cells in Italy, some Allied sources have informed us, it seems that they are organizing sabotage in our country>>, the colonel made me understand that I was a volunteer and I didn't have many options to choose: <<the fatherland is served where it is needed! .>>. I accepted".

The diary continued several days later. It told of the training: the author had been taught to use secret codes, invisible ink, and how to shoot a pistol.

On September 1st there is a notation:

"They assigned me the destination. Zurich, it seems that the saboteurs' nest is there. The boss is a diplomat named Maurig Von Sarnfeld, he works together with a naval officer, Captain Mayer. The source of these is the Deuxieme Bureau with whom we work over there."

Still a few days without any notes then the 10th:

"They are changing my destination. A report has arrived from Rome, in the city someone told our men that the saboteurs' headquarters is not in Zurich, but in Bern, so they are sending me to the Swiss capital..."

On September 27 he writes:

"Horrible day, this morning the battleship Benedetto Brin sank due to an explosion in the magazine, 421 people died, including Admiral Rubin de Cervin who commanded the naval division.

Our director Poggi is furious, to reach Brindisi the network of spies and traitors, in our beloved homeland must be well extended. He says that the tallow eaters are very well infiltrated in the Vatican, among the black nobility and together with the Germans in the Banca Commerciale.

I have a sudden doubt. It is not strange that exactly one month before the sabotage, that Information arrived from Rome that moved the headquarters of the saboteurs' network from Zurich to Bern.

I talk to Chapperon about it. He agrees, it is likely that the information came from some traitorous environment.

We need to try to understand where the head of the snake really is."

On October 15th the author resumes writing.

"They asked me to do something. Something that disgusts me, but I absolutely have to do it for the honor of my country, I have to penetrate the enemy network, provide and do something they call disinformation..."

What is it that disgusts the author of the diary? And who is he, Mario wondered.

"And if he is my father then he did not die at the front, where he ended up. Why don't they tell me the truth about his end?"

He turned and found himself facing his grandfather. He was standing, straight as a spindle, in his dark suit with a waistcoat and black tie. He was looking at him and had a strange expression, a bitter and almost furious look, which made his eyes black as coal, like the barrels of two pointed pistols.

Mario was left speechless, the diary he was reading fell from his hand, ended up on the wooden floor, covered in dust with a dull thud, raising a small cloud.

Grandpa's expression changed slightly, he took a step forward and bent down, apparently without much effort. He picked up the diary and patted it twice with his hand to remove the dust that had fallen on it. He looked at the date, turned to the shelf, looked at the volumes one by one and put the diary back in its place.

Then he turned to Mario, his expression changed, it became understanding, like the one he assumed when Mario's pranks had been less serious or involuntary.

He looked at him, her gaze had softened:

"Young man, please ask me for permission whenever you intend to poke your nose into matters that do not concern you."

Mario felt a surge of tears rising from the bottom of his stomach, tears began to come out without him wanting to, with a firm voice, and with his cheeks wet with copious tears he said:

"I ask your forgiveness, grandfather... I, I, "

A new sob of crying stopped him, the grandfather waited patiently for it to pass, then with a deep and reassuring voice like Mario had never heard, he said:

"You are still a child, it is too early to tell you things that would make you suffer unjustly, one day you will know, I myself will tell you. For now, be content to know that these are the diaries of a man who was a great injustice done to him, his name was Ervè, Ervè Vaillante...., he was your father"

3.2 Cynthia...Charlottesville July 1919 ...The Scarecrow

It was a very hot night, Cynthia's mother had left the window of her room open, and she couldn't sleep that night. She knew that her father, Captain William Uberti, was coming home that very evening, and she was very excited. The officer was returning from the French front where he had fought as a volunteer in the Lafayette Squadron. A unit framed in the French air force but composed of American citizens. Captain Uberti was of remote Italian origins, his family history was very particular.

Thomas Jefferson cultivated vines on his estate in Monticello. Some of these gave excellent Malvasia, they came from Italian vines, which had arrived there, on order of Jefferson himself. Those vines had been brought to Virginia by a merchant winemaker from Chianti named Uberti, whose father had met the future president during one of his tours in Europe. The man, a farmer with a passion for the philosophy of the Enlightenment, had decided to leave his homeland, in his opinion dominated by the Catholic Church and obscurantism, to reach America. He had embarked in Livorno on a ship that he had equipped himself, together with some of his best winemakers. The journey had followed almost the same route as Christopher Columbus, then turned north, a little before Florida and docked at the port of Norfolk. From there he had reached Charlottesville on wagons and those lands so similar to Tuscany, which were called Piedmont, a name that recalled Piedmont in Italy.

Uberti had worked on Jefferson's estate, married a local girl, who died in an unfortunate accident, before giving him children.

In 1826, when Jefferson died, Uberti had left Monticello and bought land not far from there, on the slopes of the Blue Ridge.

On Jefferson's estate there were some slaves working. Among them was a beautiful mulatto girl, daughter of a black woman from Gambia and a white master who wanted to get rid of the girl who was causing him irresistible remorse, by selling her to Jefferson.

When the house was sold to a doctor, Thomas Bercley, Uberti had bought the girl and emancipated her, he had not married her for two reasons. The first was that, although it was not at all rare for southern owners to have relationships with their slaves, this did not mean that the children born from them had the same rights as whites or that even the owners had to marry the slaves. Uberti, an enlightened and liberal, seriously convinced that all men were equal, did not want to create problems for himself and his descendants, so he never married the half-blood Miriam, but he had a son by her, who before dying he decided to recognize.

The boy was practically white, and it was very difficult to imagine that he could be the son of a mulatto slave.

In 1858 the young Uberti had decided to leave for Italy, where the second war of independence was about to break out. He had fought with Garibaldi, first in Varese in the Alpine Hunters, and then in various battles. Then he went to enlist in the Thousand.

He had returned to America just in time to enlist in the Federal Army, in the firm belief that he was fighting for the liberation of what he believed to be his people.

Things had gone rather badly for him, because in Gettysburg he had lost a leg, but in the hospital he had found a girl whom he had married, he had returned to his father's estate, in a land that was actually his enemy, but his father had welcomed him anyway with an embrace, together with his young wife.

Thus the Uberti family had proliferated in that corner of the southern USA. One of their ancestors had been a senator, the black chromosomes had been greatly diluted, but not their memory, so they had always fought for the emancipation of black people, making some enemies.

One of these, that very day, was waiting outside the fence that surrounded the farm. It was a certain Achab Boghey, a member of the Klu Klux Klan, a fanatic who wanted to make a name for himself among his infamous ideological companions, by killing one of those they called renegades of the white race, not knowing that the Uberti had African blood, even if that would have been one more reason for Achab Boghey to commit that crime.

He knew that the dirty renegade, that papist bastard, who had even had the courage to fight in the army, would be back that evening. One of the telegraph clerks was a member of the Klan, and had intercepted Uberti's telegram, sent from aboard the ocean liner on which he was returning to the United States. Boghey had taken up surveillance of the house, that was all he had to do, being unemployed and living on a miserable inheritance from his mother, who had worked all her life as a maid in the big house of a guy who was a friend of the Ubertis, and had saved penny after penny to ensure a minimum of decent living for her illegitimate son, Achab, had by a tramp who had raped her, one bad summer evening.

The poor woman had thought that the creature she had found in her womb was not at fault ,for how it had been conceived, and she hoped, unfortunately in vain, that it had not inherited its father's violent character and alcoholism.

But Achab had grown up crookedly, he had started very early to frequent the squalid saloon just outside the village and the racist scum that met there. He had beaten up many blacks, he had set fire to some crosses, but these were all things that did not satisfy his frustration and his desire for revenge and rematch against anyone he did not like, that is, nine tenths of humanity.

When his mother died he had gone to the home of her employers, the Masterson family, to ask for some money, no one knows for what reason. The landlord had received him and listened patiently to his requests. Finally he had offered him a job, which Boghey had scornfully refused, "farm work was for niggers," he had said.

Masterson had politely kicked him out, and he had gone to join the Klan.

Now he was leaning against the fence of the Uberti house, sharpening a stick with a knife and looking around. He had a gun in his pocket that he had borrowed from a guy who was part of his circle, saying that he needed it to rob a couple of blacks.

He thought about the little girl who lived in that big house that was behind the hill and that he couldn't see from there. He watched her every now and then go around town, accompanied by a driver and the nurse. She would go into the only candy store in town, and come out with tiny packages, or you could see her in the windows eating ice cream. At Christmas, parcels would arrive at the station for her, things bought by mail order, from the best catalogs available in Virginia. Everything he had never had, that damned little girl, she had. And Achab accumulated hatred, against everyone and everything, including himself, but especially against that little girl, whom he wanted to hurt: what he wanted to do was take away all the things she owned, killing the one who gave them to her and destroying that beautiful house with fire. Now he looked at that hill, chewing on his anger, making splinters fly off the wood he held in his hand. That's what life was for him, there was always a hill that prevented him from seeing and touching what he deserved, because he was white, American, Protestant, that had to be enough. All the garbage that the Washington businessmen had brought in from all over the world could at most work the land and thank the white people who let them live.

The Ford T was advancing on the dusty avenue, it was very hot. The two officers, one from the US Army Air Service and the other from the Royal Air Force, on board the car had taken off their jackets and had unbuttoned the first two buttons of their shirts, rolling up their sleeves to above their elbows, even their caps had ended up on the back seats. They were both wearing a pair of aviator goggles, to protect themselves from the thin cloud that the car's wheels themselves were raising. Leonard Uberti was driving, he was forced to hold the wheel tightly due to the poor efficiency of the shock absorber system and the poor quality of the road surface.

Uberti told himself that the first thing he would do as a civilian would be to redo the road from his house to the state highway.

The fence from where his property began was still standing, but it needed a freshening up; the heat and the rain, the cold of winter had made it grey and in some places it even looked like it was about to collapse.

However, from what could be seen from the road, the estate was in good condition. From afar you could see the vegetable gardens and the vines still in order. The latter were green in the sun, in a couple of months there would be the harvest, its vines of Chianti origin, lovingly cared for by its head winemaker Brubaker, would give the usual wine worthy of the tables of the White House.

Brubaker was Irish, descended from a family that had begun working in the Uberti vineyards immediately after the American Civil War.

The ancestor of the present vintner owned a large estate, near that of the Ubertis, where tobacco was grown. The Brubakers had sided with the Confederacy, Lyam Brubaker was a captain in the 8th Virginia Infantry Regiment, Garnett Brigade, which had participated, together with Pickett's brigade, in the legendary and desperate charge launched against Cemetrey Ridge, on July 3, 1863.

Uberti's ancestor, wounded in the battle, had found the captain who was also seriously wounded, had recognized him and had helped him, taking him to a Northern hospital and saving his life, losing the leg on which they had intervened too late.

After the war, when Uberti returned to the farm, he met Brubaker. The man had had to sell his land to speculators linked to the federal government, at a paltry price and was in financial difficulty. Uberti had generously offered to work for him as a factor. From then on, the two families had joined in a brotherly pact, from which they had never left. One of the Brubaker brothers had studied at the Ubertis' expense, at the University of Virginia in Charlotteville and had entered the State Department, in 1916-17 he had been one of Robert Lansing's assistants, at that time he was in France for the final activities connected to the signing of the Versailles peace treaty.

As he was thinking about these things, he saw someone leaning against the fence. A rather shabbily dressed man, wearing peasant overalls, a torn and torn shirt, a big hat and cowboy boots. The man was holding a knife in his hand with which he was sharpening a piece of wood.

It looked like a scarecrow to him, he had a strange unpleasant sensation, which evidently changed his expression because

William Stephenson, the RAF officer of Canadian origin who was travelling with him asked him: "What's happening... have you seen a ghost?"

"Maybe so...", Leonard said. He didn't know the man, but seeing him leaning against the fence of his farm made a strange, evil impression on him, so much so that he decided to stop and reverse. He went back, but he had disappeared. With the engine running and immersed in a cloud of dust, Leonard remained looking around, with a doubtful and worried expression. William looked at him a little surprised.

"But what's happening...?" He asked again, but in a calm voice.

"I don't know..." Leonard continued, "I saw a man leaning against the fence and I had a strange, unpleasant sensation. Something I felt the last time in 18, above Ribécourt, when the engine of my Neuport had the idea of cutting out while two Albatrosses were approaching, only that time there was a reason, this time..." he shook his head and said almost to himself: "but it must be the tiredness of the journey"

"But yes," William seized on Leonard's last sentence to defuse the situation, "we've come a long way in just a few days, it's understandable that you're being nonsense."

Leonard turned the Ford T once more and headed back toward the farm entrance.

Achab was spying from a bush, he was well hidden, if there was one thing he had learned when he was a child skipping school to wander the countryside, it was to hide. He knew all the nooks and crannies, all the hollow trees, the bushes, all the places where he could take refuge to avoid being beaten by his mother, who could find no other solution than to beat him to make him a little less lazy, a little less wild, a little less evil.

He hid... and spied. He spied on the rich and the less rich, and according to him everyone had something that he wanted and that he lacked and accumulated hatred. But he lacked the courage to do something against those who were stronger than him. So he vented his anger on the blacks, on the weak and sick. He had stolen from the house of the widow Berry, a woman who was in a wheelchair and who had nothing except an old cuckoo clock, which the poor woman was fond of and William had stolen. Then as he always did he had destroyed the clock, he had shattered it into a thousand pieces by jumping on it.

He waited for Uberti's car, which had turned back and stopped in the middle of the road, to start off again towards its destination and went out. As soon as it got dark he would go up the hill to observe the lights of the house, see those happy bastards, celebrate the return of the renegade, and savour their desperation and that of the little girl.

Leonard woke up, it had been daylight for a while, he stretched, his wife, Nora, was not in bed, he heard a gurgle coming from the door, it was the laughter of a little girl who had been badly restrained, it was the laughter of his wonderful Cynthia. A laugh that made her slightly toothless mouth slacken, transformed her eyes into two slits from which you could glimpse the sparkling emeralds of her pupils, which emitted an irresistible sensation of joy, her cheekbones rose and two dimples formed around her mouth, and the gurgle that came out of her mouth, the irresistible laughter like a tidal wave, shook the little girl's body, infected those around her, until it became like overwhelming music.

Leonard turned and opened his arms, the door burst open and Cynthia burst in like a hurricane, running and diving into the man's arms, she hugged him covering him with little kisses, which tickled and increased the desire to laugh. That little being smelled good, candy, cinnamon, soap... and Leonard felt like he had returned to paradise.

Achab looked up the hill from his usual spot along the fence. Two nights before, taking advantage of the darkness, he had climbed up the side of that hill, cautiously, hidden by the darkness, and had looked at the house. That wooden building, surrounded by trees, with the porch that ran along the front, with a tidy garden, the stables, from which came the occasional neighing of the horses, a smaller house where the farmer lived. That damned house so perfect, was an insult to Achab's damned soul. The opposite of his disorderly, full of spite, inconclusive life. Perhaps that was why it attracted him, like a distant and seductive mirage, like a girl too beautiful to be courted. And there it was, and Ahab would have wanted to destroy it and be its master at the same time. He would have wanted to go out on that porch, look around, feel the satisfaction of one who owns.

He couldn't resist, he climbed over the fence and started to climb the hill, running out of breath, he reached the top and saw the house, he saw the peace that reigned in that place, and he felt almost a physical pain, a kind of painful nostalgia for something he had never had, a terrible sensation that he never wanted to feel again and he decided that the next evening he would set fire to that cursed place.

He waited all day, at his house, that house on the outskirts of town, which after his mother's death had slowly turned into a hovel fit only for a pig or a tramp like him. But inside he kept his precious things. The gun he had borrowed, an old Smith & Wesson 38 revolver. A bowie-knife, a large hunting knife, that his mother kept in the house and used in the kitchen, who knows, maybe it came from someone in the family. It was the only object that Achab kept carefully, he sharpened it on a stone and cleaned it and cleaned it, and he carried it everywhere, in a leather sheath, he had used it a couple of times to threaten blacks, but, "unfortunately", he thought, he had never had the chance to hurt anyone.

Then there were other miscellaneous gadgets, including an old can where they kept oil for the lamps at home.

In the countryside he had found a branch, quite long and sturdy, he decided to make a torch. He wrapped some rags around one of the two ends and secured them with string, then he said to himself that it wouldn't work like that, he had to dip the rags in pitch. He had some pitch left! From the last time they had decided to sprinkle a black one and cover it with chicken feathers.

He searched frantically in the mess that plagued that den, finally found what he was looking for and prepared the torch. Then he took the oil can for the lamp; there was still more than half of the contents of the container... He thought that was enough for what he needed now he just had to wait, he looked at the half bottle of bad quality whiskey, which seemed to be contemplating him from the table, he decided to wait until the last moment to use it to give himself courage, he lay down on the bed and began to contemplate the ceiling, as he had always done since he was a child, his head completely empty, in a state of stupor that did not make him feel the pain of being in the world.

Cynthia looked at the night, the stars were veiled by the heat of that day, it hadn't rained for many days and not even the evening brought any relief. A large moon lit up the landscape like a black and white sun and she, as if she were a cat, saw the animals move under that silver ray. She heard the noises and the creaks, the calls of the owls and other nocturnal birds of prey and the squeaking of the mice. Other children were afraid of the night, but she wasn't. And now there were also her dad and Uncle William and she was sure that no one could come and steal her. There was already that story, the terrible one, that old mamy told, the colored woman who worked in the Brubaker house. The story of a scarecrow that a very powerful Indian sorcerer had once placed to guard a corn field, one day the white people arrived and chased the sorcerer away, but before leaving he had cast a spell on the scarecrow, so that in the dark nights it would come to life and go and kidnap the white people's children. When the first slaves arrived, one night the scarecrow came to life and began to look for children, but he only found black children and the evil spirit that was in him could not understand, he had to take it out on the white children, but they were all black!!! Then the scarecrow began to walk around, howling, even scaring the black people's children! One of the slaves was an African sorcerer, and all his companions begged him to free them from the torment of this howling. The sorcerer spoke to the spirit, but he could not achieve much because the magic of that spirit was tied to the earth and the earth where they were was not the land of the African sorcerer.

But the spirit thought that the sorcerer could disturb him with some magic unknown to him, perhaps making him suffer with terrible pains. He knew of a spirit nearby who had to suffer from hunger pangs, because of the black sorcerer, and he could never get rid of it until it ran away. Then he made a deal: he would not touch the black children and would only go to the homes of the white children to steal them.

Since then, Cynthia, in the winter, when the nights were dark, stole some wood from the fireplace and stained her face black, while in the summer she went out to sunbathe to get a tan. Her mother did not understand this strangeness, moreover the little girl, who like all Ubertis had African chromosomes, became very dark, so much so that she risked being mistaken for a colored girl, which could become dangerous in those parts. However, it was difficult to explain this thing to Cynthia, so her mother told her that she did not need to tan, because she was already a bit of an African girl, but she should not tell this to anyone.

However, that night there was a moon and so the scarecrow could not go hunting for children, so what Cynthia saw at that moment scared her even more... because in the garden in front of the house there was a scarecrow, who was moving staggeringly, he had a can and a stick in his hand, and he was going towards the stable.

Cynthia was gripped by terror and began to scream.

Achab was walking in the dark, he was drunk, being a chronic alcoholic it took little to start him, and he had drunk half a bottle of the worst whiskey in the county, but it had given him the courage of a lion. Now he was walking in the middle of the Uberti's garden, with the torch in his right hand and the oil can in his left. He staggered toward the stable, the animals inside began to stir, the horses to neigh, then someone above him began to scream, a scream that resounded in the silence of that garden like the blast of a trumpet, what to Achab seemed to be the trumpet of judgment. The man looked toward the source of the scream, it was a window on the first floor of the house and from that window was leaning out her, the damned child, his enemy, looking at him in terror and screaming. The lights in the Uberti and Brubaker house began to come on. Achab, as if he had just woken up from a dream. He looked at the things he was holding in his hands, dropped them, without even realizing it; there was only one thing in his head: to stop that scream, which like a sonic drill penetrated his ears, upset his brain, spread terror in his body.

He didn't know where he found the strength but he was climbing up the wooden posts of the porch, grabbed the edges of the windowsill and was inside the little girl's room, who had now fallen silent and was looking at him with wide eyes, her hands over her mouth, breathing with difficulty.

Leonard woke up with a start, someone was screaming in the house, even Nora, his wife jumped in bed, the screams were coming from the little girl's room, they both got up, looked at each other, and ran out of the room.

Achab looked at Cynthia, she was tiny compared to him, crouched in a corner, her nightgown pulled up over her legs, almost as if she were hiding inside it, her hair was long, loose on her shoulders, she was covering her face with her arms. He was paralyzed, but he heard noises on the stairs outside the door of the room, someone was running, they were going to hurt him, bastards! They were going to jump on him, they were going to beat him, but he knew how to defend himself, he took the Smith & Wesson from his pocket and emptied it in the direction of the door just as it opened.

Cynthia wasn't looking, that was definitely the scarecrow, he wanted to steal her, but why? She was an African child, but maybe the scarecrow didn't know that. And then that night there was the moon, and the scarecrow stole children only on dark nights, because he was there then, because he wanted to hurt her.

Leonard flung open the door and just had time to see the silhouette of a man, the bullet hit him in the face, broke through his cheekbone and penetrated his brain. He collapsed to the ground with a crash, while a second bullet hit Nora in the heart.

Acahb saw two people collapse beyond the door, he kept pulling the trigger, but the shots were gone, and suddenly he was faced with the enormity of what he had done, he looked around. He had to run and hide... sure, he would run to the hills, to the places only he knew, between the ravines and the woods. But then who knew that it was he who had done it, he had not told anyone his intentions.. But there was a witness, the little girl, the damned little girl, and he had faked the shots. But he had the knife, he had his Bowie Knife, yes, he would silence her forever he pulled out the knife...

William, stepped over the bodies of Leonard and Nora, was in the room, clutching his Webley gun, saw the man in the little girl's room. A dark shadow, dressed in rags, hair disheveled, you could smell the stench of alcohol and sweat coming from that being, something glinted in his hands, in the moonlight filtering through the window, the sinister flash of a knife blade, William cocked the hammer of the Webley, stretched out his arm and fired without aiming, he fired twice.

Achab lunged at the girl, but something hit him and sent him flying, like a giant fist, while a fiery point pierced his neck. A second fist hit his shoulder, shattered his bones, sent the knife flying, Ahab bounced off the wall, fell to the ground, blood spurting from his jugular, which had been sliced clean through by the Webley .45 ball. Achab didn't even notice that his filthy soul was leaving his body forever.

3.2 *Monaco…September 1919…the puppet and his master*

He had found him, that was the confirmation that the man he had identified was the one for them. The seeker had been lucky; the prince had described to him the type of character they were looking for: a man not particularly intelligent, but endowed with kharisma, a fanatical idealist, but with the stigmata of the leader. It was not an easy search, but he, Dr. Morell, who had collaborated for a certain period with the head of the psychiatric department at the hospital in Pasewalk, remembered a man like that, well. He had met him in 1918, hit by poison gas during an attack on the Belgian front at Upern. He had arrived at the hospital blind, but that blindness was not explained by the slight symptoms of conjunctivitis that the man, an infantry corporal, showed. The director of the department, Professor Forster, of whom Morrell was assistant, had treated him with hypnosis.

They had discovered a singular personality: apparently shy and withdrawn, with great difficulty in relating to others and not very talkative, but when he spoke about politics and Germany he was capable of lighting up as if he had another man inside him.

Not only did he become like a magnet that attracted everyone's attention, his eloquence was overwhelming, attractive and engaging, his clear eyes, normally almost expressionless, liquid like those of an animal, lit up with an almost mystical fire, his voice rose, became hoarse and scratchy, deeply affecting the souls of those present.

The doctor, while listening to the man, was thinking back to how he had come to that evening, in the beer hall of the Sternekerbrau Hotel. He was affiliated with an esoteric society called Thule, of which many influential people were secretly members, among them Prince Thurn und Taxis. One day he had invited Morell to his house, with the excuse of having to talk to him about a relative of his who had neurotic disorders.

Then the prince had spoken to him about something else, under the constraint of the utmost secrecy, he had told him that a group of very important businessmen, also supported by powerful international financial institutions, worried about the advance of Bolshevism and the financial instability of Europe, wanted to find a political leader who would bring the German nation back to play a key role in Europe. But they needed a man who could be controlled, a facade that would enchant the German people, and that would serve the interests of their hidden voters.

"You," said the prince, "have certainly met many men during your career as a doctor, and you can also access hospital archives without having to give explanations. We don't think it's a simple thing, but it's fundamental."

He had been lucky, the infantry corporal had immediately come to mind, he had gone to Pasewalk, from there he had followed the man's trail to Munich, where he had discovered that he was an informer for the army. Thanks to his contacts and those of the Thule society, he had had him assigned the task of infiltrating the DAP, *Deutsche Arbeiterpartei* , a political emanation of Thule itself, perhaps conceived for the very purpose the prince had spoken to him about.

Now the man was before him and was launching himself with unheard-of verbal violence against another member of the party who had dared to speak of dividing Bavaria from Germany. The bystanders listened to him spellbound. Morell waited for him to finish, he would immediately report to the prince, certain that perhaps the character could have had a name a little less banal and more German, perhaps preceded by a Von, instead his name was Hitler, Adolf Hitler

3.3 Vizzola …29 October 1922……..the mysteries in the attic

Mario finished his homework, he had only started his second year of high school a month earlier. Two years earlier he had left college, his grandfather had decided to keep him close and make him an aeronautical engineer. His teachers, who all knew his grandfather, kept an eye on him and gave him a lot of homework, especially Latin translations. He actually preferred arithmetic, but in the Italian school system, reformed more or less seventy years earlier, a lot of space had been left for classical subjects. To Mario this idea seemed a bit absurd. The world had long since abandoned ancient philosophy and classical knowledge, to replace it with science, the substitute for classical philosophy introduced by the Enlightenment, but Italy seemed to want to proudly maintain the primacy of classicism.

Grandpa wasn't there that Sunday. He had left for Rome two days earlier to join a friend of his, a certain Italo Balbo, one of the main leaders of the fascist party, a *quadrumvir* they called him. The fascists, according to grandpa, were the only ones who could restore dignity to our country, betrayed by the liberal political class, which had not even been able to reap the just reward of the victory of November 4, 1918, or better still had not succeeded in enforcing the agreements set out in the secret pact of London. The agreement according to which Italy, betraying the Triple Alliance of which it was a member, had sided with the allies of the Entente. The Great War had cost Italy six hundred and fifty thousand deaths, in exchange the so-called allies, the Western demoplutocracies, had given us the alms of letting us occupy a few square kilometers to the east, and nothing in the overseas colonies: a real stab in the back!

It was about 9 in the evening, he had just finished a version of Cicero, the last exercise, his head was falling on his books. At the door of his room appeared his grandfather's housekeeper, Mrs. Colombo. An austere woman, about forty-five, she must have been rather beautiful when she was young, you could still see the signs of it, two deep blue eyes, but full of an invincible melancholy; a straight nose and long blond hair, a little white, gathered in a chignon at the nape of her neck. The lady had lost her husband in the war, on the Isonzo, and two children because of the Spanish flu. She had had to sell her husband's few properties to survive and to take care of the children, but it had all been in vain. The grandfather, who had known her husband in his youth, had helped her, secretly through the parish priest, to avoid gossip. When the grandmother's illness had worsened, the grandfather had hired her, first to assist his wife and then as his personal housekeeper. Mrs. Colombo was incredibly efficient and clean, she spoke very little, but with an infinitely sweet tone, no one in the house disobeyed when the lady gave orders, always preceded by her melancholic smile and a "please...".

That was the same for Mario that evening: "Please, young man, I think it's time to go to sleep." Mario got up from his desk and replied: " can I have a cup of milk before I go to sleep?" The lady smiled: "Of course, young man, if you prefer you can start getting into bed and I'll bring you the cup in a few minutes..." "Okay," Mario replied and headed for his bed. He slipped into it, and sleep came in a few seconds.

He was in his grandmother's living room and Svetonio, the house cat, was looking at him with a curious expression, tilting his head slightly. He walked towards the door, stopped and looked at Mario with the same expression as before, meowing, this time. He continued to do so until Mario began to follow him, along the corridors, up the stairs, then towards the attic, when he was at the top of the stairs it seemed to Mario that the cat changed shape, becoming a sort of human shadow, which disappeared into the opening that led to the attic.

Mario felt terror block his legs, he began to tremble and realized that he couldn't move, then his legs moved by themselves and began to climb towards the attic, towards the darkness, as if something similar to a magnet was hidden in it, capable of irresistibly attracting human beings, Mario felt a kind of breath coming from the darkness of the attic, a cold breath that penetrated inside him, and he felt an unbearable anguish growing inside him, a kind of sensation of urgency, as if he had to solve a complicated problem, and he had to do it immediately, before the darkness swallowed him up. But he couldn't understand what the problem was, this increased the anguish even more. He tried to resist, to keep his legs still but he couldn't, he climbed towards the darkness and towards the anguish.

He woke up with his eyes wide open suddenly in the darkness of the room. He had a moment of confusion, he immediately understood where he was... his room, in Vizzola, in his grandfather's villa. The sudden awakening and the anguish of the nightmare made him pant. He tried to look around, he saw nothing, then slowly, slowly his eyes got used to the little light, the one that filtered through the shutters, whose lower slats had been left open, perhaps by Mrs. Colombo, to let a little brightness penetrate from outside, where the full moon flooded the sleeping countryside.

What had happened to him? Why that strange dream? It wasn't the first time he had it, since that time he had gone up to the attic and discovered his father's diaries, more or less once a year, more or less at the same time, at the beginning of winter, that nightmare happened to him. It was as if someone, or something, wanted him to return to that attic, but he had never done it, because his grandfather had forbidden him to do so and perhaps secretly checked that he didn't go up.

On the nightstand he glimpsed something white, he focused on a cup, one of those big ones, the ones he used for breakfast, he remembered that he had asked Mrs. Colombo for milk. He touched the porcelain, it was still warm, so it meant that he had not fallen asleep long ago. He drank the milk and that flavor and the warmth of the drink gave him a pleasant sensation, of reassurance. He sat up, now he could see better. He guessed the furniture, the curtains, some outlines of objects. The dream came back to him suddenly. Suetonius climbing the stairs and turning into a shadow, the feeling of anguish that came from inside the attic. He remembered again what had happened two years before, when his grandfather had caught him leafing through the diaries with his father's memoirs. The engineer had told him, "when you're older....", well now he was older. That nightmare he had just dreamed was a call from something, perhaps from his conscience or maybe from his father's spirit. He had to face that mystery, despite feeling butterflies in his stomach, and a kind of force that was holding him to the bed. He decided he had to go up there... now. Taking advantage of his grandfather's absence. He pulled back the covers, felt the cold of autumn that had invaded the house, freezing his feet. He put on his slippers, but his feet were still cold. Trying not to make any noise, he approached the dresser, opened a drawer and took out a pair of wool socks, put them on. Then he thought for a moment, took out a sweater and put it on over his pajamas. The door to his room was closed, he opened it carefully. The corridor was deserted, there was a great silence, the house was asleep. He went out slowly, slowly, holding his breath, almost fearing that the sound of his breathing could wake up the inhabitants. He ventured out of the dark space of his room into the deeper part of the corridor, trying to make out the outlines of the furniture that cluttered it. He held his hands out like a sleepwalker, to avoid bumping into them. He walked silently across the space to the stairs and began to climb cautiously. A step creaked, with a creak that seemed sinister to him, chilling and resounding like a cannon shot. He remained still. The house continued to sleep, undisturbed. Up there the attic door seemed to be waiting for him, like a riddle that demanded to be solved, but without giving him any hint other than the pale and faint gleam of the wood.

He pushed the door carefully, to avoid it tipping over with a noise that would wake the mice as well.

He ventured into the attic, barely lit by the skylight from which the moonlight came. The objects illuminated by that milky light took on a strange appearance, as if the white half were in our world and the dark half were in another place, another dimension that we could only guess at, but not perceive. A dimension in which perhaps something else existed, something that sometimes called us to give us its disturbing messages, or perhaps to push us to solve unfathomable mysteries, or to remedy some infamy committed in a remote time. At that moment he had the sensation that the two worlds had drawn closer, that those presences were very close to him. He felt a tremor in his stomach, the sensation of falling into the void... he took courage, it was only his imagination, there was no one around, only the night and his fear as a child, no, there was someone, he was moving silently on the floor and had two green, round eyes, it was Suetonius, he passed by him, and disappeared into the darkness, down the stairs. He felt himself relax.

Now he remembered that somewhere there must be a dark lantern, complete with matches.

He moved cautiously, to the point where he remembered the lantern was. It was there, it wasn't dusty and nearby was a matchbox, half full. Mario thought that evidently someone periodically went up there, and it could only be his grandfather.

He opened the little door of the dark lantern and illuminated the shelf that reached all the way to the back of the room.

He had to move carefully, the boards were old and probably loose. He took a cautious step forward, testing their solidity. They were still, he illuminated them, someone had fixed them well.

Now he was sure, his grandfather went periodically to that place, and he wanted to avoid anyone noticing. What secrets was the engineer hiding?

Mario looked at the diaries one by one, they were still dusty, but there was a book that was different from the others, it was covered in dark leather, and there was no dust on its surface. He reached out and tried to pull out the book, it came out halfway, then stopped, blocked. He was afraid he had made a mess, which his grandfather might notice, so he tried to push it back into place, the book advanced a few millimeters, Mario heard a click behind him, he jumped. He turned and lit up the room behind him, a small door had opened in the wall. He approached cautiously and opened it, there were other books inside, he took one out, opened it, it was a diary, year by year, from 1915. He looked for the one from 1916, it began in the month of October of that year...

Milan 1916.......destiny does not forget

Ervé was ready. He would leave for Bern in a few days, he was just waiting for the authorization and the necessary documents, false passport and all.

When he was summoned by Colonel Melis he thought that it was precisely for that reason, he arrived in Via Mascheroni at the headquarters of Office I a little out of breath due to the emotion.

It was not the first time he left Italy, with the Duke of Abruzzi he had gone to Pakistan for the Karakorum expedition, even if with a secondary assignment. Then he had toured half of Europe, practically any place where there were mountains.

This time, however, he was leaving with a difficult assignment, one he was not used to, espionage was certainly not his profession. He still had trouble understanding why they had assigned him to the intelligence services. Certainly because in a country where people struggled to learn the national language, there were few people who could explain themselves and understand foreign languages. This characteristic made him a bit of a waste as a fighter in the trenches. At least that's what they had told him.

He entered the offices of the service, a few square meters in the building intended for the functions of the Military District of Milan.

The colonel was waiting for him, he seemed rather bored, when he saw him enter he greeted him barely, with a hasty "rest". Then he began to rummage through the papers he had on the table, took out a sheet of tissue paper and without too much ceremony handed it to Ervé, adding a: "Please read, lieutenant".

The communication in the bureaucratic and ceremonious style in use at the time in the Italian army, informed him of a transfer to the ITO office in Rome.

Ervè looked astonished and exclaimed: "Rome... but... but I had to go to Bern?"

The colonel's expression did not change, only his eyes had a momentary glint of disappointment. Then without any emotion he said, with his strong Sardinian accent: "Officers must - I strongly emphasize the word must - do only what they are commanded."

Ervé was confused, he didn't understand, of course in the military you were expected to follow orders without arguing, but this was far beyond what he had understood.

He looked at the Colonel, he was impassive, his gaze devoid of any emotion, his long moustache that seemed like a barrier to prevent his mouth from uttering a word.

"but what am I going to do in Rome...?" Ervé thought to ask.

The stone face maintained its impenetrability: "You report to the Navy Ministry within forty-eight hours, ask the lieutenant Versace's steward, he will explain everything to you."

Then he added in a conclusive tone: "Now you can go."

Vaillante remained motionless for a moment, turned the tissue over in his hands, looked again at the colonel, who finally changed expression and his face expressed urgency for the young officer to leave.

"Commands," Ervé said in a low voice, saluted with a half-hearted gesture, turned on his heel and left.

Lieutenant Versace received Ervé in his office at the Ministry of the Navy. The officer had a very thick black beard, well-groomed and short, and a strong Calabrian accent.

His beard hid half his face, leaving practically only his eyes visible with an intense expression, reminiscent of a ferret. He had Vaillante sit down in front of his desk and began to speak, surprising the command of language, combined with that aspirated accent that would have made one think of something completely different.

He didn't let the young Alpine lieutenant say anything, but he explained to him why he was there.

The Italian network of the Evidenzbureau, that is, the Austrian imperial secret service, seemed to be coordinated by a woman: Countess Von Testory. Her main contact was none other than the Pope's secret valet, a Bavarian prelate named Rudolph Gerlach.

Countess Von Testory was an old acquaintance of the English Intelligence Service. It seems she had two weaknesses: morphine and sex. "For the first," said Versace, "we can do little, since it is the German embassy in the Vatican that supplies it to her, even if of course we have no proof of it. On the second, however, we can do something.

And here you comes: you speaks German, and apart from the irredentists who are all engaged on the front, we have no people who speak that language well and are reliable. Furthermore, thanks to the triple alliance and the passion of our sailors for blondes, there are practically no naval officers in Rome who are not well known by the ladies, who all play a double game, or rather a single game, serving their ancient homeland, Prussia or Austria.

Second, you, Lieutenant, have some experience with German ladies... right?

-Ervè blushed slightly-

"Thirdly, it seems that the lady has a weakness for sportsmen. She was only twenty years old when she met an Italian sportsman, a fencer named Alberto Vassalli from Torreantica, for whom she lost her head and who you, lieutenant, seem to resemble a lot in terms of character..."

Ervé was speechless. His father-in-law who goes around Europe, flitting from flower to flower and marrying maidens of the Prussian nobility? The stern man who had so strongly opposed his marriage to Catherine... Of course, now he understood, his father-in-law saw himself in him, he knew that people like him made women suffer terribly, and the count wanted to spare his daughter such suffering.

The lieutenant stared at Vaillante. Now he understood; a series of fortuitous circumstances made Lieutenant Ervè Vaillante the perfect copy of a man the German agent had fallen in love with years before. Ideal for a diversionary operation that the naval services had been planning for some time.

"You will be our instrument for a diversionary operation..." Versace explained

The lieutenant looked at the naval officer: "So I have no way out..."

"I wouldn't put it that way, Lieutenant. This is an important operation, if it works it will allow us to strike a formidable blow to enemy espionage, and get away with it without any damage.

"What should I do..?" asked Vaillante

"you will have to, let's say, be seduced by the lady. You will make her believe that you has lost your head for her, and that you are willing to give her information about our agents abroad, particularly in Switzerland, even more particularly in Zurich."

"how will I approach this...lady"

"If we are playing our game well, the lady will approach you. In the meantime, you will be assigned as a liaison officer with the ground forces, to the Chief of Naval Staff Admiral Tahon De Revell.

We will make up a story of gambling debts and admiration for the Germanic world. Maybe we will add some lies about your disagreement with the anticlericalism of the Risorgimento, just to make that bastard Gerlach happy".

Rome 1916....the doctor

Elsbeth was not supposed to let anyone know, not even in Germany, her real name, so as an agent of the Evidenz Bureau, she called herself Annemarie Lesser.

She looked around, the church of Sant'Ignazio di Loyola in Campo Marzio showed off all its sumptuousness, despite being covered in the sad colors of Advent, it appeared even more majestic, baroque and full of ornaments. Monsignor Gerlach had decided to organize the contact between her and the informant in that strange place, where there were monuments and relics dedicated to the Society of Jesus. According to her, a bizarre move by the Bavarian prelate, a kind of voluptuous desire to emphasize the triumph of Catholicism over the agents of modernity and oppressors of the power of Holy Mother Church, who had violated the Sacred Throne at Porta Pia.

She, on the other hand, had no particular predilection for the church, but had had to accept her transfer to Rome after an operation in England had failed due to the lack of cunning of her superiors. Here her cover name was Countess Von Testory, officially the wife of an official of the Administrative Commission for Religious Works. A citizen of the Vatican, Count Von Testory, descendant of an officer of the Swiss Guards and member of the Pontifical Palafrinieri. In reality the man was also an agent of the Evidenzbureau, placed in the Vatican, with the approval of Monsignor Gerlach. Anne, on the other hand, came from Holland, where her code name was Fraulein Doctor. Probably because of her habit of carrying around a syringe and a tourniquet, which she used to occasionally give herself injections of morphine, which served to keep her innate shyness at bay and give him the coolness necessary to face his infamous profession.

The officer she was observing in one of the pews in the Ludovisi Chapel had something that attracted her like a magnet. He had broad shoulders, a head worthy of Michelangelo's David, he seemed perfect among those marble statues that cluttered the space of the chapel dedicated to the tomb of Pope Gregory XV. She saw him from behind but it seemed to her that she could guess what his expression was like, what the eyes of such a person might be like. Perhaps it was her madness. Perhaps it was her frantic desire, which had so often pushed her towards men and women, indifferently, ever since she was only sixteen years old and had gotten pregnant by one of her father's subordinate officers. But that man, sitting in one of the pews in front of her, attracted her irresistibly, and then there was a very good reason for completing her mission: revenge!

Ervè pretended to pray, he knew that his liaison agent had to contact him there, in that church that celebrated the glories of the Society of Jesus. He found it quite theatrical. He fervently hoped that his contact would take him where this damned mission was supposed to take him: to that mysterious Von Testory. He had not yet resigned himself to the idea of being a passive instrument of that war of the European powers, which he had once hoped would have brought him honor and glory and instead reduced him to being a kind of male whore.

He pretended to concentrate in prayer, he remained for a few seconds with his face in his hands and his eyes closed, he had the light sensation of something passing by, of an intense perfume, of spices, disturbing like the movement of the hips of a bayadère. He raised his head and turned, he glimpsed the figure of a woman, dressed completely in black, she seemed slender as a willow branch, a hat that fell on one side and from which a veil protruded, hiding the shape of the head and certainly the face.

The woman took the exit of the chapel and disappeared quickly like a mirage. But in the air, very light, that perfume persisted. He saw next to him a small piece of colored paper, folded in two. It was from there that the perfume emanated.

He took the piece of paper and opened it, it only said " *tomorrow at 11 pm, Via dell'orso 60* ". The liaison officer was wasting no time. Better this way, the sooner it started, the sooner it would end. He thought of his son who had just turned six, of his wife, the courageous Caterina who had challenged the severity of her father and the customs of the time. Of course he was rewarding her well, he said to himself bitterly. A bad thought came to him, and he smiled sarcastically to himself: "The austere engineer Vassalli, *do as I say and not as I do* , was already very disappointed, after all he respected that man, This was a surprise... then he decided that anyone, after 11 pm the next day, if they had not known his story thoroughly, could have thought the same of him and decided to suspend judgment. In the meantime that perfume remained in his nose, more and more mysterious, more and more insinuating and more and more seductive.

Ervè walked calmly, to make himself as inconspicuous as possible he wore civilian clothes, very modest: a cycling sweater, a brown velvet jacket, with a few patches here and there, a peaked cap, He wondered if he hadn't exaggerated, maybe he would end up being stopped by some policeman, who would have mistaken him for a thief, in which case how would he have explained the large Bodeo leg of lamb revolver that he had tucked into his belt? The city at that hour was a desert, the war was making its effects felt even on the proverbial cheerfulness of the Romans. There wasn't a living soul, his footsteps echoed on the cobblestones. He crossed the Umberto I bridge and continued for a while along the Tiber, then he turned right and headed towards the point where the street emerged where his mysterious liaison agent was waiting for him. There was no one in the street either, Ervè didn't feel safe, the walls of the houses in the narrow street loomed over him, he approached the wall, then he thought that someone could pop out of the doors and hit him on the head. At number 60, under a street lamp there was a figure, it looked like a man wearing a coat and a lobbed hat, the brim of which overshadowed the features of his face, a flame suddenly illuminated them, just enough time to glimpse the face of a person who wore a beard, so it wasn't the lady they had told him about. It was clear that they intended to take him around a bit to lose stalkers and to confuse his ideas a bit. The man let out a puff of smoke, lowered his hand where he was holding the cigar he had just lit, waited until Vaillante was seven or eight meters away from him, then said in a strange voice, evidently faked, "stop, now I'm going towards Via dei Portoghesi, you follow me, but don't get closer than ten meters to me." Then he turned and started walking. Ervè waited a few seconds and then he too started walking, on the trail of the mysterious character.

The man walked down Via dell'Orso, with Ervè at his heels, he walked slowly, and with a gait that seemed strange to Vaillante, perhaps a little swaying, no, not swaying, he wasn't actually swaying. He shivered, he really hoped he wouldn't have to make that compromise too... They reached the corner of Via di Ripetta, stopped on the corner of Via della Stelletta was a carriage, a brumm, whose closed compartment had the curtains drawn. On the box of the vehicle was a coachman in a green overcoat and a top hat. Ervè's contact climbed into the carriage, then stuck his head out and motioned for him to get on board, "hurry up," he said in an authoritative tone and a strange shrill voice.

As Ervè got into the carriage he smelled that scent, the same one that was on the ticket in the church of San'Ignazio... ah that's why "the man was shaking his hips..", it was a woman, that woman he had glimpsed in the Ludovisi chapel.

He fixed her with an inquiring and ironic look, the liaison agent had taken off, or rather taken off, the bowler hat he was wearing and his beard.

Now she let her hair down.

She was not what you would call a beauty. Her features were very hard, almost angular. Her small, pointed nose looked like a wasp's stinger, her cheekbones were high, slightly too prominent. However, a powerful charm emanated from that woman, she seemed to attract like flowers attract insects in the summer. And then she had something, something in her gaze. Her very black eyes, like those of Arabs or Indians, shone with a strange fervor, or perhaps it was a passion, she seemed to have a fever, a furious fever that seemed to devour her inside. That singular dark light in her gaze contrasted with a severe expression, almost as if her face were ashamed of those too penetrating eyes, revealing a ferocious passion. The very white color of the woman's skin enhanced her pupils even more, like two pieces of coal in a puddle of milk. Her thin, vermilion lips, with a slightly bitter crease, completed that singular physiognomy.

Ervé started to speak, but the woman made him an unmistakable signal with her gloved hand to be silent, pointing to the coachman.

The carriage went all the way down Via di Ripetta to Ponte Cavour, where it turned. It went all the way down and turned left, following Lungotevere Prati. They stopped at the side of Castel Sant'Angelo. The woman put on a large cloak, with a hood that covered almost her entire face, an out-of-fashion and out-of-time garment, but which hid her almost entirely.

They entered the gardens of Piazza Adriana, the gate was closed but the woman had a key, she opened it and signaled Ervè to hurry up. They walked a few meters along Via Cardinal Dell'Acqua and headed towards the castle moat. There was a staircase that led to the moat, they went down it, the woman headed towards the ancient entrance of the Mole Adriana. She approached the walls, pushed something into the wall and a door opened. They entered, they found themselves in a passage.

The door closed and they fell into darkness. The woman struck a flint, and with it she approached the wall to light herself. There was a niche with a dark lantern, she took it and lit it, then she set off while Ervè followed her, passively. It seemed that the mysterious lady moved with a brazen confidence, almost as if the meanders of that ancient mass were the corridors of her house. The darkness and the slightly sinister light of the dark lantern gave him a feeling of anguish, he was reminded of ancient legends that were told in his valleys, the tales of the Lamia that populated the night. Perhaps she was a witch who was dragging him to hell. He didn't know where they were going, but he understood that they were walking through secret passages in the bowels of the great ancient building. They emerged on the walls, in front of the entrance to Passetto di Borgo and ventured there. They walked along it all the way to the Vatican. They went down a staircase and found themselves in via Sant' Anna, a little further on was the tower of Niccolo V, towards which the woman headed. Her irrational fear subsided, after all they were now inside the sacred heart of Rome... but what the hell, witches don't exist and that was an enemy agent, to whom he had to tell a plausible story.

In front of the entrance to the tower there was a Swiss Guard, the woman lowered her hood, and approached the soldier, she said something to him in a hoarse and gurgling German, swissdeutch.. probably. The sentry jumped to attention and let them pass. They continued down the corridor, to a door made of seasoned wood, inlaid and decorated with iron studs, the woman turned the handle, entered and operated a small key on the side of the door itself. The gas lights illuminated a room furnished in Renaissance style. There were old paintings on the walls and padded leather armchairs. The woman said almost without any accent: "Please take a seat...". Ervè entered and went to sit on one of the armchairs, while she took off her cloak and remained standing. She looked him straight in the eyes, with her magnetic gaze. The male suit she was wearing seemed tailor-made, making that figure even more disturbing. The long hair, thick and puffy, like a black cloud over the very white face made one think of a barbaric storm deity. Ervè felt conflicting sensations inside himself; on the one hand that being scared him, there was nothing of feminine sweetness in her, the expression in those eyes was of a hardness conceivable more for a ferocious beast than for a woman. A wind of defiance blew from her, an almost physical force that seemed to say "try to touch me if you dare..." and yet that same defiance seemed to attract irresistibly, like when in his mountains he found himself in front of a wall apparently impossible to climb and he regularly managed to tame it. He decided that he had to accept that arm wrestling with that being so impenetrable.

"So..." said the countess, "you are the man who should reveal to us the arcane secrets of the supreme command." The woman said with an obviously sarcastic tone.

"No madam...- Ervé replied- I do not know the secrets of the supreme command, because only General Cadorna knows them, who reveals them only at the very last moment.- he paused- at most I can get hold of the minutes of the communications of the naval command. The messages that Tahon de Revel sends, and also the orders that are given to the stations of the naval intelligence service, abroad, particularly in Switzerland!"

The woman looked shocked.

"Ah..." she exclaimed then remained silent for a few seconds, the hard expression cracked for an instant, a lightning-fast flutter, as if a sort of amazement had insinuated itself into that steel face and forced the facial muscles to relax for the briefest of moments.

But he recovered immediately, as if nothing had happened.

"And why should you give us this news... like this – he moved a hand in a circular motion, three fingers half-stretched and two bent, in a vague gesture to underline what he was saying – important..." and he gave a sort of smile, just a twist of the mouth, a little contemptuous"

"Come on, Countess, let's not play with words, you know very well that I have huge gambling debts, otherwise why would a moustachioed gentleman who only spoke about agriculture be so often appeared in all the gambling dens of Rome where I went to squander the family fortune!"

The countess looked at him intently: "Mr. Vaillante, I am a professional in this profession, I must tell you sincerely that there are not many professionals like me in Europe, and this means that you are not very lucky, that is, it will not be easy for me to trust you, it will take a long time before I do, a very long time..."

His black eyes lit up with a light of satisfaction, almost of victory, which Ervè considered excessive, a sort of capricious triumph.

Ervé sighed: "... Take all the time you want, even until the end of the war... but in the meantime, perhaps someone will have struck somewhere, perhaps in Switzerland, and will have taken possession of the list of your agents in Italy, those who are helping you sabotage ships and arsenals and ammunition depots of the Navy..."

Then he stood up and looked around: "Well... if we have nothing else to say, maybe I'd better go," he said.

The countess looked at him, her expression halfway between astonished and half about to burst out laughing.

"Do you really think you can just walk out of here without my permission...?" he said flatly.

"Do you really think you can make me disappear into thin air in Rome without anyone coming to look for me...?"

Ervé answered calmly

The woman looked at him again with the same expression as before:

"Yes... certainly, it wouldn't be the first and I don't think it would be the last, we are in the territory of a foreign state, which is not at war with Italy, and I can assure you that no one will come looking for you here..."

Ervé realized he was in a situation from which it was impossible to escape with his own strength, the woman in front of him had his life in her hands. She looked at him with that expression, as if he were a hare stuck in a corner and she was the fox, ready to break his neck with a bite.

It was the most embarrassing situation he had ever been in, that was the word that came to mind, not ..dangerous, not dramatic.., but embarrassing. He was playing poker with her, he had bluffed and she had called the bluff, and now he didn't know what to do or say, except that in this case it wasn't a pot of poker at stake, but his life.

He decided to give up, or rather to make her believe that she had won, perhaps the countess liked the idea of winning over men, perhaps if he had "put himself in her hands... she would have felt like the winner, perhaps at that point his ego so imperative, would have made him make a mistake... but a light dawned on Ervé: what was the point, why bring him all the way there, just for the pleasure of killing him... to show him who was in charge... No, that woman had a sense of spectacle, a victory achieved there in the silence and solitude of that room, in that ancient tower, without an audience to see her and applaud her, no, it made no sense. The countess wanted something from him, perhaps sex? It seemed like a stupid idea to him, he was the head of the Evidenz Bureau in Rome, a professional, as she said, why settle for a small success, a miserable victory when he could have done much more, why waste time in this stage setting Tosca, if she thought he couldn't provide her with interesting information, could have eliminated him on the street or if she wanted to have sex with him and that's it, there were dozens of places in Rome, outside the Vatican, in less dangerous places. Maybe she could still carry on the bluff or better still see him in turn.

He sat back down, looked the woman straight in the eyes, sighed: "Well, Countess... I'm in your hands, what do you want from me..."

The fox kept his expression: "exactly what you told me: I want to know who they are, how many there are and where they intend to operate, the Italian agents of the Navy's secret services.

They are very dangerous people for us, they could discover very serious things... and we don't want that. So dear Vaillante, we will give you what you ask for and you will give us what we need... »

Then she approached him. Ervè was hit by that scent, and by a sort of seductive wave he had the sensation, physically perceptible, of having been captured, of having fallen into a spider's web, from which something inside him held him back from escaping, something that grew when the countess took him by the nape of the neck and stuck her tongue in his mouth.

Elsbeth decided to enjoy that "unorthodox" part of the game, while thinking that with that man, in addition to becoming aware of information that the Evidenz Bureau had been following for some time, she would also get a little personal satisfaction, returning a checkmate that dated back to a long time ago...

The prelate looked through the blind mirror, now, he said to himself, came the funny part, the Pope did not know that side of his character, but that was not the only thing he did not know about him... "Thank God," he said quietly to himself.

Mario hadn't noticed the shadow behind him, he felt a very light breathing and turned around suddenly, Mrs. Colombo was looking at him, sweet and stern as always.

"Mister Mario, you know that your grandfather the Count does not want you to come to this place and read these diaries..."

Mario was speechless for a second, then he looked at the lady: "Please, don't say anything..."

The lady's expression changed slightly: "As long as you go back to bed immediately, let's say that this will remain a secret between us, but it must never happen again that you disobey the count's will."

Mario bowed his head and murmured "OK... okay" and headed towards his room, but now he wanted to know who that Countess Von Testory was, where she had ended up and, above all, what had happened to his father.

Berlin .... November 1922.......... Dinner with the apocalypse

Otto looked out the window, it had been dark for a while. In Berlin, at that time of year, evening came very early, around half past four, which meant that he and his assistant Lise did not realize that time was passing, it was getting late and they in turn were late for dinner. But that evening Otto could not go wrong, he had been invited by his friend Fabian Rinkweiser, the Swiss cultural attaché, a physics enthusiast, gifted with a great and versatile intelligence, who had become friends with Einstein during the latter's stay in Zurich and had met the brilliant scientist of the theory of relativity again at a physicists' conference, organized by the Canton of Zurich, in 1919. From then on, once every six months Rinkweiser invited Einstein, Otto Hann and Niels Bohr to dinner, who on those occasions even came from Copenhagen. During dinner they talked about a bit of everything and it was also an opportunity for the three scientists to compare notes on their study topics. The cultural attaché's daughter, Sabine, often took part in the banquet. She was a girl particularly gifted in physics and had often had extraordinary intuitions, even from the point of view of luminaries such as Hann and Einstein.

Otto Hann was forty-three years old, and certainly one of the most brilliant physicists at the Kaiser Wilhelm Institute. In

1918, together with his assistant, Lise Meitner, an Austrian Jew who had converted to Protestantism, they had isolated a long-lived radioactive element, which they had called protactinium, a discovery that meant nothing to the layman, but which had enormous significance in the world of science.

He looked at his watch, it was 6:30 pm, he had to be at the Swiss consulate within an hour.

He decided to hurry, since it would take about forty minutes from where the Kaiser Wilhelm Institute was located to Rinkweiser's home, near the Swiss embassy, and he didn't want to be late, especially with a Swiss man.

Quickly but carefully he put away all his notes. He took off his coat, put on his jacket, coat and hat and went out. It was cold, very cold. He looked for a taxi, it took him a few minutes then he saw one, he raised his hand to stop it, but it was busy and he continued on. "Damn," Otto exclaimed to himself, but the taxi stopped. He saw a full head of hair and an arm leaning out of the back window, at the end of which the hand was waving a black hat. He looked more closely, it was Albert Einstein. Otto lengthened his stride and got into the taxi on the opposite side to his colleague.

"We are going in the same direction, I suppose?" Einstein asked. "Same direction," Hann said, smiling.

The two scientists exchanged a few playful pleasantries, "Do you think we'll have fondue tonight..." Einstein asked questioningly, "No, I'm afraid we'll have some Jewish dishes instead. You know, Rinkweiser loves to adapt to the tastes of his guests," Hann replied.

"But I don't like Jewish cuisine, damn, let's hope that tonight he decides to be rude and prepares some tasty dish, his wife is half Italian, maybe she'll make pasta with meatballs..." Einstein countered,

"Well. Worst case scenario, we'll console ourselves with shnaps, last time he had a really good one..."

They continued with this idle talk until Rinkweiser's door.

They rang, a very young waitress opened the door, blushing up to her ears when she saw the two men. Albert showed off his most reassuring smile. The girl seemed to relax, in fact the Nobel Prize winner did not have the stern expression of a professor of his level, indeed with that hair a little too long and rather messy and the big moustache, he seemed like a creature from a fairy tale book.

Rinkweiser was about the same age as the other two, forty-three, but he had a youthful appearance. His cheeks were shaved, his hair was cut a bit like a Prussian, which made him the object of some irony from the other guests. He had gold-rimmed glasses and a particularly infectious smile.

The dinner was beyond the expectations of the two scientists. They talked about the prize Einstein had won that year for the discovery of the photoelectric effect.

Also at the table was Rinkweiser's daughter, Sabine, who listened all evening as the adults talked about their work and their favorite subject: physics.

At one point she approached her father and asked him something, whispering in his ear. Her mother looked at her sternly: "Sabine, you don't whisper in one's ear, it's not polite." Rinkweiser smiled. "Excuse me Mara, it's just that our Sabine would like to ask Albert a question."

Einstein looked at her with sympathy: "tell me dear"

Sabine seemed to think for a second, then asked, "Here, professor, your equation E=mc2, what does that mean exactly?"

Einstein smiled again: "To summarize, it means that there is a relationship between energy and mass or, if you prefer, matter."

Sabine looked impressed, and continued "But that means that any of us could turn into energy"

"Well in a way... yes," Einstein said thoughtfully, "if we could divide the atoms that make us up."

And... Sabine continued – so if we can transform ourselves into energy, we could disappear in a flash of light, like wizards... like in a firework?"

Silence fell in the dining room, the three looked at each other, and at that moment they all understood the same thing: "Yes," Einstein said, almost in a whisper, like a firework.

"Or in a bomb..." Hann concluded with an eerie, suspended tone.

3.5 Deer Island Maine... 1924.... The Author and His Alterego

WB was sitting in the council room of the Skull and Bones house, he was in the company of two members of the order, the two who had been entrusted with the German question.

Everyone's faces were rather gloomy. The news from Bavaria was not good, not good at all! The chosen one had made a grave mistake, but above all those who were supposed to direct and guide him had not been able to do so. The coup d'état of the 8th of that month had not been well organized. The action of the NSDAP had fallen on deaf ears, even the intervention of the powerful general Ludendorf had been of no use. WB turned to his brother sitting on his right:

"I believe that this putsch was not well organised, it was premature" he said with a tone of reproach directed at everyone and no one and which for this very reason appeared more worrying.

WB had the monstrous ability, even when speaking generally, to make everyone feel guilty.

"However," he continued, "we must look on the bright side of the situation. In the end, the sentence was lenient and not only that: it played into our plan to use communication to win over the German people. The newspapers have been talking about him for 24 days, and I understand that in prison he is treated like a head of state. However, we must keep him under control.

The man we had placed next to him… what was his name? »
he made a strange gesture with his hand, and someone suggested
« Hess, Rudolf Hess »

"That's right… he took refuge in Austria, right?" someone
confirmed again.

"Well, let him come back, we'll need him. The time has come
for our man to write his gospel, his Koran, someone will have to
suggest it to him and help him write, it seems to me that from the
point of view of the pen our corporal is not exactly a champion…"

There was the usual confirmation

« Well we will use our man in the NSDAP. Hess had worked well
up to this point, we must not leave Hitler alone, he is a very bizarre
guy and I do not want him to have dangerous exits for himself and
for our project.

Maybe we can get him some reading that will help and motivate
him. WB thought for a moment. "There's that book by Mr. Ford,
The *International Jew,* I think it's ideal for inspiring our man,
make sure it gets to him. Then give orders to Mr. Hess to return
to Bavaria and hand himself in. We'll see to it that they put him in
Landsberg with Hitler."

Landsberg am Lech…..1924

It was not a good day. Outside the fortress the weather was
gloomy, it was raining and windy. Adolf Hitler was sensitive to
the weather and on those days, his gloomy and neurotic nature
emerged in its most exasperated aspects.

He had decided to have breakfast in his cell, and his jailers
had promptly complied with his wishes.

He was not satisfied with the book he was writing, dictating
it to his friend and subordinate in the SA, Emil Maurice, a good
typist, but naturally incapable of making literary suggestions.
He, the Fuhrer, was a great talker, but when he took up the

pen his lack of sympathy for school and his little attendance at the classrooms took their revenge. His flaming ideas, which he knew how to express so well verbally, became an unreadable tirade, full of blunders, repetitions without the force that his word required. When he read Henry Ford's book he was inflamed. The anti-Semitic contents of the text of the one he considered a great man, reflected his ideas exactly. How he would have liked to have the same ability as Ford in expressing those concepts that were so clear in his mind, but that on paper lost all beauty. The same friends who had given him Ford's book had suggested that he write a text, which would become the bible of the party, the ideological basis on which to build the conquest of power. But thanks to the incapacity of those "dirty, infamous Jews" who controlled the German school, he had not been able to study and therefore did not have the gift of writing.

Rudolf Hess entered at that moment: "Good morning my Fhurer..."

He did so in his usual emphatic tone.

Then he noticed the expression in Hitler's eyes. He knew it well, it was the one on bad days. The blue and transparent eyes became glassy, the jaw was tense, the mouth took on a bitter and ferocious turn.

Hess knew that mood had something to do with the bad weather.

He saw a pad of papers in one corner of the table, written in Maurice's neat postal worker handwriting, and understood what the problem could be.

But he didn't say anything, the Führer was easily irritable in those days and it took nothing to unleash his anger.

Hitler had stopped eating, he turned his gaze towards Hess: "Rudolf... how did you go to school?"

Hess thought for a moment before answering, he had to be careful what he said...

"pretty good mein fürer." - then he added - you know... I studied out of respect for discipline"

« and how do you get by with writing... »

The moment had come, their financiers had asked him to "take care" of writing the "bible" of the National Socialist movement, they knew that Hitler was "much better with words than with writing" and he had to write that book.

« What would you say Hess about contributing to the writing of my work. You know, right? That I am dictating to Maurice a text that will be the guide of the movement and unfortunately because of the stupidity of my teachers I have not studied the literary aspects sufficiently... in short I will ask you to be my arm. Of course it would be better if I were to write this work... but... In short I am the prophet of the new Germanic religion and I must write a book that will be its guide all the prophets have done it... »

Hess noticed Hitler's embarrassment in admitting his ignorance to one of his subordinates.

« Of course all the prophets did it, but not all of them wrote it directly. The Gospel was not written by Jesus Christ. His apostles, Saint Luke, Saint Mark, Saint Matthew and Saint John, took care of it... you, mein Fhurer, will have to be content with me... »

Hitler's expression suddenly changed, his gaze lost its emptiness, and he returned, penetrating. Hess had solved the problem brilliantly, without embarrassing him.

"What will this work be called, my leader...?"

Hitler looked at him intensely: "mein kampf Rudolf, it will be called mein kampf! Try looking at that work" he said pointing to the ream of paper on the table.

Hess took it and began to read; it was a solemn piece of rubbish in ungrammatical and not at all fluent German.

up and said, "Allow me to retire to my cell, this is a job that requires concentration."

The next morning he returned to the Führer: "Here," he said, "I've given him a little fix."

Hitler assumed a thoughtful expression and began to read:

On February 24, 1920, the first great public demonstration of our young movement took place. In the hall of the Royal Beer Hall in Munich, the twenty-five theses of the program of the new party were presented to a crowd of nearly two thousand people, and each point was approved amid shouts of agreement and jubilation.

With this were laid down the guidelines and fundamental principles of a struggle aimed at putting an end to the very filth of decrepit conceptions and opinions and to all unclear, indeed harmful, aims. A new force was to be launched against the lazy and cowardly bourgeois world, against the triumphal march of the Marxist wave, in order to rebalance, at the last hour, the chariot of Destiny ."

He looked at Hess: "... yes Rudolf, you did a good job, we will continue today.

Budapest...... 1926.... It sometimes appears shrouded in mist, magical and beautiful, but if the pilot moves forward........

Even though Mario had just turned seventeen, with one of the miracles his grandfather was able to perform, he had been included as an observer in the foil team that participated in the 1926 "European Fencing Championships".

Mario was a great fencer; he and Amedeo had started one day playing pirates, then they had become passionate about it, they had been lucky that the gym teacher at the college was a swordsman, who had taught them the first rudiments.

One summer when they were both guests of their grandfather in Vizzola, the engineer had seen them duel. He had stopped to watch them, they had not noticed anything and had continued to exchange blows and parries, until, they had heard applause, they had turned and had seen their grandfather with a half smile, he never went beyond the one with the children, who was slowly clapping his hands.

"Well done! This is a real man's sport…".

They both jumped to attention, blushing up to their ears, sweating and panting.

Grandpa, tall and thin as a bamboo, always wore dark suits, made to measure by a Sicilian tailor from Varese, who came to the house to take measurements, and who never needed to come back a second time. Grandpa's carefully trimmed mustache was turning white, but his eyes were blue and piercing like two bayonets, his gait similar to that of a Hidalgo, did not betray his 53 years. His completely shaved head looked like that of a Roman bust, for example of Scipio Africanus, just above his left eye there was a thin white scar, the result of a duel fought with a socialist deputy, years before. They said that the other one had it worse, though.

He looked at them both again. Then he turned to Mario. "Where did you learn to fight like this?"

"Our gymnastics teacher, Mr. Grandpa, taught us"

"Ah… I hope that's not the only thing they're teaching you in that college for young ladies," said the man.

"Allow me, Count…" said Amedeo, with the comical air of a little English gentleman.

The man looked him up and down, raising an eyebrow: "Tell me, young man."

"It's not a boarding school for young ladies, my father would never send me to a place for young ladies, word of an officer" Guillet said with great and comical pride.

The grandfather almost seemed to smile: "That's true."

Mario continued: "Grandpa, they teach us many things. Amedeo and I are the best in arithmetic and history. We won the second quarter competition, so to reward us they allowed us to practice fencing in the evening after vespers."

The grandfather turned to Guillet: "Is it the truth...?" he asked in a voice that did not allow for pretense: "Yes, Count" replied Amedeo very seriously.

"All right, if you like fencing I will have a teacher come here from Milan next summer, if your parents allow it you will be our guest...Of course as long as you continue to behave properly" ; concluded the count, in a tone that did not allow for replies.

Mario had become a little champion, he had been noticed by the fascist authorities, who had courted him in every way, he had won the national championships of the Avanguardisti. When Mario, who was now attending a classical high school, had heard about the championships in Budapest, he had expressed to his grandfather his desire to go and see them. He had been satisfied, given that his scholastic results were excellent.

He had left with the national team, amidst Roman salutes and waving flags. In the Hungarian capital, the Italians had, as usual in fencing, made a great impression. Chiavacci had won gold in the individual foil.

The sympathies that the regent Horty had for the fascist regimes took the form of invitations to parties and ceremonies to celebrate the Italian victory at the championships, even though in reality it had occurred at the expense of the Hungarians, traditional adversaries of our fencers.

One evening they were invited to the opera house. It was a cool summer evening, along Handrassy Hut, in front of the neo-Renaissance mass of the opera house, lit up like a cruise ship and decorated with the flags of the nations participating in the fencing championships, luxurious cars, Mercedes, Rolls Royce and Lancia, Renault, with shiny chrome, stopped, from which officers in full uniform, gentlemen in tailcoats and women in elegant evening dresses alighted.

The couples climbed the few steps of the external ramp, decorated with a red carpet, and entered the large foyer of the theater, greeted by two hussars in full uniform who stood guard on either side of the door. The entrance was illuminated by the light diffused by the large suspended chandelier, which illuminated the beautiful frescoes and sculptures by Bertalan Székely, Mór Than and Károly Lotz.

Mario and his teammates wore white double-breasted uniforms, complete with black shirts and ties.

The young fencer was simultaneously excited and intimidated by that extraordinary atmosphere. Not even in his wildest childhood dreams had he ever imagined anything like it. He would have liked his friend Amedeo to be with him, who had not been able to come due to a family commitment.

Mario felt full of pride in his Italianness, he didn't understand much about politics, but as a young man with great and beautiful hopes, he was convinced that fascism was giving his beloved homeland one of the most beautiful moments in its extraordinary history.

On the program was Puccini's "Tosca", an opera that Mario had learned to love, thanks to a friend of his grandfather, confined to a wheelchair by an accident in the mountains. His sporty and indomitable temperament had suffered a serious trauma from that disability, from which the man had emerged thanks to music, when in 1924 the URI had started to broadcast music via radio, Mr. Ugo, as he was called, spent all the time possible next to the device, managing to reach even foreign radio stations. The man had become an expert in radio and radio telephony, and had a very powerful system, which was granted to him only thanks to the friendships that his father's and mother's families had both at court and in the PNF. Every now and then Mario went to visit him, he listened to those broadcasts in the strangest languages, remote emissions, whose origin appeared on the small green-lit screen, over which the tuner rod ran: radio Delhi, radio Paris, radio London... .

It was a masterly performance, and as usual when he listened to that piece, Mario could hardly hold back his tears, when the tenor, who played Mario Cavaradossi, performed the romance "E lucean le stelle..." and like the entire audience, their hands were clapped out in open applause when the singer emitted his last desperate cry of love towards Tosca and towards life: "e non ho amato tanto la vita..." (and I have never loved life so much...).

As he applauded, he looked toward one of the boxes, and his heart sank. A fleeting image had struck him. The faint vision of a white evening dress, of an almost evanescent figure, which immediately seemed to disappear.

Although, for the last part of the performance Mario continued to explore the long rows of boxes, he was unable to recover that vision.

The lights came on and people began to flow out of the boxes and the stalls, gradually crowding the splendid staircase and the foyer.

Mario went down the stairs, and the Italian ambassador, to whom they had been attached, stopped to chat with an official from the Hungarian Foreign Ministry, who was accompanied by a very tall, very "flat" lady, with a strange feverish expression, who was speaking to another woman in a language that sounded like German, but almost seemed like a Germanic dialect.

Mario looked around and suddenly felt the thump in his heart again and the vision from before reappeared: it was a girl, beautiful and dark, with green eyes like two emeralds. Maybe she was as young as him, she was wearing a white dress that she had covered with a very light stole of the same color, studded with rhinestones.

He walked down the aisle smiling, on the arm of a gentleman wearing the full dress uniform of the Royal Air Force, with a row of medals and decorations, and another gentleman in a tailcoat, a man of about forty, with a pair of round, gold-framed glasses that made him resemble the former American President Wilson.

The girl smiled, with an irresistibly seductive expression and spoke to the two, both seemed enchanted by the beauty and charm of that young woman, but the most struck of all was Mario. That girl was the same one he had seen in a dream as a child, the night after he had heard "the most beautiful", the poem by Gozzano. While the girl was coming down, he looked at her with his mouth open, he seemed to hear the voice of Professor Guzzetti again: "but the most beautiful of all is the island not found...".

The trio passed very close to him, perhaps they noticed his expression, while the girl blushed violently and changed expression, as if she too had seen a ghost. The officer noticed the scene, shook his head a little, smiled and said "Eh, Eh... Italians!", comically rolling his eyes to the sky.

As the three of them walked out of the theater doors, she turned to give him an unforgettably seductive look over her shoulder.

Perhaps the Italian consul and the lady who spoke the strange German also noticed something, because they both looked at Mario with an indulgent expression, and the lady said to him jokingly "Wie ich verstehe, ist wirklich hübsch (I understand you... she's really cute)".

He didn't speak German and was even more confused, so the lady, in a slightly haphazard and distorted Italian, said to him: "Ich, comprendo te, ist proprio *Karina* ".

They went outside, the girl and the two men had got into a Rolls Royce Silver Ghost, which had quickly driven away.

Mario's heart was in turmoil, he felt the same emotion inside him as that night, luckily he was no longer a child, so he did not have the same consequences that he had faced when he woke up in the dormitory of the college. But he remained all evening in a strange state between euphoric and dazed, so much so that one of the fencers, a sharp-tongued Livorno native, made a couple of harsh jokes that the boy did not understand, partly because of the vernacular in which the man expressed himself and partly because at only 17 years old, some of the heaviness of the older males escaped him!

They returned to the Hotel, Margitsziget, on Margaret Island in the middle of the Danube. In that hotel were lodged all the delegations of the nations participating in the fencing tournament.

Mario went back into his room. He was a little ashamed of the embarrassment he had made watching that beautiful girl go down the theater stairs. He also felt a little jealous, who knows who those two damned Englishmen he was hanging out with were. And that idiot aviator, what did he have to make fun of... "The Italians!" Mario said to himself, imitating the officer's voice: "I would have liked to see you on the platform!! I would have shown you the Italians!!"

He went to bed still agitated. He couldn't fall asleep, he tossed and turned, in that bed as if it had thorns instead of the comfortable mattress on which he actually lay.

He kept thinking about the two who were accompanying the girl .

They were probably just some of his relatives. "The English are a depraved, exploitative people, but those didn't seem so terrible! They were probably his father and uncle," he thought to himself, hoping he was right.

He had conceived that idea about the British while reading Salgari's books, he imagined that all the inhabitants of the island across the Channel were more or less all James Brookes, bloodthirsty and greedy for riches.

He managed to banish the two importunate men from his mind, but his thoughts returned to her, it was impossible, but that was the woman from his dream, he began to imagine adventures in the South Seas, and she was a sort of Marianna Guillonk and he was an Italian Sandokan.

Finally he decided to get up and go out onto the balcony to get some fresh air. From the terrace he could see the long Danube and the city of Pest lit up, and the night was warm, but not muggy, suddenly he smelled that scent again, turned around and saw her: she was leaning out onto the balcony next to his and was looking at him. Mario was as if paralyzed, then something inside him started moving, he approached the balustrade and making a huge effort asked, "but who are you?"

The girl smiled, with her mouth that looked like a pearl necklace, and answered, in Italian, with a warm, melodious accent, which felt like a caress to Mario: "My name is Cynthia and you...".

"I..my name is Mario."

Cynthia's eyes became two shining emerald lights, her gaze seemed like a wave of light that hit him and warmed him like the desert wind: "How beautiful you are..." she said, then, throwing him one last enchanting look, she turned and went towards the French window to go back into the room.

Mario, almost without a voice, said: "wait... I, I have to tell you something - but by now she had one hand on the handle of the French window -... I want to see you again", said Mario, with the childishly desperate tone of a child asking his mother not to go to bed yet.

She stopped and turned around, smiled again, giving a small, delightful shrug of her shoulders like Venus Calipyge: "Who knows... maybe one day, maybe here in Budapest again!" Mario then felt himself fill with joy, as if that were an oath, as if that promise were not pure madness, as it seemed, but a certainty of destiny: "So will we see each other again in Budapest?" "Yes," she said, "I'll see you in Budapest" and disappeared into the room.

Mario stayed awake for a long time dreaming of that girl, of that island, he felt a sort of nostalgia inside him... no it was anxiety, the anxiety of the next time he would see her again, and he knew it would happen.

Then toward dawn a sinister thought crept into his mind, like a snake in the Garden of Eden. He remembered that woman with the German accent, a woman... German, like Von Testory, yes, if that was really her name, Von Testory, who certainly knew where her father had gone.

3.6 Poughkeepsie, New York November 1927......Ivy League

The driver stopped the car, got out and opened the back door to let Cynthia and Mr. William out, then went to the trunk and took out two large suitcases. William looked at them with an ironic look, then turned to his adoptive daughter and with his usual soft and warm tone said: "... Do you plan to change often ...!", the girl smiled, showing the two seductive dimples that opened at the sides of her mouth every time she did it. "As often as I see fit ... and even more."

"Well," William continued, "if you are so keen to study, how many clothes will we have a Nobel Prize?"

Cynthia smiled again coquettishly "I will study as much as I need and change when necessary", then she turned toward the entrance of the residence where she had been assigned a room. In the afternoon there would be the welcoming ceremony of the new students of Vassar College, one of the best women's colleges in the United States. Cynthia Uberti Stephenson, hugged her adoptive father, who remained, as was his habit, a little embarrassed by that sincere display of affection, winked at him and set off followed by the gigantic driver who carried her heavy suitcases as if they were two twigs.

There was a girl at the entrance, a student who was in charge of welcoming the new arrivals, she had a pair of round glasses, a friendly and welcoming smile and she blushed every time she addressed a new arrival. Cynthia introduced herself to her, that blush had a strange effect on her, she couldn't understand what, but it was like a disturbance. The young woman's name was Caireen O'Mallei, she looked at her documents and directed her with a kind gesture towards one of the attendants who took the documents from Cynthia's hands and escorted her to a door in walnut, dark in color, with a spherical handle, in shining brass, reflecting everything around her in a distorted image that made her look like a small alef, imprisoned in the shiny metal. The door was unlocked, the young woman turned the sphere without any effort and pushed the door, which opened on perfectly oiled hinges and was in a room, soberly furnished with two bookcases, two brass beds, two desks built into the bookcases, a wardrobe divided into four doors. On one of the two doors on the right was glued a frame, which contained a small card with written in thin and precise handwriting "Ms. Uberti". Between the two bookcases was a window that looked out onto a garden, perfectly kept.

Cynthia, put the suitcases on the bed, and opened the closet, began to look at the various shelves to decide how to distribute her clothes: She heard the door open behind her, she turned and found herself in front of a girl. She was tall, she had very black hair, cut in a mop, two large eyes of an intense brown color, that seemed to shine like two topazes behind a pair of round glasses with a tortoise frame. The makeup, barely there, around them made them stand out even more. Her mouth seemed drawn, and she was wearing lipstick, which was strange for a girl of their age, at least in America. She had a pointed nose, surrounded by freckles, a small pronounced and round chin from the right of which a small wart barely protruded, which made her, who knows why, strangely attractive.

"Good morning," she said in a nice, rather high-pitched voice, "My name is Sabine, I'm Swiss."

She put the only suitcase on the floor and took a step toward Cynthia, who also stepped toward her and shook that hand, gaining a vice-like grip. She gave a pained expression, and Sabine understood, apologized "Um... my hands are a little too strong" and after a short pause "... you know I love sailing and so...". That then hung in the air, a then that was supposed to explain the strength of those hands, that made you think of bollards, hawsers, port and starboard sides, pirates and adventures in the South Seas.

They both looked at each other for a moment, their conversation remained suspended for a few seconds, as if they had not yet decided what their relationship could be. Then Cynthia felt inside a warm sensation, which rose from her heart to her lips, making a wide smile blossom, which found a match in Sabine's lips, slightly timidly pursed to show a set of perfect, white teeth.

"Well," the Swiss girl began timidly, "it seems that for a while she and I will have to live together."

"I have a lot of bad habits: I snore at night, I sleepwalk, and when the moon rises I turn into a werewolf... and you?"

Sabine blushed violently, then burst out laughing: "Well... I snore too, I'm not a sleepwalker, I'm not a werewolf......But – then making a funny expression, raising and waving her hands, and raising her voice – I am a vampire and I feed on the blood of young creatures"

Cynthia burst out laughing too. They both burst into convulsive laughter, tears in their eyes. At that moment the girl who had welcomed them entered, she was a little surprised and her eyes widened at their uncontrollable laughter.

She coughed, and the two women noticed her, they managed to stop the laughter, but this cost Cynthia a fit of hiccups. She couldn't speak so Sabine spoke: "Good morning she said" , trying to stifle the laughter that didn't seem to want to die away.

The three of them, with Cynthia sobbing, Sabine muttering and the third one looking at them amused and without saying a word, but with a smile that hovered between her round glasses and her full mouth, gave a funny impression, but at the same time they seemed to be three old friends who met again after who knows how long.

When Cynthia managed to stop her sobs and Sabine her laughter, the third arrival introduced itself.

"Good morning, my name is Caireen O' Malley and I will be your tutor. Which means I will help you with your studies. I will prepare you for your exams and I will accompany you until the end of the year in your preparation path".

Cynthia suddenly stopped laughing and sobbing, it was as if a curtain had suddenly fallen, now all three were silent and smiling, they were almost out of breath, breathing deeply after the long laugh. Sabine and Cyanthia's chest moved rhythmically to catch their breath. Cynthia in that moment caught a sensation, the same one she had had when she met her at the entrance to the College, but more intense, a kind of sudden physical perception of the young tutor with the blatant Irish surname. She didn't know if it was a deja vu or the singular idea of having always known Caireen, or maybe it was something else.

Cynthia was enrolled in the literature course, her dream was to become a writer and journalist, to travel the world and have an eventful and adventurous life, at only 11 years old, she had written a novel, set in Naples in Italy.

The land of the sun was the land of origin of her family, in particular her ancestors were Tuscan. However, she had not yet visited that country and hoped to go and see it soon. She would take a tour of the Mediterranean, first in Spain and then in Italy, where she was sure she would meet her great love, she was convinced she had already seen him, the year before in Budapest. An Italian boy, a fencer, had met him on the steps of the opera house, and she had felt a very strong sensation. She had seen him again that same night, on the balcony of the Hotel, the young man seemed ready to climb over the balcony and she had somehow had to stop him. She was still too young to do what the young fencer seemed to have in mind, but she was so convinced that the boy would have a special role in her life that she had made him a sort of appointment, something between the joking and the fatal: "I'll see you in Budapest." She still remembered that evening and that feeling of almost violent attraction for the boy in the fascist uniform, a feeling... very similar to the one she had felt when she had met Caireen and which at that moment created in her the same emotion as when you face something forbidden and irresistibly attractive.

A few months after she had arrived at Vassar that dream came back, and she felt sick, it came back every ten fortnight. She thought she had gotten rid of that terrifying vision, but the ghost, the damned ghost that had haunted her childhood had reappeared, the damned Scarecrow returned in those nights, to threaten her, that disgusting being, the murderer of her mother and father, came closer to her. With his enormous threatening knife in his hand and he stained her with his blood, like that night when Captain Stephenson, her current adoptive father, had shot him down with his gun. The dreams had become more and more frequent, the nights of terror closer and closer. When the sun set the terrible moment approached, the one in which she had to go to bed, the one in which she had her appointment with that obscene boyfriend of her nightmares. For this reason she tried to postpone the moment of sleep as much as possible, she resisted as much as possible, she studied until she fell asleep.

Sleep deprivation is a real torture and she would appear in class in the morning and give everyone the impression of being a zombie and no one could understand, even her performance had suffered, despite studying until late she had memory lapses and could not get the grades that her intellectual level would have deserved.

The only one who knew was Sabine; it was she who in those nights welcomed her tears, her terror when she woke up screaming, hugged her, while she panted and sweated and cried desperately.

That story lasted six months. The professors were dissatisfied with her results and had given him a sort of ultimatum: she absolutely had to improve.

Vassar was the best women's college in America, or at least it claimed to be, and so Cynthia's performance level absolutely had to improve or she would have to look for another school.

Cairean O'Malley finished correcting the English literature tests, as usual Cynthia Uberti had been the best and she couldn't understand how it could happen that a girl capable of writing things like that, had such a low performance. She seemed to struggle, especially in mathematics, she fell asleep and made incredible mistakes due to distraction. In the morning she arrived in class with dark circles under her eyes, she seemed distraught, and yet she was beautiful.

Her eyes were filled with infinite melancholy, but when she smiled it seemed as if a light was cutting across her face, her very white teeth flashing in contrast with her lightly tanned skin.

Cairean didn't know what to do, she should have intervened, as a tutor she had to find a way to help her, but she didn't do more than the bare minimum, because that girl attracted her irresistibly, as it hadn't happened for a long time that she hadn't been attracted by a woman and she was afraid of falling into that terrible vice of hers again. The one that had forced her to flee from Ireland when she was only sixteen, so as not to incur the wrath of the parish priest of her village. The wrath, or maybe something worse, they said that that strange priest liked to watch while women had sex with each other, took advantage of them and blackmailed them.

Sabine looked straight into Cynthia's eyes:

"You can't go on like this, everyone thinks you're stupid, the spoiled daughter of an important person in the Canadian government, but you're the victim of a crime who suffers the consequences of his misfortune, someone has to do something to help you... and then... and then you have to talk to O'Malley about it..."

At the word O'Mallei, Cynthia shook herself: "No, I don't want her to know..." she said it forcefully, almost as if she had been slapped.

"Why...?" Sabine asked in surprise.

« Because I just don't want to.. »

Sabine wasn't the type to give up: "Wait a minute, what's the point? What you're saying is absurd, if you don't tell your tutor, who the hell are you supposed to tell this to?"

"I don't want...I don't want.. not to her" and she burst into tears.

Sabine was disoriented: "listen, if you want I'll talk to her"

Cynthia kept crying and Sabine didn't know what to do, she wanted to help her friend, with whom she had built a friendship like she had never had with anyone.

They had spent evenings laughing at nothing until their jaws dropped, talking about the flaws and oddities of one teacher or another, or of their colleagues. Others moved to tears reading Cynthia's stories, confessing everything, telling each other their own lives.

Now Sabine understood that there was something deeply disturbing, beyond her nightmares, and she wanted to see the Cynthia of old return, happy and smiling, shining in her spectacular beauty.

She approached her, looked at her with a helpless look. Sabine never cried, it was impossible for her. She didn't even cry when she was a child, the maximum expression of her desperation was that helpless look and Cynthia knew it. She understood that her friend felt almost as bad as she did, maybe she was giving her a chance to unload some of the weight that was afflicting her, maybe that would help her release some tension, she had to tell someone.

She held back the tears, dried his eyes as best he could with the soaked handkerchief she was holding in his hand, sniffed, took a breath: "Well, I don't want to talk to O'Malley because... because... -

the words wouldn't come out

"Why?!" Sabine repeated with an almost impatient tone.

"Because I'm attracted to her, I'm attracted in a way that's wrong.. she's a woman and I'm a woman and I shouldn't feel for her what I feel..."

Sabine was silent for a moment, then sighed: "You mean you're a little lesbian?" she asked in a relaxed tone, as if it were the most natural thing in the world.

« I don't know if I am... if I am that thing there.. »

"Listen Cynthia, it's possible that this situation is the cause of your nightmares. I mean, an internal conflict could have stirred up bad memories that were deep in your subconscious. I think you need to face this conflict and work through it," she looked at her friend who was staring at her with her mouth open, "you know, resolve it."

"How do you hope for these things?" said Cynthia.

"You know, I'm a very curious person, and I also speak German, so when I found some books by a certain Sigmund Freud in my library at home, I read them all. It's a new science, called psychoanalysis, it says that our behaviors derive from our experiences, from childhood traumas, and that apparently inexplicable phenomena can be the consequence of the resurfacing of these traumas or vice versa. In short, I'm not really an expert... but I could be right, my father always says: when you're afraid of something, face that thing or the fear will kill you, without you even knowing if what's killing you is really something to be feared or is just a sick fantasy"

"Do you mean I should go to O'Mallei and confess everything to her...?"

Cynthia said in a slightly exasperated tone

"I say that you have to face this fear of yours, maybe this attraction of yours is a passing fact, or the consequence of a phase of your growth, or you really are a lesbian... never mind. The poet Sappho was too, and some other famous female character, who I don't remember now..., and in any case I don't think it's the case that you go crazy just because maybe she has a sexuality... well, a somewhat particular sexuality."

Sabine's words seemed to break through Cynthia's wall of pain.

"You mean I should go to O'Mallei and tell her straight out that I had dreams in which I happened to do unspeakable things with her?"

Sabine started laughing: "Well no, not exactly like that. But you could at least tell her about the scarecrow's nightmares, that you're not a stupid person, but just that you're sick, that's why your performance has dropped, that's all, I don't think she'll bite you or that anything will happen, and maybe as a side effect you'll get rid of your obsessions. You'll feel better and maybe they'll stop believing that you're a stupid Canadian daddy's girl."

"I am not Canadian..."

« Exactly... Anyway it has nothing to do with it, in short ask her for help with your studies.. »

« What if something happens to me that has to do with that other thing? »

« It means that I will have a lesbian friend, or rather bisexual, since you also have dirty dreams with that Italian boy... the one from Budapest, dressed as a fascist »

« Yeah, there's that too... I mean, I'm really depraved... »

"No, you're an idiot.. but you're my friend and I love you"
Sabine concluded.

Cynthia felt tears welling up in her eyes, but this time it wasn't despair, it was emotion, she hugged Sabine, who hugged her back. They stayed there, in silence for a few minutes, then Sabine's very un-Swiss sense of humor decided that the situation had to be resolved, she looked Cynthia in the eyes and said: "Hey... don't get any strange ideas", the American responded with a flirtatious look and said: "And don't get any illusions...".

They burst out laughing, meanwhile breakfast had now been had and they headed towards the canteen.

3.7 Deer Island...1928...the vultures

WB closed the report coming from Germany: the elections had gone very badly, the communists and social democrats had won, not only that, the Nazi party had lost votes, it was not going as WB had hoped.

"The Dawes Plan has worked, contrary to what we had expected, the situation in Germany is improving and this does not favor the progress of Mr. Hitler, but it will be a temporary situation, I predict that within the next year a financial crisis with all its trimmings will break out. Stock market speculation on Wall Street will eventually explode, the bubble cannot last much longer, and the shock wave will reverberate throughout the world. We did not want this crisis, but we do not want the federal government to interfere with market forces either, so we will choose in each country how to behave. Crises are good for nations, they eliminate inefficient companies and if a nation is healthy it survives, even if someone will have to suffer a little – he paused and winked at the man closest to him – but it will not be us.

Germany is still a weak country, the war debt still weighs and the Dawes Plan has only shifted the problem.

The wrath of God will be unleashed there, banks and companies will collapse, fear and anger will spread again: the ideal breeding ground for the populist ideas of Hitler and the Nazis to become popular."

The other diners looked at him, as always, perplexed.

Harriman, as usual, took the floor: "We all think we are heading towards a crisis, but we have no idea how to deal with it..."

WB interrupted him: "We will face it as usual, as we have faced all crises, emerging from it richer and more powerful than before..."

"And Germany... are we sure it will end up the way we hope?"

WB seemed not to have heard Haryman's remark

"The NSDAP must seek allies among the right-wing and centrist parties, they are the same ones who asked us to help them when we "invented" Hitler. He is crazy, but he is not stupid, and I continue to believe that he is the right man for Germany and for Europe, at least Europe as we conceive it and as we would like it to be, that is, weak, divided but strongly anti-communist. This will allow us to give more and more power to the United States, that is, to us."

Haryman always had a puzzled expression.

"But this crisis could give rise to exasperated protectionism, nations will close in on themselves, which could mean a new war"

WB made a questionig face

"Mister Haryman, Europe has emerged from this last war politically and financially weakened. We bought the continent with a few million dollars and with a very limited number of casualties. If they make another war they will finish demolishing what remains of their own power, we will stay out of it and when it is over we will buy a continent at a bargain price"

"But this is vulture behavior!" protested Haryman.

"Vultures are useful animals and extremely economically wise. They make the least effort and have the maximum yield, the economy is like that and we can only adapt to the force of nature that it is."

3.8 Pougehspie.....summer 1931...the cop and the butterfly

For three years Caireen and Cynthia had been seeing each other openly every day, because Caireen was her tutor, and clandestinely every weekend, spending them in long, exhausting and satisfying sessions of lesbian sex and equally long and exhausting discussions of politics, but on this the two of them had very different views, in fact diametrically opposed.

Cynthia was a republican and Cairean was decidedly and irrevocably an anarcho-communist and feminist. This did not prevent the two girls from being sentimentally, almost violently, attracted to each other. Sabine Rinkweiser often took part in political discussions. Coming from Europe and having seen what was happening in Germany, she found herself on positions a little closer to those of Cairean. She was a social democrat, but this meant being very far from both of them politically, at least as much as she was sexually, preferring men by far, who, she always repeated to her friends, were endowed with an interesting appendage, which the girls did not possess.

Cynthia's nightmares were gone, but it was opium that had brought the Virginian girl back to sleep, Cairean's third passion after politics and women, a passion that she nevertheless managed to contain to a few visits to a New York smokehouse, once a month. A frequentation in which she had involved Cynthia.

Special Agent George Ruch rubbed his hands together, he had found another one! Another anarchist feminist bastard, the boss would have been happy as a clam with his discovery, also because among other things this one was also a lesbian, a fucking pervert, like that Cairean O'Mailley on whose trail he had come to this new suspect.

Hoover was totally homosexual, capturing communists and persecuting homosexuals was his way of hiding this inclination, which for a fanatical reactionary like him, was not exactly edifying and had to be very well hidden. Then the depraved, he felt a kind of perverse pleasure in persecuting homosexuals like himself. A way to unload his own feelings of guilt for what he was. A way of pouring on others the hatred he felt for what he himself considered a vice and to conveniently absolve himself. Cairean O'Malley frequented an anarchist circle and wrote under the pseudonym of Corday, the assassin of Marat, the symbol of the revolutionary female rebellion against the males.

The new arrival was a beautiful woman, tall, with a perfect and athletic body, honey-colored skin, jet black hair and two spectacular emerald eyes and Ruch thought it was a real waste that she preferred women, even though in reality he was convinced that the young woman did not disdain men either and this time Ruch would take advantage of it.

George was organizing a trap, he had infiltrated the cultural circle, the Kropotkin Literary Society, in reality a completely harmless circle, in which meetings were organized, often of a feminist nature, during which however violence was never discussed. Ruch however was a real tempting demon, it was Hoover himself who had the idea of recruiting him into the FBI, to do what he called "active investigation". In reality these were real provocations. Ruch infiltrated completely harmless political groups, identified the characters most easily manipulated and pushed them to carry out dangerous subversive actions, promptly making sure the police were found in the places where these actions were to take place.

This time, however, he was convinced that he had found a truly exceptional lead, what in the journalistic field would be called a scoop. He was in contact with a woman he himself had infiltrated, a foreigner, a European, whom he had met at a scientific conference.

He had passed himself off as a medical student who was passionate about new discoveries and science in general. The girl was a true genius and at first he had had a lot of difficulty keeping up with her. He didn't understand anything of the things she was telling him about atomic physics and European scientists. He didn't like those people very much, he had informed himself and they were all or almost all Jews, dangerous people, an inferior race. Naturally George didn't say anything to the girl about his ideas about the Semites, on the contrary he passed himself off as a fervent revolutionary, constantly pulling out phrases from Marx and other revolutionary authors that he studied in the evening, taking them from the subversive books that they had confiscated in the latest operations.

He would reveal himself as soon as he was sure he could use her as he pleased: first he had to get her into bed, then he would blackmail her by threatening to reveal to some relative of hers the perverse things she would make him do. It seemed that she was the daughter of a jeweler who had settled in New York and who intended to open a store that would compete with Tiffany. Of course, like all rich snobs, she had strange ideas, about "social justice" and " women's rights" and even, most disgustingly, about the rights of "colored people", yes, he called those people Negroes.

The girl's name was Herta, Herta Simmering, she was Austrian. That day she had arranged to meet him in front of St. Patrick's Church and he was walking along Fifth Avenue calmly, observing the movement of the great arterial road. There was a certain amount of traffic, even though America was in the midst of a crisis. However, you could see lines of people in miserable conditions everywhere, waiting for the employment offices to open, hoping that there would be a place, even for just one day's work. He passed in front of the construction site of the Rockefeller Center that only the year before the magnate John D. Rockefeller had decided to give to the city of New York. Ruch thought it was a waste of money, it would have been better to pay more police to keep all those starving people at bay who were roaming the streets, and who would kill for a cent. However, the construction site with all the comings and goings of workers, machines and cranes rising into the New York sky, struck his imagination; it was the great America that managed to grow even in times of crisis.

His young friend was waiting for him. She was very elegant, with a white fur coat open in the front, worn over a brick red suit with a skirt just below the knee, a clutch hat, a pair of white and black shoes, little makeup and tortoiseshell glasses that gave her a sexy look.

She came closer and smiled at him: "Good morning Herta, how are you...?".

The girl replied with a smile: "Good, also because I have some news"

"Ah," Ruch said, "what kind?"

"Listen George, I think it's time to move beyond the chatter we have at the Kroprotkin Circle..."

"Ah, eeeh: did you wake up like this, this morning? With the desire to start a revolution?"

"Well, it's not from this morning, but the fact is that yesterday I met an emigrant, one who comes from Russia. They are changing the world. Here we continue to wait for we don't know what. We need to give a strong blow to the capitalist system... the financial crisis continues, the people are suffering, but soon they will understand and rebel: we are on the eve of the revolution!"

George couldn't believe it, his ears were hearing a sweet symphony, there was a Russian infiltrator, maybe a Jew, there was a daughter of the bourgeoisie who wanted to start a revolution and maybe...

"Cairean was with me too, we are both thrilled..."

...Well there was also the lesbian, hurray, bingo!

"But," asked George, "what does the Russian have in mind?"

Herta looked around cautiously: "Let's get out of here, take a taxi and go to Central Park, so we can move and talk without anyone hearing or seeing us."

Ruch was over the moon, he already saw himself as Hoover's deputy, if not in his place, given his boss's unorthodox habits.

George decided to make a good impression, he wanted to appear as a shrewd and cautious person, he was sure that this would be the best way to push the Austrian to commit some imprudence and expose her accomplices.

"But excuse this...immigrant...if he was so happy in Russia, why did he come here..."

Herta smiled slyly: "And that's the extraordinary thing, he passes himself off as an emigrant but he's here on behalf of the Communist International... you know, Stalin pretends to follow the theory of communism in just one country to make people believe he's not dangerous, but the Bolsheviks want only one thing: world revolution."

Ruch's heart sank, well, he and Hoover were right. The communists in agreement with the Jews wanted to overturn the natural order of things, to unleash the world revolution, and now he was about to discover a branch of that evil plant, perhaps the most important branch, since it was to strike right in America, the country of capitalism par excellence.

Herta looked at him: "What's the matter?" she said. "You look worried." George congratulated himself, what a formidable actor he must have been, he managed to disguise his satisfaction so well that one would have thought he was worried.

"No...oh, and you know, ideas are one thing, however revolutionary...and actions are another, in short, violence...

"Violence is the midwife of history!" Herta exclaimed, raising a hand to stop a passing taxi.

The woman got into the taxi and nodded to George as if to say, "Now be quiet so the taxi driver can hear us..."

"By the way, Cardinal Hayes thanks you for that generosity from our Irish friend..." Herta said with a wink, then ordered the taxi driver to take them to the Plaza Hotel. The man turned and looked at Ruch with an ironic look, perhaps thinking that the rather wrinkled suit that did not denote particular refinement, had little to do with the luxurious destination address, however without saying anything else he started his Ford.

The journey was quite short, Herta paid, shelling out a sum that was certainly too high, given the short distance between St. Patrick's and the southern entrance to Central Park, generating further glances from the taxi driver between pity and envy towards his companion in adventure.

They pretended to enter the hotel and as soon as the taxi drove away they set off at a brisk pace, toward Grand Army Plaza and entered the park via the wide avenues that ran parallel to 5th.

George pretended to be distracted and looked around, it was a beautiful day, there were a few people in the park, many idlers, wandering aimlessly waiting for a better future that was always slow to arrive. The depression, despite President Hoover's claims that the crisis was over, did not seem to want to adapt to the statements of politicians and bankers, superstitiously tied to the idea that all that hell unleashed by the collapse of Black Monday, was nothing but the psychological effect of rumors spread, of course by the usual Jews, defeatists and socialists.

The queues of poor, unemployed and various outcasts at the Charity offices grew longer day by day.

Herta seemed to have gone mute, it was cold, February is a hard month in New York.

Steam came out of people's mouths, which mixed with the fog coming from the water basins in the park.

The young woman took another look around: she had a way of looking that excited George, she turned around nonchalantly, threw a haughty glance, raising an eyebrow, like a gentlewoman who had been dared to annoy someone, even by their mere presence.

« So George...what do you think of a tremendous coup on a day that makes headlines all over the world... »

"for example?" Ruch replied

« for example St. Patrick's Day, exactly one month from now! »

« St. Patrick ?... »

« Certainly a celebration that involves all of New York, the Irish in particular and the Catholics above all »

George was trembling, now he was sure he had the shot of his life in his hands, he felt his legs trembling and his throat tight with emotion, what did this crazy woman want to do on a day that would bring the entire large Irish community out into the streets and also many other communities of the Catholic religion, who would join in the celebrations?

Ruch did not like Catholics, papists who were in fact enemies of the true faith, however the idea of combining something revolutionary that very day made his wrists tremble. How many people would have died, surely including women and children, but he would have avoided all this by acting in advance together with his colleagues at the FBI.

His colleagues already, maybe someone could steal his shot... he decided that he would talk to his colleagues at the last moment, when he really couldn't avoid it.

The agent now wanted to know more.

« But what are you planning to do, may I know... »

Herta looked at him slyly: "Fireworks...inside St. Patrick's Church..."

"Do you mean an attack on the church?"

She continued to make a sly expression; "what do you say?"

George decided to continue the game: "but we'll make a lot of victims..."

Herta's expression suddenly became hard: "Listen George Ruch, I like you, but not to the point of not making a move like this to go after your fears... you either go along with it or you melt away. But if you melt away, you really should disappear, those people from the Cheka are no joke, by now you know what the plan is and so you are tied to me either you go along with it or..." and she made a very explicit gesture with two fingers under her chin.

George wanted to burst out laughing and scream with joy, he reasoned to himself: should he run to Hoover and tell everything or wait until things matured a bit more and go with evidence in his hands? Certainly the second!

He showed a doubtful expression, the joy had made him blush strongly and he managed to mystify that skin expression, making it pass for embarrassment.

After a few minutes of silence, Ruch began speaking again: "Um, okay, you convinced me, I'm in."

Herta turned to him and smiled broadly: "Oh... here is the true man and revolutionary I met at the Kropotkin circle..." and she kissed him on the mouth. George decided to take advantage of the situation, his was a dangerous job and one with great responsibility, taking advantage of it to gain some advantage was completely legitimate, indeed it was due, an extra reward for his courage and his loyalty to the country. So he took the initiative and tried to stick a little tongue in the mouth of his "companion".

Herta blushed violently, but did not back down:

George felt encouraged: "Listen Herta, why don't we go and celebrate this agreement of ours, maybe in the meantime, since I'm in the game, you could tell me something more.

The young Austrian girl smiled: "You're such a naughty boy... OK, where do you want to go?"

"Let's go to my place...," said George, "I have an apartment in the Village."

It was a service apartment, rented by the FBI, to allow him to do his "dirty" work, it was perfect to give the idea of a bohemian character, a revolutionary intellectual, a traitor out of boredom of his own social class, the prototype of the enemy, more dangerous than the established order.

They took a taxi, but had it dropped off some distance from George's apartment, so that Herta could tell George more about the plot.

"So," Herta began, "the means for the attack will arrive on board an Irish ship, to divert any suspicion from us. Imagine the irony, it will be the Irish themselves who will provide us with the means for a coup that will ultimately harm them most. After all, the Irish are among the poorest and most unfortunate in American society, so they are angry and hitting them will increase their revolutionary propensity, which is already in their blood. The idea is to strike in front of St. Patrick, the "fires" will explode in the evening, the evening of March 17, we want to avoid too many problems with the parade, it must be a sensational event but without exaggerating.."

George hesitated for a moment: "But it will have less effect this way..."

Herta looked at him in admiration: "Ah, I see you have fully embraced the cause. Of course, doing it during the parade would be quite sensational, I will speak to the emissary of the Cheka about it..."

"But what is the name of this emissary?"

Herta hesitated for a moment: "Well, here's the thing: he made me swear not to reveal his name to anyone, under any circumstances. He said it's the revolutionary cell system, three people for each cell, and only one of the three knows the leader. But he swears not to reveal his name to anyone, unless he's tortured, in which case he'll hold out for at least twenty-four hours before confessing." Then she looked suggestively in the direction they were walking. "And I hope that where we're going, you don't intend to torture me..." she said in a whisper.

George shivered and smiled knowingly.

They entered the house, Herta didn't have time to say anything that George started kissing her and putting his hands all over her. She pushed him away gently: "Oh my God, what an impetus... give me time to get used to it"

"You'll get used to it later... let's go to the bedroom," Herta laughed and followed him into the alcove, they undressed with passion, the young Austrian had an exceptional body, with breasts that were neither too big nor too small, perfect legs, a flat and muscular stomach, she looked at George and thought to herself that this sexual intercourse would not be too long nor particularly memorable.

It was raining, but weather experts said that the next morning it would be sunny and the St. Patrick's Day parade would go ahead as usual, with all its music, its bagpipes, its characters dressed up as leprechauns, shamrocks and other figures from the culture of the green island.

Hoover was impatient inside the Ford parked near the New York Cathedral Church, there were two other cars full of agents parked in strategic positions, ready to intervene. George Ruch was sitting behind the wheel of Hoover's car and was nervously biting his lip.

Edgar J. with his bulldog face was impassive, but the frequent movement of his eyes denoted a certain impatience.

"Ruch, are you sure that the explosives are hidden in the basement of the church?" the FBI chief said gruffly.

"I brought the boxes together with a group of three terrorists, members of the gang. We entered at night, a sacristan who is on the side of the terrorist group opened the door for us.

"It's 11:45 and this mysterious Herta has still not been seen...."

"Because the appointment is for midnight and the revolutionaries are very cautious. They arrive at the exact moment to avoid being spotted by unfortunate coincidences."

Hoover looked at him with an expression of distrust, but at that moment young Herta appeared along Fifth Avenue, walking relaxed toward the church, occasionally looking around nonchalantly.

"Ok," Ruch said with satisfaction, "when I get close to the door, follow me and intervene."

He got out of the car and walked toward the girl, Hoover saw him approach the girl, kiss her and take her arm.

They turned onto 50th Street, walked a few yards and headed toward a side entrance.

The young woman approached a door and knocked, first twice, then a third.

The door opened and a little man leaned out, Hoover decided it was time to act. He got out of the car and motioned for the other officers to move, in a few minutes they were all in front of the door. The girl looked at them in amazement, then looked at George, and made an expression full of anger and disappointment shaking his head, the officer smiled triumphantly and turned to the little man who had opened, showing his badge.

"Let us in buddy, FBI"

The old man was very surprised: "FBI... and why?" he said with sincere surprise.

They were in a sort of antechamber of the sacristy, which became too crowded. Hoover ordered: "Take us to the basement".

The elderly assistant sacristan tried to complain: "but I should notify the archpriest and then... really"

"Silence," Hoover raised his voice, "you will not warn anyone, not before you have delivered the explosive to us."

"Explosive...?" the old man became more and more surprised.

"Move...!", Hoover growled.

The sacristan decided not to resist further, he accompanied them along a corridor, then they went down some stone stairs and found themselves in a large cellar, there was the light on and three men were looking at some boxes, talking calmly.

"Everyone stop!" George shouted.

The three men turned and saw that there was a fourth man with them, wearing a cassock, trimmed in red, and it was His Eminence Patrick Joseph Hayes, Archbishop of New York, who looked Hoover straight in the eye and exclaimed: "What's this uproar, ah Mister Hoover, have you come in person to collect the invitation to the St. Patrick's Day ceremony? But you are not a Catholic, if I am not mistaken."

The bulldog's expression changed to that of a beaten dog, but Ruch was not impressed:

"Your Eminence, I believe you are the victim of a hoax." He approached the crates and took a crowbar that was nearby, opened the first crate, lifted the lid and tore off the paper... and beautiful fireworks appeared.

The cardinal expressed a certain impatience and condescension on his face: "These are fireworks, built by an Italian craftsman and donated by the Archdiocese of Dublin for our feast of St. Patrick, are you Catholic, sir...?"

"Ruch...-George said softly- my name is Ruch and I am an Evangelical."

"It doesn't matter, we are tolerant, this evening you can come and watch the fireworks display, which will take place at Battery Park."

The FBI men at Hoover's command turned and left, their chief leaving last, "I hope you won't be offended but I have an engagement this evening" Hoover said to the cardinal.

Ruch saw her walking with a proud and elastic step along Fiftieth Street, in the direction of St. Patrick, he went towards her and stood in front of her: "Damn, German bitch..."

The girl looked at him haughtily and said: "Excuse me, I'm actually Swiss... what problem is affecting you, sir?"

« You got me in the shit... »

« Oh you mean for this evening...well I told you it was fireworks...right? »

Joseph Kennedy smiled, and pushed his tortoiseshell glasses down to the tip of his nose and grinned broadly at William Stephenson.

"Mister Stephenson, I really have to thank you. The idea of making Hoover look bad was excellent, but above all, allowing your daughter to be used as bait," the businessman said, turning to Fabian Rinkweyser, "was truly generous of you."

Stephenson bowed his head slightly: "It was a pleasure, I don't like Mr. Hoover, we are working with the army to create strategic secret services and he is scheming to get his hands on this activity."

"Well," Kennedy continued, "we had a strange coincidence of interests, I had commercial ones, since EJ was starting to bother me more than necessary about my alcohol trade between the United States and Canada, she had her political objectives and Mr. Rinkweiser..."

« An exchange of favors between secret services, we Swiss and MI6 collaborate, sometimes, do ut des! »

The ocean liner Gange, of Lloyd Triestino, was waiting at dock number 34 in the port of New York.

The passengers leaned over the bulwarks greeting the people on the platform, there was an hour left before departure. Sabine smiled at the two girls who accompanied her: "You had a lot of courage to lend yourself to that joke, Hoover is a beast, he could have taken revenge and made you have a bad time", Cairean said with a worried expression.

« I have a Swiss diplomatic passport, they can't do anything to me and then, I knew I was going to leave for Italy, I'm going to study physics with Enrico Fermi, in Rome Hoover will have a hard time reaching me! »

« Yes - added Cynthia, as for me I am well protected by my stepfather, rather you Cairean, with your political background don't you think it would be a good idea for you to get out of the way a bit... ? »

« I wouldn't know where to go, my life is all here in the United States and at Vassar »

« Why don't you go to Russia, you'd be fine there, wouldn't you? »

"I don't know what to do, I have no contacts, my communism stops at ideas, I have never had contacts with the Cheka"

"It can be fixed," said Cynthia, "my stepfather has some acquaintances in the Moscow area."

He smiled and planted a kiss on the mouth of the astonished Irish professor.

3.9 Rome ... February 1932 the Saracen and the fire of the stars

The assistant wrote numbers and Greek letters on the blackboard at lightning speed; he was definitely a handsome man, Sabine thought, very dark and thick hair, a regular nose, very black eyes, the face of a child, a Saracen child, and the brain of Leonardo da Vinci or perhaps even more.

They said he had a somewhat grumpy character, his companions called him "the grand inquisitor", his name was Ettore Maiorana.

Like everyone else, Sabine's classmate had the bewildered expression of someone watching a Martian explaining how he had gotten to Earth from his distant planet. Only she didn't miss a beat, while Maiorana continued with her calculations.

The bell rang and the young assistant seemed not to hear, he continued for another five minutes, almost until he reached the result, then he turned to the hemicycle and said: "Well, you can go, finish solving this calculation..."

At that moment the door of the classroom opened and a tall, lanky young man with a pair of metal glasses and a smiling face entered, Maiorana turned:

"Good morning Rasetti, what a pain in the ass are you bringing me?"

"Do you want to come with us to Lake Bracciano..."

"With you who..."

"The usual Segre, Fermi and company....."

"Yes, but I don't want any of your stupid jokes..." replied the professor with a slightly gloomy expression.

Sabine didn't listen to anything else but remained there waiting for the professor to finish talking to his colleague and take her into consideration.

"Okay, I'll see you at noon outside the faculty."

Then the professor turned to Sabine, with the tone of one who did not have much time to waste, but when he saw her he seemed to have been struck, and his expression changed:

"Good morning... miss...?"

"Rinkweiser..."

"Ah, you are a foreigner...?" he asked with a sort of embarrassment

"I am Swiss....."

"And how could I help her...?"

"By inviting me to dinner this evening..." Sabine replied with the most cheeky face, handing him a sheet of paper with the solution to the calculation done on the blackboard.

Ettore Maiorana darkened slightly: "Are you trying to corrupt me...?"

"I don't need it," Sabine said with a smile, handing the professor the paper.

Maiorana looked at him and her impenetrable expression seemed to crack for a moment, the grumpy Saracen had a moment of hesitation, she took advantage of it: "elegant no..." the girl whispered.

Incredibly Maiorana smiled, just, just: "I would say yes, have you solved this problem...?"

"And who else?"

"Well, I'm very surprised, he's the first student, to solve something like this...but I - the voice took on an embarrassed tone - well, I can't go out to dinner with my students..."

Sabine smiled again, then wrote her address on the back of the paper, placed it on the desk, next to a book, then politely bowed her head and headed towards the exit: "Have a good day, professor" she said, sticking her head out of the door she was leaving and smiling mischievously.

Rasetti chuckled: "Damn, the Grand Inquisitor is having success with the female sex...a foreign one at that!"

Maiorana looked at Rasetti with disdain: "Okay, you've convinced me, I'm coming to the lake with you, now stop bothering me and let me work".

He had skipped dinner, as often happened, then went to his room. Mrs. Dorina, the mother, cleared the table, then went into the living room, to listen to the radio as was her custom.

She was listening to dance music on the radio, saw Ettore pass by, and head towards the front door.

"Where are you going at this hour.."

"What time, it's half past eight, it's not even dark yet... anyway I'm going for a walk."

Ettore walked for a while through the streets around his house. That freckled face and those intelligent eyes behind the tortoiseshell glasses, and above all the solution to that mathematical problem, kept coming back to his mind. He had never met a person of that girl's age, who was able to understand and solve his complex mathematical problems, in fact he had never met anyone who was able to do so and this attracted him even more to that mysterious "Swiss" lady.

He reached a public car park and after some hesitation, decided to have himself taken to that address in the Parioli district, written in firm and elegant handwriting on the sheet of paper that the mysterious student had left on his desk, with discreet nonchalance.

The taxi driver drove Maiorana to the Swiss embassy. Ettore paid, ignoring the public driver's attempts at conversation, then looked at the gate of the villa that housed the diplomatic headquarters and hesitated for a moment.

After a few seconds the taxi driver interjected: "Ah doctor, what's happening? You don't like this embassy. If you want, we can change it. Do you prefer the English one or the French one?"

"No, no, that's fine, thanks," and he got out of the car.

In front of the gate Ettore had some hesitation, certainly the time was not the most suitable for a visit, he walked up and down a couple of times, then decided that if she had given him the address and wanted to be invited to dinner he would have to put up with the strangeness of the man with whom she intended to spend an evening at the restaurant. He approached the concierge and rang. An usher in a gray suit, a sort of uniform, came to open the door and looked him up and down: "Good evening, what would you like?" the man asked in a deep voice, looking down at the young professor, who, not at all intimidated, replied: "I'm looking for Miss - he looked at the piece of paper furtively - Rinkawasser"

"there is no Miss Rinkwasser here..."

Majorana had a moment of perplexity: "It may be that the name is not exactly correct..." he hinted.

"Young man," the guard continued, somewhat snarling, "this is an embassy, let me explain, it is neither a girls' college nor any other place where you can find ladies, not in this neighborhood."

Maiorana was quite embarrassed when a shrill voice behind him exclaimed: "Pedroni, don't worry, this gentleman is an acquaintance of mine, I gave him our address"

"Ah..." said the usher Pedroni, not very convinced, "should I let him in...?".

Maiorana turned around and found himself in front of the mysterious "Swiss" student: "Ah, here, excuse me but I ..."

Sabine Rinkweiser looked at him with a cheerful and ironic look: "You have decided to come and see for yourself who I am: here I am, the daughter of the Swiss cultural attaché. The ambassador is hosting us in this building so that he can have my father whenever he needs him."

"I was curious to have a chat with a woman who could solve an equation like the one I proposed to the students, it doesn't happen often, not even among men.."

"What?"

"that they can solve the problems I give them..."

"Does it surprise you that a woman can do it?"

Maiorana made a vague expression: "Well... actually yes."

The young woman flashed her particular smile again and let it fall into the void: "Professor, I had suggested inviting me to dinner...or are you just here to snoop around?"

The professor seemed slightly embarrassed: "No, well, I mean, yes, I wanted to invite her to dinner and..."

"And find out my secret, okay, where are we going?"

Maiorana looked around, still embarrassed: "I was thinking of going to Trastevere, but here we are

a little far away.."

"No problem, there will definitely be a service driver available"

The girl turned to the caretaker: "Mr. Pedroni, could you please send me someone from the car park?"

The man did not flinch, spoke into the intercom and shortly after a black Mercedes, with the Swiss flag, appeared at the gate, the driver was wearing an impeccable black uniform buttoned up to the neck with two rows of buttons; riding trousers and highly polished boots.

He got out of the car and opened the door. Sabine got in without hesitation, while Maiorana looked around with a certain embarrassment:

"Professor, come on, they say you are a new Galileo, you won't be embarrassed to get into a car..."

The professor went up: "Well, actually at my house in Catania we have four, more or less like this, but I don't use them much."

Sabine ordered the driver in German to take them to Piazza Santa Maria in Trastevere.

The restaurant was crowded, despite the late hour, there was a pleasant and festive atmosphere. The Italian scientist had spoken little along the way, he seemed to be thinking. Sabine after having eaten a fantastic "coda alla vaccinara" without haste; watched the young professor as, with extreme calm, he wrapped small bites of bucatini alla matriciana, with the same attitude of a child who had been punished for eating. Ettore appeared like this in all his attitudes, a kind of caution emanated from him, as if the world was observing and spying on him. Only when he began to do mathematical calculations did he change his attitude. It seemed as if another person had taken possession of him, he ran over the blackboard or the paper or the cigarette packets that he used from time to time, as if he were listening to music, which note after note appeared on the surface where he was writing. Sabine pointed this out to her. Ettore looked up

:"mathematics is music and music is mathematics"

"And physics..." asked Sabine

" ...Physics....., physics is like a song you write with mathematics, what matters are the notes, the whole world is mathematics, but everyone uses it to debase it for practical purposes, for physics, for engineering and maybe they will end up using it for cooking too! »

« but you're a physics assistant... »

« ....better than doing it in engineering... »

Then Maiorana, cautiously started eating her matriciana again, stopped with the fochetta in mid-air: « Why, what do you think of mathematics... »

Sabine was impressed by the fact that the professor used the formal "Lei" , but that was normal in a language like Italian, where the difference between the familiarity and the confidentiality to be used in a relationship that was just starting out was reflected in the language.

He popped another piece of oxtail into his mouth and chewed calmly, appearing to think about his answer: "For me, mathematics is the key, a key to discovering the secrets of the world..."

Maiorana interrupted her almost rudely: "You see, you are also wrong, you are thinking of prostituting a pure science!"

Sabine swallowed and looked Ettore in the eye: "Professor, pure sciences do not exist, a science without a finalized purpose is intellectual solipsism, this is the snobbery of top-of-the-class students"

"It is not believing in perfection, every time science has been mortified in practical applications, evil things have happened, from Archimedes' burning mirrors to gunpowder"

"But these are alchemists' reasonings. Physics, chemistry, science in general, are the way in which God wrote in the great book through which he created the world. They represent the explanation of what God wanted to do, and mathematics is the language through which the Eternal Father wrote this book. If we discover how the world works we will understand why we are here and how we are here, and we will also be able to live better. So mathematics must be used to describe science, as words are used to describe reality. If someone makes an evil use of science this happens as with any human thing, even the most banal object can be used for an evil purpose."

Maiorana's coal-colored gaze seemed to light up: "This is what Fermi also says, when he talks about his studies on the nature and conformation of the nucleus of the atom, but I have doubts that this science can improve the world. I'm not sure, he thinks that in atomic physics there is the secret to dominate nature. The explanation of how the stars work, but he is certain that this can make the world better... I'm not so sure."

"Funny, it's an idea that I've always had too. You see, professor, I've been hanging out with scientists since I was a child, my father used to invite Einstein, Hanh, Meitner to dinner, that's why I handle mathematics well. I remember one evening in 1922 in Berlin, a strange thing happened, they were having dinner at my father's to celebrate Albert's Nobel Prize, they were talking about the equation of relativity, and at a certain point I said something... and suddenly everyone fell silent..."

"What did you say?"

"I said that if there is a direct correlation between mass and energy, theoretically we could all suddenly transform ourselves into energy, like a bomb, everyone had a shocked expression, it seemed like I had said a swear word. Then Hanh added in a low voice, "theoretically yes", maybe I had said the same thing that Fermi says and also, at the same time, what you say"

Suddenly, the same expression that had appeared on the faces of other scientists like him that distant evening in Berlin appeared on Ettore Maiorana's face. He went pale, then grimaced, as if he felt pain: "Theoretically, yes..." he said in a low voice.

It was very late, Ettore was walking slowly toward home, he had the Swiss embassy car drop him off not far from his house, so he could take a walk. The evening had gone by discussing science and philosophy, they had said goodbye promising to see each other again in a few days, but the conversations with Sabine about the relationship between matter and energy continued to come back to his mind: "..transforming ourselves into energy", already like a firework... or like a bomb, an evil voice told him, and this word returned again and again, and what power could this bomb have? The physicist wondered.

Was the possibility that Sabine feared so remote? Radioactivity was a sign that matter was somehow transforming, slowly, but it was. This transformation could be induced, Rutherford had already done it.

Hector thought of a fire, It slowly transforms one substance into another in a certain sense, emitting energy, when this happens slowly you have a simple bonfire, but when it happens at high speed you have an explosion, that is, a bomb. How powerful could a rapid radioactive transformation have been?

Ettore returned home, his mother was in the living room listening to the radio, Maiorana passed by trying not to be heard:

"but do you think it's time to go back, it's two o'clock" came the voice of Mrs. Dorina

"Yes mom I was just out for a walk"

"Up to this hour... and why have you turned around all of Rome? Was that a girl you took away?"

Mrs. Majorana's voice sounded hopeful.

But Hector didn't answer, he took some paper and began to write down calculations.

Suddenly he stopped, for the first time in his life he did not reach the result.

Sabine and Ettore saw each other again several times, they talked about many things, but never about physics again, because every time it happened Ettore changed the subject, until a few years later Dr. Rinkweiser was transferred again, this time to London.

3.10 *Glamis Castle...Scotland September 1932...*
the puppeteer and the princess

WB looked around, castles were his favorite places. Places that expressed the strength of the ruling classes for centuries in Europe. Time and history had radically changed the organization of society, and those sumptuous rooms, overly furnished and full of memories said "look, this was the world, before modernity advanced with its load of vulgarity."

WB belonged to that ancient caste, he descended from a family that had emigrated to America from Scotland more or less at the same time as the Pilgrim Fathers. During the so-called "American War of Independence" his family had sided with the loyalists, they had understood very well that that pseudo revolution of grocers and cheap bourgeois was only a way to avoid paying taxes to the crown, and to take over, without too much trouble from Her Majesty's government, that continent that extended boundlessly towards the West. To help these parvenus had intervened the French and Spanish, the historical enemies of England, the Empires of the idlers and the papists, who while England was slowly, slowly expanding its prior civilization in the world thought only of inflating the stomachs of their idle and incompetent nobility, and of their tyrants. Even though the so-called revolutionaries had won, his ancestors remained a very powerful family, so much so that Washington himself had intervened against the hotheads who wanted to exile them, demanding that they be left in peace and entrusting the head of the family with an important role in the new government of the thirteen states.

England, on the other hand, was the driving force of history. The bold and enterprising English nobility at that time invented the joint-stock company, colonized the East, using the bare minimum of force and infinite cunning, sending the scum of the country to act as its vanguard throughout the world and using that formidable instrument of power which was their model of democracy.

A tool that had allowed the whims and greed of the royal families to be kept under control. To make the so-called people believe they could self-determine, to give those who governed a legitimacy unknown to all the other forms of tyrannical government on the continent. The best among the bourgeois became part of the ruling classes, obviously paying a price that they could not have afforded without the help of the nobility and ending up being hostages and playing their game. To write laws and organize the government of the country in that way that had allowed a small island to become the greatest power in the world.

Democracy had also arrived in America, fortunately it had been brought under control there too. It had certainly happened that sideshow characters like Davy Crockett had reached the congress, however thanks to the cost of political campaigns and the low salary of those who represented the voters, the control of the big families had remained firm and decisive.

Becoming president of the United States was still a very expensive undertaking, which could not be undertaken without the support of those who had the means to sustain campaigns of interminable duration and prohibitive cost.

His family was among those who financed these campaigns, each time choosing those candidates who gave them the greatest guarantee of maintaining their role and of orienting the United States in the right direction. They had supported Lincoln's and Roosevelt's campaigns. Now they would support that of another Roosevelt, although his ideas were quite far from the conservative vision of WB's family, it was clear that he was the only one who could restart the American economy after the two inept Coolidge and Hoover had failed to reverse the depression of '29. Incidentally, neither of them had been supported by WB's family who had preferred to remain neutral and exploit the financial crisis to make golden deals on the stock market.

The trip to Scotland was necessary because of the turbulence that Europe was still going through. The Nazi party in Germany had won the July elections, gaining the chancellorship, but had had to ally itself with other minor parties, including Von Papen's. WB's plan to create a political force in Germany capable of restoring stability to that country seemed to be coming to fruition. However, the excesses of the SA and the Fhurer, worried some of the most important members of the Order, that is, of that pact between the most powerful families in the world, twelve in all, of which he was at that time the representative for the United States, in the Council, the body in which the heads of the families met to decide on a common attitude on the most important events in the world.

The spokeswoman for the British group of these cautious supporters of the ORDER was Cecilia Cavendish Bentik Bowes Lyon Countess of Strathmore and Kinghorne and mistress of the castle where WB now resided: the woman who within a few years would become the mother of the Queen of England.

The Countess entered through a small door into the drawing room and very politely addressed WB, welcoming him, accompanied by young Elizabeth. Both women had blue eyes, with a very intense expression, aristocratic noses and mouths curved in an indulgent smile. WB bowed slightly and thanked Her Grace for having wished to receive him. In fact, "Her Grace" had been rather explicit, in the telegram inviting him to Glamis Castle.

Tea was served, and the Countess opened with a seemingly out-of-context speech, asking after WB's family. It was Elizabeth who entered the subject, rather directly, in the style which, it was said, strongly characterised her.

"So Mister WB, you don't mind if I use your pseudonym... right?"

"No your grace," WB replied, swallowing a sip of tea.

So I was saying, it seems to me that your creature is... so to speak, getting out of control?"

WB feigned surprise: "Your Grace perhaps mistakes me for Baron Frankenstein...?"

Elizabeth took the hint and smiled back.

"You are right to compare yourself to Frankenstein, Hitler is not an artificial creature, but, according to what they say, his brain, or at least his ideas, have in you a... paternity... or am I wrong"

"Allow me, Your Grace, I think my role in this affair was, let's say: a little... exaggerated. However, I admit that I had a significant role of influence, both on the creation of the NSDAP, and on the path of the Fhurer. I am aware of the concerns that the behavior of the SA, creates for our German contacts..." he said sipping a sip of tea.

Elizabeth took advantage of the suspension to introduce herself to the discussion: "There is not only the problem of the SA, there is also the violent anti-Semitism of the Nazis, which worries us a lot"

Wb swallowed his tea calmly, then looked young Bowes Lyon straight in the eyes.

"Your Grace, allow me to explain my position..." he paused for a moment, waiting for the young woman's assent, which came with an almost imperceptible movement of her head:

"Well, Germany is the pillar of European security, that is, the linchpin on which the world order hinges. If it were to fall into the hands of the Bolsheviks, all of Europe would end up under the influence of socialism, or rather of the much more dangerous variant called communism.

When it was decided to support the Nazis' seizure of power, these elements were well in mind. Germany is a country allergic to democracy. Centuries of rule by the Junker caste have accustomed the Germans to obey, certainly not all Germans, but to think that in Germany, at this time, we have a system of the type of the English or French is pure illusion. There are therefore no alternatives. Germany must be firmly in the hands of a strong man. This man did not exist until we identified Hitler. A character who is not strong, in himself, but who also thanks to our help has become so in the German imagination, which is what counts. Unfortunately, anti-Semitism is an unavoidable element of Hitler's winning ideology. A demagogue always needs scapegoats, and the Jews have been the ideal scapegoats throughout Europe for nineteen hundred years. Both the Catholic Church and later the Protestant Church pushed in this direction, with the legend of deicide and other nonsense that has always been part of the populist imagination. Precisely for this reason, it was very easy, by leveraging anti-Semitism and a few other simplistic ideas, to give Hitler a perfect ideology to conquer the majority of the German people..."

Elizabeth seemed struck: "But you yourself say that Hitler's things are nonsense, it is really essential to have a character like that to dominate Germany... and from what you say, even Europe, in the end, the cavalier Mussolini for example is a dictator, but he seems a little different from Hitler.."

"Because Italy is different from Germany...your grace. You see, sir - and he turned his gaze to both ladies present - the alternative to a strong Germany and in some way our ally, would be to greatly strengthen the English fleet and its armed forces, and divert resources from the empire towards Europe. Tensions would also be created, which would not be good for business, neither ours nor yours. Moreover, the English parliament has voted to renew the "ten years rule", that is, the law that establishes that for the next ten years England will not have to face major conflicts, that is, that it will not invest in strengthening the armed forces. This means that stability will have to pass through paths other than those of force, that of a stable Germany is the only seriously practicable one."

The two ladies looked at each other, the mother spoke: "You seem quite convincing mister WB, however I think we should have more control over this madman... even if I don't know how"

"I have an idea," WB said, "we have to try to infiltrate one of our men into the Fuhrer's closest entourage. We already have one but it seems to me that he is not exactly the right man. If Your Grace would like to support this operation by guaranteeing us the support of His Majesty and using the MI6 network, we would have greater guarantees of success..."

Countess Cecilia thought for a moment. "I will ask His Majesty's permission to let you speak to Sir Hugh Sinclair, the Director of MI6. I hope that will be sufficient."

Elizabeth had a gloomy expression, the Dowager Countess looked at her: "You don't seem convinced dear"

"I'm not at all, I'm sure that madman will get out of control and start a war, another war... worse than the last one"

WB grimaced a little. "If that happens, we'll try to limit the damage..."

"And make as much money as possible," Elizabeth said bitterly. "Right, Mr. WB...?"

"If we really can't do without it...", the man replied, in a low tone.

3.11 *Marblehead Massachusetts.... December 6, 1932..*
the puppeteer and his marionettes

WB scratched his head, a gesture he made whenever he learned that things weren't going exactly the way he wanted them to.

The dispatch said that Von Papen's attempt to form a government had failed.

They had entrusted the task to General Von Schleicher, who had a bizarre idea in mind: to form a government of the trade unions and all the parties including the Nazi one.

Of course, that was no good. So he sent his German contacts a phonogram, informing them that he would pressure Congress to ensure that the United States would not support such a government.

Two days passed and a phonogram came back.

It asked whether the Order would foster a positive attitude in the United States towards a government with Hitler as Chancellor, Von Papen as Vice-Chancellor, two Nazi figures as Minister of the Interior and Commissioner for Prussia (the names of Frick, a Munich lawyer and Goering were mentioned), and the government would also include the press magnate and head of the small right-wing party DNVP Alfred Hugenberg, with a very important post, namely Minister of Economics, Agriculture and Food.

The idea was that the latter together with Von Papen would moderate the Nazis' aggressivity.

The phonogram was signed by all the main representatives of the German industrial groups.

WB scratched his head, it wasn't ideal but it was better than nothing. That government, he thought to himself, would last the space of a morning. His German friends would understand that the only solution was a government entirely in the hands of the Nazis, this would have serious consequences, but WB told himself that none of them would be to the detriment of the Order's plans.

Perhaps the first to lose out would be the German Jews, but... you couldn't make a mess without breaking eggs... In any case, someone very close to Hitler had to be inserted to keep him under control.

3.12 London August 1933 ....Operation Martingale 1

Admiral Sir Hug Sinclair, was Director General of MI6, better known as the Secret Intelligence Service from 1923.

Previously he had headed the Naval Intelligence Division.

What they were proposing to him was, in his opinion, absolute madness: infiltrating the leadership of Nazi Germany with a man who was supposed to replace one of the leaders and work to the advantage of England, already seemed like a huge gamble, but the fact that this project had been conceived by a man who had nothing to do with the secret services, belonging to a mysterious organization whose name they had not even wanted to tell him, seemed even crazier to him, especially since Prime Minister Ramsey McDonald was not informed of the matter, because that operation was too delicate to involve a politician who could have changed at the first elections.

On the one hand his English soul rebelled against this highly undemocratic procedure, on the other his soldier soul shared it, he owed obedience first and foremost to the King and apparently the orders came from there.

He looked up from the file and picked up the intercom microphone: "Good morning Mrs Moneypenny. Mr Fleming has arrived..."

"Yes sir, it is right here in front of me..."

"Let him in," said the admiral.

The door at the end of the office opened. The man who entered Admiral Sinclair's office was tall, blond, his hair combed to the side, parted and held in place with brilliantine. A prominent nose, a strong jaw, and the cold expression of his blue eyes gave the impression of a person with an aristocratic and aloof character.

He wore a suit made by a Seville Row tailor, a hand-made shirt, probably by the same tailor, and a bow tie.

"Come in, Mr. Fleming," the admiral said politely.

Fleming sat down politely opposite the Director of Her Majesty's Intelligence Service. He had the same relaxed expression he would have had if he had been sitting opposite his tailor.

Sinclair had his arms resting on the large desk and his hands clasped together, he seemed more anxious than the young man in front of him.

"Mister Fleming, do you know why you are here?"

"They told me to come to you because you have a job to offer me. I know you have my resume and they told me you are the director of a company that deals with import export"

The Admiral let out a short sigh.

"No Mister Fleming, I do not run an import export company, I am the director of MI6, also known as the Secret Intelligence Service"

"Ah..." said Fleming "and I...what should I..."

May I offer you some tea, Mr Fleming?"

"No thanks sir... I'm fine like this"

"a whiskey?"

Fleming's expression changed to surprise, "Well sir," he said, looking at his wristwatch, "perhaps at this time..."

"Well, maybe not at this exact time, but I'm sure that in a few minutes you will be asking me... So Mr. Fleming, Mister Jan Fleming, if I'm not mistaken... what would you say to going to Germany and making contact with one of our men who is infiltrated into the highest Nazi hierarchies?"

Fleming's expression changed from surprise to astonishment. "Well, maybe that whisky...but first, if you don't mind, could you tell me why me?"

"For three reasons: the first is that you speak German perfectly, having studied at the University of Munich, you also know that city very well, and also Berlin. Furthermore, you are not part of the service staff and therefore we can entrust you with a mission that you and I and His Majesty the King will be aware of. Finally, because you were recommended to us for this mission by an important member of a family very close to the royal family. Finally, because it seems you know this person."

Fleming asked in a low tone, "I know him...and who would he be?"

The Admiral told him..."

"Ah, Fleming said, it was really a passing acquaintance, an interview..."

"but that... let's say sir, that gentleman mentioned his name..."

"then I fear....", Fleming's sentence remained suspended in the air, faded into silence, while the man moved a hand with a vague gesture.

"Am I to take his attitude as consent?" Sinclair asked again.

"I really think so," replied the interlocutor.

"From now on, you will be the only one who will have contact with that man, and you will receive orders and inform me exclusively... are there any questions?"

"Can I have my whisky?" asked Fleming.

3.13 Walter Westerhaupt…. Heligoland, autumn 1933..the sailor's son

Walter looked out to sea, the steel-colored Nordsee, reflecting the gray of the clouds, driven by the wind toward the east. The waves crashed down below, against the breakwater that defended the red sheer walls of the Lange Anna, a tower of sedimentary rock, which seemed to have been placed by the gods of Whalalla to guard the Sacred Island, as that strange land off the coast of Schlewing Holstein was called.

It was not cold, the climate of Heligoland was moderated by a gust of the Gulf Stream that ventured northwards, tempering the effects of the nearby polar areas, a gift of the warm tropical waters to the inhabitants of those lands, which would otherwise have been completely inhospitable.

Walter thought that perhaps that would be one of the last times he would see the beauty of his land blessed by nature. He was about to leave for Murwik, the Reichmarine academy, where he would become *an Offiziersanwarter* (Aspirant Officer). A career in the navy was the rule in his family, ever since an ancestor of his who was a fisherman, one day got tired of the hard work of catching herring on the German coast and enlisted in the Danish navy, then moved on to the British navy, becoming captain of a frigate that fought in the battle of Cape Trafalgar. All his descendants had served in one of the two navies (the Danish and the English), until 1864 when the duchy of Shleving Holsetin of which Helgoland was an appendage was incorporated into Prussia, following a war won by Bismark against Denmark.

From that moment on, the Westerhaupts had faithfully served the Kaiser aboard the most diverse ships. His father had also followed the same path, which was why Walter did not remember anything about that man, since he had barely had time to see him, before he embarked on the cruiser Konisberg, sent to German East Africa to guard that remote corner of the Empire. Karl Westerhaupt, gunnery officer, had died at his combat post, when the ship had finally been sunk by the English navy, after a series of epic clashes in the delta of the Rufiji River, in Tanganyika.

So Walter had grown up in the midst of the war, on that island that had been fortified to protect access to the ports of the North Sea from possible attacks by the Royal Navy. In 1918, the war had ended with the defeat of Germany. An event that according to what all Germans said, had more to do with the betrayal and the infamous tricks of the powers that were above the nations, than with the courage of the German soldiers, who emerged undefeated from the battlefields and oceans of the world. At least that's what Walter thought, who at 20 years old was able to listen more to the voice of feeling than to reason. A voice that responded to the flattery of the new Chancellor Adolf Hitler, who after the German humiliation of Versailles, returned to speaking of a great Reich.

Walter had grown up with the frustration of seeing his mother, Freja, left alone and with her father's small war pension, having to struggle with the frightening inflation of the Mark and struggling, even in a place like Helgoland, far from the big cities and therefore less expensive, to make ends meet.

At only fourteen years old he had embarked and begun the hard life of a fisherman, to help that heroic woman, with the beautiful transparent blue eyes, to lead a dignified life.

At seventeen one day he met a naval officer who had come to visit his mother, his name was Wilhelm Canaris. He had met his father at the academy and was a family friend of Freja, a Danish family, also sailors. Canaris had talked to him at length, telling him about the battles that had seen the Kriegs Marine, face a heroic and unequal fight with the very powerful Royal Navy, giving him a hard time in the Falklands, in front of Jutland, in the Coco Islands and off Juan Fernandez and finally in the delta of the Rufiji River, deep in Equatorial Africa, where his father had died.

Walter had asked the veteran how he could join the Navy, too, and Canaris had assured him that as soon as it was possible, there would certainly be a place for a Westerhaupt.

That day had come, now the austere building of the Marineschule awaited him. He took a last look at that sea that for six years had fed him, and forced him to the daily toil of every fisherman, but that also gave him the joy of its boundless grandeur, of its spectacular storms, of its continuously changing and always surprising colors.

He walked slowly back to Sudhafen, where he lived with his mother in a small, brightly colored house like those of all fishermen. He entered and went into his room to get his suitcase. His mother Freja was waiting for him, standing, wearing the modest cotton dress she wore every day and a rather worn sweater. She was smiling, even though her emotion was clear. She had already seen a man of her family leave so many times. The last time was in the spring of 1914, when Walter's father had left his home to reach the port from which the Konisberg would set sail for Africa.

He hugged his mother, who remained frozen, as if she did not want to respond to that hug, or as if she did not expect it. Freja put her hands on Walter's shoulders and pushed him away from her, but not harshly, slowly, like the farewell to a ship, which leaves behind a pier and slowly, slowly disappears on the horizon. She looked him straight in the eyes, without saying anything, the expression in those eyes that despite the glacial color, transmitted a great love for her son, sent him a silent message "Come back!"

He boarded the boat, no longer looked at the white sands receding, now he looked south, towards the German coast. He disembarked at Cuxhaven where he took a train to Hamburg.

Arriving in the port city he decided to take a look outside the station. The train to Flesburg didn't leave for another three hours, he had some time and was hungry. He wanted to find a cheap place to eat something and drink a beer. He left the Hauptbanoff and took a random direction.

He had walked a few meters when he saw a group of men wearing the brown shirts of the SA. They had surrounded an elderly man and were threatening him. The man looked terrified, stammering something at the insulting phrases of the men in uniform. At a certain point one of the Nazis gave him a violent slap, the man staggered, amid the laughter of the other members of the group, who began to kick him. To Walter this seemed like an injustice, and he did not like that type of action, with an indignant expression he took a step towards the group, but felt a hand on his right shoulder that held him back, forcefully. He turned suddenly, in front of him was a man in civilian clothes. A black suit, a brown shirt, a black tie, on which stood an eagle with outstretched wings, which held in its talons the laurel branches that surrounded a swastika, a small badge of the Nazi party in his buttonhole. The man showed him a badge and said harshly: "Shutzstaffel", Walter had heard that name, they were the men who took care of the personal security of the Fhurer and he wondered what they could want from him. Then he looked at him, there was something disturbing in the face of that man, perhaps more or less his age, but who seemed to have a face marked by experience, who looked at him in turn with the same somewhat uncertain expression, then he seemed to recover and his features became hard, almost ferocious: "Do you intend to defend a Jew, comrade?", the SS man did not wait for the answer: "I think it is better for you to continue on your way, do not turn this beautiful day into a bad adventure" he said continuing to look him in the eyes, while the strange, disturbing sensation grew in Walter's soul. He gestured vaguely across the street, where the attack seemed to have ended and the elderly victim was now lying on the ground, but his words caught in his throat when the SS man stared at him again with an insurmountable hardness. Walter decided that he had had enough for the day, turned around and went back to the station. He hadn't eaten, " *Schaisse* !" he muttered to himself. He went back into the main station building, he needed to wash his face. He went into the bathroom, took off his cap and washed his face, looked at himself almost involuntarily in the mirror, and was astonished, he instantly understood what had upset him in the SS: he and that man looked alike like two peas in a pod, except that while the man was blond and had blue eyes, he had dark hair and eyes.

3.14 Horst Luderiz ...Hamburg 1933....the son of guilt

She watched him walk away from the colorful house, she was looking at him, her hands one on top of the other held in her lap, her head slightly bowed, Hans was far away but he was sure that she had a melancholic look.

Hans had been returning to Heligoland for a while; more or less three years, almost every month he took the train from Munich and went to that island, a long journey, but which was for him a kind of drug, the only situation that awakened a remote and until then almost incomprehensible sensation, he didn't know what to call it, but he felt he needed it.

How did it begin? Many years before, practically the day he was born.

Her mother was a waitress in a beer hall in Walvis Bay, a place where local white sailors and fishermen gathered. A light cruiser of the Kriegsmarine had dropped anchor in the bay. That night the town had filled up with sailors and officers, the town didn't have much to offer, so they all ended up meeting in the beer hall where her mother worked.

Hans didn't know what had happened that night, but his mother said that he had met a very handsome naval officer and nine months later he was born, she even remembered the name and surname of that officer Helmut Westerhaupt. The next day the ship left again.

Hans had grown up on the streets of Walvis Bay. His mother had taken care of him for a while, then the excesses, especially in drinking, had destroyed her and he had grown up on the streets of the city, among the poor and the colored people. One day he had come home, he was desperately hungry and hoped that his mother had something to eat. It was night, he had entered from the kitchen, and he had noticed that in his mother's room there was a light on. He heard voices, but they were strange screams, like he had never heard before, animalistic moans, so he had ventured to the room, where he had witnessed a scene that had left him shocked. There were three naked men, with erect penises, in the middle his mother, who was doing things with those men, simultaneously with all three, and she was panting, she was sweaty and.. and at a certain point he felt his legs moving by themselves, which took him out of the house. He walked for hours, unable to stop, finally he collapsed from exhaustion near the pier near the fishing material warehouses. When he woke up he had a strange sensation, as if something inside him had broken forever. No one ever saw him smile again. No one could ever see an emotion in his face; he remained in a corner, his eyes lost in nothingness. Sometimes the fishermen gave him something to eat, he accepted in silence and returned to his corner.

But he didn't always stay in a corner, during the winter all the white children in the village went to school, one day Hans was wandering around the school building, he saw an open window and sat there to listen. From that day on he always went to listen, the teacher, an intelligent and sensitive woman had noticed him, she had made him enter the classroom, Hans had sat in a corner and that's how he went through elementary school, in a strange way because he didn't do as the other students and didn't let them get close to him, only the teacher could talk to him, she had also given him pens and notebooks, Hans liked arithmetic and it had become his favorite game: the only one he played.

One day a non-commissioned officer of the colonial troops, the Schutztruppe, had picked it up.

He had become the regiment's mascot, an ice mascot, who did not play like other children and had continued to go to school, with good results.

He behaved like an adult soldier, a child who made you shiver just by looking at him, there was nothing childish about him. He had grown up crossing the territory of the colony. Taking part in operations that served to maintain order among the local tribes, tamed for the first time by General Von Trotha, but remained endemically ready to create disorder whenever the authorities were distracted. When the war broke out he had been attached to the troops and captured, with the other soldiers by the South African forces and sent to a concentration camp in Pietermaritzburg in South Africa.

He was very young and strong, the camp commander had thought it a good idea to send him to work on his brother-in-law's farm, he was a sort of farmer's assistant and they had taught him to treat the colored laborers as if they were not even human. Hans had no political ideas, he did not understand racism, he was not able to formulate thoughts with ideological content. They involved an emotion, something that was completely foreign to him.

It's not that he mistreated blacks, he had the same attitude towards them as he had towards horses and cows, tools of the trade and nothing more.

When they released him he returned to Walvis Bay, he didn't know where to go, so he thought of going to his mother's old house.

The door was open, the thieves must have entered several times, but there was almost nothing to steal, in a closet he found a trunk, who knows why the thieves had spared it. It was closed but it didn't take long to force the locks.

Inside there were a couple of old photos of the mother, very faded, some clothes: a guepierre, long panties with lace at the bottom, a corset, some stockings.

Hans rummaged around with detachment, as if he were a detective investigating a crime: the murder of the child who had been inside him. At a certain point something caught his attention.

It was a book, bound in leather, closed with two ribbons, held in place by a bow knot.

An anxious hurry took hold of him, he had difficulty untying those simple knots, then he tore off the bows, with an anger he had never known.

He looked at the first page, it was written in Gothic characters: Tagebuch (diary).

He put it down. As if it were burning. He thought about what could be in there, his mother's story, a story he didn't want to know. He didn't want to know anything, he didn't want to know who she was and why she was like that, why she had had that strange and wild life, he had a remote image of her, like a Liebig figurine and he didn't want a ghost to emerge from that figurine to disturb his distant soul, his frozen feelings that for this reason didn't generate pain.

There was one thing that could have been in that book, though: his father's name. His name

They called him Luderitz, it was the name of the founder of the colony, that's what they called all the orphans.

But he, to whom life had given nothing and who wanted nothing from it, wanted at least a name, at least one that made him feel he existed, more or less like the others.

Being careful not to read anything he looked at the pages, discovered that there were dates, and looked for the one that approximately concerned his conception, he read trying not to give any meaning to the words. Finally his eye fell on a name: Helmut Westerhaupt, he read a little more: his father was an officer of the Kriegs Marine; he did not want to go on.

Hans watched the ferry pull up to the dock, the lights of the city could be seen from the ship, the port was still bustling despite it being dark. He had a military bag on his shoulder and was wearing a worn and not exactly clean suit, his work shoes were almost worn out, and if it hadn't been for the presentation he was carrying in his pocket, intended for the commander of one of the Freikorps, General Von Der Goltz, he would have looked like one of the many unfortunates that the crisis was throwing onto the streets.

He greeted the ship's captain who was on the bridge and set off along the dock.

He walked calmly out of the port and ventured into the streets, and immediately understood where he was, he read the sign "Reepebhan", there were windows and inside there were girls and it seemed to him that he had fallen into his childhood, he did not like it and continued until he left the Sankt Pauli district. He found a hotel, it was not a big hotel but it gave the impression of not hosting prostitutes and clients, The next day he would go to the headquarters of Von Goltz's Freikorp.

He did this every month, taking a train in Munich and travelling to Bremerhaven, then hitching a ride to Cuxhaven, where he took a ferry to the island, and spent the weekend watching his half-brother and his mother live.

Taking advantage of the fact that he was a member of the SA, Lieutenant Commander Helmut Westerhaupt, a hero who died in the Battle of the Rufiji River aboard the cruiser Koenisberg, of which he was the gunnery officer, had managed to find out everything about his father.

The first time he had gone to Helgoland with a great desire to go to that man's wife and tell her the whole truth, to tell him about her husband's sordid adventure and the life of a disinherited man that had been the fruit of this adventure. He had expected to find a villa by the sea, an arrogant and well-dressed Junker, and a boy who could have been him, but was not, and who enjoyed all the privileges of the German military caste, those, more or less, he would have earned thanks to his membership in the Nazi party and the SA.

So when he saw the little colorful house by the sea, the boy who was his brother coming home in the morning dressed as a fisherman, the woman in modest clothes, he wondered if he had got the wrong person, he investigated, no, he had not got the wrong person, those were the Westerhaupts: no villas, no millions, no arrogance, no Junkers, just a little more than what life had given him, very little more.

He came back again, he had nothing in mind, neither anger, much less compassion; that was just his pastime.

One day, it was the winter of 1926, he had been offered to join a select group within the SA, a unit that would take care of the Fhurer's security, that unit would be called Shutzstaffeln. He had accepted, the one who had proposed it to him was Hitler's right-hand man, Rudolf Hess, a strange man apparently stupid but sometimes surprising.

Nazism came to power and Hans had a certain career in the SS, he had become Sturmhauptführer, a very rapid career, thanks to that rank and his membership in the SS he had had wide access to all the information he thought it appropriate to know, so he had investigated his brother, he didn't want to do him any harm, it was curiosity, it was a way of satisfying that one "vice" of his, that one way of experiencing a remote, faint emotion.

Walter had applied to join the Kriegs Marines, why? Maybe to follow in his father's footsteps, maybe to spread poor wretches like his brother around the world?

Supporting him was Kapitän zur See, Canaris, commander of the training ship Berlin and an officer of the naval intelligence services.

Hans decided that he would "supervise" his younger brother's career, he would make sure he went where he wanted, a kind of revenge on life, the satisfaction of a delirium of omnipotence, his little vice. He knew well that sooner or later the war would come and deciding where to send a soldier was like deciding his life and his death, he would decide from time to time whether his brother should live or die and how he should live.

In the autumn of 1933 the time came when his brother Walter had to leave Sudhafen. He asked for a few days' leave and, dressed in civilian clothes, set off for Northern Germany, and then to Heligoland.

He saw Walter leave, hugging his mother Freja, he followed him step by step, keeping an eye on him and that day in Hamburg he decided to save him from very serious trouble, perhaps by looking at his face he would have noticed the resemblance, or better, he would have understood that somewhere there was a guardian, someone who was watching over him, benignly or malignantly? That would be up to him, Hans, to decide from time to time.

3.15 *Berlin ....May 1934 Operation Martingale 2*

He had chosen the name "martingale operation" the martingale is a mathematical tool linked to probabilistic calculation, in fact a game strategy in use since the seventeenth century.

He loved the game and he loved mathematics, maybe because there was a strong correlation between the two, what he was doing was exactly this, a bet, but whoever had decided to play it did not like gambling and had decided to have all the aces in his hand; how? Simple by playing the game from both sides.

The idea seemed too sophisticated to be the Admiral's brainchild; no, there was someone much more subtle and much more powerful shuffling the deck.

He looked at himself in the mirror, the SS uniform he was wearing was elegant, if a little funereal, but he much preferred the clothes from Seville Row, but if that was the game he had to play it.

Speaking of gambling: the agent they had identified was codenamed *Baccarat.*

He, Ian Fleming the contact with Admiral Sinclair would have been *The Bank.*

No one knew Agent Baccara except him and Admiral Sinclair, no one knew that Obersturmführer Jakob Bindung, who was in charge of the Fürer's secretariat, was actually an Englishman whose real name was Ian Fleming. Obersturmführer Bindung was one of the adjutants of SS-Gruppenführer Karl Wolff, at least when he was in Germany, which happened very rarely because direct contact with Agent Baccara was very rare.

That day Bindung was in Berlin to close the deal with Agent Baccara, the demands of the mole infiltrated in the top of the Nazi party and now of Germany itself were quite high, five hundred thousand dollars a year, Neville had accepted without batting an eyelid. Now Fleming / Bindung had to meet Agent Baccara to confirm Neville's acceptance of his conditions, and he also had to tell him how he would be paid. Every four months one hundred and twenty-five thousand dollars would be deposited at the Lisbon branch of the Banco do Espirito Santo, on a coded number, the person who would pay this money would be Mr. Fleming who would win those amounts at the Estorili casino playing Baccara. This was to prevent anyone from discovering the source of the money. The owners of the casino, a few months earlier had received a visit from a very well-known lawyer from Lisbon, very close to the Portuguese Prime Minister Antonio De Oliveira Salazar, who had announced that an American company based in the Cayman Islands would enter the board of directors of the casino, in exchange the casino would have a special consideration for a German gentleman, named Jakob Bindung, who would periodically visit the Casino. The American company would automatically cover the losses caused by Herr Bindung, needless to say that Mister WB had a share in that anonymous company, together with eleven other partners. The company was called ORDER.

Commander Fleming was partly informed of all this, but he didn't ask questions about the part he didn't know. He liked to play and Estoril was a highly regarded holiday resort.

He calmly left the apartment, which was located in a building on Kurfürstendamm, right in the center of Berlin, a rather inappropriate location for a spy, however his rank as an SS officer and member of the Führer's secretariat made it difficult to have him live in a working-class neighborhood on the outskirts, where he would certainly have aroused much more curiosity than in the Charlottenbourg neighborhood where he lived during his Berlin interludes.

He took a taxi and had himself taken to the chancellery, he showed the guards his special pass, eliciting clicking heels and greetings, the reactions of the German security personnel always amused him, they were deferential, expressionless, totally stiff, they seemed like robots, he often wondered if so much haughtiness corresponded to the same amount of attention, but he preferred not to delve further. Accompanied by a Scharführer he walked along marble corridors, polished to a shine, with very high solid wood doors. The area reserved for the Fhurer and his secretary was separated by a sort of portal to the right of which was a desk where an SS non-commissioned officer sat, while two ordinary SS men stood guard, impaled like two statues. He showed the special pass and was given access to the door, where he was taken over by another non-commissioned officer who accompanied him to Agent Baccarà's office.

He was seated. The man was sitting at a desk immersed in work. The office was rather modest, there was nothing sumptuous about it, it seemed like a place intended exclusively for work. The conversation was not very long. Baccara took note of the acceptance of the economic conditions then moved on to something else.

"What guarantees do you give me...?" he asked suddenly

Fleming remained suspended for a thousandth of a second: "In what sense?"

He asked in a low voice

Baccara stood up, put a finger on his lips, as if asking for silence, walked towards a door and opened it, there was a rather large bathroom, he signaled Bindung/Fleming to come in. The British temperament of the English agent made him move with a certain embarrassment, but Baccara's expression made him understand that it was a necessary thing.

He entered the bathroom, Baccarat had turned on all the taps.

"You see Bindung, in this building all the walls have ears and they are the ears of Reichfürer Himmler. Very dangerous ears"

Fleming understood the reason for all those open taps and the use of the bathroom for that singular conversation: the roaring of the water would prevent unwanted listeners from catching its contents!

"So, dear friend," Baccara began, "as you know, I have blind faith in the Fhurer and in the destiny of Germany. But the power of Jewish money and its holders is great, and could succeed in preventing the realization of the destiny of our great Aryan race and of Germany."

Fleming thought to himself that perhaps, there was something incongruous about the fact that Baccara did not disdain a substantial portion of that money which "threatened the success of the Aryan project", but since he was a man of the world, he decided to gloss over the matter.

"So, Herr Bindung, I want guarantees that in this unfortunate event, my collaboration with the Order will be recognized and rewarded with my physical salvation... - he paused - you understand that all those dollars that your bosses will pay me are of little use when I'm dead.. "

Fleming found this to be unquestionably true: "So?" he asked.

« so you guarantee me safety in a suitable place, in case the Reich should collapse, the contract is written in detail how this must happen, if this does not happen the press of the whole world will know that you have financed one of the most important leaders of the Nazi party and considering what the Fhurer has in mind I do not think that England would make a good impression. You come from a family of bankers, so you know well what a life insurance is, this is mine »

"But who can guarantee us that she will respect the agreements?"

« On leaving here you will go to the notary Wesser in Hoenzollern Strasse at number 14. The notary will give you a contract in two copies which you will have signed by the Admiral and authenticated by the notary Ferndale in Carlos Street in Mayfair, then you will take one copy to Cascais and deliver it at the casino to a person who on June 4 will be at the reception of the Hotel Villa Albatroz.

If everything goes as planned, on the morning of July 3rd you will know from the newspapers that I have respected the commitment requested of me by the Order.

He turned off the taps and showed Fleming outside. The English agent was quickly dismissed. He left the chancellery building and went to the notary. That evening he was aboard a Dehavilland Dragon Fly which took him from Tempelof airport to a military airfield in Kent. He took a train and disembarked in London. The next morning he presented himself to the admiral, who carefully read the notary's document: "Give me two hours," said the high officer, picked up the telephone and said: "Miss Money Penny, call me the code Whiskey Bravo .. "

Then he politely asked Fleming out. Miss Money Penny escorted him into a sitting room, Ian watched her go and thought that the young clerk had all the right curves in the right places, as well as a rather sexy expression.

Three days later Fleming was in Portugal.

On the morning of July 3, the news appeared in all the German newspapers that during the night the main leaders of the SA had been arrested and shot; history called that event the *night of the long knives* ; Hitler had freed himself from the SA and the least controllable part of the party; the German establishment and the leaders of the Order had secured for themselves a chancellor who was docile or almost docile to their will...

Or so they thought.

3.16 Glamis Castle ....June 1937...the princess and the statesman

Cecilia Cavendish Bentik Bowes Lyon, wife of the recently crowned King George VI of England, sat in the drawing room of Glamis Castle, opposite her were Sir William Samuel Stephenson, Royal Canadian Air Force officer KBE, CC, MC, DFC and Canadian businessman and Sir Winston Leonard Spencer-Churchill, KG,

OM, CH, TD, DL, FRS, RA, Conservative politician and MP. Between them was an elegant neo-Edwardian table on which was placed a lovely Limoges porcelain tea service.

"So Sir Winston and Sir William, you believe that Europe is heading for war?"

asked the Queen: "In our opinion there is no doubt, the bombing of Guernica was an experiment, Marshal Von Sperle and General Von Richtofen are charged with testing Douhet's ideas on air warfare in the field, and this means only one thing, they are preparing a large-scale war in Europe" said Stephenson

"According to some, this war is directed against the Bolsheviks," said the Queen.

"The Germans have always had only one goal, to conquer space in the East and sooner or later they will do it, but this will provoke a reaction from the French, because France does not want to allow Germany to be more powerful than it, for reasons of national pride and for historical reasons, which are the same thing. When the Germans attack France their army will crush the French one in a few months, at that point Europe will be in the hands of a single great power, what England has been trying to avoid for five hundred years, at that point there will be only two people who can help us: God and Joseph Yugasvili Stalin."

Churchill concluded.

The Queen looked at both her guests: "Sir Winston, are you saying that we should ally ourselves with the Bolsheviks...?" asked the Queen

"Yes, your majesty," replied the politician.

"Sir Winston, we are used to some of your outbursts... let's say strange, but this one is really enormous, you mean that we should go to Moscow and ask those godless people to make a pact with us against Germany...."

"No, Your Majesty, the godless would send us to the devil without hesitation..."

"So what should we do?" the queen continued.

"We have to create a channel, an informal one, initially, a channel with the Russians, Sir William here already has very intense business contacts and as Your Majesty knows business has no ideas, from this channel, probably at the right moment we will be able to activate direct contact with the Soviet Foreign Ministry and of course with Stalin."

"For these things there is MI5, and the Foreign Office"

"Excuse me, Your Majesty," Stephenson intervened, "the Foreign Office is an official channel, and therefore would only receive an official response from the Russian Foreign Ministry. As for MI5, the secret services are easy to infiltrate and this... operation must remain secret. And that is why we are here with Your Majesty, if we were to go to Sir Neville (*Chamberlain* , *Prime Minister)* he would oppose us with a series of observations of common sense and rules of international relations, and, Your Majesty, to be honest with what awaits us, common sense and international rules at this moment......" He paused for a very significant moment of silence.

"Gentlemen, you know well that the crown has no executive power in the English system..."

"Your Majesty," Churchill continued, "knows the secret clause of John Lackland..."

The queen and her mother looked at each other

"Si periculum sit in regnum rex eximi, the king can in extreme cases of danger take action on his own initiative if this is in the interests of the kingdom" added Churchill.

"As long as you inform the chambers sooner or later..."

"Sooner or later, your majesty, sooner.... or later," Churchill said with intent.

They got into Churchill's Rolls Royce, both in good spirits:

"His Majesty has been generous to us," said Stephenson.

"Of course, we didn't even have to remind him that the Windsors are one of the twelve families that form the Order, nor of the recent visit of the Grand Master, the mysterious Mr WB"

"He already did it - Stephenson - it would have been embarrassing to do it though.."

"Embarrassing," Churchill exclaimed, "my family has been English long before the Windsors and if we are talking about quarters of nobility I would say that the Windsors are not even close to it."

"What will this organization be called?" asked Churchill.

"Pijelesk our Russian contact suggests *Ottepel* in our language which means Thaw.. he says that this war will be like a very hard winter and when it ends it will be like spring, thaw is an auspicious name.."

"I agree," Churchill replied. "Thaw seems like a nice name to me."

3.17 *Princeton...1937...the puppeteer discovers and the genie of the lamp*

The ceremony had just ended, the board of trustees of Princeton University had concluded as usual with the communication of the resounding results of the budget, the students who had graduated during the previous academic year had all found their place in the richest and most prestigious institutions in the United States. In the ballroom the meeting with the faculty was underway, some of the most excellent minds of the time were there.

WB had just finished discussing with a couple of eminent professors of economics, both of whom had different ideas on the solution to the financial crisis that was still weighing on nations around the world. He had no opinions on the matter, he was only interested in where to guarantee the best returns for the considerable finances of the twelve families that formed the Order. In this regard, he was starting to take an interest in the latest advances in science. It wasn't easy to understand, but his instinct told him that physics was on the threshold of an extraordinary leap that would radically change the world. A leap that would drag the other sciences with it, radically changing technologies and industrial development. In the council, he had been one of those who had pushed most insistently for Albert Einstein to be hired. Now he wanted to meet him.

He saw him among the others chatting amiably with other professors, approached and introduced himself. The scientist had an open character, loved to chat and was particularly happy to answer WB's questions.

"It seems that an extraordinary prospect is opening up to the world, you are telling me that in a few years we will be able to control matter and energy..."

Einstein was smiling, but slowly his expression changed, it was as if a remote vein of sadness had crept into the apparently jovial character of the great scientist.

"You see sir, nature, unfortunately, does not have its own ethics, in nature good and evil are confused. What is good for a lion, can be evil for a gazelle... Nietzke said that moral phenomena do not exist, but only moral interpretations of phenomena"

"Do you love Nietzke...?"

"I wouldn't say so..." Einstein replied with a smile

"However, do you mean to say that these discoveries could also have... let's say... bad effects?"

"The control of matter and energy, if we ever succeed in obtaining it, unleashes great and terrible forces that can be used for progress, but also for destruction. When he left Germany, Heisenberg was studying the splitting of the atom and was beginning to glimpse developments that in the long run could be disturbing, especially if they were handed over to Hitler."

"Ah," WB said, "unpleasant..."

"Enough," Einstein replied with a bitter smile.

3.18 *Marblehead, Massachusetts ,mister WB's residence... operation Martingale 3*

He was sitting on the patio and looking out to sea, it was a beautiful day and the ocean was flat and reflected the sun like a sheet of steel. He preferred days when the sea was rough, the waves crashed against the shore, with high breakers, and the sky was a continuous scenario of changing clouds of all shades of gray and white. The calm made him anxious, he preferred to look the storm in the eyes, just as he liked to do in life, the storm created challenges and you knew how to solve them for better or for worse, the flat calm was more dangerous than the storm because you never knew what to expect. For example, the pleasant chat with Albert Einstein had opened up extraordinary scenarios: extraordinarily exciting and extraordinarily worrying. It was necessary to know more, if what Einstein said was true, and it could hardly have been otherwise.

The energy that the great scientist was talking about was now at the center of discussions among the small group of nuclear physicists. Those who were most advanced in this research were the Germans. Many of them were Jews and had already fled Germany, but some, including Verner Heisemberg, who had understood better than anyone else, were not Jews and could soon arrive at practical conclusions, that is, begin to produce energy or perhaps build weapons that would use this energy.

In Hitler's hands, weapons that used atomic energy would have been a threat to the entire world and would have blown up the Order's project to create a weak but stable Europe, so much so as to be a good market for the United States but not a competitor. Furthermore, it was unthinkable that the Anglo-Saxon powers were not the holders, or better still the monopolists of those weapons and that power.

It was necessary to play a complex game, which would allow the objective of order to be achieved without Germany becoming an uncontrollable power; in short, it was a question of playing, as always, on both sides of the table.

The *Martingale operation* was one side of the table, on the other it was a matter of working on Jewish scientists exiled in the United States, making sure they would get the support of the administration and the president, but this was not a problem, Roosevelt would very quickly remember the support given to him by WB in the elections, and he was also intelligent enough to understand how important it was to work on atomic energy.

Estoril....

Fleming rose from the gaming table, Herr Bindung had won for the umpteenth time, also thanks to the fact that he remembered all the cards that came out, and for the umpteenth time he would make the payment to Agent Baccarat.

He went to deposit the chips at the cashier, took the money. He checked that the walter ppk under his armpit had a bullet in the chamber and took off the safety. Portugal was a quiet place, Salazar did not allow thieves and robbers to circulate freely in the country *of the Estado Novo,* Guardia Nacional Republicana and the Policia kept watch, both on the criminals and on the very few surviving political opponents and kept away the possible refugees "not compliant" with Salazar's political choices from Spain shaken by the civil war. The surveillance extended above all to the streets of places like Estoril, where the rich of the whole world, there were very few of them left, but those few were very rich, they were not to be disturbed in any way. The possible enemies, however, were not the common criminals, but some hostile secret service, and in the world where Fleming moved, one never knew who the opposing side was. *Operation Martingale* was a well-kept secret, but in the world of intelligence services, secrets were a weapon to be used from time to time against whoever it was deemed useful to attack, directly or indirectly.

Along with the envelope of money, the cashier handed him another anonymous-looking envelope addressed to Herr Bindung, sent from Zurich.

Fleming arrived at the bank and deposited the money, then went into a private room where he opened the envelope and read. Well, he had to take a trip to Berlin, a way to break the monotony of that job as a messenger.

Berlin-

The Führer closed the scientific report and looked at Reich Führer Himmler: "Dear Himmler, this report on the so-called discoveries of Einstein and his ilk is a true masterpiece. It is obvious that depraved Jews cannot have had correct intuitions about nuclear physics. It was clear from the beginning that Einstein's discoveries were totally wrong. Well, let's not waste time with this nonsense. Germany has other things to do."

"Of course my Führer..."

The Reich Fhurer walked out. That report had been drawn up by a dangerous adversary of his within the Reich leadership, a man who was a real threat to his power. Those discoveries needed to be investigated further. He knew that not only Jewish scientists, but excellent Aryan scientists, had been interested in that subject, and from what he understood there were extraordinary developments on the horizon, the possibility of giving Germany a power that no one in the world could have countered, perhaps the same weapon that had possessed Atlantis and led to its destruction and forced the Aryans to take refuge in the mythical city of Agarttha.

He decided to turn to Dr. Walther Wüst, the scientific director of the Forschungsgemeinschaft Deutsches Ahnenerbe

e. V., commonly called Ahnenerbe, the scientific association that Himmler himself had founded in 1935, with the aim of bringing to light the glorious vestiges of the ancestral heritage of the Aryans.

Luderiz looked at the dispatch that the Rottenführer on duty had given him a few hours earlier. It was an order from the chief of staff Obergruppenführer Karl Wolff, who invited him to report to him by 4 pm that same day for " *important communications* ".

Now he was in the antechamber of the high officer, sitting in the only chair in the room and watching the Schütze on duty who was gluing stamps onto letters that had been handed to him by a non-commissioned officer a short while before. He was bored, but as a good SS man he didn't show it, he just stared at the shiny tips of his boots. He had risen rapidly in rank, for some time he had been entrusted with extremely delicate tasks, for a while he had attended physics courses at the university with the task of supervising the professors and students of what was called a nest of Jews. He had become curious about that singular science that seemed to be trying to explain how the world worked, what was behind the complex and almost always incomprehensible veil of reality. Naturally he hadn't spoken about this to anyone, but he had managed to get hold of some books, he had a hard time but he was starting to understand something.

The massive door of the Obergruppenführer's office opened, Wolff himself had done it:

"Have a seat, Luderitz," came the hoarse voice of the high officer.

There was another officer sitting at the desk, Luderitz didn't know him, he was slightly surprised, Wolff, came around the desk and sat down: "Allow me, dear Luderitz, to introduce you to the Obersturmführer Bindung, he belongs to the foreign service of the SD...

So dear Luderitz, I have called you to inform you of my intention to assign you to a special department of our corps.

You have done a good job at the university. Your reports are very accurate... - he paused - among other things, by chance, by attending the lectures, have you understood anything about this so-called Jewish science?"

The question was rather strange and embarrassing and Luderitz, despite his stony character, had a moment of hesitation: "Well, mein commandant, really..."

Wolff looked at him - "mein Luderitz, please, we are among ourselves, every officer who does our job must know his enemy, the better he knows him, the more effective he can be, so tell me, are you passionate about physics?"

"Yes sir..."

"All the better, so the Reichfhurer has decided to create a section of the Anenherbe that will deal with the most recent discoveries in physics, Herr Himmler is convinced that this science can lead to equipping the Reich with the same weapons that the ancient Aryans had, you will be part of this special team, which will be called Schwartze Sonne. It goes without saying that this is a huge responsibility, we will soon be adding other agents to your team, your task will be to identify among the Aryan scholars those who can best serve the Reich and lead it to equip itself with these extraordinary weapons. Whatever discovery you make, whatever happens to you, you will have to inform me and me alone, you will accept instructions only from me and from Herr Bindung here, even if you will have to verify Herr Bindung's orders with me.

In three days you will meet Professor Heisenberg, who will help you to understand these topics a little better, the next day you will appear here and I will receive you and give you further instructions

Are there questions...?"

"No mein Obergruppenfhurer..."

"Luderitz can go"

Hans stood up, walked towards the door and greeted both Wolff and Bindung with an outstretched arm. It seemed to him that the latter hesitated for a moment before returning the greeting. The officer had remained silent the whole time. He gave off a strange impression in Luderitz. There was something about him that made one think of a foreigner...

3.19 Copenhagen .... 1937. The Saracen's Notebook

Grete had been a maid in the Bohr household for a few days, the Bohrs were a well-off family, but with many children, which gave Grete a lot to do, but what she took up most was the professor's study, to clean it she had to put in order the papers that the professor left on the desk every evening. It was not easy to put things in order, Grete did not understand anything of what was written and was afraid of making a mess, especially not putting the papers in the right order and making Bohr angry as had happened the second day, she found herself working for that family. The professor had to work half a day to put his notes in order.

Luckily, the brilliant Bohr was a good-natured person, he understood the young girl's difficulties and therefore numbered the sheets as he went along, this did not prevent the girl from becoming anxious.

That morning there was more of a mess than usual, the professor had stayed on until late and there were sheets of paper everywhere, he had numbered them, but the problem was managing to get them all, at that moment Grete was looking for page fifty-three, she had looked under the desk, under various pieces of furniture, on the various shelves of the bookcase, nothing, all that was missing was to look under the sofa, Grete knelt down, and put her cheek on the floor and saw the sheet of paper, she reached out and touched something, she took the sheet of paper and sighed, she looked at the sheet of paper, it was page fifty-three, finally... then she decided to take the other object she had touched out from under the sofa, there was a lot of dust, no one including her had dusted under there already. Maybe it was better to do it, before getting a scolding, with some difficulty she managed to take the object out, it was a notebook, with a black cover, she opened the cover, on the first page there was something written, it was written in a language she didn't know. He dusted off the notebook and put it on the desk, finished collecting the papers and putting his notes in order, just as Professor Bohr entered the room.

"Good morning Grete, how are we doing...", the girl blushed violently.

"well, well your excellency, um professor..."

Bohr smiled, "Leave your Excellency alone. I see you have tidied up nicely, thank you, I know I left a lot of mess last night."

"No, no, your excellency, erm, professor, of course, it's my job"

Meanwhile Bohr had approached the desk, saw the notebook and was a little surprised: "Grete, is this notebook yours...?"

" oh no sir, and also written in a foreign language, I thought it was yours... it was under the sofa, here, it was next to a piece of paper I, um I thought of dusting under the sofa and I found it, here.."

"Oh, okay, Grete. Are you finished in this room?" The girl nodded and politely asked permission to leave, which was granted immediately.

The professor looked at the notebook, told him something, opened it at random, it was full of calculations, which ended suddenly, under the last line there was something written, in another language: in Italian.

Bohr immediately understood that it was a notebook of Ettore Majorana, he had been a guest at his house some time. Before. That notebook must have been there for a long time. Who knows what the hell that curious and brilliant Italian had astrologized. He went to the first page and began to follow them, little by little as he proceeded his expression changed, those calculations, they reminded him of something, the hypothesis that the German chemist Ida Nodak had published in *"Nature"* four years earlier, there was something regarding the mass of the elements, they had also spoken about that thing with Lise Meitner.... The calculation developed on the next page and... it ended there and underneath there was a sentence in Italian, a short sentence, where there was a word that was not Italian, something like Apocalisse.

3.20 Balearic Islands....1937...the island rediscovered

Mario had arrived in Majorca with the first contingent of SM 79, the *cursed hunchback* , with the group of Colonel Biseo and Bruno Mussolini, the 205 bomber known as the *green mice*. Those who, only a few months earlier had won the Istress-Damascus-Paris, a speed race between planes, in which the best machines in the world took part. A trophy that had brought great popularity to Italy and fascism. Now it was a question of testing the military capabilities of the SM79, an aircraft in whose design his grandfather had also taken part.

The Cursed Hunchback, whose official name was Sparviero, had many merits and some defects.

One of these was that it was not very easy to fly, especially in strong winds and bad weather. On the other hand, the canvas fuselage was certainly not suitable for giving stability to the vehicle. The second defect was the bomb bay, the plane had been originally designed as a fast passenger aircraft, so the bomb bay was an adaptation. The bombs were vertical, instead of horizontal and the release mechanisms did not always work at their best.

The complicated and dangerous job of manually releasing the bombs was carried out by his radio operator, Sergeant Major Salvatore Pascalis, known to his friends as Totò, a boy from Carovigno near Lecce, who was worth as much as ten people, because in addition to having considerable acrobatic skills and being an excellent radio operator, he was gifted with exceptional aim, which had earned him numerous leaves of absence after shooting exercises, and which had saved the lives of the entire crew during a raid a few days earlier on the port of Tarragona, when with the dorsal machine gun, the one that protruded from the legendary hump of the Sparviero, Pascalis had shot down two Ratas of the Republican Air Force, earning himself a war cross.

It was cold, the weather was not particularly favorable for missions, but the needs of the battlefield were pressing, so the planes took off in disastrous weather conditions, aboard that canvas shell stretched over a metal skeleton. It had been a tiring day, starting at three in the morning. They had returned to the target four times and during the last incursion one of the *hunchbacks* had taken several hits. Captain Pareto who was piloting it, had been wounded, a shot to the collarbone and a graze to the head. His second lieutenant Valletti was dead. Pareto had struggled, flying with only one eye and a paralyzed arm, but he had miraculously managed to return to base.

They were all quite tense and tired, and when Mario suggested going into town he found himself alone.

He decided to stop by the airport to see if Pascalis was there. The sergeant was staying in the non-commissioned officers' quarters, near the airport, and did not enjoy the same privileges as the officers, who were staying at the Royal Hotel just outside the city in a place with a spectacular view. Mario was watching him from the balcony of his room, the sea was rough and was hitting the beach and the rocks below with force, it was a moonlit night, which every now and then appeared between one cloud and another and illuminated the dramatic scenery of the coast. The port of Palma not far away was in the dark, there was a curfew.

He pulled his heavy flight jacket tighter around him, he had decided to go into town and have some fun. The good boy from his college days in Piacenza would have had a hard time recognizing this young man who was about to venture into the backwaters of Palma de Mallorca. He had abandoned certain qualms a long time ago, after entering the aeronautical academy in Nisida. One evening they had officially been given leave to go out, unofficially they had been taken to the best brothel in Naples, where a big girl from Bassano del Grappa had introduced him to the world of adults. It had cost him dearly, but for him money had never been a problem.

Since then he had had several adventures, paid and unpaid, even if in the back of his mind he was always the girl from Budapest, more than ten years had passed since that night.

He had been around all over Europe, piloting various planes, but especially the S79 Sparviero, in every city he had looked for the woman with the emerald eyes, he had found eyes of every kind and every color, he had had a lot of fun, always being careful, as his grandfather had recommended, and never bringing home any other gift than the passionate participation of his companions in adventure.

But the woman with emerald eyes wasn't the only one Mario was looking for, there was another.

They called her Madamoiselle Docteur, no one knew her real name. Perhaps Elisabeth Schragmuller or Anne Lesser, but in Rome she was the Countess Von Testory. The woman who had ruined his father's reputation and killed him. Mario had sworn revenge, and that was one of the reasons why he had undertaken a career that had taken him around the world thanks to the support of his grandfather and General Italo Balbo.

The two women appeared alternately in his thoughts almost every day.

When he thought of his enemy he imagined killing her without mercy, after making her suffer the same pain that his mother Caterina had suffered. The same humiliations that his father had suffered, left dead in a garbage dump making everyone believe that he had fallen victim to a homosexual vendetta. But he and his grandfather knew well that it had been the revenge of the Austrian secret services, which he had deceived by allowing a group of Italian agents to penetrate the Austrian embassy in Zurich and locate numerous enemy agents in Italy.

What made him deeply angry was that only a few of those agents had been arrested. Most were protected by the Vatican and by illustrious relatives. Luckily, his grandfather, Count Vergotti di Santa Tecla, was also a powerful figure, close to Italy's new allies in the Great War, and so he had managed to ensure that the story of Mario's father's death was not too publicized and Ervè's death was recorded as having fallen in service during a skirmish on the Adamello front.

Mario had already tried to understand why the German spy had been so determined to disgrace Ervè Vaillante, in that world, the world of spy, It was not customary to eliminate the opponent. There was a chivalrous attitude and they were content to accept defeat in a sporting manner, postponing any rematch until the next match. Von Testory had wanted to shame his father, to make him look like a two-bit faggot, and when his grandfather asked him for explanations on this aspect of the story, he became gloomy and changed the subject. But his friend Amedeo, who had contacts in the world of espionage through his uncle, a general of the Carabinieri, had told Mario that in that world there were rumors that there was an old score to settle between Mademoiselle Docteur and Vergotti di Santatecla.

Mario had a motorbike, a Guzzi Sport 15 bought brand new a few days before leaving for the Balearics and brought by ship together with that of Bruno Mussolini, at the expense of the Crown. The motorbike was parked in the hotel garage next to that of the son of the Duce, together with other military cars and various vehicles of the commands present on the island, the only two civilian vehicles.

Mario rode that motorbike around Mallorca in his rare moments of freedom, especially in the evening when there were no missions planned for the following day, and he hadn't been out for a while, and the weather forecast for the following day was terrible, so the Gobbis would be left stranded.

He decided to go out in civilian clothes, the places he frequented were not places to go in uniform. They were places a bit unusual, where fights broke out every now and then, and the formal involvement of one of the pilots of the Duce's son's squadron could irritate Colonel Biseo and cost a few days of delivery, even if, with the need for pilots that there was, the whole thing would have ended in a dressing down. But he preferred to avoid it, also because the name he bore was rather important.

As an officer he was free to move around in civilian clothes, they were in a war zone and discipline was quite loose. People who risked their lives every day couldn't possibly behave like a schoolboy at the college, so it was enough to respect the forms.

That evening none of his colleagues intended to follow him, he made a phone call to the base where Pascalis was staying, as a non-commissioned officer he did not enjoy the same privileges as the officers and did not sleep at the hotel, even if he risked his life in the same way and that was why Mario took him with him whenever he could, and often wondered if it was Pascalis who was taking him with him, given that he was a few years older than him.

As always, Pascalis was available, he was waiting for him in front of the base entrance, also wrapped up in his flight jacket and with a yellow and red plaid scarf, he had put on his flight cap exactly as Mario had done, they wanted to be recognized as pilots, this made a particular impression on the girls. Those who were around at that time and in the places they frequented could not exactly be called girls.

Mario preferred to call them adventurers. Pascalis, more prosaic, called them *sluts* , but the substance did not change: the pilots were impressive.

Salvatore climbed onto the back seat and off they went, that evening they had decided to go to a place called *El Paraiso*.

It was a place where you could find rather available girls, who Mario and Totò always approached with extreme caution, at that time adventurers from all over the world were wandering around Mallorca. Franco did not have many men at his disposal and so he recruited in the Tercio Estrangeros both idealists and the right-wing scum from half the world, the idealists and the left-wing scum had been recruited in the international brigades. Naturally where there were soldiers there were also whores, despite the heavy Catholic moralism of the Francoists, which always stopped at the doors of the many brothels that had now opened throughout Spain. The confessionals of this country must have been clogged, but the massacres of priests and nuns perpetrated by the "progressives" of the *popular front* , which also included bloodthirsty bands of anarchists, probably made it difficult to confess or perhaps it was enough to kill some communists, maybe even someone who vaguely resembled them to obtain plenary indulgence for all sins. So they all went on killing and fucking, each with the justification closest to their own vision of the world and all with the same hypocritical belief that they were right.

It was around midnight, the streets of the old city were deserted. There was a curfew and the Guardia Civil was enforcing it...with the necessary exceptions, all generally very well paid.

The entrance to the place was an anonymous looking door, lit by a red shaded lamp... to respect the curfew. A guy hidden in the shadows watched the street to keep away the pests and to be ready to "guarantee" to the guards that the place respected the rules.

Mario and Salvatore knew the rules, Vaillante gave them the usual tip, and the man, a skinny guy with a moustache and sideburns and a cigarette hanging from the side of his mouth, knocked on the door: two knocks, then two more, then one.

The door opened just wide enough to let the two Italians in.

The place was immersed in darkness, there were several tables where groups of men were sitting, who were jeering and chatting loudly, languages from all over the world and all the same conversations: women, war, bets.

The tables were around a sort of platform, at that moment poorly lit by small lights, at the back of the room there was another platform where there was a group of musicians: a violin, an accordion and a drum kit, they were not playing; at the counter there were a couple of girls. The manager approached the two soldiers: « good evening teniente, bien vindo »

"Thank you Manuel" Mario replied in Italian, "How's the movement this evening" Mario asked just to say something.

« Many Kameraden, and the usual adventurers...but tonight we have a special number, two women dancing the tango with each other...Phew » Manuel said with a wink.

« Hey, aren't you afraid that the Guardia Civil... »

"The lieutenant of the Civil Guard is in that corner," Manuel said with a wink, "to ensure order, of course," he said in a comical guttural voice like a priest in the pulpit.

The host concluded and walked away, winking at the two Italians, then reached the center of the platform.

It was illuminated by a spotlight and began to address the audience asking for silence, announcing the crucial event of the evening: two women dancing the tango together: "un tango de fuego..."

You can see two figures covered in cloaks from head to toe entering and standing next to Manuel.

The lights went out and the orchestra began to play a milonga. The spotlight came back on, illuminating two female bodies embracing like couples dancing tango. At the same time, Mario's heart sank. The two girls were wearing two tango dancer dresses, in the style of *the Four Horsemen of the Apocalypse*, one was black, the other fire red. Their hair was identical, one was a blonde like Marlene Dietrich, but with a statuesque body and ice-blue eyes. The second one had jet black hair and eyes the color of emeralds, and it was Her: the girl from Budapest. The two dancers began to evolve, chased by the spotlight along the dance floor.

Silence had fallen in the room, the milonga accompanied the movements of the two with its sinful and sensual harmony.

When the music ended on the brunette's "casqué", there was a moment of silence, then a sort of ovation exploded and the room was lit up. The two women got out and walked away, going to sit at a table. Mario, his heart pounding, stood up and started to head towards the table. Salvatore followed him, and in a leap they were in front of the two girls.

"Good evening..." Mario said to the brunette, who was smoking a cigarette inserted into a holder. The girl turned around with an annoyed expression, then her expression changed.

"Good evening!" she replied with a slightly hoarse voice and a tone of pleasant surprise:

"You see," said Mario, "we are not in Budapest but we will see each other again."

the blonde girl had taken on a strange worried expression, jealousy? No, it wasn't that, there was something different.

"My name is Cinzia and she ..." the brunette said with the same irresistibly seductive tone

"My name is Mario, I would like to dance with you, Miss", at that moment the little orchestra had started playing a slow, Cinzia turned towards the blonde and said softly "alles in ordnung". She was in Mario's arms and they began to twirl.

Mario looked her straight in the eyes: "Who are you?"

"I'm Cinzia" she repeated smiling

"Come on, don't make fun of me. Where are you from?", the smile was like a light dancing in the darkness, the teeth were very white, a necklace of bright pearls

"I'm American, with distant Italian origins... "

Mario had a completely dazed expression, but he wanted to know more, who was this ghost that mysteriously appeared in his life, at the most unexpected moments, leaving him with an indomitable nostalgia after each apparition.

"But what is a woman like you doing in this place, you're not a dancer... in Budapest..." the sentence remained hanging, Cinzia put a hand and a finger on his mouth, then kissed him, like no one had ever done in his life.

"I am the lady of your dreams, and you are my swordsman... the swordsman of my heart"

Mario decided not to waste time asking any more questions, they continued dancing until the end of the song.

"Can I offer you a glass of Champagne?" Mario asked, Cinzia nodded, she seemed to be in the grip of great emotion. Mario offered him his arm and they were heading towards the bar, when a German sailor appeared in front of them, he was visibly tipsy. He turned to Cinzia

"Fräulein will tanzen *vuole (dance, Miss)* ?" he said with an awkward bow.

Mario looked at him as one would look at an annoying insect that crosses your path: "Fräulein ist mit mir beschäftigt ... und curiosiert sich nicht für Tanz (*the young lady is busy with me... and is not interested in dancing)*"

The German made a disdainful expression. Then he turned to the table of his comrades, and repeated Mario's sentence in a mocking tone, then turned back to Mario: "Eih Spacchetti, signorina ist here per todos...", he said with an arrogant grimace. Mario let go of Cinzia's arm and prepared to start a direct train, but behind the sailor's shoulders a calm and authoritative voice was heard: "Franke, hast du nicht gehört, was er sagte, die italienischen Kameraden. Die junge Dame ist nicht daran interessaert, Ihre Aufmerksamkeit, zurück zum Zwinger (*Franke, didn't you hear what the Italian comrade said? The signorina is not interested in your attentions, go back to your kennel)*"

The German turned around, there was a man standing at the sailors' table, he had a firm expression and was looking at him with two calm eyes but similar to two steel blades.

The German seemed to run out of breath, then stood stiffly at attention: "Ja, Herr, Herr Kommandant"

He turned and sat back down.

The Kommandant walked towards Mario and held out his hand: "I am Captain Westerhaupt. Please forgive my men. They are under a bit of pressure but they are good comrades."

Mario shook the German's hand, he had a hand like a pair of pliers, but politely he shook it in a frank and friendly way.

They stayed at the bar for a long time drinking champagne, they discovered that they had both had premonitions in the past about their meeting. Cinzia laughed thinking of herself walking along a tropical beach, dancing to the sound of a flute.

The decision came almost without them realizing it, they looked into each other's eyes and Cinzia said: "Do you sleep in the barracks or in a decent hotel?"

"I sleep in a castle on top of a cliff overlooking the sea, where every evening I watch the sunset and cry for my lost love," Mario said in a rather comical tone.

"Ah, damn, I didn't think I'd meet Lord Byron in the midst of the Spanish Civil War..."

"Listen, do you want to see my castle? It's called Hotel Royal but it's a fake to mislead my enemies..." Mario said, lowering his voice

She smiled again: "Hey, I think this Byron has a little too much Italian blood... tell me what you have in mind, we girls from the islands are very difficult to bring to the castle..."

"I'll tell you on the way I have a motorbike out here..."

"I'm disappointed, a motorbike? Not a black thoroughbred that only you can ride...?"

Mario decided to lighten the mood a bit: "No, I have a Guzzi Sport 15. With the horsepower it would be a bit long from here. Tomorrow morning at 10 I'm going on a mission to the continent and if we don't hurry I'm afraid I'll have to take you and the bombs on board my Sparviero..."

They went out and walked to the motorbike, jumped on it and flew away.

The blonde looked at Commander Westerhaupt and nodded in agreement.

Pascalis was negotiating with a rather Moroccan brunette. Black girls had always been his passion, with this one he didn't get along well. He thought it was time to go back, he looked around; Captain Vaillante had disappeared: "fuck..." the sergeant muttered under his breath, he had to go back to the base on foot and he had to hurry before he was late and reported for desertion.

It had been a tough day, repeated attacks on the Republican lines, Mario's physical resistance had been put to the test. He got out of his plane and glanced at the fuselage, it was riddled like a colander. Pascalis had been slightly wounded in the head, but a lot of blood had come out and the right side of his face was dirty as if he had been slaughtered. He had wrapped himself in a silk scarf that he always wore around his neck, he had a slightly depressed expression:

"what's up pascalis, are you worried about the wound? Go easy, inside that head there's only bone, it takes an anti-tank bullet to break it..."

"What the hell, I ruined my entire scarf, it was a gift from a friend and I really wanted it..."

"Well, Totò, you'll get another one, won't you..."

"and that one left with the last fortnight...you know how some girls are"

Mario laughed, turned around, a sergeant was running towards him, stopped in front of him, saluted military: "Sir, the colonel urgently wants you"

"Now...?" Mario asked, surprised.

"Yes sir, Captain"

He headed towards the command building, with his parachute askew and his flight suit stained with grease, without a cap and holding his pilot's cap in his hand, his hair disheveled, he looked like he had just come out of a fight, which was true enough, except that the fight had taken place at an altitude of fifteen hundred metres.

He entered the building, the adjutant was reading the reconnaissance dispatches that verified the effects of the raids on the port of Barcelona. Mario appeared in front of the desk, stood at attention: "Commands, Major, the colonel called me.

The major looked up from his paperwork and fixed Mario: "Ah, Captain Vaillante, take a seat, the colonel is waiting for you."

Colonel Biseo was on the phone. Mario stood at attention in front of the desk. Biseo looked at him and gave a half smile, but he didn't give him rest. He ended the call.

"Rest" began the commander "so dear Vaillante, it seems that we will have to give up your precious collaboration"

"As Mr. Colonel, what do you mean?"

"I mean dear Captain Vaillante Vergotti of Santa Tecla, that his excellency comrade Italo Balbo, Minister of Aeronautics, seems to suddenly need your presence in Rome"

"I'm amazed, Colonel, with the need for staff we have here..." Mario said in a disappointed tone.

"Yes captain, with the need we have, you, one of our best pilots must suddenly leave for Rome"

"Colonel, you don't think that I..."

"No Vaillante, I don't think so, but I'm pissed off with Ettore, it's a joke that he shouldn't have played on me, but never mind, it's you who's missing out, we're moving to Logrogno in the north soon and there's going to be some fighting there!"

"What a pain in the ass," Mario said out loud, looking at himself in the mirror. He had shaved carefully, he had an appointment with Cinzia and he had to give her the bad news. They hadn't seen or heard from each other for four days, and he couldn't wait to meet her, but he didn't like having to give her that bad news. He sprayed himself with lavender and combed his hair in a Mascagni style, using plenty of Linetti brilliantine. He had put on his clean, starched shirt and was about to put on his jacket. Both had been ironed to perfection by the orderly, a Spanish boy from the legionary air force.

He got on the motorbike, decided to go slowly, meanwhile he thought about how to give Cinzia the bad news, he arrived at the Paraiso, went in, there wasn't much movement. He saw Elke, Cinzia's blonde friend, she was at a table with Captain Westerhaupt, they were drinking Malaga wine.

Mario walked towards their table, put two fingers to the peak of his cap in a little parody of the military salute: "Good evening, how are we doing?" he asked out of pure politeness. "Cinzia..?" he asked.

Elke gave him a little smile, « gestatet..Partrtita »

Mario was stunned: "But when?"

"Your days have passed," Elke said, "but I left a message for you." And she handed him a sealed envelope.

Mario opened it, almost tearing it with anxiety, and read:

My dear love, I have to leave, I can't tell you why, I'm sure we'll see each other again, maybe in Budapest, so Seeyou in Budapest Aurevoir, Cynthia »

"Oh shit!" Mario exclaimed with a disappointed expression.
"Yah," said Westerhaupt – Scheisse!

They stayed all night drinking sangria and talking about Cinzia, the war, the sea and planes and everything that alcohol dictated to them.

The sun was rising when Mario said goodbye to the two and got on his motorbike and returned to the hotel. He had to pack his suitcase because at 10 an s84 would take him back to Rome, together with the mail for the families of the legionaries in Italy.

Elke and Walter looked at each other and the blonde said: "our little eagle was really in love, one of those Mediterranean passions, which are born and die in the space of a few days, they burn like the straw and then Aufiderseen.... »

Walter gave a half smile: "You know, something tells me those two aren't done here..."

3.21 *Rinkeveiser...Rome winter 1937....The adventure begins*

It was one of those days when it really seemed that Rome was a paradise. Even though it was around Christmas, the temperature was not particularly low, for someone who was used to the cold of Neuchatel it was a spring warmth, in fact he still went out without a coat.

It was 7 o' clock, like every morning Fabian Rinkveiser entered his office at the Swiss embassy in Rome. He had some paperwork to take care of, concerning musical and literary events and the possibility of a series of conferences on Borromini, the Swiss sculptor who had worked so much in Rome in the 17th century.

Fabian loved that city, he was born in Switzerland, in Corcelles-Cormondrèche, canton of Neuchatel, a place not bad, but where in winter it was freezing cold and he hated the cold. He didn't know exactly why, he was convinced that it was a consequence of his half-Jewish blood. He descended from a family of Marranos, Spanish Jews forcibly converted, who had emigrated from Spain in the fifteenth century. Then they had toured various countries of the Mediterranean, and in the eighteenth century they had settled in that fiefdom of the King of Prussia, then passed in 1815 to Switzerland.

Rinkveser was the result of a series of adaptations of the name to the circumstances. The original Spanish name was Ashkenazi, evidently too Jewish not to risk lynching. In Barcelona where they lived in 1430, they had therefore changed their name, they had called themselves Valencia, also this a name too obviously artificial. Then they had changed their name several times, depending on the country where they were going to settle. When they had passed through Switzerland someone had begun to notice the fact that their ancestors did not drink alcohol, so they had nicknamed them Trinkwasser, another completely improbable name, which had been adjusted to Rinkveser.

Along with their name, the Rinkveser had also forgotten their origins, or rather they had made sure that they were not too well known, since in Europe every time some scoundrel needed an excuse to cover up the consequences of his misdeeds, he accused the Jews.

Fabian had discovered this family secret while rummaging through old papers in a trunk in the attic of their lakeside house.

Fabian's mother was a native of the city, and a Protestant, which meant that according to the Torah, he was not Jewish. However, this did not stop her from disliking anti-Semites around the world, especially Nazis.

Fabian was a singular character, he had two degrees; one in physics from Zurich and one in political science from the Sorbonne. In Paris he had met some officers of the Deuxieme Bureau. He had maintained close relations with them, so much so that he was at the origin of a counterespionage affair of which two colonels had been "victims": Friedrich Moritz von Wattenwyl and Karl Egli of the Swiss general staff, who collaborated with the German and Austrian military attachés in Bern. The two colonels had not suffered any particular damage, but the allies had remembered the help provided by Rinkveiser. In the twenties the man had come into contact with Hans Hann, a publicist who had set up a strange private agency, closely linked to the general staff. An embryo of a secret service, with which he had begun to work from the beginning.

Alongside this activity, Rinkveiser had maintained close relations with several scientists, in particular Albert Einstein, with whom he had studied at the University of Zurich. His profession as a diplomat was naturally perfectly compatible with his collaboration with the service set up by Hann.

Rinkveiser had sensed from the beginning that the discoveries of physics would end up having a fundamental strategic role. He had spoken about this with Stephenson, who had included him in the new transnational secret organization formed under the patronage of Winston Churchill: "The Thaw".

Rinkveiser's presence in Rome was not entirely unrelated to the discoveries that the group on Via Panisperna was making, her passion for new discoveries was unstoppable. Sabine had graduated in nuclear physics and had met those scientists, in particular she had had a relationship with one of them, Maiorana.

It was early morning, at least for Rome. Unfortunately at that time the cafes were closed and so he would have to wait even longer before going to eat a croissant and cappuccino in the city. He would have taken advantage of the time to read the mail that had arrived in the afternoon and that he had not been able to read, because he was busy with a meeting with the musician Zandonai who he wanted to invite to conduct a concert in Locarno.

He leafed through some envelopes that he put aside, it didn't seem like anything urgent, then he saw the envelope, it was rather bulky, as if it contained several sheets of paper, the address was written in the unmistakable handwriting of Niels Bohr: "strange", Rinkveiser reflected, it had been a while since he had spoken to his friends from "Jewish science", as the Nazis called it. He calmly opened the envelope. The letter was twelve sheets long, it must have been something important, Bohr wasn't the type to write uselessly, as a good scientist he preferred numbers to words.

It took him half an hour to read everything, and to understand: Bohr had found a notebook by chance in his house, he wasn't sure, but it seemed to belong to Ettore Majorana. The strange thing was that the notebook contained calculations that seemed to lead to an extraordinary discovery. An evolution of the studies of Einstein and other colleagues of Kaiser Wilhelm Institute. Apparently the calculations in those notes demonstrated the possibility of the existence of a new energy. But there was a strange detail, the calculations suddenly, right at a crucial point stopped, and there was a writing, in Italian, whose meaning escaped the illustrious Danish scientist who did not know the language of Dante.

Bohr asked Rinkveiser to contact Maiorana in Rome and ask him to go and visit Bohr in Copenhagen, Bohr himself would cover the travel expenses.

Rinkveiser was perplexed, he read and reread that sentence, it was terribly disturbing, it was written: " questa è la formula dell'apocalisse" *(This is the formula of the Apocalypse!)*

Maiorana, Ettore Maiorana, was the scientist with whom three years earlier his daughter Sabine had had a friendship, or maybe something more. Sabine right! As he thought of Sabine he was struck by a lightning bolt of inspiration, a dinner came to his mind: in the winter of 1922, Einstein and Hann were present. Sabine was a child and had asked a strange question, about the fact that a person could transform themselves into a firework. They had all fallen silent and Hann had said: "or into a bomb", a bomb, was it the same thing that Majorana meant when he spoke of the formula of the Apocalypse?

It was very important news, he had to inform some authority higher than him: The Swiss Government? No, his was a minor nation, it did not have the resources to develop a project like a new weapon, but there was someone who would be very interested: Disgelo *(Thaw)*. He had to inform William Stephenson, but above all he had to speak as soon as possible with the Italian scientist, he would go to see Senator Corbino, the dean of the Faculty of Science in Rome.

Rinkveiser called the faculty, Corbino was quite free, he just had to see Professor Fermi for a few minutes. He made an appointment with him in Via Panisperna.

He had the driver accompany him. Corbino was waiting for him, he was with Fermi, the great scientist greeted Rinkveiser with his usual cordiality, his recent discoveries were making people talk about a possible Nobel Prize.

After a few pleasantries Corbino got to the point: "So dear friend, how can I be of help to you?"

The Swiss had prepared a convincing story, he said that the University of Zurich wanted to offer a chair in physics to Majorana. Corbino and Fermi looked at each other with embarrassed expressions. Corbino rolled his eyes: "you see Rinkveiser, as far as I know Ettore has refused the offer of a chair at Cambridge, one at Yale and a grant from the Carnegie Foundation, in the end, well, let's say he chose to go and teach in Naples but... we know little or nothing about it. He rarely shows up at the faculty, he always complains of more or less serious ailments, in short Ettore has become even stranger than he was, in the last few years..."

Rinkveiser felt a warning signal inside him and decided to probe a little deeper: "Well, I knew he was a somewhat singular guy, but gifted with extraordinary abilities, especially of a mathematical nature...

Fermi intervened: "You see, dear friend, there are different categories of scientists. Second and third rank people, who do their best but do not go far. There are also first rank people, who arrive at discoveries of great importance, fundamental for the development of science. But then there are geniuses like Galileo and Newton. Well Ettore is one of them.

Majorana has what no one else in the world has. Unfortunately, he lacks what is common to find in other men: simple common sense... I have had personal relationships with him for a long time, even very close ones.

He even lived in my house for a while, then he started to be more and more absent and nervous, sometimes he seemed to be concentrated on one thought to the point of not noticing what was happening around him. Things got even worse when he returned from Germany, but at that point I cooled my relationship with him"

"Why?" asked Rinkweiser.

"I read a comment of his on the Jewish persecution in Germany and I didn't like it, my wife is Jewish..." said Fermi in a rather harsh tone.

"I see..." concluded the Swiss, "do you have any idea where I can get it in Naples?"

Fermi looked concentrated, scratched his head and ran his hand over his face, as if to help himself think, looked at Corbino and said: "but I think he is a good friend of Professor Carelli, in any case he works at the physics institute"

Rinkveiser decided that he had enough information and that he couldn't get any more from there. He chatted a little more about this and that so as not to be rude and not to arouse suspicion, then he left. Something strange was evidently happening to the Italian scientist, it had been like this since his return from Germany: what could be the reason?

We needed to contact him, talk to him and understand more.

Rinkveiser decided to return to the embassy and get organized.

He entered the office and found a message from the ambassador's secretary.

They had called him at the British Embassy: a certain Stephenson. He picked up the phone and had the switchboard give him the number of the British Embassy, asked for Stephenson, they told him that Mr Stephenson had gone out and would be back around midday.

Fabian decided to walk directly to the British diplomatic headquarters. The embassy was on Via 20 Settembre, right next to Porta Pia, about twenty minutes' walk from Via Panisperna, where he had met Corbino and Fermi.

He walked down Via Panisperna, Via Del Boschetto and came out on Via Nazionale, went up towards the Quirinale and began to walk along Via del Quirinale. He felt a strange sensation, as if someone was following him, he was not a professional secret agent and therefore had not learned anything of what the English called *tradecraft,* that is, the techniques that spies used in their profession, including of course the ability to identify tailers and lose them. So he thought of stopping, pretending to tie a shoe. He looked around a little furtively, but there were only ordinary people around... yes "ordinary people", exactly what expert secret agents knew they looked like.

He was somewhere near Porta Pia, when he came across a familiar face, the man was wearing a Borsalino, which partly hid his face, but Fabian had the distinct feeling of having seen that man before. He was trying to remember, when he found himself in front of the embassy. He introduced himself to the clerk at the entrance to the diplomatic headquarters. The man closely resembled a Dikensian character. Very old-fashioned dressed, very old and very haughty.

He ceremoniously asked Rinkveiser for an ID, who showed him his diplomatic passport. The clerk did not seem particularly impressed. He calmly handed the passport back, bent down and rummaged under the counter: "Mr Stephenson left this message for you."

Fabian opened the envelope, it simply said: "Greco coffee, 5 pm".

He had a couple of hours, he decided to walk to Via Condotti, at the appointment, if he had arrived earlier he would have had a coffee, he was Swiss and like all his fellow citizens he was a good walker and then the road between the English embassy and Via Condotti crossed some of the most beautiful places in the world. It was at the top of the Spanish Steps that the illumination came to him. The man he had crossed paths with was the German cultural attaché: his name was Wirth, Herman Wirth, a Nazi fanatic, although not one of the particularly crude ones.

He was interested in ancient archaeology, they had talked about it at a conference on Germanic culture to which he had been invited because he was Swiss. He remembered that Wirth wore a strange badge on the lapel of his tuxedo. An ellipse in the center of which was written a sword and a kind of bow that formed a ring, then they had explained to him that it was the badge of an organization called Ahnenerbe.

What could that guy be doing around the British embassy?

He was about half an hour early, he decided not to go into the cafe, it seemed like a good idea not to go to the appointment right away, he wandered around a bit and finally saw Stephenson arriving. He recognized him immediately by the way he walked, slow, almost cautious, as if he were walking on eggshells. Apart from that William moved with ease, like any other passerby.

He walked past the café, completely ignoring the place, the same with Fabian, however he looked at him with a suggestive expression turning his eyes towards the café, Fabian looked, right in front of it was Wirth, who seemed to be putting on an attitude: curious.

Stephenson had his hands behind his back, he was moving a finger in a strange way, Fabian understood, he wanted to say "follow me".

He saw him enter the Piazza di Spagna and head towards the Spanish Steps. He started off in the same direction, but first he turned towards the Caffè Greco. The German was still there, nervously looking at his watch. Fabian walked away quickly towards the Piazza di Spagna, every now and then he turned around to check if the German had moved, now he couldn't see him anymore, maybe he had gone into the café.

Up above he saw Stephenson standing still, looking out over the square as if he were admiring the view, he saw him turn and walk towards the top of the steps.

He followed him when he was at the top and saw him leaning on the parapet and was motioning for him to come closer: "Good morning Rinkveiser, it's been a while since we've seen each other..."

"Yeah, when was the last time...

"In New York, in front of that imbecile Hoover, who was eager for our little joke"

Fabian nodded towards Via Condotti: "Is anyone interested in our friendship?"

"I don't know, it could be a coincidence, but the presence of one of the heads of the Ahnenerbe in Rome worries me"

"and here as cultural attaché," Rinkweiser replied

"It seems like a bogus job to me, he is too high up in the Nazi hierarchy to do that job in Rome. There must be something more, and it could be the same thing that interests me..."

"That is...?" asked Rinkwieser

"shall we talk about it in a quiet place?"

Stephenson's house overlooked Piazza Navona, Christmas was approaching, from the balcony you could hear the noise of people and traffic and you could see the first stalls

They had some whiskey brought to them and were sipping it.

William spoke first: "Dear Fabian, you are certainly well aware of the progress made in physics in recent years..."

Rinkveiser looked at him in surprise: "You also want to talk to me about this."

William was also shocked: "Because who else told him about it...?"

Rinkvesiser told about Bohr's letter and his contacts with Corbino and Fermi.

"Well, it seems that the whole world is moving in the same direction," Stephenson said, "someone, it seems, Einstein himself, has mentioned to Mr. Churchill about possible "dangerous" developments in the discoveries on the atom, and in Germany it seems that Heisenberg is moving in the direction of a formidable discovery, but the one who seems to be ahead of everyone is a certain Ettore Maiorana, whoever manages to involve him in the research team could arrive at sensational results years before the others."

Rinkvesiser looked at his interlocutor worriedly: "Do you know what Maiorana wrote at the bottom of the notebook that

Bohr found in his house?" - without waiting for an answer Fabian continued - it was written "this is the formula of the apocalypse".

"My God, do you understand why the Ahnenerbe is in Rome?" Stephenson said

"But aren't they some kind of esoteric brotherhood, a band of madmen looking for traces of the Aryans?"

"Yes, but some say that there is a special scientific section, which deals with new discoveries. The cover story is that nuclear energy was perhaps the power that was in the hands of the Aryans, that destroyed Atlantis, etc., etc., but among those fanatics there are also some clear heads and the energy of the atom in their hands would be a misfortune for humanity"

"That Maiorana seems to have had sympathies for the Nazis," said Fabian.

"So, dear Rinkveiser Thaw must find it and convert it...or"

"Or...?"

William made an unmistakable gesture with a finger under his throat.

The Swiss felt a shiver run down his spine: "Well, like all my fellow countrymen, I served in the military, but there's a long way to go from that to cutting a throat in the cold. By the way, who are we going to send to look for Majorana? He's a strange guy, getting close to him will be as difficult as touching a unicorn."

William reflected as he sipped his whiskey: "Your daughter didn't graduate in physics here in Rome... maybe she met him..."

"I think she knew him in the broadest sense of the word, then they drifted apart.

The character was quite difficult as I said, and his colleagues confirmed it to me today, however I think that Sabine alone, even if she wanted to lend herself, would not be enough. Especially if we had to..." and he made the same sign with his finger to his throat that Stephenson had made.

"No, that won't be enough, but we have other candidates, one is officially on the other side of the barricade, an officer of the

German naval intelligence services, the other... well the other is an Italian character, a man who owes me a debt..."

"But just any one?"

"No, he's someone who has secret agent work in his blood, he doesn't know it, but he'll find out soon."

Horst Luderitz got off the train, he had traveled first class from Munich, but that didn't stop him from being rather tired. He looked around, Termini station greeted him with its smell of coal and iron and the metal vaults, in the style of French stations, he had a suitcase of modest size and ignored the porter who offered to help him.

He went outside and looked around, an embassy car was parked at the curb, a driver of imposing height and blond hair straightened with brilliantine was waiting impassively by the door of the Mercedes. Horst ignored him and continued towards a taxi: he did not want to be identified immediately as a German agent!

He was accompanied to a not particularly luxurious hotel, a little out of the center. He went up to his room, after having faced a less than warm welcome from the doorman, an ex-combatant of the Great War, as could be understood from a badge flaunted on the lapel of his jacket.

He dismissed the waiter without a tip, as a true German tourist would do, and decided to sleep for a couple of hours. He thought back to Colonel Dollman's instructions, and was very curious to meet the person who would be in charge of this operation.

The person had a cover name: Von Testory, but her nickname, she was a true legend: Mademoiselle Docteur.

Horst thought that the woman was no longer so young, but they said she still had a great charm, but above all that she had a profound knowledge of the Roman environment, ideal for that mission. She was an Italian scientist, whom Heisemberg had called a new Galileo. He had to be convinced to return to Leipzig, to deal with a new extraordinary discovery, a discovery that the

Führer had included among those of the Jewish tax, but which, it seemed, concerned an energy of extraordinary power, which would have given Germany the power to win a war without firing a shot and to subjugate Europe.

What was the Italian name called, but a strange name: Maggiorana?... Oh no, here's Majorana, Ettore Majorana.

3.22 Mario....Rome 1937.............a heavy legacy

He was bored to death, he had been on duty at the SIA, the Air Force Information Service, for about a month, but he still hadn't understood what he was supposed to do. General Balbo had received him briefly a few days after his arrival in Rome. He had told him that his appointment was necessary for a very delicate service that required precisely his qualities: "Boldness, initiative, sharpness of thought not disjoined from a certain savoir faire", so comrade Balbo had told him.

Mario was quite upset, he only added: "and the ability to pilot...?"

The Quadrumvir had looked at him, become serious and changed his tone: "that too happens... in its time, that too..." leaving a thought hanging in the air like a premonition.

It was lunchtime, Mario was undecided whether to go to the usual restaurant or skip that daily ritual, which made him sleepy for the rest of the afternoon. He heard a knock at the door and: "Come in!"

He found himself in front of Italo Balbo. He jumped to attention and raised his right arm in the Roman salute: "To us, Your Excellency," he said in a stentorian tone.

Balbo smiled at him and in a good-natured voice replied: "Rest assured, Captain... I'm here to make you a proposal, what would you say to spending an hour in the fencing gym?"

"At your disposal, Your Excellency"

"I approve of the arrangement, as for excellence I hardly excel in anything, so leave it alone"

They went to the gym, in the first assault Mario was rather cautious, at the end of the assault Balbo took off his protective mask and looked at him with a falsely severe expression: "Captain, do you think that your minister is not skilled enough in fencing to be faced as if he were a young Italian girl?"

Mario took off his mask and smiled and said: "General, if it's trouble you're looking for, I'll get it to you."

The next assault was extremely challenging for both, feints, thrusts, parries followed one another without interruption. Until Mario managed with an almost circus-like acrobatics to hit his opponent.

The high official took off his mask again, his Mascagni-styled hair was disheveled and he looked like a sweaty, smiling lion.

"Oh, finally we see the Count of Santa Tecla in action. They told me you were a tough nut to crack, but here we are at Olympic levels"

Mario bowed and smiled in return: "Always at your disposal, comrade," he said with a playful, challenging tone.

After showering and getting dressed, the two officers met in the corridor overlooking the gymnasium. In their perfect blue uniforms, with their rank insignia in shining gold and their white shirts under their carefully ironed jackets, they looked like the modern image of warrior gods.

"Vaillante," asked Balbo, "aren't you hungry?"

"enough etc..." Balbo pretended to glare at him "comrade"

"Well, let's have something brought to us from the tavern nearby. I should have a little chat with you about your career."

They ate a matriciana and drank some good Frascati, they talked about planes, about flying, Balbo told about the Atlantic cruise, about the welcome from the Americans and that of the Soviets.

Balbo remembered Mario's grandfather, who had collaborated with engineer Marchetti on the design of the SM55 hydroplane.

"It was a pity for me when your grandfather died," Balbo said almost suddenly.

Mario was a little saddened, he had a great affection for that man, his sudden death had come while Mario was acquiring the patent on multi-engine aircraft, and it had been a bolt from the blue.

"You comrade," Mario said at one point, "my grandfather took a secret with him, which he had promised to reveal to me. Something very painful, I believe, that concerned my father. His disappearance, I mean, involved a German spy, a woman... a dark story."

"Are you speaking of Countess Von Testory..." asked the general.

Surprise appeared on Mario's face: "Do you know anything about that story?"

"I know a lot about that story. Your grandfather and I had formed a strong and virile friendship, he was a man of integrity, and he had had a very adventurous life. Unfortunately, adventures sometimes leave victims, the story of your father and Von Testory, few people know it but it was a scandal that went around the secret services of all Europe. Your grandfather didn't like to remember it, he felt very guilty"

"I had understood something, but I never managed to get it told to me..." Mario said thoughtfully

"I'll tell you, so you'll also understand why you were assigned to intelligence."

Paris...1909

Paris sparkled in the night, it was the height of the Belle Époque. The taverns were full of dancers, officers, businessmen, politicians, who spent the night drinking champagne and having fun. For Captain Carlo Vassalli that mission was the greatest opportunity of his life, he served as an artillery officer at the general staff, with technical duties. This was his official role, but the royal house, which could not stand the Triple Alliance, had chosen some career officers and diplomats to maintain relations with the opposing nations. Carlo had an English mother, a gentlewoman who had fallen in love with his father during a trip to Italy, while the country was fighting the battles of the Risorgimento. His father belonged to the Lombard nobility, but he wanted Italy united and independent from Austria, which imposed taxes, internal customs barriers and did not allow the necessary economic freedom to the nationalities it subjugated. When the third war of independence broke out, the young countess of Caradon, a fiefdom in Cornwall, rushed to Italy as a journalist for Time, met the young lieutenant, the count of Santa Tecla and........ Charles was the third of the four children born from the union.

His English relatives had invited him to their home several times and during one of these visits they had offered him a job for the Secret Service Bureau. He had declined the invitation, but upon his return to Italy his commander had summoned him, who had invited him to accept the offer: "His Majesty would have been very happy", added the colonel.

It was in 1909 that the Secret Intelligence Service, also known as MI6, was established, the service was responsible for foreign espionage.

Charles was in Paris with a specific task: he had to evaluate the military proposals that the English and French were making to Italy, to leave the Triple Alliance and move on to the Entente Cordiale.

It was a very delicate task that had been entrusted to him despite his being rather young and of a low rank, but the English trusted him and would not have accepted anyone other than him to discuss the matter.

He lived on Rue Vavin, practically in front of the Luxembourg Gardens. Every morning he walked along Rue D'Assas to Boulevard

Raspail, which he followed until it crossed Rue De Varenne which he entered, arriving at 51, the seat of the Italian Embassy. Every day, always around nine in the morning, twenty minutes later, disguised as a driver, he accompanied the ambassador's wife to Faubourg Saint'Honore, where the lady went to mass in the church of Saint Philippe du Roul. There, Carlo exchanged with the lady's real driver and went off to go to the British Embassy nearby.

A very habitual behavior, which Carlo detested and he also detested that masquerade, something that had very little to do with the chivalrous style that he would have loved to be able to maintain as an officer. But the man who had been with him during training, a Turin official of the royal guard, who had collaborated with General Govone during the wars of independence, had explained to him that being a secret agent was very different from being a cavalry officer. He had adapted, but he was beginning to no longer tolerate that theatricality, he would have liked to deal with a new invention: the airplane. In America two brothers had made the first motorized flights, and even in France they were beginning to do demonstrations of this new machine. Carlo was convinced that a vehicle of that kind would revolutionize the way of waging war and the way of traveling, and he would also be able to return home. He loved adventure very much, but he was beginning to get tired of it. His wife had given him a daughter: Caterina, and he had seen her very little, the child was now a woman, and this worried him a lot. Considering the many love adventures, in which he had been the protagonist despite everything, it was not difficult for him to think that his peers had intentions that were anything but chivalrous towards the beautiful Caterina

He was thinking about these things as he passed the College Catholique. Suddenly, he found the girl in front of him. She had run out of the building, probably chasing a group of her colleagues who were a little further ahead.

She could have been sixteen, with a huge mass of black, raven hair, shiny as if it were made of pure coal. She was thin as a bamboo cane, but under her school uniform you could see two notable breasts. She looked into his eyes for a moment and had a strange impression, as if he had been punched in the stomach. The girl smiled and apologized in a Frenchman with a curious accent, very hard, very un-French. Then she turned and ran away towards the other girls, but before she reached them she turned once more and looked at him.

Carlo let the group of students continue for a while, then decided to follow them for a while. He saw them emerge onto Boulevard Raspail, he accelerated to see where they were going. They crossed, and turned onto Rue de Sevres and entered the church of Sainte Ignace.

They were waiting for him at the embassy and he decided to let it go, but those piercing eyes remained in his head as if they had branded him.

He spent the day in a boring meeting with French and English officers, an interminable discussion about how the front would be organized if Italy entered the war alongside the allies of the Entente Cordiale. But Carlo, instead of thinking about where the artillery would be deployed, imagined how large, soft but firm the breasts of the young woman he had met must be. Like every evening, he dined at the Italian embassy, stopped to talk with the cultural attaché, a professor of literature and Latin, with whom he had frequent discussions about the excessive literary content of the programs of Italian schools.

The clerk said that mathematics was a science for mechanics, and boasted that he couldn't solve a first-degree equation. When he had had enough of the professor's ramblings, he decided to return to his boardinghouse. He retraced his morning route and passed in front of the College Catholique. He thought he could feel the girl's gaze on him, a pure illusion he told himself, but he had goosebumps. The next day was Saturday, there would be no meetings because the English didn't work on Saturdays. He decided he would take advantage of the opportunity to sleep a little longer.

But there was no way he could sleep, she kept coming back to his mind, each time he imagined taking her without inhibitions and with all the fury of his young man's passion, while his remorse had ended up in a corner, like an old and worn out dress.

It was no use continuing to tell himself that the girl could be more or less the same age as his daughter, the temptation was strong. But then, how could he follow that young siren, he was busy all day with the Allied officers and certainly she couldn't go out in the evening. At six, after having slept for a few hours, he was awake again. He decided to get up and go for a walk in Paris. He stuck his nose out of the hotel, turned right, turned left and almost without realizing it he walked along the usual road, towards the Luxembourg gardens, he thought of going to have breakfast at the kiosk. He ate a coissant and cafe au lait. It was seven-thirty when he got up from the table and headed towards the exit of the gardens, finding himself once again in the rue d'Assas, walking towards the place of the fatal meeting of the previous day, he passed in front of the college, he met no one. Patience, he decided to continue, but when he reached the rue de Sevres he decided to go into the church. A mass was in progress. The girls were sitting in a row of pews on the right. He sat down not far away, he couldn't recognize her, then one of them turned and looked at him, she put a hand in front of her mouth, she was obviously smiling. At the end of the mass Carlo waited for them to come out, he too was about to leave the church, when a child pulled his sleeve and put a note in his hand, it was written in a very feminine and round handwriting:

« Demain, Jardin de Luxembourg, at kiosk heure 10 ».

Carlo couldn't help but smile.

He went to lunch at a restaurant in Faubourg Saint-Honore, then returned to the hotel. The concierge handed him an envelope. He thanked her and headed for the stairs. He opened the envelope, it was a message from his English contact, from the Royal Navy intelligence service, Captain Mansfield, who was expecting him at five in front of the Louvre.

They met in the large square in front of the museum. Mansfield spoke to him in French, he wanted to be sure that no one would be suspicious of the contacts between an Italian officer and an Englishman in a city like Paris. Carlo knew French, his father had learned it fighting with the troops of Napoleon III, he was passionate about that language and wanted his children to learn it. This made the Vassalli family a singular example of polyglots in a country like Italy, where many did not even know the national language and expressed themselves in dialect.

They walked, chatting, towards the Tuilerie Gardens. Mansfield told him that from London they had informed him that the Germans suspected contacts between the Italians and the Franco-English to betray the Triple Alliance. They had received information on this from sources linked to the Vatican, and had sent a team of agents to Paris, to monitor the Italian embassy, and he recommended extreme caution to Carlo. They had lunch together, and Carlo returned to the hotel after a brief visit to the embassy.

He thought about the meeting the next day, his conscience suddenly made its bites felt again. He told himself that he was getting old, once he would have taken this thing more frivolously. After all, what was wrong with chasing an adventure, other times it had happened to him and he had had no problem. All stories that had left little or no trace. He had difficulty remembering the names of most of those women and had completely forgotten many of them.

It was cold, Paris, which in many ways was a place of delight, was climatically a disgrace, it was a miracle that it hadn't snowed yet.

He went to the kiosk and had a grog served. It was a little early for alcohol, but the cold meant that the intoxicating effect of the drink didn't manifest itself in the slightest.

He didn't know exactly where to stand, he looked at the path from which his mysterious lady might arrive. A couple arrived with a tiny dog, who they had dressed in a little coat; he followed an elderly gentleman, who proceeded with a slow and haughty step, leaning on a stick perhaps more out of habit than necessity.

It was getting colder and colder, but the young lady did not show up.

Carlo thought that perhaps the young woman, after having set up the thing, had regretted such brazen behavior and had given it up.

He felt a touch on his shoulder and turned around, almost frightened: she was there in front of him, as if she had emerged from one of the spirals of fog that was beginning to spread across the park.

Dressed entirely in black, which made her look even slimmer, with a hat of the same color, her face hidden by a veil.

"Good morning," said a low voice from behind the veil.

"If you don't mind, can we get away from here?"

Carlo understood,

"certainly," Carlo continued. "What do you say if we take a taxi and go to Montmartre?"

The girl offered him her arm.

"May I ask you what your name is, Miss..."

« My name is Elisabette... »

"My name is – he thought of saying a different name – Alberto, I'm Italian"

"Very happy," the voice still whispered behind the veil.

The café was at the top of Montmartre, they sat at a table and Carlo ordered a coffee, she asked for an absinthe. Carlo thought to himself that the girl seemed to have no inhibitions, and he shivered.

She had raised her veil, her face was very white, like that of people with red hair, but her thin eyebrows and the coal color of her eyes left no doubt that she was brunette. Her eyes, those were like daggers, penetrating, Carlo was not a boy, but he had never met a woman with a look like that.

She was smiling, but he was struck by the fact that the smile seemed to stop at her cheekbones, which were particularly high, rather pronounced, but not excessively prominent.

"So," said the young Elisabeth, "you are disappointed in me, monsieur italien."

"Not at all," Carlo said, "but I was wondering what a young woman like you could have in mind when approaching a man of my age in such a bold way."

She laughed, in a childish way, putting, with a very graceful and studied gesture, one hand in front of her mouth and showing just a set of small, very white teeth, then the enigmatic smile returned: "At your age, can't you imagine it?", in her voice there was a distant, almost contemptuous tone.

Carlo blushed slightly, no, he had never met a woman like that.

"I didn't dare to hope so much"

"Dare," she replied, "See, sir, I'll tell you a little thing about myself. Last summer I was at my parents' house, a villa where my family and I move in the summer, so as not to suffer the heat and the sultriness of the hot sun. One day I woke up with a strange feeling of uneasiness that pervaded me. I couldn't understand what it was, I had never felt it before.

During the day that feeling passed, and I didn't think about it anymore, that night I had a dream that I had never had, a man who hugged me and kissed me, and wanted something from me, I woke up just when I was about to give it to him"

Carlo was quite embarrassed, but also quite excited. Who was this girl who emerged from nowhere and spoke to him about such intimate things? And why was she speaking to him about these things.

It seemed that Elisabeth had noticed his thought:

"You may be wondering why I am speaking to you so...so...so explicitly, but let me finish telling you and you will understand.

So I woke up, I wanted to understand what had happened to me and so I wanted to go to the library to see if I could find some book that could explain these strange things that were happening to me. My parents had left to go visit their friends, they would return only in the evening.

I entered the library and looked around, I didn't know where to start, then I remembered that my mother had forbidden me to look at the books that were on a specific shelf in the library. The only one that was closed and whose doors had a lock. It wasn't difficult to find that key. There were some books, on medicine, others on various sciences and then a series of erotic books. I began to leaf through Diderot's The Nun, and it didn't take me long to understand what that mania was.

I thought about those things for a few days and secretly read some more of those books.

In one of them I discovered how some women fantasized about having intercourse with a stranger, who would possess them and then disappear. I decided that this was my case.

That stranger is you"

Carlo felt a sensation that was difficult to define. Like those women and many men, he had often desired a fleeting encounter with a stranger. He had had encounters, more than one, but he had never liked them very much. There was not enough confidence with his partner for the encounter to be that liberation and give that sense of completeness that Carlo liked in sexual relations.

The woman remained silent. Carlo looked at her, decided to explain his embarrassment, his lack of passion for fleeting encounters and so he did.

The enigmatic smile reappeared, but this time the look became like a waterfall of heat and passion: "You say that because you don't know that I will make you feel what you have never felt and will never feel again..."

"Damn," thought Carlo, "She really doesn't mince words."

He looked straight into her eyes, in that strange look there was a kind of desperation, like a child who has been given an incomprehensible negative answer, which slowly became confidence, as if that child had realized that the no they were saying would become a yes.

"Okay miss, but I'm afraid our meeting can't happen now..."

"Of course not," she interrupted him, "but tell me that the next time we meet you won't say no."

"I promise you."

The girl stood up, smiled at Carlo, lowered her veil and went out, moving her bottom as if they were the coils of a snake.

He returned to the hotel, he had had all sorts of experiences with women, but this one was really bizarre.

She then disappeared, giving him no indication of how she would get back in touch with him. Maybe she was just crazy, maybe he should be careful, but there was something about her that irresistibly attracted him, he felt inside that she was not crazy.

The chief looked at the report and smiled slightly, so the contact had been made, now it was a matter of waiting, the shot would put the opponents out of the game... for a long time.

He went down the stairs, his stay in Paris was coming to an end. He was happy to be returning to Italy, the London Olympics were approaching and he, who would have participated as a fencer, was rather behind in his training. However, there was a thorn stuck somewhere in his brain that was troubling him. It was a feeling difficult to define. A relief that resembled a disappointment: the mysterious girl from the Luxembourg garden had not shown up again and had not contacted him, disappeared into the fog from which she had emerged. Yes, she was probably crazy, or more simply a girl in the mood to play...

The scent of vetiver hit him, like a violent deja vu, a soft slap. She had been there. The concierge smiled at Carlo: "Sir, excuse me, a...er, person left this note for you."

It was made of scented paper, an indefinable color between yellow and pink, closed with a sealing wax seal on which stood out the image of a phoenix. Carlo waited until he was outside the Hotel and opened it, it was written in the usual round handwriting: "Rue Jacob, 21, top floor, today at 3, ring Berton". It was an address in Saint Germain de Pre.

He looked at his pocket watch, it was eleven o'clock, the day was free from meetings at the embassy, he decided to go and look for some flowers and sweets, to bring to his young prey. Prey... yes, curious, in reality he had a hard time understanding who the prey was.

Bastian, the hotel concierge, picked up the telephone receiver: "switchboard" he heard a pretty female voice say in the earpiece: "Pass me cublay four hundred and ninety", the call was put through quickly.

"Hello here dufour" said a male voice with a hard accent

"Here Bessier," continued the doorman, "our man has received the message."

"Good," replied the man with the hard accent.

Carlo looked at the entrance to the building, it was a glass door, inside a small courtyard, in which they had placed large rectangular vases, which in the summer must have been full of flowers.

He approached the bell plate, made of highly polished brass, and rang. The door was opened by an electric command. Carlo thought that this system of welcoming guests was a great idea, it avoided the concierges and their gossip.

He climbed the stairs to the top floor, along wide marble stairs. There was no sound from the various apartments whose doors opened onto the landings. Finally he reached the top, there was only one door, in black mahogany. He rang the bell, heard a light sound of heels on the floor inside. The door opened: in front of him stood a black girl, she could have been seventeen, she was completely naked, except for a pair of boots, a small white apron in front of her pubic area and a crest of the same color on her hair. She smiled at him with very white teeth and with a small bow invited him to sit down: "S'il vous plait".

Carlo smiled in turn, and thought that the afternoon was looking interesting.

The girl took her outer clothes, hat, coat, gloves, a stiffelius with a silver knob and a cashmere scarf. She accompanied him, shaking her bottom, towards a room at the end of the corridor. The room was large, wallpapered in a blue, almost black color, on one wall hung a rack with whips hanging from it, on another side a St. Andrew's cross to which were attached some convict bracelets. In the center stood a bed, on which Elisabeth was lying, wearing only a very transparent black lace Negligee, and a mask of the same material that made her look like a cat.

"Take a seat, my master," Elisabeth said in her usual sensual voice.

Carlo was quite impressed, he hadn't expected that "jardin de Suplices" setting, and it wasn't even his kind of thing, but he told himself that perhaps in life you had to try everything.

He placed the flowers and sweets somewhere, the ceiling above him was a mirror.

The girl got up from the bed and took a whip from the rack; "My master, why don't you start by punishing me for my daring..?"

"Well, look, madam, maybe I'm not ready to be so severe yet," Carlo glossed over, not being very fond of that kind of transgression.

"Then perhaps you would like to let my maid serve you," the little black girl was behind him and began to undress him.

Kurt watched his sister from the ceiling of the room through the mirror. The camera they had given him was a German copy of the Eastman Kodak 1888, with many optical and film improvements, which allowed him to take pictures even in not very strong light. Watching his sister Anne do those things had always excited him quite a bit, this time there was also the taste of adventure. He would photograph the embraces of the Italian officer with Anne, then they would blackmail him and make him tell them what the intentions of the country of Pulcinella were towards the triple alliance.

That day was a test so Anne didn't push the Italian to do any particularly unseemly things, but next time, Kurt told himself he would have a lot of fun.

Carlo was exhausted, it had been quite intense and holding his own against those two hadn't been a walk in the park, but... how much fun he had had! Elisabeth had made him promise that he would return three days later and that he would be very strict with her.

He had promised, as for the severity, well, he would get over it.

Mansfield was waiting for him in front of the Hotel. Carlo saw him from afar, smoking his pipe and looking around, with his usual relaxed air. The Italian had a certain admiration for the calmness of the Scottish naval officer, he found his hard accent amusing, with those rolled r's that reminded him of his cousin from Parma, Matilde.

"What a good wind Mansfield.." said jovially Carlo

"A wind of vetiverrr mister Vassalli"

Carlo didn't get the hint right away, then he understood, so the SIS was monitoring him? He had a moment of irritation, Mansfield understood: "Captain, please, don't get angry, we have to protect our informants, especially from honey traps..."

Carlo looked at Mansfield with a raised eyebrow. "Honey traps?"

"Yes, like the ones that flies fall into, go on top of the paper to suck the honey and get stuck..."

Carlo understood: "Does this mean that Miss Elisabeth...?"

"Elsbeth Schragmuller, also known as Anne Lesser, born in Schlussemburg, Nordrhein-Westfalia, her father seems to be an officer of the Reichwher, as is her brother, with the consent of the family she lends herself to this kind of thing to provide information to the Nachrichteindiest, that is the imperial intelligence service, in her case I believe they are trying to... emh unmask Italy's attitude towards the triple alliance..."

Carlo was shocked: "I should have imagined it, it was too strange for such a young girl to behave that way..."

"Not very strange," said Mansfield, "but certainly worth checking before tasting the honey..."

"And now....?"

"If Her Majesty's Secret Service is perhaps made up of amateurs...you would be in trouble...but we are watching, when you return to Miss Lesser's pleasure nest they will not again propose to you to amuse yourself with two young women, but they will present you with a series of rather, er, interesting photos for some close relative of yours, in exchange for the diplomatic protocol of Italy with the understanding."

"So, what should I do...?"

"She will go there, but we will follow her and... we will fix things"

Anne or rather Elsbeth had demanded that before moving on to blackmail, he take some more photos, she said "to make things more effective" and Kurt, who did not disdain the idea of a little more "effectiveness" agreed. So when Carlo arrived he found more or less the same situation as the previous time. Mansfield had told him to pretend nothing had happened, no matter what happened, this time she had herself tied to the St. Andrew's cross, Carlo entered, Kurt was ready with the camera and was so excited that he did not notice that the young black maid was not in the room and when the girl stuck a ten-centimeter needle, placed on the tip of a hypodermic syringe, containing a lethal dose of morphine three fingers below his left ear.

He simply died without even understanding what was happening to him.

The fake maid had dressed and ran downstairs to open the door for four men, criminals in the pay of Her Majesty's Royal Navy Intelligence Service and Captain Winston Churchill Mansfield, head of the Paris branch of the service.

Carlo smiled at the young woman chained to the St. Andrew's cross, and said, "What a shame, I would have gladly beaten you this time." She returned his look with a scornful look and a string of insults in German.

Mansfield's men searched everywhere, they were professional thieves and knew where to look. They found the photos, in the room where Kurt probably slept. Perhaps the man had become a little too passionate about his work, Mansfield threw them into the fireplace where the fire had been lit, he smiled at Carlo: "A gentleman is not curious about certain things, which concern the privacy of another gentleman"

Carlo smiled back, then they all left.

The French police, alerted by a mysterious informer, found the situation in the Berton family home on the top floor of 21 Rue Jacob surprising.

Prosecutor Cagnol, who was charged with investigating the strange affair, did not delve too deeply; the girl was a minor and, moreover, she could not have killed the man in the room on the upper floor, where there was a transparent mirror on the floor that looked into the young lady's bedroom on the floor below. He also thought it was not worth resisting too much to the Minister of Justice's insistence.

"Amusant," thought Cagnol to himself as he closed the file.

Italo Balbo finished the story.

"So Mario, Elisabeth Scraghmuller, Alias Anne Lesser, Alias Madmoiselle Docteur, in Rome she called herself Countess Von Testory. But that's not all, you know that your father was not lost on Montello..."

"Certain...."

"But don't you know how he died...?"

"No, I know that somehow the Austrians killed him, here in Rome, and that perhaps it was Von Testory who killed him..."

"You only know part of the story. That woman is extremely determined and vindictive, she decided to send a message to those who had humiliated her in Paris, and were somehow responsible for her brother's death. She put the two together. Your father was found in the cellar of a church, chained to a St. Andrew's cross, poisoned by a lethal dose of morphine..."

Mario received that revelation like a punch in the stomach; he had been harboring the desire to take revenge on that woman for years.

"Well..." concluded Balbo while Mario had fallen into silence. He looked at his watch: "Comrade, I'm afraid I have to leave you, I think we'll have a chance to see each other"

He stood up and gave the Roman salute.

Mario was quite surprised, he also stood up and gave the Roman salute, a slightly flaccid gesture that matched his surprised face, Balbo smiled: "Comrade, sorry if I have to interrupt this conversation, I see I've upset you a bit..."

"I knew part of the story as I told you, not in every detail as you told me, I can't understand what connection there is between my work as a secret agent and this story."

Balbo took on an enigmatic expression: "You'll find out soon enough, comrade."

Mario lived in the Prati neighborhood and rode his motorbike to Via del Pretoriano, the seat of the ministry. He wore a helmet and an air force jacket, large pilot glasses, and a Scottish silk scarf with a tartan with red and brown squares on a yellow background.

For a couple of days, after Balbo's revelation, he kept thinking about the dark story of his father, about the German spy who had taken revenge on him for a humiliation suffered by his grandfather. What was the point of bringing up that story again now?

He was walking along Viale del Muro Torto, that day he had decided to go slowly and look around a bit to see the city, when he thought he saw her, on the other side of the street, she was going in the opposite direction to him, it was as if a breath of the woman's spectacular beauty had hit him, like a perfume that remained in his memory, like a deja vu full of nostalgia, it was her: Cynthia!

He almost caused an accident with a taxi: « li mortacci tua... ».. the taxi driver's insults chased him, while after having made a scary u-turn with the motorbike, going back over the crooked wall. But she had disappeared, where the hell had she ended up?

He saw a public car up ahead, he had a fleeting vision of a figure dressed in white disappearing into it, the taxi proceeded along via del Muro Torto until it turned into via Vittorio Veneto, continued until Palazzo Margherita, home to the American embassy, in front of which it stopped. He saw her get out and pay and head for the entrance. He stopped the motorbike, he certainly couldn't enter the grounds of a foreign embassy, racing like a rocket astride his Guzzi.

What the hell was the Majorcan tango dancer doing in Rome, at the American embassy.

At that moment it occurred to him that he knew practically nothing about her, he had seen her once in Hungary, together with an English officer and an unknown civilian. In Mallorca they had talked about many things but she had never spoken about herself, except vaguely and mostly making jokes, then she had disappeared, without telling him anything and without leaving any obvious traces.

She saw the taxi that had transported her go back towards the crooked wall and disappear. If she had come in, she had to come out too, unless she was the ambassador's daughter.

He had been sitting on his motorbike for an hour, smoking and watching, no one was coming out of the embassy.

He thought to himself about the madness he was doing, what sense could there be in waiting for a woman who was basically a complete stranger, on a street in Rome, someone who had appeared in a dream, then on a balcony of a hotel in a remote village, and then on an island in the middle of a war; a story from an adventure book, yes........ from an adventure book.

He waited in vain for two hours, then got on his Guzzi and went home.

The next day he arrived early at the office, the guard greeted him at attention and informed him that the minister was waiting for him, Mario went directly to Balbo's office without even taking off the clothes he wore for riding his motorbike.

"Here we are," the hierarch greeted him, "have you recovered?" He didn't even let him finish. "Here, it's an invitation from the American embassy, tomorrow is President Day, there will be a reception, you will represent me... I recommend you, I know you won't make me look bad, I have an engagement with Benito and I won't be able to be at that event..."

Mario turned the envelope over in his hands, in precious paper, with the seal of the State Department, that event was just right, at Palazzo Margherita he could investigate his mysterious beloved.

She spent the day thinking about what would happen the next day, imagining the halls of Palazzo Margherita full of elegantly dressed guests; would she be there, or had the day before just been a casual visit? No, a casual visit doesn't last more than two hours.

Had she changed...? No, you don't change in eight months, why had she disappeared? Why was she in Rome? What had she gone to do at the embassy? The questions piled up, with the hope and anxiety of seeing Cynthia again.

Balbo had put the service car at his disposal, the reception began at 7 pm, he put on his full dress uniform, with the decorations he had earned in Spain, with the brevet eagle tilted to the right, instead of a coat he wore a dark blue cloak, as was customary for the evening gala.

He heard the bell ring, it was the driver, he looked at his watch, a golden Wiler Vetta chronograph, a gift from his grandfather. It was 6:45 p.m., he was not of Balbo's rank, so, even though he represented him, he was not authorized to be late for an official ceremony.

He arrived at 6:55 p.m., they drove the car into the embassy. All the lights in the building were on, the official cars were following one another. A marine sergeant verified his invitation and let him pass with an impeccable military salute. He handed over his sabre to the cloakroom along with his cloak, and walked towards the reception room, where he was met by a thoughtful official who greeted him cordially in Italian. Mario wanted to surprise him by answering him in perfect English, which did not seem to surprise the man. He was accompanied by the ambassador, who greeted him warmly, thanking him for his presence, Mario excused Balbo's absence, but the ambassador was already aware of the matter and expressed understanding for the commitments of the famous hierarch.

After a brief ceremony to congratulate the president, the buffet was opened. It was a custom Mario was not familiar with. He found it rather unpleasant to throw himself headlong into a laden table, contending with rather robust and intrusive ladies for food, however he managed to help himself while avoiding a clash with the matrons obsessed with canapés and strange American foods, which Mario was not familiar with.

There were a few tables where he could sit and he chose one, trying to spot friendly-looking people sitting at them. At one there was a fat "monsignore" who looked like he hadn't eaten for a few days, along with a lady, who despite the outside temperature not being the most suitable had not given up an ample cleavage, which showed off two arms similar to ham and an oversized breast. From the way she gorged on the canapés you could understand the reasons for the superfetation of her limbs and breasts.

He moved away from the table, then saw another one, a Royal Air Force officer sitting there, and some people in tuxedos speaking with a strong Quebecois accent: Canadian.

He looked at the officer, and had a strong feeling that he knew him; who was he? Where on earth had he seen him before? It was strange, he didn't know any English officers... but that man had a familiar face, that uniform full of decorations, he distinctly remembered the effect of multi-colored ribbons on the blue of an air force uniform, that uniform was... There, my God, it was him... it was the uniform worn by the man who was on Cynthia's arm as they walked down the stairs of the Budapest Opera House.

The man saw him, smiled politely and continued chatting with the other diners.

If he was there, She had to be there too. He began, trying not to attract attention, to wander around the hall and the open rooms nearby. He met people of all kinds, ambassadors in livery from the strangest nations, elegant women speaking incomprehensible languages, but there was no sign of Her. Somewhere an orchestra was playing swing, he bumped into a couple of people he knew, officials from the Foreign Ministry who were friends of the family, with whom he exchanged a few pleasantries, but he was not very concentrated. He was sipping a glass of champagne and listening to the orchestra, when a voice behind him said, with a strange accent somewhere between French and English: "Good evening, how about we meet in Budapest?"

Mario started and turned in front of him was the RAF officer from before, he was holding a cigarette in his hand and smiling imperceptibly, he had noticed the reaction of the Italian officer, and said to him: "What do you say we go and talk in a less crowded place?"

They moved to the office, upstairs, the man sat down and motioned for Mario to sit in an armchair in front of him.

« My name is William Stephenson, I am in Rome with a post as assistant to the English military attache....at least officially.... »

« And not officially... ? » asked Mario

"I am in charge of assembling a team of agents, for a vital operation..."

Mario looked at him without hiding a certain surprise: "Are you about to suggest that I betray my country?"

« Not exactly, the operation is also in the interest of your country... »

"I'm a pilot, do you need a pilot?"

"As you see," Stephenson said, pointing to the badge above the decorations, "this is something we have in common, and it's not the only one."

"What else..." Mario said with a slightly sarcastic tone

« We share a friendship with Italo Balbo... who knows well that I am talking to you to propose that you join the team »

« You seem a little too sure of my availability... »

« I will tell you about other things we have in common: for example an enemy, or rather to be precise a female enemy, a certain Anne Lesser, cover name of Elsbeth Schcragmuller, known to the French services as Madamoislle Docteur or Fraulein Doctor.... »

Mario continued to show a lost expression

« Known in Rome during the last war as Lise Marie Von Testory »

Mario changed expression: "I would say that this is certainly my enemy, but that doesn't mean that I have to accept her offer." Then he changed expression and became vaguely thoughtful. "Unless..."

"Unless I told you that the lady is in Rome and leads the team that has the task of preventing the vital operation entrusted to me from succeeding."

"Certainly if I had the opportunity to make that woman pay for her crimes, it would be an attractive way to engage me, but what should I do?"

"it's about finding a person who seems to have disappeared and convincing him to escape with your group"

"Escape where?"

"Where we will convince him to work with us...naturally"

"Who is this man?"

"Well now you are the one who takes too many things for granted, you'll know more if and when you joins the team."

"but why did you choose me?"

« As I told you, we have a lot in common, but above all with your family there is a rather consolidated relationship of trust, dating back to your grandfather Carlo. There are professions in which, in addition to skill, a certain sense of belonging counts and I would say that from this point of view you belong to this world.. »

" Which ? "

"That of the spies, distinguished captain, I mean the professional spies"

Mario was quite dazed, his idea of adventure had to do with flying, air raids, direct confrontation with danger, dive attacks, the unique sensation of the plane regaining altitude after a bomb-dropping maneuver. This meant that in that war he would not have fought in that way, for him it would have been a war of masks and daggers, of stolen information, of backwaters and dark places where he could meet informants, traitors, and people like Von Testory.

"Do you think I could refuse?" he asked the English officer.

"It would be unpleasant..- replied the other with a serious expression, and I would like our relationship not to be unpleasant, because there is one last thing we have in common, her name is Cynthia..."

Mario was startled, that's what he was doing at the embassy, it had been a honey trap to lure him there, and what do they have in common with Cynthia?

"What do you mean, Commander," said Mario with a frown

"I mean we both have a close relationship with her, mine are different from yours though, because I am her adoptive father. And that's not all, do you know why Cynthia disappeared from Spain?"

Mario thought for a moment, while the Englishman lit a new cigarette.

" I would not know… "

« She was pregnant, dear Captain, which means that you will soon be a father, and in some way I will be a grandfather. Well, if a final blow was needed, this was it, in the truest sense of the word.

4

THE HUNT

It was one of those days when Naples seemed like paradise. Even though it was November, the temperature was mild, but he didn't even notice. He had been wearing the same suit for months now and never went to university, where he had the chair of theoretical physics, after having refused many other positions in much more prestigious places. But he didn't want to go, because there he would have had to reveal his secret. They would have forced him to work and sooner or later they would have realized that he knew. He had realized it one evening, when he went out for the first time with Sabine, the Swiss girl with whom he had had a relationship a few years earlier. He had ended the relationship and gone to Germany, precisely because every time he saw her that phrase came back to mind: "we could explode like a firework... or like a bomb."

He went home and began to do calculations, and as he got closer to the truth he became terrified and stopped. He made the papers disappear; he burned them in the stove. He liked Sabine very much. He liked that brain that was capable not only of elaborating mathematical calculations that only he could understand, but also of being cheerful, of telling jokes and, most difficult of all, of making him laugh.

But he had turned on that terrifying light in his brain, and one day while he was in Denmark as a guest of Niels Bohr, he had come to the conclusion: Fermi had not discovered a new element, by bombarding uranium nuclei he had simply split them. Uranium absorbs a neutron and splits in two, giving rise to two neutrons that had a lower mass than the starting one, with atomic weights between 38 and 58. According to Einstein's formula, this separation gives rise to an energy equivalent to about two hundred million electron volts for each fissioned nucleus. How many nuclei are there in a kilo of uranium? If we imagine shattering even a kilo of uranium, what power does that produce? Something very close to a few thousand tons of any powerful explosive, for example those used in war.

Of course it wasn't such an easy job and he kept thinking about how to do it. He went home and wrote, notes on sheets of paper that he brought back from the university.

He had never kept a calculation in his life, he always threw everything away, he remembered by heart, but this was different. It had become an obsession, he wanted to get to the conclusion, to understand in depth how to do it, how to make a bomb: why? He wanted to see in depth if man really held the key to the apocalypse, unleashing the same force that powered the sun and the stars. And when he understood how it worked and if it could work? He would go to Fermi, he would beg him to stop the research! Or he would turn to the newspapers, he would tell the whole world that there was a threat looming over the future of humanity. A secret like the one revealed would effectively prevent everyone from appropriating it individually, it would be common knowledge in the world. Two things could happen: that everyone would understand that it was time to stop any idea of starting a war, but this seemed rather unlikely to him. Or everyone would have had the bomb and discovered that a war waged with these weapons would have annihilated everyone, there would have been no winner and therefore there would have been no point in waging war.

The thoughts in his head overlapped. The splitting of the nucleus gave rise to two nuclei, and at this point what would happen: maybe nothing, or maybe not, maybe those nuclei would hit two other nuclei and so on, causing a "chain reaction", a very rapid and divergent reaction that would lead to an enormous production of energy if his calculations were correct.

He had thought about it over and over, that was not a mathematical problem. The calculations could come later, but it was necessary to understand how after the first split, the neutrons produced hit other nuclei, and so on without stopping, producing the explosion.

In the end he understood, it was simple, it was a problem of probability that neutrons would hit nuclei, so the nuclei had to be close to each other; it was a problem of concentration of the mass of Uranium and of shape and also of quantity, such a mass, with a shape that would favor the chain reaction. A geometric problem, a shape was needed that had a low surface-volume ratio, he had thought about it, but not for long, the ideal shape was a sphere. He had done some calculations... something was missing. If the neutrons had dispersed after the first impact, almost nothing would have happened. It was necessary to find a way to avoid dispersion, so that round mass had to be covered with a substance that would avoid dispersion.

So with a little uranium you could almost destroy the world? He had started the calculations again,... The uranium did not have sufficient mass and concentration, Raw uranium could not produce anything similar to an explosion, an isotope was needed, a uranium with a higher atomic number. Natural uranium is made up of three isotopes, U234, U235 and U238. The latter represents the majority of the mineral, about ninety-nine percent. To make a bomb it was necessary to have a few kilos of U235, because the others, according to his calculations, were not fissile, he stopped there. It was a problem for chemists and he understood almost nothing about it, an isotope was needed, an artificial heavy metal, you had to start with a normal mineral and make it become an isotope. A complicated problem, did it take an engineer to solve the problem? No, not at all, he could figure it out on his own.

Meanwhile, another problem had come to mind: a bomb had to be taken somewhere, to a target, then the mass brought to criticality, after having dropped it from an airplane or something like that. But the mass had to become critical at the moment of the explosion, because as soon as it became so it would explode violently, so two or more subcritical masses had to be taken, to be kept separate until the right moment, then find a devilry that would push them against each other, violently to make them become a single, critical, mass.

And then there was another problem..

All these ideas had been going through his mind for a long time. He had written everything down in notebooks, all the calculations, all his deductions, three notebooks, which he had never had the strength to destroy. He carried them around with him everywhere in a bag.

4.2 Mazara del Vallo……. 1937: Tommaso Lipari…….the player

Tommaso Lipari looked around, it was dawn, even though it was late in the season it wasn't cold, and in that place it never got very cold. They were a few kilometers from Africa and you could tell not only from the temperature, but also from the architecture of that large fishing village, which had been, in times gone by, when Sicily was something different from Italy, and Mazara was the seat of an Ikrim, a sort of provincial capital, of the emirate of Sicily. And you could also tell from the physical appearance of many of the inhabitants of that town, Tommaso included: slim, with very black hair, olive-colored skin, eyes the same color as coal and sparkling like little diamonds: a Saracen, a descendant of the knights of Asad Ibn al Furat, the emir of Ifriqa, today's Tunisia, who had invaded the island in 827, starting right from Mazara.

He decided to take a walk along the canal port, where the fishing boats that had spent the night out filling their nets with fish were returning. Soon the merchants would arrive to buy to supply the fishmongers with the darting fruit of the night's labors of those tireless sailors. He too had spent the night trying to fish, not fish, but good cards, at the nobles' club. But it had gone badly for him. And yet he understood the good cards immediately, his formidable mind remembered all the cards that came out, that same mind had a monstrous capacity to elaborate complex statistical calculations, so when the game was played correctly he always won. But in that place someone was cheating and who knows why the good cards never came out. Yeah... who knows why.... because someone was cheating, damn it! And he even knew who: Baron Galluzzo, a fucking "curnuto", but he couldn't tell him: "curnuto you're cheating... I know because you keep track of all the fucking cards you draw, and a two of spades that has already been drawn twice can't be drawn a third time, because there are only two spades in the deck."

It was already impossible to tell him that he was a cuckold, son of a whore, because not only was he the owner of half of Mazzara, but he was also a friend of the "friends", of all friends: politicians, priests and even mafiosi, those who had become crafty and had sketched out with the fascists: "change everything so as not to change anything". This, the Baron Galluzzo, had understood this very well and therefore could also allow himself to continue cheating.

Tommaso Lipari, on the other hand, was little or nothing compared to Galuzzo, he was the son of a small nobleman from the province of Trapani, who owned some land and a couple of boats in Mazzara and who had had the good idea of dying when Tommaso was still attending university in Naples and studying mathematics. Because he had a mathematical mind and his father had understood it and wanted that gift to be useful to his son to make his way in life. Instead, the damned Spanish flu had taken him away and Tommaso had had to return to Trapani, to take care of the family business. The only thing that remained of his life in the Neapolitan city was his knowledge of Newtonian physics and his vice of gambling. What as a student had helped him to support himself in style and have fun. He had also tried to have fun in Mazara, he had succeeded for a while, then the bastard, the cheat, had arrived and he had started to lose and someone had even made him understand that it was not the case to act like a hero, Galuzzo had to win at cards at the nobles' club: period.

That evening Tommaso had also gambled away the last of his family's assets and now what the fuck could he do? Maybe one thing he could do: go back to Naples and try to rebuild himself there, as he had done years before, he had some money left that he had managed to steal from himself, from his self-destructive gambling rage: with that he would start over again, in the face of that curnutu baron.

4. 3 Rome.......... 1937 Rinkveiser....the hunt begins

Rinkveiser reorganized his thoughts: Majorana had left Rome and never returned. He seemed to have disappeared, or rather: at the physics institute everyone was sure that he taught in Naples, but there was little contradictory news about him.

The first problem was to find him, and then he had to be convinced to leave and go where Stephenson wanted, but from what Corbino and Fermi said, the scientist was anything but easy to convince and if what the two colleagues of the Sicilian professor had told him was true, he must have become even more grumpy and difficult to convince.

It occurred to him that his daughter could be the key. She had graduated with Fermi, the leader of the boys from Via Panisperna, the group Maiorana was part of. For some time she and Ettore had been seeing each other, a bit secretly, because Maiorana didn't like socializing much. It had been an impossible story. Ettore was a bizarre character, shy, introverted and often unkempt, capable of lighting up only when talking about physics and mathematics. He spent almost all his time writing on all kinds of paper, from cigarette packets to bread wrappers.

Although, at a certain point, he had sometimes started to write in notebooks which he then put in a bag that he always kept in a closet in his room and which he took with him when he moved.

However, he had a weakness for Sabine, probably also thanks to the young woman's extraordinary propensity for numerical calculation. In the end, however, they lost sight of each other. Ettore seemed very reluctant to meet her, Sabine had decided to let go of that story too complicated for a linear young woman like her. She had graduated with a thesis in spectroscopy, with Franco Rasetti, but despite her brilliance, physics did not light any sacred fire in her. She preferred Roman archaeology and spent her free time rummaging through the ruins of the city, working with an archaeologist friend of her father.

He called the American embassy and asked to speak to Stephenson, they put him through and agreed to meet that evening at the Swiss embassy.

4.4 Luderitz…the devil and the puritan

ObersturbanFhurer Luderitz was reading the latest dispatch from Berlin. Wolff was informing him of a new development, since the operation was supposed to take place in Naples they would send an agent who knew the environment well, codenamed Contessa, she would be officially responsible for the operation....however the Obergruppenfhurer informed him that he would receive instructions directly from his representative on the matter.

"Well," he said aloud, "I wouldn't like having to obey a woman."

His relationships with the female sex were difficult; the memory of his mother and of that pornographic scene he had witnessed had blocked him forever, with women he had the same relationships he had with men, as distant as possible, as little warm as possible, as far as sex was concerned it had the effect of a magnet of the same pole on another magnet, he felt repelled by it.

The phone rang, it was Wirth: "Luderitz," he said without even greeting, "I have to see you right away, there's something new that I don't like."

They met in the office of the Anenherbe representative: "Heil Hilter," Wirth said, "I have something I would like to talk to you about. Today I met a man, a Jew," he said in a contemptuous tone.

Luderitz looked at him questioningly: "You understand, Luderitz...." The SS officer was quite used to a certain singularity in the communication of the Nazi puritans, but this time he had some difficulty understanding. Calmly and without showing the profound boredom that discussions with Wirth generated in him, he said: "It seems to me an event not particularly relevant", the other made a resentful expression.

"I mean to say," Luderitz continued, searching for words to calm his intemperate interlocutor, "that in itself the meeting with a representative of an inferior race, in itself," he repeated, underlining with his tone the allusion to absolute irrelevance, "has nothing particularly interesting."

"The Jews, wherever and whoever they are, are plotting against the Reich," Wirth said confidentially, as if he were revealing a celestial truth. "And in any case, this is a particular Jew, in reality he is not known as such, but his surname, Rinkweiser, makes me suspect him. But there is more, he is a diplomat in the service of Switzerland and works for the Swiss security services."

Luderitz interrupted him: "I didn't know that Switzerland had security services."

Wirth looked at him with a certain pitying look: "Her Luderitz, the Jewish plutocrats have all the possible weapons to harm the Reich, and this Rinkweiser is one of them," Wirth concluded with the tone of someone who knew a lot. Then he continued: "He was close to the English embassy and I know that he is a friend of all the representatives of Jewish science. A series of coincidences that make me doubt that he is here to take possession of the knowledge of the Atlanteans."

Luderitz, despite a certain obscurity in the official's speech, understood where the man was going with this.

"Well," he said, "you can never be too careful, we'll check," Luderitz said conclusively, then he saluted Wirth in the Roman style and with a loud "Heil Hitler" he left. He returned to his office and decided that, despite his low esteem for Wirth, it was worth investigating. He would start with the English embassy, then the Swiss one... while he was thinking about these things he heard a knock at the door, it was Wirth again: "Perhaps, comrade, you'll be interested to know that the crypto-Jew Rinkweiser also visited the Faculty of Science, where Professor Fermi is located, one of the pseudo-scientists who is also a crypto-Jew."

"Ah, replied Luedritz, thank you Wirth"

The Anenherbe man was as heavy as a plate of Sausages and Sauerkraut at three in the morning, however, if you overlooked his verbal excesses he also provided some interesting information. Yes, it was definitely worth investigating the Faculty of Science at the University of Rome and Rinkweiser's visits to the British Embassy. He began by sending an urgent dispatch to the SiPO (Sicherheitspolizei), the office that dealt with internal security directly dependent on Himmler, asking for information on a certain Fabian Rinkweiser.

Then he called the military attaché, the officer was in the office, he was a ship's captain, his name was Marken, he was a nice guy with a big, well-groomed beard, who had lost a leg in the battle of the Falklands, he had an artificial limb and this had taken away his chances of being sent on board. The fact that he was a naval officer made Horst Luderitz feel a bit uncomfortable. He wondered if his father had been like that, but he had also learned to overcome these idiosyncrasies, but he kept his distance. They exchanged a few pleasantries, then Horst asked him if he had any news of any espionage activity going on at the British embassy.

Marken looked slightly surprised; "no more than usual... business as usual."

Horst also decided to ask about the Swiss diplomat. Marken had met him only once the previous Christmas at a party of the Italian Foreign Ministry, he told him that he was the cultural attaché and that he had exchanged only a few words with him.

Then Marken thought of a tip he had received from an undercover agent in the embassy, concerning the visit of a Canadian official named Stephenson, a strange thing, considering the man's past as a secret agent.

He pondered whether or not to break the news to that strange SS officer with his uncertain assignments. He thought it was best to be safe and mentioned the matter.

When Luderitz had left, however, he decided to inform his real boss, Admiral Canaris of the Abwehr, of this kind of impromptu investigation by the SS, and sent a top secret coded message using a confidential internal code to the service, informing the admiral of all Luderitz's movements.

The head of the SiPo forwarded a copy of Luderitz's request to General Wolff, adjutant to Reichsfürer Himmler.

Horst had sent the same message to General Wolff for information... luckily for him

Even a non-commissioned officer infiltrated by the SS into the Abwehr decided to pass on Marken's information to General Wolff.

Wolff found himself with the three messages in his hands and decided to inform his contact in Lisbon, Jackob Bindung.

Commander Fleming was just returning from his night of gambling to finance Operation Martingale, read the briefing and passed it on to his superiors in London. An urgent phonogram was sent from London and arrived in Scarsdale along with the latest news on the stock market.

WB took a quick look at the market reports, the usual disaster, according to him it would take about fifty years to recover the losses of Black Monday. He, fortunately or more than anything because he had understood, had come out of that sewer much earlier, he had invested in other types of assets, in particular in a company founded by a crazy genius, named Oward Huges, who dealt with airplanes and cinema. How can you think that a genius is not also crazy? WB himself, wondered what his crazy side was, he looked at himself in the mirror and saw the most normal face in the world, he went down to have breakfast and met his perfect WASP wife, his three perfect children enrolled in IVY league schools, there was no alcohol in the house, the maid was a black woman, silent, almost invisible and totally submissive, physically she resembled a table. He was an evangelical, who went to church punctually every Sunday.... and what else? Perhaps his madness was there, in its total, leaden, unshakeable normality, and he wondered if one day it would not explode in some uncontrollable gesture, in some totally absurd action, as sometimes happened to someone in some city in America. Deep down, WB thought, America was like him, everything in order, everything "normal", and underneath, underneath the madness, the gangsters who controlled the cities, the big capitalists with secret manias vented at night in the villas of Hollywood, the cocaine, the whiskey, which flowed like rivers. Deep down, Hughes was simply an American, like so many others, and what was he, WB? He picked up the reports from London and that intrigued him, something was happening, on the front that interested him most, that of physics, that of those new surprising discoveries.

Apparently other people were starting to take an interest in the subject, Himmler the madman, but also someone who wasn't mad: Stephenson, and Stephenson meant Winston Churchill, a man with boundless pride, but also an intelligence that was very difficult to find in anyone else, a political genius, who was worth comparing himself with. WB decided it was time to go to Europe and talk to that English Bulldog. It was time to set up something to work together on the nuclear physics project, that discovery was the future, not only that, if it went in the wrong direction it could mean there would be no future. He went down to the cellar where there was a private switchboard, he called a number in England.

Portugal ...

Jan had gone to bed at 7 that morning, the usual night spent doing his job as a gambler to finance the Martingale operation. He was dreaming, meaningless dreams; a carousel was spinning, there were wooden horses and on the horses were girls in corsets and suspenders who were smiling, smiling at him, they were beautiful, blondes, redheads, brunettes and they all smiled at him, and when the horse passed they turned and looked him in the eyes and continued to smile. Jan felt a thought rise from deep within him: how long had it been since he had been with a woman. The carousel went around again, one of the women was holding a phone that was ringing, it kept ringing... Jan's eyes suddenly widened. The phone on the bedside table rang, Jan suddenly sat up, tried to grab the receiver which slipped from his hand and fell to the floor, Jan rolled with difficulty out of bed and grabbed the receiver and in an otherworldly voice murmured: "Haloo".

On the other end a cold, flat female voice said, "Good morning Senor Vinculo, may I put you through to Mr. Sinclair."

It took him a few seconds to figure out where he was. ..Vinculo, who the hell was he...? He was about to say that they had the wrong number, then the fog cleared, ah here is Vinculo, yes his name as a Portuguese citizen. Bond in English and Bindung in German. The secret service men really had strange brains, they probably enjoyed making anagrams and charades, two things that after only a few hours of sleep were not easy to unravel.

"yes, pass it to me, thanks"

"Good morning," Sinclair said jovially, "there's some news..."

Jan ran her hands through her disheveled hair, what the hell kind of news must it have been, to ask to be communicated at that time of the morning, she looked at the clock wetta placed on the bedside table.... shit it was 1pm...

"I am at your disposal, Mr. Sinclair..."

"Go to the post office, you will find a long telegram for you..."

At that time, in Portugal, the post office must have been quite closed, ..however, since he had been working for Sinclair, he had become accustomed to surprising events.

"Excellent sir,,,," replied Jan

"Good and.... please, check his passion for the game, lately we've been winning a bit too much"

Fleming got up, took a shower and went out, the outside temperature at that hour was quite pleasant, the Portugal had a beautiful climate. The post office was in Sao Joao, quite far from the center. He got a lift in a taxi. The post office was closed, but in front of it was sitting in the sun an old man, dressed modestly, with the classic black duck-billed cap, which all Portuguese farmers and fishermen wore.

Fleming looked around, heard a voice coming from under the duckbill cap:

"Are you Mr. Vinculo?"

Fleming looked at the old gentleman, it seemed very unlikely to him that that small, thin guy of uncertain age, but certainly closer to that of Methuselah than to that of Peter Pan, could be dangerous, he decided to overcome his distrust and, while maintaining his distance, he answered "Yes"

"This is for you," said the little man, getting up and handing him a yellow envelope and disappearing around the corner with surprising speed.

The fishing boat was waiting for him at the dock of the Club Naval, in Cascais, the captain and the three sailors, on board the fishing boat looked like photocopies of the old man from the post office, they were just dressed a little differently, and with bare feet on which they moved quickly on the damp deck of the fishing boat.

The journey lasted just over half an hour, Jan saw their destination in the distance, a large seaplane, floating peacefully on the waves of an ocean, singularly calm, on the right wing of the airplane could be seen a small figure, leaning on the support spar, scanning the sea.

As they approached, the figure became more and more distinct; he was a rather tall man, on his head he had a felt hat, with a wide brim, of the walking type but rather worn. He had a thin mustache, Hollywood actor style; a leather jacket open in front revealed a long white silk scarf that hung down the front, partly hiding a Hawaiian flowered shirt. He wore riding breeches and high leather boots. He lowered the binoculars with which he was observing them, and with his free arm and hand, he made a wide greeting movement.

The fishing boat came as close as possible, then they put a dinghy into the sea, on which Fleming climbed together with one of the fishermen, with a few strokes of the oars they were close to the boot, on the side there was a sort of ladder to climb on. The man with the mustache shouted "Hey, here, take the ladder..."

It was quite difficult for Jan to jump on the boot without getting wet, in fact he didn't succeed, he put one foot in the sea and got the espadrilles he was wearing wet.

The mustachioed man smiled: "Good morning, my name is Howard, Howard Hughes, come upstairs, my girlfriend will show you some clothes to change into."

Fleming shook the man's hand, climbed up the ladder, at the top was the hatch from which protruded a pretty, slightly angular face, very clear and lively eyes, an enormous mass of red hair.

"Hello," she said, "I'm Katharine, come in, mister...."

"Bindung- he said in his usual relaxed tone, Fleming- Jacob Bindung"

The woman looked at him and her face broke into a wide, very white smile, accompanied by a questioning expression: "Are you German...?"

"Sometimes..." replied Fleming. Katharine burst into a loud laugh, clear as a waterfall.

The Englishman had the impression of recognizing that woman... ah, of course he had seen her at the cinema, several times, the last time in the company of his friend Cary Grant, who pretended to be a zoology professor and a leopard who pretended to be... a leopard.

The lady showed him a pile of clothes and shoes in a corner and said: "You know, we're going to the house of a friend of Oward's, a certain...., a kind guy, but a little formal and he expects his guests to show up in jacket and tie..."

"I know people like that too... so formal, I'm used to it," Fleming replied.

The trip was pleasant, Huges was intent on watching the route and did not say much, Katharine on the other hand was as garish as a magpie, however the conversation was anything but boring. She told little gossip about Hollywood and of an evening when she had tried to seduce Grant, but had been beaten to it by a bold engineer from the Troupe. The woman screamed a little to cover the noise of the engines, but it did not seem to tire her.

Jan wondered where they were going, not that he had a problem, since he had been working for Sinclair the strangest things had happened, he didn't know much about secret services, but he had understood one thing immediately: there was no point in asking questions.

After about two hours they spotted a group of islands, Huges turned to them and, pointing with a wave of his hand at the archipelago, shouted: "... Azores, we're stopping to refuel, it's almost two thousand miles from here to New York, we'll refuel halfway, just to be safe. There'll be a small tanker waiting for us about four hundred and fifty miles from Nova Scotia. You know, buddy, it's a bit of a bold operation, but it's to test the range of this plane, one day it could become an anti-submarine patrol plane..." he winked. Kataharine made a funny expression like a disappointed child and said almost in a whisper: "Wow... if I'd known beforehand I'd have dressed up as a spy"

"Fleming looked at her ironically: "Me too, but I didn't have time to stop by Seville Rove."

There was also a small bar on board, they drank gin, ate a couple of sandwiches and then drank more gin, while Huges seemed to be in another world; he held the control stick in his hand and checked the instruments at regular intervals.

Katharine was a little tipsy, she looked at him and giggled: "Look at him... the pilot, when he's at the controls it seems like the world disappears, he's the richest man in America and he plays with this thing like it's a child..."

Jan was starting to feel sleepy, he was suffering from the previous night spent at the gaming table. The copious amount of gin he had ingested along with that diva who drank like an Irish sailor, did not cooperate in keeping him awake. His head felt heavy and he began to nod to the woman's chatter, until he collapsed, his chin on his chest.

The woman looked at him and shook her head: "..men,...damn, that would be cute but it can't hold two glasses of gin..."

He woke up with a start as the plane bobbed through the clouds, gliding toward the sea. Rain was hitting the plane's windshield with a machine-gun noise, the windshield wiper was doing its Sisyphean job, moving rivers of water that would immediately reform.

Katherine had turned pale and looked like she was about to vomit, and this seemed to be the only good reason for her not to scream in terror, while the madman at the controls had replaced his hat with a pilot's cap and was speaking into a microphone asking for information on the position of the tanker.

The sea below them was incredibly calm, Hughes turned to him: "We are in the eye of the storm, here the winds stop we will have time to fill up with petrol and escape before the storm starts again...." He looked at Fleming's puzzled expression... "don't worry, it's just a summer storm"

So it was, as the plane floated quietly on the grey waters a lifeboat approached from the small tanker, dragging a hose connected to a hand pump. The two men in the boat had decidedly worried expressions. They did it as quickly as they could, and as soon as they had finished they began to row furiously towards the ship, while the sea began to get rough.

The next four hours of the journey were relatively uneventful, as they climbed above the storm, but they had to don a thermal suit and oxygen masks, a rather complicated operation for Hughes who was simultaneously busy at the controls.

When God and fortune willed they were in sight of the American coast. They flew over New York, then glided and landed on the sea. They landed near a village on the coast where they were joined by a large motorboat. After about an hour, time to change into the formal clothes that Katharine had shown at the beginning of the trip. The woman had started smiling again, and commented with stinging jokes on the fact of having to change on board that contraption, while she did so she took off and put on her clothes with the ease of a stripper, doing everything to make the Englishman notice her athletic physique. But he had a family-sized headache and thought that in a slightly less complicated moment he would have taken advantage of the young star's all too theatrical advances, even if redheads were not exactly his ideal.

A large cabin cruiser approached the plane. Fleming noted that the craft was a real marvel. The deck and frames were Virginia oak. Polished to a high gloss, the brass fittings had been polished to a high gloss, but in a way that seemed subdued, as if the polisher had been instructed not to make them too visible.

The pilot of the craft maneuvered with great skill, bringing the vessel close to the seaplane's boots so that the guests would not risk getting wet. Before they disembarked, a young man wearing a flight suit climbed aboard. He greeted Huges, and they exchanged some information, then their crazy host also joined the group on the vessel and they all set off together towards the coast.

It was a few minutes before land came into sight, they entered a small bay, surrounded by hills that sloped down to the sea, closing the bay to the north and south. A low building could be seen in the distance, built almost on the beach, which rested on a platform from which a pier started. Behind the house were trees, which extended like a curtain for a few meters to the left and right of the pier.

Now they were very close to the pier, in front of the building there was a man, a person of medium height, bald, dressed in white, shirt and trousers of the same color, he seemed busy doing something. He looked down, and every now and then he threw something with his left hand, taking it from the right hand, perhaps he was feeding some small animal. Fleming found it curious. The man by the building raised his head, stopped what he was doing and calmly walked towards the edge of the pier. He waited standing, until the pilot of the motorboat had finished pulling over, had the cable thrown to him and tied it himself to one of the large poles that supported the pier. Then he threw the pilot a rope ladder.

Katharine shouted good morning at the top of her lungs. "Good morning, Miss Epburn," the mysterious amphityrion replied with a slight smile.

The men on board stepped aside to let the young woman pass, who, barefoot, climbed up the ladder and, generously showing off her legs, stepped onto the dock.

The host went up to him and gave him a perfect kiss on the hand.

Then, noticing that the young lady was having a bit of difficulty putting on her shoes, he offered to help her and let her lean on him to put on her elegant pumps, with rather high heels.

Meanwhile Fleming and Huges had climbed onto the dock, the man turned to them with the subdued smile he had shown the lady.

"Good morning, gentlemen, and welcome to my home."

Huges waved his hand broadly: "Hello WB," he said jovially, "How are we doing, my friend?"

"Well," replied the other, "it seems that your company's stocks are gaining despite this awful market, and that's music to my ears..." he said with a mischievous smile and making a circular sign with his right hand around his ear.

Then he turned his gaze towards Fleming and with his usual polite smile, held out his hand.

« Very pleased to meet you, Mr. Fleming.. » and he shook the Englishman's hand vigorously, demonstrating an unexpected strength in his hands, given his not particularly imposing physical structure.

"How are you, Mr..." the man omitted to say his name and replied: "Very well, thank you."

Fleming was a very controlled person, but he was beginning to get tired and he would not have minded understanding why he had crossed the Atlantic Ocean, after a sleepless night, passing through a storm and risking his life in a drafty contraption.

"May I ask you the reason for your kind invitation...?" he asked.

« Today, dear friend, is the anniversary of the start of the collaboration between me and Mr. Huges, I would say an exceptionally successful initiative, both with regard to airplanes and with regard to cinema... » and he stopped

Fleming waited for him to continue but nothing happened.

"Well, thank you for sharing your success with me, but I'm afraid I had no influence on this ... thing."

"No, in fact you are here for another reason. The fact is that they tell me that you know very well a person with whom I would like to get in touch.... "

"I know a lot of people, mister...."

The man continued not to say his name: "That person is not just anyone, his name is Winston Churchill..."

« Ah, well, yes, I would say I know him. To say that we are friends would be excessive, it is not easy to get into the good graces of the third son of the Duke of Marlborough »

« Exactly, but I know that his father and Sir Winston were comrades in arms, so much so that it was Churchill who wrote his obituary.... »

« Yes, it's true, he had a lot of respect for my father ... »

« So...do you think you can bring him a message from me...? »

« It depends on the message.... »

« Listen, I'd suggest we talk about it later, if you don't mind. In the meantime, this evening you'll be my guest at a party to celebrate Oward. We'll talk about it tomorrow morning after breakfast, we'll meet here on the pier... »

Fleming shivered: "... I suppose at a rather early hour..."

WB smiled: "I know everything about you, dear Fleming... is ten o'clock okay?" he said, looking at the Eberhard chronograph he wore on his wrist.

Jan smiled in turn: "I'll make do with them..."

The party was less boring than Jan expected, Katharine buzzed around him all evening, but she was a smart girl and so the conversation was brilliant, full of little suggestive jokes, to which Fleming always responded with the right tone, the conversation between the two seemed like a tennis match between two champions. She talked all evening with anyone who would listen about movies and airplanes. They all went to bed rather early. Jan had the doubt that Katharine would decide to follow up on his advances. This did not happen, and Jan was a little hurt, yes after all he was used to rather insistent female assaults, and his ego remained a little resentful, but perhaps this was just the decisive blow of the tennis match... smash... she had won.

He ate breakfast with gusto, avoiding the pancakes, scrambled eggs and crispy bacon. He decided to eat continental, also because there were croissants that were incredibly well made considering which side of the Atlantic they were on.

Mister WB had provided each of them with a complete wardrobe, which was placed in the closet of the assigned rooms.

Jan had found underwear, socks and shirts made by her supplier in Seville Rowe, exactly in her size and in her favorite color.

There were canvas trousers and a pair of espadrilles, which Fleming dressed in and then went down to the marina. A black waiter was waiting at a small table on which were a couple of packets of Chesterfields, a coffee service with cups and a coffeepot in Limoges porcelain, from which a delicious smell emanated.

Fleming had just enough time to drink a cup of coffee and smoke the first of many cigarettes of the day and WB appeared, still dressed in white, clothes identical to those of the day before, but perfectly clean and ironed.

He greeted Fleming cordially. He took a cup of coffee himself and then began to speak.

« Well Mr. Fleming, lately you have been busy maintaining relations between Admiral Sinclair and an important figure in the Nazi regime... »

Fleming looked at him slightly surprised.

« Don't be surprised, international politics does not have a life of its own, and not even internal politics. Everything is strongly influenced by finance, and I influence finance, together with a few other men.

Let's say we have some control over the German government as well. You are working for something that is above nations and governments... »

« It means I'm working for you.... »

« I am not above anything, I am only a coordinator, of a pressure group that tries to direct the world towards some interests... what is above governments, nations, churches and peoples is money, because it allows you to buy power, and the so-called powerful are very weak and greedy creatures.... »

Fleming remained silent, he had always had this vague suspicion.

« But now something has happened, something partly unexpected, that no one can do anything about. It's called science. Scientists have discovered a terrible energy that is uncontrollable today. Whoever could do it would have the keys to the world in their hands, and if this were an unmanageable character, the world would fall apart, we would arrive at the apocalypse.... »

« And who could be the one to take control of the atomic energy... »

"Did you want to surprise me, Mr. Fleming?" WB said with an indulgent smile. "Yes, I'm talking about atomic energy, and there are two people I wouldn't want to take control of it, one is Hitler and the other is Stalin."

« But, we, that is, aren't you supporting the Führer? »

"It is one thing to support a man to govern a country and direct some aspects of the politics of this country towards our interests, another to give him the same power as God."

"And what could Churchill and I do?"

« You bring him a message from me, as far as Sir Winston is concerned I will speak to him directly if he accepts my proposal... »

"That's all...?" exclaimed Fleming.

"For the moment... The captain will arrive shortly with my pilot boat, who will accompany you to the vessel with which you will reach England. There you will go to Sinclair, and give him this letter."

He handed him an envelope wrapped in gutta-percha and sealed.

"Sinclair will then find a way for you to talk to Churchill, I'm sure it won't be difficult. You will give him this other letter..." This one was also wrapped in gutta-percha, but it was of a different color.

« If Sir Winston accepts my proposal I will know very soon, in the meantime you will return to Estoril, and continue your war at the green table...then you will receive instructions. »

Along with the two envelopes WB gave him a military canvas bag: "this will be useful to you."

Fleming put the two envelopes back in his saddlebag, slung it over his shoulder, and at that moment the pilot boat appeared and quickly reached the dock.

WB waved goodbye to Fleming, and walked away toward the building, stopped and looked down, there was a small animal at his feet, he put his hand in his pocket and took out something that he threw on the ground a little at a time. The little animal grabbed them one by one and then raised its head, waiting for the next thing. Probably a peanut. Strange character, Fleming thought, then he got into the pilot boat, which with a quick maneuver moved away towards the open sea.

After about an hour they stopped. The captain of the pilot boat took from under the bridge in front of him a round and heavy object with a ring hanging from it, the captain snatched it and threw the grenade into the sea a few meters from the side of the pilot boat, a few minutes passed, then a dull thunder was heard and a small column of water emerged from the water.

Five more minutes passed and the turret of a submarine slowly emerged from the sea. It was painted black and had a white writing: H28.

Two sailors came out of the turret, took a dinghy fixed on the deck, and rowed to the pilot boat.

"Commander Fleming...?" asked one of the two, a sergeant.

« Fleming, not commander, however I believe I am the person you are looking for... »

"Then please come aboard."

4.5 Rome …1937 Mademoiselle Docteur ………the queen of spies

The woman was about forty-five, maybe a little older, not particularly beautiful, at least not at first glance. But as Horst looked at her more closely, he noticed that a kind of magnetic fluid was exuding from her. Maybe it was her eyes that seemed to almost sparkle with fever. Maybe it was her general attitude, strangely detached, almost haughty, and yet powerfully attractive. Or maybe it was the way she looked at him, she reminded him of the way lions looked at zebras in Southwest Africa, where he came from. No woman had ever had that effect on him, he didn't like it, not at all. The memory of his mother had suddenly resurfaced, and it gave him something he hadn't felt for a long time, a painful feeling of loss, a feeling that took him back to the alleys of Luderiz, when he ate garbage, before the sergeant saved him. And something told him that the one who brought back those forgotten sensations was that woman: Anne Lesser, sent by the Reich Führer himself to direct Operation Schwartze Sonne, that is, the capture of an Italian scientist who, according to Heisenberg, had discovered the secret of a very powerful and unknown energy.

Anne was wearing a black suit, buttoned up to the neck, rather tight, a white lace blouse and a small hat with a veil. Her skirt fell below the knee and revealed a pair of black sheer stockings with a line. She was sitting with a cup of coffee in front of her at a table in a meeting room of the German embassy in Rome, and was looking around, without letting it show, with a rather bored expression. Ambassador Von Mackensen, on the other hand, gave the impression of being there by chance, and probably was.

He was there only because he was the son and brother of two important officers, and because his predecessor Von Hasael had made an enemy of the Nazi government with his uncooperative attitudes. Von Mackensen understood foreign policy as well as a Swiss cow could understand the philosophy of being.

Wirth sat next to him, agitated and disdainful as usual, he looked at Lesser with a look full of distrust, he couldn't hide the annoyance he felt at the idea that the command of the operation had been entrusted to someone other than him.

He had provided all the information he had, but speaking in a confused and disorderly manner, giving much more emphasis to ideological facts, completely irrelevant to the operation, than to important information.

Anne let him finish his report. She took a sip of coffee and turned to Luderiz.

"Mr. Luderiz, I would like to ask you two questions.." - then he turned to Wirth - you know, professor, our comrade is an operative, I'm sure he has some important information - he emphasized the word with his tone - on two things that particularly worry me. "

Wirth blushed: "Of course... of course he said," unable to hide his anger. It was known that Lessere was a favorite of the head of the SD, Hedrich, a difficult pill to swallow perhaps even for Himmler, let alone for a not particularly important figure like Wirth.

Lesser continued: "First of all: I would like a complete picture, as far as you know," she said in a falsely amiable tone, "of where this scientist is.

Then I would like to have some more information on the, um, competitors.... » then she smiled charmingly.

Horst was embarrassed, he had the feeling of being an animal surrounded by wolves, and that the only way out was through that woman; probably through a narrow passage between her long, shapely legs.

He began by talking about Maiorana:

« Ettore Maiorana is considered the best of the group of Italian scientists working with Professor Fermi. He is highly gifted in mathematics and they say that he has already solved, thanks to his calculations, 90% of the questions regarding this new energy.

He left Rome a long time ago, it seems that he had some disagreements with Enrico Fermi, but above all it seems that for a long time he has undergone a singular change, no one can talk to him. He no longer publishes anything, apparently he lives in Naples, where he teaches at the university.

I have already been to that city once but I was not able to find out much, I plan to return soon, a letter of introduction from the German embassy or even from Professor Heisemberg could be useful to me, to contact Majorana's superiors and have a... let's say friendly treatment. »

He stopped, took a sip of water from the glass in front of him, and continued on.

Lesser was staring at him, her gaze had changed a little, now she showed interest, but a different interest than before, like a sort of professional admiration.

« As far as the opposition is concerned, there are no major movements at the moment, we know that the man who is looking for Majorana is a Swiss citizen...

"Of Jewish origin..." Wirth rudely interrupted him, Lesser glared at him.

"Yes, it seems he is of Jewish origin and that he is connected to the Swiss security services. He has frequent contact with an English officer, a rather dangerous man for us, his name is Stephenson," continued Horst.

Lesser almost seemed to startle: "Stephenson? William Stephenson?"

"Yes ma'am..." Luderiz replied

« Well this is interesting news. It means at the very least that there is an important operation underway in Rome by the British

Services, and this operation can only concern your ... Marjoram.. is that what it's called? »

«nein meine herren, Maiorana.. »

« Maiorana already. But it also means that we have to expect some annoying competition »

"If we have to use strong methods, we will..." exclaimed Wirth.

Anne looked at him with pity: "My dear Wirth, when I speak of annoying competition I mean that they will make life difficult for us, we can use force as much as they can and we are in a foreign country, a friend..., but a foreign one. It will be a difficult and complicated game, where violence could be more counterproductive than useful. Unfortunately for you, Wirth, we will have to try to be more cunning."

Wirth evidently didn't understand the joke, he half-smiled, with the obvious expression of someone who hadn't understood a damn thing.

London *Winston Churchill...the lion and the puppeteer*

Winston Churchill read the message given to him by Lord Hugh Sinclair. The head of Naval Intelligence was transmitting him a message from America, the author of the message was WB

The English statesman was quite surprised, Mr.WB was a person he had known for a long time. Even personally, he was part of the Order. A secret society that controlled enormous resources, governments and whose members were many noble families and even royal European ones. Among them the English one.

He proposed to meet him on the island of Jersey to talk to him about an extremely important matter. Chirchill was sure that it was, WB was not a man to waste time with chitchat. He therefore decided to accept the appointment, the following month in Jersey.

Rome....Sabine Rinkweiser

Fabian Rinkweiser scratched his head. Professor Maiorana hadn't been seen at the university for several days, no one knew where he was. He hadn't been able to get his address from the hateful secretary of the physics department: "That's his business," the woman had said with a certain rudeness and cutting short Rinkweiser's insistence.

Finding that man in Naples was like looking for a needle in a haystack, and he didn't know where to start. Someone had to help him, he thought of his daughter Sabine. She was a brilliant girl, with great instincts and courage. She still remembered the little prank they had played on Edgard Hoover in New York, and she still remembered the angry bulldog face of the head of the FBI, in front of the cardinal archbishop of New York.

He called the embassy in Rome, and by pure chance he managed to catch her when she hadn't left yet, to go and dig in her favorite archaeological sites.

« Sabine what do you think about taking a trip to Naples »

« Well it could be the right season, here in Rome it's quite cold, but what should I do there? »

« Keep your father company for example... »

« Dad, you know I adore you, but you also know that being a companion to a Swiss cultural attaché is not exactly my passion... »

« Well it's not my fault if I'm Swiss, but I don't think you're a citizen of Courland... »

« Yes, but you know very well how little Swiss I am... no, here in Rome I have a lot to do, you have to find something more attractive than your freckled face... »

« well, there is one thing but we need to talk about it face to face »

« what kind of thing.... »

« What if I told you about swashbuckling adventures... ? »

There was silence on the other end of the line.

"So..." Fabian continued.

« New York-like stuff... ? »

« maybe even better... »

"Tomorrow morning I'll be with you, where we are, in Mergellina in front of the church of Santa Maria del Parto. Do you know where it is ..."

"I'll find out tomorrow, see you at three in the afternoon in front of the entrance."

Rome ...Chyntia

She was there in front of him, looking at him with her teasing smile and caressing her round belly, her emerald eyes laughing, her gaze indulgent and affectionate.

Mario felt his legs go weak, he wanted to run towards her and hug her, right there on the spot but the Capannelle racecourse at that moment was too crowded for this scene, so he settled for a perfect hand kiss. Cynthia noticed how excited he was, she smiled at him: "I see she's in good shape, it's been a while since we last saw each other"

Mario would have liked to tell her a lot of things, but the words died in his throat, he barely managed to say: "I would say yes, many things..." and he gestured to the woman's belly.

Then she recovered: "Pregnancy suits you very well, lady..."

"Oh thank you, I consider it a gift, a gift from a man I love madly..."

His legs were shaking even more: "Your husband will be happy..."

She approached him and, murmuring so that only he could understand, said: "Mario, my husband is completely homosexual, but the man who got me pregnant seems quite excited."

"Excited is a very limited word to describe what I feel"

Commander Stephenson had come over and was chatting amiably with Balbo:"

"Comrade Vaillante, I see you haven't wasted any time, you can't be left alone for a moment without finding yourself next to a beautiful woman" said the quadrumvir and bowed, kissing Cinthya's hand.

The woman glared at Mario, "Ah, they told me that all Italian aviators are womanizers..."

"But with class and respect..." added Balbo

"Of course," the woman concluded with a kind smile.

They chatted about trivialities and watched a race, Cinthya had bet on a horse named Gladiator, she had also won...of course.

That meeting at the racecourse was not a coincidence, Stephenson's great prudence had made him imagine that little trick, he, Mario, and his daughter were supposed to meet in a public place and pretend that a certain friendship was developing, so that if the Italian captain and the American lady were to see each other around, at most some gossip would arise, but no suspicion.

It was about three in the afternoon, they were sipping a drink when Cinthya suddenly faltered and brought a hand to her face. The men who were with her rushed to her aid, William supported her: "is everything okay?" Mario asked as soon as the woman showed some signs of recovery.

"Yes but I think it would be better if I went home...you know in these conditions" she said allusively"

Stephenson seemed to be preparing to accompany her, but Mario stepped forward: "Excuse me, commander, I can accompany her in my car, my orderly will be happy to return and I can easily give up these races, at the racetracks you always lose..." he said, dramatically tearing up the betting slips he had just lost.

"Allow me, Miss.." he said, offering his right arm.

"So you don't mind, Captain..?" Stephenson asked.

"He certainly doesn't mind..." Balbo winked.

The two walked away chatting.

Aminta Brocca della Fonte was the worst gossip in Rome. Descendant of an ancient family of the black nobility, she had never done anything else in her life but observe others and gossip. Her rather masculine physique, and the face that strongly resembled that of a horse, did not give her the success she would have hoped for with men and perhaps that was why at thirty she was still a spinster and sour as a lemon.

She saw Chynthia walking away with Mario towards the exit and his tongue began to cut and sew.

"What whores these foreigners are, they come here and steal the best of our boys... but how can the Duce allow such things, what is an Englishwoman doing with an Italian pilot. Such a handsome boy like the Count"

The woman accompanying Aminta turned around: "What do you say dear...?" she asked nonchalantly.

"But yes, that English whore who is going away with the Count of Santa Tecla, not only allows herself to be seen pregnant at the hippodrome without her husband, who everyone knows is a bit of a faggot, but she also has one of our best officers accompany her. Who knows who impregnated that cow..."

Aminta turned to her friend, she noticed that she seemed even paler than usual, her lips were stretched and her gaze seemed to blaze: "Everything's fine Lise..."

"Yes, everything is fine....", replied Anne Lesser alias Lise Marie Von Testory.

North Sea: Westerhaupt

Westerhaupt looked into the periscope, the target was moving at ten knots, towed by a heavy tug, there were approximately five hundred meters between his submarine and the wreck that served as the target, at the speed at which it was moving Walter had plenty of time to calculate the precise moment of the launch.

He decided to take a quick look around, they were on the shooting range off Kiel but there was no point in taking any risks, it always happened that during an exercise some surface craft that had nothing to do with it would slip into the firing range at the last moment and there was a risk of tragedy. In fact there was a craft that was rapidly approaching at forty-five degrees to starboard of the UBoot.

Around the bow of the object two large foam whiskers rose, Walter increased the magnification. It was an E boot, the insignia that was waving attached to the antenna that protruded from the small bridge, was that of the department that was to act as adversary in the exercise, but underneath you could see two signal flags, one half yellow and blue, divided vertically, the signal of the letter K, which meant attention I must communicate with you, the other, half blue and half red, the letter E, which meant I am turning to starboard.

He enlarged the image even more, and he thought he recognized Oberleutnant Khulm standing on the small bridge of the vessel. The officer signaled to a sailor next to him, the man was holding a signal light and transmitted in Morse: "surface, urgent orders for the commander"

Walter turned away from the periscope eyepiece: "Engines stopped, rapid emergence, controls on the bridge..."

The submarine discharged compressed air into the emergence chambers, with a deafening roar, in the absence of movement that would have helped the inertia of the engine to raise the submarine, all the upward thrust came from the rapid emptying of the emergence chambers.

Khulm saw at 150 meters at thirty degrees port side of the lookout, an air bubble emerge and immediately afterward the submarine's turret appear. Not yet all the water had drained from the turret when Captain Westerhaupt's cap appeared at twenty-three.

The shnellboot slowed down and came to a stop a few meters from the submarine with a turn. The waters were not very calm, as was usual in the North Sea.

Khulm took the megaphone and shouted to Westerhaupt: "I have to take you to the base, an important person has to talk to you"

The submarine commander looked around: "It's not that easy to get onto that tub from here."

"Use a dinghy..."

"I'll get wet like a seal..

"It's what you are..."

The officer disappeared from the turret bridge. A few minutes passed and he reappeared on the deckhouse of the submarine's hull, exiting through the gunner's hatch.

"There are no dinghies on board, I'll go to the bridge, throw me a line, I'll try to go down that"

Khulm turned to his sailors: "You heard, we have an acrobat, pass me that rope and a life jacket because we have to fish the commander out of the sea soon..."

Walter tied the line to the hatch, then motioned for Khulm to step away so he could tighten the line. He climbed over the turret rail and began to descend the line, a real acrobat's maneuver, which Khulm made easier by carefully operating the rudder and the motors of the patrol boat. Walter came aboard. He cut the line with the sailor's knife he kept in his pocket and saluted his second, who was watching them from the U-boat's turret.

"Who is looking for me?"

Khulm made a mysterious expression: "I don't know, an admiral's aide came to me and asked me where you were. I said you were on duty and he told me there was an important person who needed to talk to you urgently, he told me he would wait a couple of hours and to get me back immediately. And here I am"

Then he made a strange movement with his hands: "And here you are."

Walter smiled: "But let's hope it's not a nuisance, admirals bring trouble..."

They arrived at the port in an hour, Walter saw that a large black Mercedes was parked at one of the docks.

An officer was nervously checking his wristwatch and looking out to sea.

The lookout pulled alongside and they quickly moored, aided by a sailor on the dock.

The waiting officer walked toward Westerhaupt. He saluted him, and the submariner returned the salute.

"Strange," he thought, "no Nazi salute, well, that's better."

The officer held out his hand, which Westerhaupt shook: "I am Kapitanleutnant Von Vetter, I ask you to follow me, a person you know wants to speak to you..."

Walter didn't ask any questions: "Well, where is this person?"

Von Vetter pointed to the Mercedes: "I have the task of accompanying you to him, if you want to follow me."

"The problem is that I would have to explain my temporary disappearance to the commander of the U Boot flotilla on which I depend... eh.."

Von Vetter remained impassive: "We have already thought of that, you just have to follow me."

"Dressed like this..." Westerauapt said, spreading his arms and pointing to his singular uniform, typical of submariners, half civilian, with a checked shirt and a leather jacket and half military"

The other officer looked at him indifferently: "Your conversation with the person I was telling you about is more important than the form."

"Okay," Walter replied, and walked toward the Merceds.
They drove in silence the hundred and eighty kilometers that separated Kiel from Cuxaven. They entered the little harbor. There was a fishing boat waiting for them at one of the piers. Walter knew that type of vessel, he had often been aboard one for a considerable part of his youth and almost of his childhood.

The captain, a tall, stocky, bearded man, started to help Walter aboard, then recognized the uniform and gave up. He waited until he had set foot on the deck and ordered the crew to depart.

From the direction the bow of the vessel was taking, Walter understood where they were headed: Helgoland. The fishing boat was going about ten knots, it would take at least three hours.

He looked at his chronograph, they would arrive around three in the afternoon, that is, when it was already dark. He had a vague idea of who might be looking for him, but he wondered why in Helgoland.

There were a few lights on along the pier. The wind was violently shaking everything it hit, and the light from the lamps spread here and there following the capricious movement of the air, illuminating corners of the colored houses that overlooked the pier, giving birth to corners of pink and blue, hidden until that moment by the night. A yellow flash illuminated a dark figure at the edge of the dock, it was a man of medium height, his white hair was being tousled by the wind, his heavy dark blue navy coat was also being shaken by the cold gusts. Walter recognized him, it was Willhelm Canaris, the man who had opened the way for his career in the Kriegsmarine, the man who had sent him to Spain to work for the secret services. On a strange mission with indefinite contours, in which enemies and friends seemed to be dancing a ballet, made of curtsies, bows, waltzes, swapping couples.

In the shelter of the breakwater they moored. The fishermen went their way and Walter found himself only a few steps away from the enigmatic figure waiting for him. He had beckoned him closer then had turned and continued to look out at the agitated North Sea.

Walter wanted to smoke, he took out a pack of Ernte 23 and took a cigarette, put it in his mouth, took out his windproof lighter, it was an American petrol zippo. He lit the cigarette and walked towards the man who was waiting for him.

"Good evening Admiral..." said Walter

"Stormy evening, huh..." said the man, with an oddly thoughtful tone.

"I would say yes, getting here was an adventure"

"I didn't expect this wind, but we're safe here and can talk freely."

Walter pointed with his hand holding the cigarette toward the road that led inland: "This wind can only get stronger for a couple of hours, what do you say if we go and take cover. There's a tavern, assuming it's open..."

"No, let's go to your house, your mother is waiting for us"

They set off in silence. Freja's little house seemed to be waiting for them, with a pale light on. Walter could already see his mother waiting, her hands crossed on her belly, her apron clean and ironed, as if she had just put it on.

They entered the era there, "Grüß Gott, mutter" said Walter, they had always greeted each other like this: "God may be with you" was their greeting since always, with that subjunctive, which left to the will of God every possibility of future. A humble wish, without presumptions, without the pretension of changing the future, without asking permission from the supreme being.

"Grüß Gott, Walter, and to you too Willhelm"

"Thank you Freja.." Canaris replied simply.

On the table were two steaming plates of soup, some dark bread, a plate of herring, two carafes of beer.

Freja approached Walter and hugged him briefly: "I'm going to sleep, see you tomorrow morning?"

"I really think so," Canaris replied, "thank you for your hospitality."

The woman withdrew.

They ate in silence. Walter waited patiently. He knew his interlocutor and knew that he would get to the point when he deemed it appropriate.

Canaris ate everything, calmly and hungrily, drinking the beer in small sips. He waited for Walter to finish. He ate even more slowly than the admiral, every bite of that humble green cabbage soup took him back to his childhood, poor but happy, protected by the reserved love of Freja, who was always present almost without being noticed, like an invisible angel.

He also finished and took the last sip, he looked at Canaris: "So you want to tell me why we are here, or you were missing my mother's soup..."

The Admiral smiled: "No, I mean I always like your mother's soup, but I had you brought here to talk to you about something else. There are two things, the first is the mission I intend to entrust to you.

"It is a top secret mission, because it will be conducted against internal adversaries..."

Walter was used to the antics of the German spy prince, and so he was not surprised; he could imagine who the internal enemies were.

"I have to tell you something in advance, it concerns science. Perhaps you don't know that extraordinary discoveries have been made in the field of physics. The Germans are particularly advanced in these discoveries..."

"Good!" Walter said.

"Not at all," replied the Admiral.

"It is about the discovery of an energy that is the most powerful in the universe, the basis of the combustion of stars, it is called atomic energy, and it could also be used for military purposes. Which means that in our beloved Germany, it would be used mainly for military purposes. The Bohemian house painter intends to unleash a European war, and this could also be understandable, given how the Entente powers treated us after the last war. The fact is that he is raving about conquering the world. Putting that energy in the hands of our Fhurer would be like putting a P38 in the hands of a child, it would cause a massacre. In fact, much worse, the world that would emerge would be a nightmare place"

Walter was quite surprised: "Well then... what should we do?"

"Germany is not capable of winning a world war, it does not have sufficient resources. We could fight until we destroy ourselves, but it will not be enough, we have powerful enemies, we looked for them, or perhaps it was fate or geopolitics that gave them to us. The idea of conquering Russia is pure madness. Many have tried, for a thousand years now. Only the Mongols succeeded, a vast and ferocious people, but they came from the east. Going from west to east is much more complicated. Going from the more or less temperate environment of Europe to the frozen steppes is very difficult. Russia will never fall, communism must be contained, you cannot think of conquering a continent that extends for a quarter of the earth's surface as if it were Austria."

"Sure but with that energy available we could do it"

"We would conquer a desert. Devastated by our bombs, there would be nothing to conquer, only death and destruction"

Walter was perplexed, he trusted Canaris, he knew his lack of sympathy for the Führer and his circle of hierarchs, in particular Himmler, Goering, Rosenberg, but this, to the young submarine commander, seemed like pure and simple betrayal.

He told him: "Admiral, but here we are talking about treason, it is not like in Spain, where we played a double game but the aim was to make our side win."

Canaris sighed: "My dear Walter, in Spain there was something else at stake, everyone, both us and our English partners, were working to make the republic lose. At stake was the risk that Stalin would win a war in a country of strategic importance, like Spain. Other times, other circumstances, Franco won, the war was so devastating for the Iberian peninsula, that one cannot even imagine the Generalissimo participating in a European war. I know Franco personally. He has many defects, but he is not stupid, he knows well that he needs peace to consolidate his regime. Furthermore, he has the Catholic Church on his side, which instead would withdraw its support if he sided with Germany.

Because the Vatican has understood very well that it is Hitler. It has understood that Nazism is a neo-pagan religion, a madness that has a lot to do with the darkest side of the German soul. If Hitler's circle manages to take possession of this powerful energy, no one will be able to stop this madness. Hitler is evil. It is for Germany and it is for the world. If you knew the true origins of Nazism you would have no doubts"

"But at the beginning you were also on his side..."

"Like Rommel, like other Wehrmacht officers, but now we know who these madmen are, and we know that they must not win."

Walter was shocked. His duty as an officer would have been to arrest the man before him, but his conscience, his old friendship with the admiral, and a strange distant feeling told him to trust. He decided to do it.

"Okay Admiral, what do you want to do..?"

"Wait Walter, I haven't finished shocking you this evening..."

What the hell else could that man tell him; that his mother had been a whore; that his father was an English spy, that he was the son of nobody... what the hell did he want from him?

"Tell me Admiral, I'm listening to you"

"There is a man, a close associate of General Wolff, his name is Horst Luderiz. He is responsible for very special tasks."

"Well..."

"At the moment he is busy capturing or rather convincing an Italian scientist to come and work in Germany to produce a weapon that uses atomic energy.

That man is an SS officer and we believe he is your half-brother..."

Walter had a strange feeling. It was as if someone was confirming a suspicion he had had for a long time. Ever since that day when he had met his double at the Hamburg station.

That memory had faded. Walter had finally convinced himself that it had been some kind of hallucination, but it had remained in the back of his mind, like a photograph, slightly out of focus.

"How do you know...?" he wondered.

"The Admiral rose, went to the kitchen cabinet he knew well. He opened it, took out a bottle of brandy and two glasses, sat down again, placed the glasses between himself and Walter and filled them both, then swallowed the first one in one gulp.

"When I got the news from Heisemberg that the SS were interested in the new weapon, I had some discreet investigations carried out. I discovered that Wolff has long since created a parallel structure, unknown to anyone within the Gestapo. I don't know exactly who finances it, nor how large it is, but there is the suspicion that the money comes to him through very private channels, from abroad. Wolf has managed to have his man included in the team that is supposed to capture the scientist. I don't know what Wolff's plan is, perhaps he just wants to be present in this operation for reasons of prestige. Or perhaps there is something else.

Walter could not understand, something escaped him, indeed a lot escaped him. Wolf, Himmler, Canaris; they were all Germans, they were all high ranks of the Nazi system, it seemed instead that they belonged to different countries, enemies of each other.

"I don't understand, who are we? Who are the enemies?"

"Walter, the problem is that right now it's not Germany or England or France or anything else that's at stake. In this story, the future fate of the world is at stake. There's a clash that goes beyond the clash between nations. That's the show, the theater. Behind the scenes, there's a thousand-year-old clash, between forces that have been fighting for world domination for at least five hundred years. But maybe even before that. We could say it's a clash between good and evil. A clash that's been fought forever. We have to prevent evil from seizing power that would lead the world to disaster."

Walter was astonished, what he was hearing seemed completely absurd to him. If he hadn't known the man in front of him practically forever, he would have thought he was crazy. Canaris seemed to read his thoughts.

"Westerhaupt, you think I have lost my mind, I have not. Those who have lost their minds are those who support Nazism. They lost it a long time ago. Tell me, Westerhaupt, what can you think of those who want to conquer the world, of those who seek the Holy Grail, of those who imagine that there is a land under the earth, of people linked to sects of crazy exalted, like the Rosicrucians or Thule. People who imagine an era dominated by pure Aryans. Madness, Westrahaupt. A concoction of medieval beliefs, of sick aristocratic minds, because they descend from cross-breeding between relatives. These people led Germany to the disaster of the First World War. Now they want to unleash a war again. In a few months there will be an operation against all German Jews, there are thousands of people among them, including your mother."

Walter snapped his head up.

Canaris handed him a file: "Here is evidence that your mother has Jewish origins. I managed to replace the file with a false one, but it will not be possible to do so for the other one hundred thousand German Jews. Then it will be the turn of the rest of Europe, we are talking about about ten million people."

Walter opened the file, it was extremely detailed. Yes, his mother was a quarter Jewish, and that meant he too was at risk of losing everything.

"Okay Admiral, but now tell me about my stepbrother..."

"You will meet him by chance one day at the naval headquarters, I don't know why he was there. When I saw him I was about to greet him, then I saw the SS uniform. I just had time to stop, then I investigated and discovered his story..."

"So what...?"

"It's a story I don't want to tell you. Your father was a hero, but he was also a man, it wouldn't make sense for me to tell you things that would destroy his image in your eyes, a father you never knew lives in an unreal world, he lived in the real one. What I can tell you is that he didn't do anything different from what any sailor does when he goes around the world and I suppose you did too. But it happened that in one of these, let's call them adventures, fate wanted to play the worst cards.

Luderiz is the result of that game. They say he is a man incapable of feeling, and one of the best officers of the damned SS corps. He is also said to be gifted with considerable intelligence."

"So I'll be up against my brother on this mission?"

"He and others. They chose the best. The mission leader is a woman, her name is Elsbeth Schragmuller, alias Anne Lesser, but the Abwher knows her as Fraulein Doktor."

Walter poured himself a glass of Shnaps.

"What do you expect me to do..."

"You will be part of an international team, you will have to make sure that Professor Majorana does not fall into the hands of the Anenherbe team. They are the ones directing this operation. You will have instructions on this when you are on site, remember one thing: Majorana must not fall into their hands... Even at the cost of killing him.

The operation will take place in Italy, I will take care of your coverage, tomorrow you will take a plane that will take you to Vienna. From there you will reach Rome by train.

I gave Freja a bag with fake documents and instructions. Follow them carefully...

You will leave at dawn with the same fishing boat you arrived with. Tonight the storm will stop tomorrow the forecast is for good weather. We will see each other after the mission, for now good luck. Now let's go to sleep."

Freja had prepared a camp bed in the kitchen for Canaris. Walter went to the little room where he had slept all his childhood. It was not a quiet night; dreams troubled Walter until his mother woke him at four.

Rome....Mario and Cinthya

They remained in silence all the way to the American embassy. The orderly got out of the car and opened the door for Cynthia, she turned slightly, even though she was pregnant she moved with agility. She looked at Mario, with a look that spoke, it said get out and follow me, I have to talk to you about a world of things, first of all about what I'm carrying in my womb. Mario was furious and at the same time enchanted, he wanted to scream and at the same time hug her, touch that belly, which looked like a watermelon hidden under a dress, because her body was the same as before she got pregnant, apart from the swollen breasts and that almost perfect round protuberance, which contained her son. A part of him and a part of her, the fruit of a distant dream, had in a boarding school in northern Italy, which became an swashbuckling adventure and now transformed into a boy... or a girl? It didn't matter, whatever it was, it was his and the woman he'd dreamed of all his life, just the two of them and no one else.

He told the orderly Possenti, go ahead, I'll go back on my own. He saw the soldier's dark eyes smiling in the rearview mirror, "commands, captain." He got out on the opposite side of Cynthia, they found themselves facing each other in the inner courtyard, they both felt an irresistible force inside that pushed them against each other, but there were two marines in white uniforms watching them from the top of the porch.

"Come," said Cynthia, holding out her hand to him.

The Stephensons' apartment occupied a part of the building far from the entrance, with a balcony that looked out onto Via Boncompagni. The shutters were half-closed and the living room was dimly lit, it was cool, and there was a smell of freshly ironed linen, of furniture polish, of things a little old, that gave Mario a sense of deja vu, reminded him of the rooms in his grandfather's house.

They entered and Cynthia turned around smiling, Mario felt himself melt, that smile, those teeth that seemed like pearls, those emerald eyes that shone like stars and smiled completely disarmed him, he hugged her and kissed her passionately, he felt her hard and round belly pressing against him, and he felt an infinite tenderness for that creature that was inside there,

"la melunera" (the emmellon place) as the housekeeper of my grandfather's house, Mrs. Bianchi, called her, blushing and lowering her voice.

He pulled away and looked at the woman: "you're crazy, you're pregnant, how can we go hunting for a man who's hiding, in those conditions, you can't even run. And then we have dangerous opponents. You have no idea... what Mademoiselle Docteur is capable of"

"Do you think it's worse than the Cheka men in Spain...?"

Mario snorted: "You..Were'nt..Pregnant.." he almost shouted. She smiled, she always did when someone got mad at her, and her face took on an incredibly beautiful expression. The dimples near her mouth deepened, her eyes widened and her mouth took the shape of a small o..."

I know I wasn't pregnant... I hadn't yet met the most handsome and most careless Italian in the world..." and she approached him.

Mario was somewhere between desperate and amused, he burst out laughing: "Damn you, do you realize... but your father agrees...?"

"If you mean Commander Stephenson, no, but I convinced him, it's a way to ensure your cooperation... and it's also a perfect camouflage, no one would believe that a woman with a small child would get involved in an adventure like this.

"Exactly.....," Mario said exhaustedly, sitting down on a sofa and placing his head in his hands.

"We'll go to Naples pretending to be a couple on their honeymoon... we'll be a lower middle class couple and we'll stay in a small hotel, maybe in Marechiaro or Posillipo..." the woman continued.

"It seems like a Neapolitan song to me..." Mario replied

Cynthia suddenly became serious: "Listen my love, I am much stronger than I seem, in New York I frequented environments where you would never have even approached, opium dens are not nursery schools... In Spain I have been to the dives of all the cities of the republic and those under Franco's government, nothing has ever happened to me... nothing will happen to me this time either"

Mario looked at her, astonished: "What the hell are you telling me...?"

"I'm telling you what my life was for a certain time...."

"But...but the smoke shops, the taverns, what were you some kind of..."

"Prostitute..?... No my love, in New York I ended up in those places because I hoped to free myself from the nightmares of my childhood, I didn't succeed, and I risked ending up even worse, a university friend of mine saved me.

In Spain you know very well what I did, or at least you know part of it...."

Mario felt his world collapse, he wanted to run away, maybe they had framed him in an operation using that woman as a trap, and then what the fuck was the guarantee that that son was his, with what he had done for the world he could have been anyone's.

She looked at him and almost as if she could read his mind, she said: "You're wondering if, with all the adventures I've had, this son is yours...right?"

Mario was embarrassed and nodded a sort of yes.

Cynthia went into another room, and returned shortly after. She had a medical report in her hand, written in English, the heading was Good Samaritan Hospital, 255 lafayette Avenue, Alliance, Ohaio. It was a blood test of the child.

"In America we started doing this kind of thing a while ago. I have to tell the truth, the researchers are not exactly good people, they do this research to verify that there are no traces of African blood among the children of the families who send their children to Harvard.

But Stephenson wanted to be sure he wasn't fooling you. He knew your grandfather, as many English agents did, and he didn't want to fool you.

All British foreign agents in Europe were classified by this system, to ensure that they were protected from infiltration and camouflage by enemy agents. Every man has a precise mark in his blood, and this system identifies him."

She gave him another sheet, same hospital, name of the owner of the blood Carlo Vassalli of Santa Tecla. Mario looked at the two reports they were almost identical except for one detail, Cynthia pointed it out to him, that data indicates that a part of your son's blood comes from Africa... it's my contribution. Cynthia smiled a little bitterly.

"You don't have to worry, though, because your son will be born in a few days, so we won't have any problems. My mother was working in the fields with my father two hours after giving birth to me. We come from a family of slaves, and there's great strength in our blood.

The party had been going on for about an hour. The important people hadn't arrived yet, but Countess Von Testory cared little about the so-called important people. They weren't effective sources of information. When they were big mouths, they limited themselves to telling trivial gossip that everyone knew. When they were smart, they provided all the news that was convenient for them and nothing useful. But there was a group of people who did interest her. They were people who wanted to make their way in the "high society." Especially the wives of second-rate hierarchs, who had understood that gossip helped, made them accomplices and this tied them together inextricably. It was a psychological bond made of trust and fear of betraying each other. Of shared envy for those who were already someone, usually by birth, for those who had made it and occupied a social space that others, less fortunate, who had come out "from the wrong hole" as someone, a little more direct than the others, said, couldn't occupy.

The "truth", which is very often a very uncomfortable thing, for them was a way of qualifying themselves as "people to trust" and therefore who could be recruited into high society, and possibly by the secret services, Lise Marie Von Testory, born Elizabeth Schragmuller, known in the world of intelligence services as Anne Lesser or Madamoiselle Docteur, was thinking. For example, there was that giraffe called Aminta Brocca della Fonte. She was married to a guy who belonged to the fallen Roman nobility. People who had gambled away everything or almost everything in the long Roman nights. The guy, however, strangely enough, did not have the vice of gambling, but was a merchant

With extraordinary swindling skills. He had started trading in food, between the Roman countryside and the province. In Rome he had opened a business that traded in "delicatessen". Products from all over Europe and the world, which supplied the tables of many newly rich, who emerged from the First World War with their pockets full thanks to war speculation.

The Quadrumvirs of the March on Rome had benefited abundantly and gratuitously from the Della Fontes' activity, it had been: "...an investment" that had brought good results and had made Della Fonte the official supplier of the PNF bosses in Rome and the surrounding area, and his wife Aminta a regular presence at all the celebrations, and also an inexhaustible source of information, mostly malicious and consequently true.

Von Testory had immediately sensed the woman's spy potential, which was all the more valuable because it was involuntary and therefore probably reliable.

The spy had established very close relations with the woman, providing him with some openings among the German relatives of the black nobility who had faithfully served the Kaiser during the First World War.

But above all he had given her "attention"; he complimented her on the clothes, often expensive and undoubtedly elegant, that the woman wore. Her good taste in dressing was indisputable and aroused the envy of many bourgeois women, who with the advent of fascism and the war profits, had invaded Roman high society, who never missed an opportunity to denigrate Aminta, gifted by nature with a masculine physique and an excessively long neck that gave her the appearance of a giraffe, also supported by an elongated face and a nose that was not exactly French. In short, Aminta was ugly but elegant, the wicked gossips of her circle had begun to nickname her, even with some good reason: "Giraffona"(big giraffe).

The psychological refinement of the German spy had made her understand that inside that body, not exactly that of a nymph, there was hidden a certain good taste, at least in clothing.

But the good side of the woman stopped there, for the rest she knew how to cultivate a deep hatred towards any woman who was slightly less ugly than her. This hatred pushed her to investigate through her knowledge the lives of these phantom adversaries of hers.

She decided to unleash the ferocious Giraffona against his target, the young American woman he had glimpsed together with what must have been a descendant of his lifelong enemy, Count Carlo Vassalli di SantaTecla.

Aminta was with some "friends" intent on criticizing the outfit of Achille Starace's latest lover,

Von Testory saw her and signaled for her to follow her.

"Hi Aminta, I wanted to give you some news..... I have the name of the new lover of......" he remained hanging

"...well, then,..." said the other

"No, I'll only give you the news if you give me some information...."

"Tell me...what do you want to know" said Giraffona with a sly grimace

"I need news about that foreigner we saw the other day at Capannelle with that air force officer..."

"Ah, the American..."

"Exactly, a certain monsignor is interested..."

When something interested Aminta her ears turned red, at that moment they took on the color of fire.

"Well, you know, it's not like I know much... it seems like he's in the Air Force Minister's circle. You know, Balbo, after the transatlantic flight, has a lot of friends with the stars and stripes..."

"Ah if that's the case, it means I'll tell my monsignore that my sources only have generic information..."

"And no my dear... no one says that Aminta is generic..."

Aminta asked, sniffed, gossiped in exchange for information, spread false news to obtain denials that would confirm his news,

Then she made an appointment with Von Testoty at the church of Santa Anna in the Vatican. Since she was officially the wife of one of the "Palafrinieri" of the Vatican, precisely Count Von Testory, that was her parish, where, from the day of her return from Germany to the Roman theater, she went regularly to mass, to observe and lengthen the ears.

"So," Aminta began, "I know who she is......." And she reeled off a series of information about Cynthia.

"So it seems she is the daughter of an English diplomat. It seems that at a certain point she disappeared from Rome for a certain period of time, then she reappeared quite pregnant..."

"And the air force officer...?" asked Mlle Docteur without showing her interest.

"Oh but is the monsignore interested in the American woman or the aviator..?"

"No, just curious..."

"The aviator is a Nord Italy's Nobleman, a certain Mario Vaillante, the nephew of a great friend of Balbo, Count Vassalli...."

Mlle Docteur felt as if a sword of fire was piercing her heart, but she skillfully concealed her confusion.

"However," added the Giraffona, "your monsignore will have to forget about this fuck, unless he wants to move to Naples......."

The German woman flinched.

He pretended to have seen someone and quickly greeted the gossip girl who remained there, as if stunned.

Anne Lesser quickly returned to her apartment and ordered her maid to pack her bags. The time had come to move to the city of Vesuvius.

4.6 Naples, Chiaia seafront….. Sabine enters the game

It was late morning and people were walking along the Chiaia seafront talking and gesticulating, it was Sunday and almost everyone had a small bag containing pastries. They went to relatives' houses for the festive lunch, a typical ritual of the place, it was part of the family spirit of southern Italy, something that Sabine didn't mind at all. She had traveled the world with her father and mother, when the latter had died still quite young the last ties with her hometown and the families of her mother and father had been lost. It seemed nice to her that people of the same blood met every Sunday in front of enormous plates of spaghetti, seasoned with "do Ragù" that usually the eldest of the women had made with the help of all the others, daughters-in-law, sisters, etc.

He was walking along Via Caracciolo, and the street urchins were circling him: "Miss, how beautiful you are, but are you a foreigner...? And give me ten cents, you are rich...", they asked, holding out their hand.

A rather elderly and elegantly dressed gentleman approached: "Guy, come on, I'll take care of the young lady... excuse me, madam, I can accompany you" he said, offering his right arm.

At that moment Sabine saw the athletic figure of her father appear near the Santa Lucia dock and head toward her.

He turned seriously to the mature Don Juan: "If you allow me," he said with a strong Suisser Deutsch accent, "the young lady is with me."

Sabine grabbed her father's arm and looked at the intrusive Neapolitan with a certain detachment. "Scussate…" (I'm sorry) the man said with an eloquent gesture, and walked away mumbling "sti cazz e tediesc…"(thay fucking german)

He looked at his daughter with a feigned stern expression, accentuating the Suisserdeutch accent: "Young woman, you are not here to pick up seasoned Don Juans."

"No…?" Sabine asked, with a questioning tone. "Too bad, how about you explain to me what I'm here to do?"

"Let's go to the hotel, and I'll tell you everything," Fabian concluded, and quickly hailed a taxi, dodging a couple of street urchins who were offering to find him a public car.

4.7 Naples Central Railway Station……the devil lands in Naples

Luderitz yawned, the train was entering the Naples station, on the platforms there was the most varied humanity imaginable, vendors of everything from lemons to water, to pizzas and so on and so forth. That crazy mess, that noise and those colors reminded him a lot of the African markets where he grew up. Instead of Herero women, there were ladies in modest clothes, and other very elegant ones, who wore very original hats and were accompanied by equally elegant men who chatted happily among themselves.

Two Carabinieri in full uniform, with lantern hat and plume, and with imposing moustaches, walked, looking around, with a stern expression, which had the magical effect of making the crowd part before them, like the biblical Red Sea.

Fraulein Doktor had ordered that they arrive in the city on different trains. There were three of them: he, the woman and a young physics professor, Kurt Diebner, who had accompanied

Wirth at the request of the mission leader. Diebner understood much more about physics than Wirth did, he was less fanatical, even if his loyalty to Nazism was proven, he did not feel the constant need to prove it.

Diebner would arrive last, he was coming directly from Germany, brought by a plane, piloted by Rudolf Hess himself. It seemed that they wanted to include the entire top brass of Nazi Germany in that adventure, all that was missing was Hitler himself.

He did not agree with these appearances. The fewer people entered and the less known these people were, the better. Needless to say, the Fraulein agreed with him entirely.

They had arranged to meet at the German consulate at 2 pm. The diplomatic office was located in Via Medina, a central area of the city, not far from the seafront.

The lady had taken lodgings near the consulate. At the Hotel Isotta & Gèneve.

He hadn't decided yet, but he was thinking of looking for a guesthouse not far from the University. In order to be able to keep an eye on the area where their target could be moving.

His problem was moving freely around the city, he looked too German, street urchins, salesmen and scoundrels of various kinds tormented him, asked him for money or just his attention. It didn't bother him, but moving around the city with that crowd wasn't the best way for an agent who had to be noticed as little as possible. So he decided to get some cheap clothes. He dyed his hair, brown, he couldn't do anything about the color of his eyes. He decided to use dark glasses, like blind people, he would say he had an eye disease and the light bothered him

4.9 *Steamer Ostenbug........ sailing in the Southern Tyrrhenian Sea, close to the port of Naples*

Anne had taken it easy, she had decided to follow the most tortuous road possible to get to that southern city. Italy had been the scene of her exploits many years before, she had worked further north, in Rome and Florence, and she had also been in Milan and Venice which was then Habsburg Empire. A lot of time had passed, she had changed a lot, but the world in which she moved did not allow for mistakes, a banal coincidence was enough, a memory too sharp, a person too curious, a nostalgic lover or nostalgic, and everything could be lost.

She arrived at the port aboard a transport ship that had left Rio a month earlier, had stopped in Hamburg to unload wood and load coal, which would be transported to Naples where the ship would load other goods to be taken back to Brazil. A triangulation that allowed the shipowner to have his ships always loaded, and profit from every passage of goods. The ship was a modern and well-built steamer, the crew was made up of German sailors, all ex-servicemen of the Kaiserlische Marine. She had entered the ship disguised as a man, a disguise that she was particularly good at, which she often used to frequent the brothels of Hamburg, it had always worked well for her and she had never had any problems. She knew the shipowner personally and he had helped her by introducing her as one of his inspectors, Mr. Kunzer, who had to go to Naples for an inspection of the company's warehouses. The captain, a taciturn and incurious man, had simply nodded and taken a couple of puffs from a small pipe made from corn cob, then accompanied her to the purser.

The latter had grumbled a bit, because he would have to give up his cabin for the duration of the voyage to Naples. But the German navy, even the merchant navy, was not a place where one could argue.

So Mr. Kunzer stood on the bridge and calmly watched all the docking maneuvers, the newly built maritime station welcomed her as soon as she was able to step off.

She left the port on Cristoforo Colombo Street and had a street urchin help her find a public car. She had him take her to the consulate and then walked to the Hotel Isotta & Gèneve, where she had her luggage delivered by another route. Naturally, the reservation was in Kunzle's name; she intended to keep that disguise for the entire time necessary for the mission, which gave her a subtle and slightly perverse pleasure.

The doorman greeted her with a greeting in very good German, did not try to make conversation, and pocketed the substantial tip that the strange guy slipped into his pocket, with the request to protect his privacy as much as possible. She told him one of her favorite stories: he was looking for his daughter who had run away with an Italian immigrant of Neapolitan origins. He wanted to bring her back to Hamburg, whether she agreed or not and therefore he would need to not have any problems, if it was a question of being a little "authoritarian". The man signaled that he understood, the tip had made a strong contribution to the understanding of the problem...

Berlin 76/78 Tirpitzufer

The admiral was concentrating on reading a phonogram coming from Argentina, the local agent reported the movements of English merchant ships, which were carrying coal and one of them that had stopped in the Falkland Islands, alias Malvinas, unloading personnel, whose activities were completely mysterious.

He heard a knock at the door: "come in..." trying not to lose his concentration on his reading.

A sailor entered, snapped to attention and saluted.

"A package for you, Admiral"

The officer looked up: "Go ahead, Schaubele..." The sailor approached and handed him a yellow envelope.

The admiral turned the unaddressed package over in his hands. "Where did this come from?"

Schaubele shrugged. "The orderly at the main door told me that a distinguished gentleman with a party badge had brought it in and told him to give it to you... oh, yes, he also said that it was the poems he was expecting..."

The officer did not change his expression: "Oh, okay Schaubele, go ahead."

He returned to his desk and opened the envelope. He began to read, his face relaxed and then a smile appeared. "Old comrades in arms are a precious resource... now he knew what the Nazi team in Naples was made up of, what they were called, and the code name for the operation: "Schwartze Sonne!"

He quickly put on his coat and went out. He turned left and walked along the Tirpitzufer, along the Landwher Kanal, to the Benderlucke, crossed the canal on the bridge, and walked along Genthiner Strasse. He entered a private building. He greeted the caretaker. An elderly gentleman, wearing a tattered sailor's cap, smoking a meerschaum pipe and sporting two mighty Teghetoff sideburns.

The man saluted calmly, without showing too much deference. The officer entered a basement, descended twenty steps, and found himself in a rather large office, with a series of teletype machines and four telephones.

"Put Parhenope on me, please..." he ordered the young man sitting in front of one of the telephones...

Rome.... *The Hunter and the Prey*

The baby was born a few weeks early, but had no problems. She had very dark skin, but very light eyes. She slept a lot and was content to be breastfed, falling asleep immediately afterwards.

Mario, however, was equally worried. He understood little about children and fatherhood, even if the emotion he felt in seeing that little creature asleep, or that smiled at him when she was awake and looked at him, caused him a very strong emotion, such as he had never felt before.

Cinthya had wanted to take care of the child herself. Her stepfather had put at her disposal the best nannies in Rome and all the service personnel she had requested, but she had declined the offer. She had kept her personal maid, a colored girl from Virginia who had been with her practically forever, her name was Charman, she did not in any way resemble the colored nannies that American cinema would soon throw onto the screen, with a deep vein of racism, masked by Uncle Tom's Cabin do-goodism. She was thin, tall, with a stern expression, and an education that would have made a professor envious. But she was colored, and in America, the so-called homeland of democracy, that meant having no chance in society.

Stephenson was counting on the fact that as soon as Mademoiselle Docteur spotted Mario among her adversaries, she would be attracted like a decoy. She would listen to her instincts and her anger instead of her rationality. Stephenson knew that woman inside out. He had applied himself, the English secret services had a great deal of information about her, often contradictory. Then there were the missions in which she apparently had participated. Stephenson had found a series of common elements, a precise style of behavior. The spy was always very precise, very careful, she made no mistakes. But she showed a singular passion for the bizarre. She always left a mark, like a signature, and it was always something singular. She never stopped humiliating her adversaries, but always leaving very specific marks. It almost seemed as if every time she wanted to remember the treatment that Mario's grandfather had reserved for her, leaving her tied up in that obscene way in the hands of the French police. She had only killed an enemy agent once and she had done so by tying him up and leaving him obscenely dressed as a prostitute, hanging from the door of a convent.

Another time he raped a British agent with a fake dildo.

In short, she seemed to feel the need to break out of her German precision and coldness with some unusual behavior.

Stephenson was certain that she would not miss an opportunity to make Mario pay for the humiliation inflicted on her by her grandfather, and to pursue this lust she would distract herself, she was too much a slave to her impulses, despite everything in the end she gave in to them, she tried to do it only at the end of the game, so as not to compromise the operation. But this time the temptation was too strong, Stephenson was certain that she would fall for it.

Mario knew it, Stephenson had told him, he knew he was exposing himself and his family to the cruelty of the enemy spy, but the operation was too important and so in the end Mario had accepted, after the officer, who was practically his father-in-law, had sworn to him that the little girl would not run any risk.

4.10 Naples December 1937.... Professors, thieves and spies

There was a bit of a queue, after all on Sundays it was difficult not to find a crowd in what was considered one of the best pastry shops in Naples, Scaturchio was famous for a series of excellent specialties, both traditional and created from time to time, such as the Ministeriali, delicious chocolate medallions, filled with a liqueur cream, whose recipe was one of the best kept secrets of the Neapolitan city.

Professor Carrelli had bought a box of them and was walking away, making his way toward the exit between couples of bourgeois men in their party clothes. Dandies who wanted to impress some young lady of high society; families who, having left the church of San Domenico Maggiore, in the square in front of the pastry shop, had decided to invade the shop for a collective ritual of purchase that involved long and complex discussions between dad who wanted " Babbà", mom who preferred the pastiera: "which mom liked ecchiù (the most)..." and the children who wanted to gorge themselves on sfogliatelle. The professor extricated himself skillfully from that crowd, even hastily greeting some acquaintances, and trying to avoid the bothersome and intrusive people of every kind, who all seemed to have arranged to meet in that place, at that time.

Finally he reached the door and stepped out, but bumped into a remarkable pair of breasts. He looked up and saw that they belonged to a girl of about twenty, with a dazzling smile, freckles and a pair of tortoiseshell glasses, behind which shone two beautiful blue eyes. Carrelli looked at her embarrassed and heard a voice coming from his left that he thought he recognized, the accent was German, or rather, it was suisserdeutch... and it was that of, "Rinchweiser... What are you doing here in Naples?"

"Carrelli dear. How nice, long time no see. Expectations from that conference in Zurich on the electronic Raman effect..."

"And the other one already replied, it's been six or seven years... but I still remember your hospitality" meanwhile the professor was glancing sideways at the young woman he had bumped into, who was arm in arm with the Swiss diplomat.

"Oh by the way, you don't know Sabine..." the Swiss said in a somewhat ceremonious tone,

"Sabine, Professor Carrelli"

"Professor, my daughter Sabine"

Carrelli's face widened in a dazzling smile: "Ah, good morning, you are famous, they say you were the only one who could follow Majorana's lessons without collapsing exhausted after five minutes..."

Sabine gave a small, humble smile: "Mathematics has always amused me a lot... it's cooking that unfortunately..." and she made a typical Italian hand movement, thumb and index finger in a pistol shape and a rotating movement of the wrist.

Carrelli, looked a little more serious: "Well, I hope that at least in Switzerland women are no longer measured by their culinary skills....."

"Noooo, not from those, but the real test of fire is knowing how to do the laundry....And I know that too..."

"Well, it means she will marry a Russian, they say that there women are considered the same as men…"

Sabine shrugged.

"By the way, I was told that the professor teaches here…" Rinkweiser said nonchalantly.

Carrelli seemed to be completely taken aback: "Excuse me, which professor…"

"Majorana, no…"

"Oh yes, of course, they gave him an honorary chair, theoretical physics. The trouble is that the results haven't changed. The students still don't understand anything, and he's getting weirder and weirder. Since he came back from Leipzig… well, Ettore wasn't easy to understand, but after Germany, he's become an enigma. He wanders around the Spanish Quarters, always hunting for books on the most varied subjects, from shipbuilding to medicine. I don't see him often, I know he's locked up in a room at the Hotel Bologna, on Via DePretis. He's a hypochondriac like an eighty-year-old. He always carries a leather bag… who knows what he's got in it…"

Then he looked at Rinkweiser: "but… maybe he'll keep some breakfast there…"

Christian had memorized all of Carrelli's statements, without attracting attention.

"You know, a few days ago we were talking about him with Fermi in Rome…" Rinkweiser hinted.

"But what is Ettore Majorana's month," Carrelli said, "the day before yesterday a German came, a curious guy… his name was …… wait… panzer maybe or something similar, he said he was the administrative director of the University of Leipzig and he was looking for Ettore because they had to give him back some money, I don't know how much, because he had paid too much for the accommodation… but it seems bizarre to me."

Sabine tried to investigate: "It's strange that the administrative director of a university comes all the way to Naples to return four marks… what kind of guy was he?"

"but not too tall, beard and moustache, well dressed, too much so to be a German, he gave me the impression that he was... let's say a little effeminate" he said with a wink.

"For heaven's sake, a German queer man looking for Majorana, surely he hasn't changed sides in Germany?"

Carrelli smiled: "I doubt it very much, Ettore is very strange, but I could swear that he is not in that sense"

Chatting they crossed the square and headed along Via Mezzocannone.

"But you," said the professor, "why are you in Naples? Don't tell me you're on vacation, in February..."

"Sort of, I came to pick up Sabine, who was in Rome for some archaeological research... while we were there we thought we'd pop over to Naples...."

"Are you staying a long time...?"

"Some days, Sabine doesn't know the city and I wanted to show it to her..."

"Then you have to come visit me," Carrelli replied. "I'll take you to Zi Teresa's for dinner, she makes a wonderful pizza."

Luderitz

Tracking down the scientist was the equivalent of hunting for a needle in a haystack.

Madame had also made her attempt. Disguised as her Kunze, she had gone to the university, asking for Majorana, with the excuse of a reimbursement of expenses for her trip to Germany. A flop that too, and perhaps also an inappropriate performance, which had discovered them with the competition.

Horst thought of disguising himself as a beggar and starting to guard the university. In Naples, being a beggar was not easy. After observing a few, he realized that a German would never have succeeded. Too much folklore, too much warmth. The

Carabinieri and the Police did not leave them much space. And then the monopoly of the market was in the hands of the scugnizzi, orphans from the poor neighborhoods of the city: "the Spanish neighborhoods", who had a real professional paradigm. The idea of using this disguise to guard the university without being recognized was to be discarded.

Could he recruit some? No... he wasn't sure how to control them and he risked getting "ripped off" as they say in the local language.

In a foreign city, and a southern one at that, it was really difficult for a German policeman to gather information.

He had read everything he could about the city and its peculiar habits, but he couldn't find the right balance. He had learned Italian, but his "crukko" accent was too strong and risked giving him away.

He had spoken to some local informants, connected in some way to the Nazi party. They were essentially people who traded with Germany. None of them had been of any help to him.

He had gone to the places where all the Neapolitans usually gathered, restaurants, churches, pastry shops. But he had not intercepted anyone who even remotely resembled Majorana

He was doing amateur work.

Then he had an idea. A banal thing, to ask one of the Nazi sympathizers to send one of their errand boys to find out more. Going round all the hotels, to begin with, hoping not to have to investigate the bed and breakfasts as well, in Naples there were more of them than pizzerias.

The man had an office, at the port.

Luderitz went there on a cold day when he had discovered that the REX was coming into port, which would probably mean a large crowd, which would have better allowed him to blend in with the crowd.

The sympathizer was a former policeman. An austere character quite different from the average of other Neapolitans, rather cold and detached, while collaborating he kept his distance.

He listened to Luderitz's request with his elbows on the desk and his hands clasped together as if in prayer. He let him finish calmly and then, in a low, grave voice, he said.

"Comrade, you should have contacted me first, you would have saved a lot of time.

As I imagine happens in Germany, the police headquarters is informed daily of the arrivals of people in the city. Hotels and bed and breakfasts must hand out information sheets, which are collected in a special archive called: Guestbook.

Do you have any idea when he arrived in Naples?"

"I guess early November..."

"Imagine or are you sure..."

"Let's say I'm eighty percent sure..."

"It's a good chance....I'll turn to a friend and we'll see where this gentleman is.

Naples....Walter

He made a complete circle around the horizon with the periscope, twenty degrees to starboard of the submarine a fishing boat was approaching. From the bridge of the vessel, light signals in Morse code started: two dots, a dash, a dot, pause two dots a dash a dot.

Thirty seconds passed and the signal was repeated. The letter f of the Morse code.

Walter retracted the periscope and gave the order to surface.

He was wearing civilian clothes, his second looked at him: "Are we back with masks and daggers?"

Walter smiled: "No. They are offering me a holiday in the Mediterranean sun, a reward for my faithful service to the Führer's orders..."

"Yes, in the Spanish taverns, next time I want to go..."

Walter winked at his colleague, and quickly climbed the ladder to the bridge.

Luckily the sea was calm, he climbed into the dinghy which he had brought alongside to starboard.

It took them three hours to get to Naples.

He greeted the captain of the fishing vessel, who responded with a grunt.

Leaving the port area he began to walk towards the city, it was morning, the city was in motion. The appointment was at the Church of Santa Lucia a Mare. The contact was a priest, his name was Don Salvatore Vitiello. He was of medium height, with a crew cut and a square head, like his torso. He gave the impression of a sort of futurist monument. He welcomed Walter with a big smile.

"Dear Mr. Muller, how are you? Have you received the graces you asked of the saint?" he asked with a questioning expression.

"Not all of them, but a good part of them," Walter replied with his German accent.

"Well, I'll take you to your residence, first we have to go to Parthenope. There are instructions for you..." continued the futurist monument.

There were people on the streets, a bit of everything. Bank clerks in uniform with briefcases under their arms. Dandys going who knows where. Well-dressed ladies with their waitresses carrying their shopping baskets. Street urchins begging. Street vendors. Walter loved that city, he had been there a couple of times on duty.

He liked that strange and variegated humanity, that human mix where there was a bit of everything. The good and the bad that each did their part, like in a "commedia dell'arte", having as a backdrop the ancient stones of a contradictory city that bore the signs of a grandiose past, similar to a very beautiful woman, badly aged, but still capable of surprising you.

Don Vitiello spoke, he told of his relationships with some German believers, very devoted to Saint Lucia, because of their sight, these believers "were regaining their sight" he said in an allusive tone, even if "it would have been better if they had not lost it in '33..."

He saw him on the left. He was a man badly dressed, everything he wore was either too tight or too loose, and patched, he wore a pair of dark glasses. But there was something wrong with him, an inconsistency between what he wanted to appear to be and what he was. A bell rang in Walter's head... well, damn the way he walked, he was straight as a spindle, tall with a straight back and the firm step of a soldier, It had nothing to do with those poor man's clothes.

Walter interrupted Vitiello's chatter.

"Excuse me, how long until we get there...?"

"It's here, a few meters away..."

"Don't stop, go ahead, let's take a ride..."

Vitiello made a surprised expression, but didn't say anything, obeyed and accelerated.

The man's tone of voice had suddenly changed. His expression had gone from jovial to attentive, his features had hardened.

Walter said: "Do you know if Parthenope is known outside of Abwher...."

Don Salvatore didn't turn his head, looking at the road he asked in a calm voice: "Do you mean to the competition..?"

"Yes but, the internal one"

"We never had this feeling, but in our profession there is never any certainty. Have you seen anyone you know...?"

"I'm not sure, but it's better not to risk it."

Instead he was absolutely certain, what he had seen was his stepbrother, he had felt him, in the same way as that evening in Hamburg.

Naples *Consulate General of Portugal...*

Anyone who happened to be in Via Santa Anna di Palazzo and observed the entrance to the Portuguese consulate that day would not have had any particular surprises.

At the diplomatic headquarters they had arrived one by one. An elderly lady, dressed entirely in black, with an aristocratic appearance, underlined by a pair of gold-rimmed glasses; a Portuguese naval officer in an impeccable uniform with a thick and well-groomed beard; a couple in civilian clothes, rather modest, pushing a wheelchair. A very elderly gentleman who walked with the help of a walking stick. The consul himself who chatted amiably with the military attaché at his consulate, an officer whose height was certainly above the average of other Portuguese.

Portugal was a neutral country, but with an ancient tradition of friendly relations with Great Britain, dating back to the eleventh century and culminating with the refusal of the Lusitanian country to join the continental blockade decreed by Napoleon Bonaparte. The consul in charge of the Naples office interpreted this friendship in a particularly personal and extensive way, maintaining a particularly close relationship with a former classmate of his from the prestigious college of Harrow, where his parents, wealthy producers of port from the upper Douro, had sent him to study.

The Marquis Francisco De Mello had been a companion in Sir Winston Churchill's heavy mischief.

And at that moment he felt like he was back in the good old days at Harrow,

he also hated the Germans, following an ugly incident involving border incidents with German colonial troops on the border between South West Africa and Angola.

He was therefore thrilled to lend a hand to Stephenson's team. Hosting them for their meetings in the building of his diplomatic headquarters, which no one would suspect.

The theatrical gimmick of the disguises had been Stephenson's idea, who, rightly, believed that one can never be too careful.

"The dress rehearsal," as Rinkweiser called it, was held in the consulate dining room.

They looked at each other, laughing like kids at a Christmas play.

Stephenson let the jokes settle like dust after a gust of wind.

"So we are guests of the Portuguese consul at this meeting to make an initial assessment of the situation, Rinkweiser has some information to give you..."

The elderly gentleman proved to be much more agile than he might have seemed when he entered the building a short while before.

"So gentlemen, Ettore Majorana is definitely in Naples. Carelli confirmed it to me during an exquisite dinner at ZI' Teresa - the Swiss smiled under his fake moustache -

He received a position at the physics faculty, and, at least once, he showed up.

The problem is that he has no friends. He only maintains official relations with Carelli. His students have seen him only twice, once in class and once in the library.

Unfortunately, it is difficult to obtain information from the world of physics scholars. Majorana has been isolated since some of his statements that appeared to be pro-Nazi and anti-Jewish have spread. In reality, I believe they are just naive statements, but anti-Semitism is a sore and very sensitive issue at the moment. Apart from that, neither Sabine nor I have been able to find anything about him. The city is big, we would need some good local contacts...

Westerhaupt ran his fingers through his beard with a puzzled expression.

"I had some contacts in the city a while back. I might try to get him back..."

Sabine spoke up: "As we knew, we are not the only hunters. A strange character with a German accent and effeminate ways asked for him at the university, with a rather childish excuse..."

Stephenson had a frown on his face: "I'm worried, the character you mention could be Mademoiselle Docteur. She loves disguises - he looked around, unable to hold back a smile - well, a bit like us.... Anyway, we have to do something more effective and soon. Mario, do you have any ideas...?

The Italian pilot looked around: "We could turn to some of our contacts in the police. Since fascism has existed, they have controlled everything, but there is the risk of running into some double-crosser..."

Stephenson looked pleased: his Italian son-in-law was learning quickly.

"Okay, let's get organized, without wasting any more time:

Walter tries to fish out your contacts. Cynthia, you have to move a bit in the high society linked to the papal nobility. I would like to understand how far ahead Mademoiselle Docteur is. She has reappeared in society with her stage name from the last war. Countess Von Testory. That woman is a professional, if she decided to show her flag there must be a reason. I think she wants to attract someone and gather information among her old German friends of the black nobility. But this time we have the priests on our side: right Walter?"

Walter nodded.

"Well," the Englishman emphasized. "The Catholic Church has set up an anti-Nazi network in Germany, which apparently even refers to His Holiness himself. It is called Schwartze Capelle, and you would be quite surprised to know the names of its members.

Walter, can you get some references from your boss?"

-Walter nodded.-

Stephenson resumed:

"Sabine.. would it be a problem for you to go back to college?"

"No," replied the young woman, "Physics Faculty?"

"I see you're still as intuitive as you used to be. Don't let yourself be too obvious. Our little bird will have to stop by his workplace someday, right?"

"Mario, you follow the police lead...but very carefully."

By the way, from now on we will have a password for everything that requires it, we need something....easy to remember"

"How about 'See you...'" Sabine said

"Yes it's easy but it can be confused with something that is not a password, it should be clarified..."

Mario looked at Chynthia and said: "See you in Budapest...."

The woman smiled: "yes, I like it...."

Naples........... German Consulate ......

The guard saw the little man enter and raised his head from the newspaper he was reading: "Bitte..?" he said.

The man took off his bowler hat and muttered "Arian feuer."

"Ah," replied the guard. "You are first, Mr. Wirth is waiting for you in the consul's office."

The little man looked around. Then he started towards the stairs.

He stopped in front of a door, on which was a brass scroll, which bore the inscription "Ervin Kunzer, Secretary of the Chamber"

He took out a key and entered the office.

The office had a second entrance, from which a lady emerged wearing a somewhat unorthodox black SS Helferine uniform, with the rank of standartneFhürer.

Wirth was reading a dispatch sitting at the consul's desk.

He noticed the woman after five minutes: He almost jumped in his chair, but controlled himself.

"Damn, madam... good morning" then he looked at the woman critically:

"Since when can SS female soldiers wear the rank of standartenfhürer?"

"Since when can a little professor sit at a consul's desk!"

the woman replied with a hard accent: "where are the others?".

"His physics teacher went to the bathroom, he says he can't stand Italian food"

At that moment the door opened and Diebner entered, the man's round, bespectacled face did not show its best expression, and was rather livid in colour.

Lesser fixed him with her usual penetrating gaze. "Good morning Kurt, ...too indulgent towards the hug ...?"

"It's called lamb," the man replied gloomily, "but that's not what hurt me, they don't even eat it here...I'm more inclined towards mussels, but I'm feeling better and ready to work...mein herren".

Luderitz was still missing.

Luderitz arrived soon after, with his usual detached air. He greeted those present. Wirth responded with his usual ill-concealed impatience toward the SS officer.

"Is there any news?" he asked.

Madame smiled sharply: "I really expect them from you...."

Luderitz reported the solution of the police offices,

"How long will it take...?" asked Madame

"Well it's not that simple, there are many hotels and many people coming and going from Naples"

"We don't have much time..." Wirth said acidly.

"We don't have many other solutions," Luderitz replied.

"Calm down, Wirth," said Madame. "Do you have any other solutions to propose?"

"The Reichsfhüre urgently needs to have the energy of the Atlanteans in its hands, Germany cannot wait for its destiny to be fulfilled...."

Madame raised a hand: "Wirth, keep your propaganda rants to yourself. When you were scrubbing toilets in the barracks, I was running a spy school that produced the best agents of the Nachrichtendienst Bureau. Don't come and lecture me about my duty to the Reich. I know Himmler personally and can have you sent back to scrub the same toilets in the same barracks with a phone call..."

Wirth turned pale and fell silent.

"Luderitz, go ahead and try to do it as soon as possible..."

"Madame...-he bowed his head slightly- by the way, it seems we have some strong competition in the field..."

"I know," Lesser replied, "I'll take care of that...."

Westerhaupt

What the hell was that guy's name... The one whose life he had saved one night in an alley in the Spanish Quarter? He remembered the nickname. "O' maestro". Maybe he had never known the name, now that he thought about it, but that guy had said to him "if you need me and I will do you a favor, in every way that a "Maronna"(the Holy Virign) wants to make us repay you...."

She wondered if it was a good idea to go looking for him, but maybe it was the only way.

The problem was "where" to go looking for him.

He thought about it all night. A restless night with many awakenings and strange dreams, in which he met his brother at the lighthouse of Helgoland, and his brother stared at him and pointed a finger at him in a threatening manner.

He had sent a message to his contact in the Abwhere, expecting a reply in the morning.

After this dream he got up to go to the bathroom. He started to pee and his gaze fell on an object that was right there, next to the toilet.

A bidet, the word passed through his head without leaving a trace.

He went back to bed and turned over a couple of times, and that word came back to him: bidet. Italians already put in hotel rooms what others put in brothels... brothels.

Shit, here's where to look for Aniello Spavone, known as "O'maestro", at the most popular brothel in Naples, in Vicolo Sergente Maggiore

Wirth

He was not satisfied with the way things were going. Himmler had entrusted that woman with a task too high for a female. How could he, they said that the woman had been Hiedrich's lover, and therefore.... But this was not a good reason to entrust him with an operation of this magnitude. He decided that he would not follow the orders of a woman. The scientist would look for him on his own. He would find him and kidnap him without the help of others, he would do it using the ancient wisdom of the Atlanteans.

Naples was a magical city, the crossroads of narrow streets that characterized the center: *Plateiai* and *Stenopoi* , in the ancient language of the city: Greek, represented the chessboard symbol of the universe, the representation conceived by the Pythagorean architect Hippodamus of Miletus, and if the city had been built by a Pythagorean there must have been a secret numerical system to solve any mystery.

He would have questioned Arithmomancy, or rather the technique called *Isopsephy*.

Marjorana

He woke up too early as usual, around six o'clock. He had been living at the Hotel Bologna, via Agostino Depretis, 72, for a day.

He had visited a few, but he didn't like any of them. This one wasn't exactly his favorite, but it had the advantage of not being far from the university. He had asked for a large, comfortable room, with a desk where he could work on his calculations. The window looked out onto Viale Depretis, and in the distance he could see the monument to Vittorio Emanuele in Piazza Bovio, or Piazza della Borsa, as the Neapolitans called it.

He had fallen asleep late, he was working on some calculations that served to demonstrate the existence and characteristics of a bizarre particle called neutrino.

He worked for nearly two hours, then decided to go out. He shaved, dressed, absentmindedly, thinking about the elusive particulars of the enigmatic particle.

He went out, lost in thought, then something called him back. The bag, the calculations that were in there, he couldn't run the risk of someone coming into the room and snooping or stealing them.

He returned to his room, did not take off his coat, looked at the worn leather of that object that contained the revelation of the worst danger that had ever threatened humanity. That object had been with him for years now. He opened the two latches, lifted the lid, and took out a notebook. He remained there looking at those accounts, as if he were enchanted,

"just enough to make a bang...what is the magic number of the apocalypse?" he mused....

He had stopped there, the last time, but he would soon return to it. He could not resist the urge to know...

Hotel Bologna

Like every day, the doorman of the Hotel Bologna, Otello Tripodi, finished his shift and put the "notification forms of customers requesting accommodation" in an envelope, there were only two. One was from Professor Ettore Majorana and the other from a French citizen, named Pierre Dusetienne.

He left the hotel, greeting his replacement courteously, and turned left, walked a few hundred meters and took Rua Catalana, which he followed all the way until it came out on Via Medina, at the intersection with Via Diaz. He stopped in front of the police station, greeted the officer on guard, who was about to stop him, then recognized him and let him pass. Tripodi went up the stairs, walked down a long corridor, smelling of old stale papers. The office of the "guest records" was still inhabited only by the officer on duty. Soon the other doormen of the city's hotels would arrive to do the same job that Tripodi was about to do. Hand over the records to an officer, who would put them in alphabetical order, and then go and cross-reference them with the wanted records, to verify who had arrived to cause trouble in the city.

After handing over his cards, Tripodi went out and almost bumped into a not very tall guy, dressed in dark clothes, with a very well-groomed beard and a bowler hat.

Othello muttered a "schussatemi" and continued on his way.

The man muttered something and continued on his way. After a few meters he entered the building at Via Medina 40, where the German consulate was located.

"O Maestro"

Walter had put on his old sailor clothes, which were certainly more suitable for entering a brothel than a Portuguese naval uniform.

In the antechamber there were about ten men, and two or three girls. The men were middle-aged.

At that time of the morning, the young people were probably at university and the older men were at work.

The girls tried to convince the visitors to make a decision and go upstairs. But they hesitated, perhaps they were afraid of making a bad impression or perhaps they didn't like the price.

Walter approached the counter where the Maitresse was.

The lady was over forty, but she maintained a lively expression. She looked at everyone with a kind, but firm expression as if her eyes were saying, "don't get any strange ideas..."

"Good morning sailor... but... we don't know each other"

"Maybe," Walter said with a sort of sigh.

"but yes, you've definitely been here at least two other times... and what do you want today, handsome young man... are you looking for some female in particular, some...- he paused and made a strange movement with his hand- some particularity "

"I'm looking for someone..."

"There are no people here, there are whores... professionals, you come here for a reason and that's it.." said the lady, emphasizing the enough with a gesture, as if she were cutting the air.

"I'm looking for a man..."

"Hiiii," the woman continued, "and you come here looking for him? And if you're a newbie, this isn't the place for you..."

"I'm looking for the master"

"Ah," the woman remarked, "nothing less... and who do you think is here..?"

"nobody.....an idea"

"Guagliaò, master, he's not a rich man.."

"Me neither, in fact I'm not looking for it to have sex..."

"Oh no....?"

"No.."

"And what a mess..."

"I can only say this to him in 'perzona'," Walter said, imitating the Neapolitan dialect.

The lady looked at him with a suspicious expression: "You know a lot...."

She turned and pulled a pendant behind her.

A man of considerable size, dressed as a waiter, appeared. The lady murmured something in his ear, alluding with her eyes to Walter.

"Do you understand...?" he concluded

"Okay... sir" said the giant.

"Follow the garsonne...." The lady nodded at the giant who was waiting for Walter, with visible impatience.

They descended some stairs, then followed a tunnel, little higher and wider than the giant's shoulders.

They came to a clearing. At the end there was an old door, but made of metal.

The giant took out some keys, opened the door, turned to Walter, moved away from the gap and signaled Walter to come in: "Come in." The man's deep voice resounded in the small cave.

The German wasn't very happy, but having no other alternatives he slipped into the gap.

The door closed behind him.

Leaving him in the dark.

Was it a trap?

He breathed slowly, there was no noise around. There was a faint underground smell, but also a strange scent of lemons.

He didn't know whether to move and grope around his surroundings or stay still.

He took a step

"Nicht bewegen" (*don't move*)

The sentence spoken in his language paralyzed him.

"warum suchen Sie nach dem Lehrer" (*why are you looking for the master*)

"Ich kann nur ihm persönlich sagen" (I *can only say this to him in person*)

There was no answer. Walter wondered if he had made a fool of himself by answering in German, that was how he revealed himself, and if these were adversaries it was like confessing.

The light suddenly hit him hard in the face. Strong hands blocked him.

From behind the light the previous voice said:

"Oh master, I want to know who you are and why you are looking for him. Don't make a mistake in answering, because you won't get out of this alive."

This time the voice had a Neapolitan accent, even though the sentence had not been pronounced in dialect.

Walter reflected, there was nothing to do but tell the truth at this point...

"I have known that man for many years, he owes me a favor and I need to find someone, here in Naples."

The light went out, the hands let go of him.

"You still haven't told me your name..."

"My name is Walter, but he knows me as O' Swede..."

"And why does he call you a Swede if you are German...?"

"Because I told him that my family was of Danish origin, and he started calling me Swedish.."

A slightly dimmer light came on, and in front of him, sitting at an imposing desk, was Aniello Spavone, elegantly dressed in a well-cut pinstriped suit, a white shirt, and a Marinella tie.

"Since when have you been speaking German, Maestro?"

"For a long time," the man replied, "I speak French, English, Spanish and some other languages.

In my job you have to understand everyone a little..."

"What job?" asked Walter, who had never understood exactly what Spavone made a living from.

"My job...." Concluded O master

"So how can I help you?"

"we are looking for a man...."

"We are....-said Spavone with a pause that seemed like a question mark_..who?"

"I fear this is part of my *professional secret...*"

"You are right, the fact is that Naples is a port, everyone and everything passes through here and my profession involves relationships with everyone, but in order to be taken seriously I have to be very careful about possible conflicts of interest..."

"I understand, let's say then that I and my ... companions in adventure, are certainly not on the side of the official representatives of the German government... to tell the truth, we do not like the Nazis."

Oh master reflected...: "OK, we can work together... tell me who you are looking for"

"A scientist. He is a man quite well known among physics professors.

He recently moved here, he teaches physics at the university, but he is rarely seen, both at the courses and among the few friends he has..."

"And, if it's not too much of a bother, what would this professor's name be...?"

"Ettore Majorana..."

"Ah.. and you know you're not the only ones looking for it, right?"

"Of course, we also have a pretty clear idea of who the competition is..."

"You know that Ovra was also involved..."

Walter was gripped by a certain uneasiness.

"Officially....?"

"No, it seems that someone asked for news about a traveler who was supposed to be staying in Naples in recent months... who has the same name as your man."

"Do you have any idea if they found him?"

"Not yet, but it's a matter of time..."

"Eeeeh – Walter said pointedly – are we still in time??"

"I'll find out and let you know, take a walk on Via Toledo, in two hours..., I'll let you know"

Totonno

Salvatore Esposito, known as Totonno, was the son of nobody: in Naples they called them scugnizzi, they lived by their wits, thefts, scrounge, and alms.

But he wasn't just anyone, he "got the shame of being a fool and a fool and a poor man" if he had to screw someone over he chose them well, with a well-fed wallet and well-dressed.

That day he had spotted one, he must have been a foreigner because he had come out of the German consulate, on Via Medina.

He seemed a little short for a German, he wasn't blond, and he walked in a strange way... Totonno thought he might be a little "faggot". He didn't make money with them, like other street urchins did, he was "a man" who wouldn't be touched for four cents: he offered services, and he got paid for those, not for anything else... At most he would steal a wallet, and that was exactly what Totonno was thinking.

The man turned to his right, walked towards the town hall square, while Totonno kept an eye on him, at an appropriate distance, he entered, always walking with his strange slow pace, in via SanGiacomo, staying close to the wall, but without giving the impression of being worried. He moved naturally, as if Naples were his city. He emerged in via Toledo, turned right while Totonno followed him at a distance, without difficulty, because the man did not seem to be in a hurry.

He turned right into an alley, and ventured into the Spanish quarters: something didn't add up; those were no places for foreigners. Above all, there was the risk that someone would arrive first and screw everything there was to screw before he could...

He was gone.." oh shit, he had disappeared with a ghost.

He thought and said all these things to himself, looking alarmedly along the walls of the alley: to the right, to the left... Suddenly an unexpected force threw him inside a door.

Someone had a hand over his mouth and, lifting him between his legs, squeezed his balls in a threatening grip.

"What do you need, kid..." a female voice whispered to him.

He tried to speak but couldn't: "a strangely soft hand prevented him from breathing, and the other advised him not to move, so as not to get his balls crushed.

"You're old enough to have balls...kid, so you understand that you're in a bad situation. Right...?" the voice whispered in his ear

He moved his head forcefully to confirm the words of his mysterious opponent.

"Well then," the voice continued, "I'll give you just a little bit of air to talk, but if you're clever, tonight you'll sing "soprano"... and it won't be easy for you to explain why to your mother."

"Don't care about your mother..." the urchin stated as soon as he could open his mouth.

"Oooh, but what a touching thing, an orphan, well it doesn't matter, if you're smart I'll squeeze your balls so much that you won't be able to produce orphans like you.."

Totonno attempted a touching tone: "Leave me alone, don't do anything, just walk down the street..."

"Of course not, look, I'm a foreigner...not stupid"

"All right, sir, you understand, but now I swear I won't do anything to you..."

"There you go, good job, ..." the hand continued to squeeze the balls, and the grip at the top did not loosen.

"Now listen to me. How far can you count?"

"up to a hundred lords..."

"Good now I'll let you go, you count ten times to one hundred- Totonno moved and his hand tightened around the family jewels- I'm not finished yet, the voice continued, while the hand lightly and very expressively squeezed its prey.

"I was saying that you count ten times to one hundred out loud, without moving from here and with your eyes closed. Then tomorrow morning do a nice thing. Go to the German consulate and ask for the doctor. Maybe wash yourself because you stink like a rotten fish.....And don't be smart because I know that you hang around Via Medina and next time instead of my hands I'll use a razor."

The hand loosened its grip. Totonno felt his persecutor moving away and began to count, screaming like a madman, to one hundred.

He had done it twice, when he heard a familiar voice. It was that of Assunta, the older sister of his friend Gennaro.

"Guys, you're becoming stupid..."

Totonno opened his eyes. The girl was looking at him curiously

"No.. and why didn't I take it any further and no more and I was doing a repasse..."

"I understood, the big man I rewieving. Listen to me as a scholar. O Maestro, I'll speak to you as soon as I hear from him..."

"Shit, he's not really at Christmas.." thought the street urchin.

"What the hell do you want with me...o "maestro""

"I'll have some supplies and a counter...what's waiting for you?"

Totonno looked around to make sure his mysterious kidnapper wasn't around. Then he started walking. O'maestro wasn't someone to joke with, but he was a fair person, if he asked you for something he paid and, normally, he didn't hurt the urchins: At least I hope.." thought Totonno.

Ascione

Corporal Ascione had been rummaging through the files for hours. He had checked the hotels in half the city.

But not all of them yet, the man who had given him that order was someone who was not part of the Naples police headquarters. He had introduced himself as Carlo Magri, an inspector who had come from the Pescara police headquarters. At least that's what he said. He had given him the order to find out where this professor was staying. Naturally he had given him no explanation.

He had found a first card, it was from a hotel near the Chiaia Riviera, but the professor had left from there and now where the hell could he be supplied.

Enter agent Viggiano, a Pugliese, on duty for a few months in Naples. A smart guy, and also nice, he joked with everyone and teased them, but without malice, and when he could he also gave a hand.

"What the fuck are you doing Ascione, are you trying to figure out if your wife is cheating on you in some hotel....?"

"I don't have a wife, I prefer to leave certain troubles to exuberant young men like you..."

"The truth is that you don't like women...you prefer faggots! And don't make yourself decency-wise, no...!"

"The "anema e sorete" (fuck your sister), slap me to break me my balls, with this fucking professor..."

Viggiano became serious: "Which professor...?"

"Some idiots who tell us he disappeared, and fuck if one of them is a schumper and if you see that he didn't want to piss off a dick..."

Viggiano half smiled, "Oh well Ascione: orders are orders, but excuse me, what do you have to do with the missing..?"

"Well, it seems that this guy hasn't really disappeared, maybe he just changed hotels."

"Oh my God, how many complications and it was obviously uncomfortable, they must have found a hotel closer to the schools...

"Who's not a professor and a student, he teaches physics at university... what the fuck is this physics anyway or does he know..."

"Okay, look in the hotels near the university...no"

"Damn Viggia, you're a genius, be right, hurry up, hurry up I'll see the hotels near the station..."

"Well done, leave it and thank you...", Viggiano said, laughing loudly and leaving the office.

"go fuck yourself – Ascione muttered to himself – you're a faggot... okay, let's see the hotels near the station"

It took a few seconds, and there he was, Ettore Maiorana; Hotel Bologna, via De Pretis 72, a stone's throw from the University.

Viggiano saw Ascione come out. He had nothing in his hand. This meant that he had not taken the hotel card he had consulted.

He waited until he had turned the corner of the corridor and entered Ascione's office. He was curious to know where the hell this mysterious character had ended up: this professor.

The Master and the urchin

Totonno looked at the tips of the big, worn boots he was wearing; they were a couple of sizes too big for his feet and he had put some rags in them.

His thin, dirty legs were sticking out from under a pair of shorts, also baggier than they should have been. He had two sweaters, which had seen better days, one over the other.

The "Master" observed him: "Totonno, what is it? Is business going badly...?"

"No, master," the child replied in a low voice without looking up.

"So what do you have for me? Look at my face, otherwise I'll come and think badly"

Totonno looked up suddenly: "No, maestro, it's...it's just that he gets scorned..."

Oh master burst into a loud laugh: "You...you take it as an insult? But do me a favour, face up to me like Pulcinella's ass... Come on, tell me the truth. What are you talking about?"

"Nothing, Master, and...and this morning...." And he told of the strange woman dressed as a man and of the threats.

The Master remained silent for a good two minutes, then sighed and began to speak:

"So, in the morning, you wash yourself like a bride on her first wedding night . Then you go away, to Vico De Zite and stay in Rosaria's, the ones who keeps the shop in the road, let's say that she'll give you a few better clothes, then you go to the fucking German and ask her what she is looking. You sey yes to everithing , and after come to me and i'll tell you what you have to do. Take it easy, no one cut your bals ... I comand in the alley not the Germans..."

Viggiano

He saw him pass in the corridor. He had never seen that man before, he was not a policeman from the Naples police headquarters and he should not have been in that corridor. He pretended not to see him, let him pass and looked where he was going. He entered the office of Commissioner Carretto, the official who followed the cases of those seeking accommodation. Ascione's boss, in short.

The man stopped for a very short time, came out with a cautious look, he had a piece of paper in his hand. He saw him going down the stairs and into the rooms that were normally reserved for the men of the OVRA.

He decided he had to talk to Ascione.

He found it in the archive where, as usual, he put away the hotel cards.

"So, did you find this professor...?"

Ascione didn't answer and made a face that was meant to be stony, but betrayed a certain embarrassment.

"Leave it... what do you have,...."

"Nothing," said the agent with a haughty expression, "I can't tell you all my things...there are secrets here...."

"Damn...what is this secret...or does the professor sleep at the mayor's house?

"I said I know secrets, don't tell you anything..."

"Hey "Madonna".. what a story, what do I care about this professor...!"

"There you go, you fucker, you live better...."

Viggiano went out, the naïve Ascione had revealed a half-truth, he knew where the professor was, and this was a secret. He had not even noticed that Viggiano had noticed that he was putting away the card of the hotel Bologna where Mairoana was staying.

The agent decided that the time had come to do the job he had been placed in Naples to do.

He left the police station and walked along Via Medina, came out in Piazza del Municipio and continued straight, passing in front of the San Carlo theater. He turned left onto Via Cesario Console, continuing until Via Santa Lucia. He was in front of the church of Santa Lucia al Mare.

He entered the church and approached one of the confessionals where there was a plaque where was writte: "Don Salvatore Vitiello"

The priest was not there, he looked at the clock, there were about ten minutes left until confession, he decided to wait patiently. Right after him a man entered. He was dressed as a sailor, a blue jacket, corduroy trousers and he was holding a peaked cap in his hand, a beard that covered half his face.

It gave him the impression that he was a foreigner. He saw that he sat down in a pew at the back. He was not praying, he was simply turning his cap over in his hands.

Wirth

He was sure, the professor had to be around there, his calculations, the intersection between platelai and stenopoi, that is, the streets and alleys of ancient Naples could not be wrong, he had done arithmomantic calculations, that is, he had put together the names of the streets transformed into numbers and those numbers had a magical meaning from which he had derived a geographical position. The professor had to be around there. His secret science was one that could guess, much better than getting help from those savages, from those short, dark-skinned characters, who spoke in that strange way, and who had probably been infiltrated by some Jewish diaspora, because they were too dirty, untidy and charlatans to be Aryans. According to his divination, the professor had to live near the sea, his calculations said so. He was walking along the Chiaia coast, looking for some sign of the professor when he saw Luderitz......Was it him? He seemed strangely different. He had a thick, dark beard that covered half his face, his hair was black. Strange, Luderitz was not like that, and yet that seemed just like him. And where was he going dressed in that strange way and made up like a vaudeville actor? Maybe he had discovered something... maybe with the help of some corrupt local policeman with a few lire and a few capons, he had managed to obtain the results he was looking for with the power of the Atlanteans.

He decided to follow him. The man was walking rather quickly, along Via Chiatamone, he seemed to have an appointment. Wirth followed him along the whole of Via Santa Lucia. He saw him enter a church. On the pediment of the building was written "DIVAE LUCIAE DICATUM VIRG. ET MART. PAT NEAPOLI DICATUM".

He approached too, and hesitated for a moment whether to go in or not. Then he saw a group of women coming in and slipped in among them.

He looked around and saw a police officer walking away from a confessional and Luderitz, or his double, slipping into the confessional itself.

Ten minutes passed and the man came out making the sign of the cross. He stopped in front of one of the altars and seemed to be praying.

Wirth was confused, strange... strange that Luderitz went to confession, strange that he prayed. Something was wrong: an SS man praying and confessing!?

So this man was pretending to be a Nazi and he was a Catholic believer. How could this have escaped the GESTAPO? He thought that it would shame him in front of........Then he thought. If he had done that, the female would have taken credit for the matter. No, he should have informed his superiors, so they would have rewarded him for the discovery and punished her for not having understood who she was dealing with.

He got up and quickly left the church.

Walther

As the priest had suggested, he pretended to recite prayers. He had an unpleasant feeling that he could not understand.

He had been hearing her for at least an hour, he had the feeling of being followed.

He looked at the people in the church. Only pious women, but someone had come out of the door,

He started walking and went out, outside he saw only ordinary people walking, the usual vendors and some beggars.

Well anyway now they knew where Maiorana was, Hotel Bologna, via Agostino Depretis.

Madame Doctor

The boy had done as she was told. He had followed the American girl wherever she went. And she wandered around Naples, went shopping, had only been to the university once, but only to go to the library to ask for a book. Then she had met the aviator several times. They had stayed in a couple of hotels, the best in Naples.

No contact with the professor! She was sure, what those two were doing was beating around the bush. A diversionary action. But there was someone else hunting the professor.

Luderitz had managed to find out where he lived: Hotel Bologna. They had put another urchin, Totonno's friend, to check that hotel. The professor had gone out twice to go to a tobacconist, but the rest of the time he stayed in his room, having his food brought there. Kidnapping him was not possible; the order was to take him to Germany with his consent. Heisemberg had said that it was impossible to keep him from doing anything. Diebner had to talk to him and convince him.

The good thing was that not even the others could get close to him, for the time being, and so they fiddled with diversionary actions.

Better to play defensively or better to go on the offensive? Eliminate the opponents and then approach him calmly. How many were there? Wirth had identified a Swiss diplomat, but then who else was there. Stephenson seemed not to be operational, probably coordinating the others. The Italian airman limited himself to fucking with the American. As far as they knew they had no idea where Maiorana was, so maybe it was useless to eliminate them, having them found dead would only have created noise. But it was strange, it seemed like they didn't do it. That's why she had decided to check on the girl a bit, to stick her nose in. She thought about these things while she observed her

About nose That American girl had a beautiful, perfect nose and emerald eyes and breasts of the right size and a perfect ass. She was Venus come down to earth.

And she had a great desire to touch her, to put her tongue in her mouth, to feel the taste of her sex and to enter inside her.

Mademoiselle Docteur was fifty years old, a life that had never been easy, too many men, too many women, too much morphine, too much violence. She felt corrupted to the root of herself.

Look at the girl who was talking to her enemy, yes the descendant of the one who had mocked her when she was still a girl. But she also felt for him the same desire that she felt for the girl, she dreamed of a partouze that would end... how: in a massacre?..Again?

And then, what would be left for her? The same feeling of incompleteness that she had felt irremediably after she had taken pleasure in killing someone. The same ferocious headache, which passed only with the long, soft numbness of morphine.

She contemplated that woman, young, beautiful and full of life and it seemed to her that she could see the desert that she carried inside. A desert full of carrion, which was beginning to give off a stench too strong, to make her feel dirty like a pond of still water.

She had to stop staring at the ruins of herself and think of a plan, to knock out the competition. One way or another.

Naples...the boss and the player

Lipari looked at the man in front of him, his gaze impenetrable, the other two, one to his right and one to his left, were shitting themselves. Lipari knew exactly what cards the dealer might be holding. That is, the man in front of him.

They had been playing since eight o'clock at night, and it was five in the morning.

Lipari could have won by a landslide but he had always been cautious, losing every now and then and always winning interesting sums but not enough to break the bank for everyone.

He had been frequenting the club for six months now and had managed to make up for the losses he had suffered in Sicily due to that cuckolded mafioso from Mazara.

They often met with the man in front of him. He too was prudent, shrewd, knew how to win and lose and was a fearsome opponent, Don Aniello, called O'Maestro. That evening, however, he seemed strangely imprudent and at that moment he had raised the stakes to a level that was not usual for him.

Lipari was tempted to see the game, that could be the opportunity of his life. Take the money and go to Monte Carlo to play in a richer environment, where he was not known and where he could make real money.

He decided to go and see Don Aniello's game, and made a tragic mistake, at least on the surface.

The man had a poker of kings, he just had a trio of aces, but most importantly he didn't have the money to cover it!

He was also sure that the three aces were fake. What did Mr. Spavone have in mind?

Luderitz and the fanatic

He was walking calmly and had decided to go and do a check-up in the area around the professor's hotel.

He would then go to his local contact, the same one who had helped him with the police, to organize Maiorana's exfiltration, which had to take place without attracting attention.

He saw Wirth coming towards him with an evil smile on his face.

"Good morning, Herr Luderitz, are you leaving so early to go to mass?"

Horst stared at him in amazement: "To mass? Her Wirth, did you overdo it with the grappa last night?"

The man took on a furious expression: "Who do you think you're kidding? I saw you the other day, you were wearing make-up and disguised...but you didn't fool me!"

Luderitz didn't understand, but there was something strange in the outburst of that madman, too strange not to have some reason. He decided to play along and pretended to try to divert the conversation:

"Santa Lucia? I don't remember ever being there..."

"In the church Herr Luderitz, you confessed and recited your penance..."

What the hell was in this guy's head? What church, what denomination, he had only been to some church in his life to be given a bowl of soup and that hadn't happened since he left the streets in West Africa.

"But maybe you got confused..."

"It was you, the dyed black hair and beard...you, you went to confession!"

Luderitz pretended to be completely astonished: "Ah, well, I was careless... it's a priest who works for us, I went to give him some orders and, of course, I had to play the part..."

"Aaahhh there you were acting, I understand... well what orders were you supposed to give him?"

Horst's expression became hard: "It's none of your business, you think about doing your job while I think about mine..."

"You think you can fool me with your tricks but I will reveal your game to my superiors,,,they will throw you out of the SS..."

"I advise you not to do anything stupid...you could suffer serious consequences..."

"We'll see," the professor replied angrily, turning and walking away in a hurry.

Horst remained still and thoughtful: what was the point of this farce, who the hell had that idiot seen and what did Santa Lucia have to do with it.

Unless......yes, unless.....

Walter...sliding doors 1

Maiorana's exfiltration was to be done in such a way that his adversaries would not find out where he had ended up. The Rinkweisers had to convince him to cooperate. He was to take a ferry to Palermo, get to the Sicilian city and be seen around. Then leave the city on another ferry to Naples and disappear on the sea route between the two southern cities, it was to look like suicide. Then no one would look for him anymore.

Luderitz...sliding doors 2

He decided to go and take a look around the church, Wirth must have seen something, and he wanted to understand what.

There was a remote possibility that the professor wasn't seeing double, but it made no sense, it made no sense at all.

Walter..sliding doors3

He had to go to Parthenope to get in touch with Berlin. He decided to take the seaside road, via Partenope, up to Castel dell'Ovo then right up the large Viale Santa Lucia.

He and Father Vitiello had a regular appointment every day at 11:00. If he was available, the priest would display a sign outside the confessional: "German." It was a way to talk about confidential matters without anyone understanding.

It was a bad day February was not nice even in Naples the sea, from which came a wind full of salt water, had a leaden color, marked by white streaks of foam. Walter raised the collar of his sailor jacket and pulled his cap down over his eyes.

Luderitz....sliding doors4

He decided to take a taxi. There were a couple of public cars near the consulate.

As usual, he had to get rid of the dozen or so street urchins who offered him help, asked for alms, and offered goods of all kinds.

He got off at the corner of Via Santa Lucia and Via Cesario Console.

There were few people around, a few muffled-up women trying to shelter under large umbrellas from the rain that had begun to fall.

There was a man wearing a jacket and his cap pulled down over his forehead who was entering the church, two beggars had taken shelter in the porch.

Walter....sliding doors5

Walter saw him getting out of the taxi and recognized him immediately. He immediately slipped into the church.

Damn, his stepbrother was going to stick his nose into the Parthenope headquarters, bad sign.

He slipped into the church quickly. He looked at his watch, it was 10:20, he looked for a place to take shelter so as not to be seen by his dangerous stepbrother.

He saw that Father Vitiello's confessional was free, he slipped in, hoping that the priest would not arrive early. The card outside was turned to Tedesco.

Luderitz...sliding doors6

He entered, there were some old women who were counting their rosaries and murmuring prayers. The church was imposing, in its baroque style. There were sacred paintings on the walls, probably valuable works. Horst thought he understood little about them. But above all he was finding it increasingly difficult to understand what this church had to do with him, and what Wirth had seen.

Then what was Wirth doing there? Maybe he had seen someone, had mistaken him for him, had followed him to the church to look for some good reason to cause him trouble.

However, he must have been observing that person for a long time, so he couldn't have been wrong.

But there was only one possibility, too remote...but in his profession, remote possibilities not taken into consideration were the basis of all failures.

The background hum of prayers had an almost hypnotic effect.

He began to walk down the side aisle, saw two confessionals. On one of them he could see a small sign. It said "German", what did it mean. Was it possible to confess in German?

He thought about confessing, but he had no idea what he was supposed to do. He saw a woman in another confessional muttering something at a window.

He entered the confessional from the side. There was a small rectangular window in the wooden wall, and inside there was a net that prevented the view of anyone who was probably inside the confessional.

But probably in the confessional there was some kind of door that closed the window itself, and which had to be opened by the confessor.

Was there anyone in the confessional?

Trying to find out could be risky.

Walter...sliding doors6

The curtain of the confessional was slightly ajar, and through it he glimpsed Luderitz approaching, looking around. He had taken off his hat and was holding his gloves in his hand. He had a puzzled expression. Walter took out the Mauser he had in his pocket. He couldn't let himself be discovered. A shooting in the church of Santa Lucia would be the worst thing he could imagine. He hoped he wouldn't have to resort to violence.

Luderitz....sliding doors7

He didn't know what to do, if there was a priest in the confessional he would have understood that he had no idea what a confession was. He would have had to run away and he would have seen him. This was not good.

He decided to leave. He heard movement further down in the darkness of the church. Someone was coming, he walked away quickly, trying to avoid appearing suspicious.

Walter....sliding doors8

Father Vitiello pulled aside the curtain of the confessional and found Walter in front of him. He had a movement of surprise.

Walter put his index finger in front of his mouth in an unmistakable sign for silence.

The priest stopped, seemed to hesitate and looked around.

Luderitz...sliding doors9

He turned back, a priest had approached the confessional, but was standing in front of it, he was turning around, he retraced his steps in the direction of the sacristy.

An old woman approached him and asked him in a low voice for alms. The German pushed her aside and headed toward the exit.

He had accomplished nothing.

He had to turn to his contact, the one who had dealings with the police.

Wirth...sliding doors10

He finished writing his report, put a seal on it and addressed it. It was addressed to Reichsfürer Himmler. Confidential, Personal.

He looked at her and sneered he had made a nice torpedo for that lesbian slut madamoiselle Docteur.

He handed the envelope over to the office in charge of diplomatic communications to Germany.

He then decided to return to his numerological research to locate Maiorana.

Luderitz... a strange sensation

Yet something must have happened, the only possibility that Wirth was not delirious was that his brother, the commander of U BOOT was in Naples. Doing what? He would think about it another time, now he had to deal with something else: he wanted and had to go ahead with the Maiorana exfiltration plan.

Did he have to be convinced first? He thought it would be better to use a minimum of force. The best way was on a ship, the problem was how to hide it.

Maiorana...the night

He always went out at more or less the same time. He had an agreement with the night porter who would leave him the keys, in exchange for a substantial tip.

He wandered around a mysterious and deserted Naples, over which the silence of rest had fallen.

It was cold but he didn't feel it, he walked until he was exhausted. His thoughts were whirling in his brain. The picture was now clear. Building the bomb was not easy. The real complication was obtaining the fissile material, that is, the explosive. It was necessary to have heavy elements, in which in simple terms the fissile nuclei were numerous enough and close enough to each other to trigger a chain reaction.

There were two possible types of explosive: enriching uranium-238 to U235, or extracting some other isotope from uranium already used in a controlled reaction.

Producing this material was very complex. It required high energy potentials, complex industrial processes and a lot of money. This was a major obstacle to producing the bomb. There were not many nations capable of producing an industrial effort of this size. Probably America and Germany, England and perhaps France. Others were to be excluded. Perhaps it would take more than one allied nation.

Ettore ended up going to Santa Lucia every evening. He would go to Pallonetto, then stop to look at the panorama of the city. Stretched out along the gulf, illuminated, with Vesuvius in the background.

He stood there, no one bothered him and he let his thoughts fly, which sometimes became dark. He was in a dead-end alley. He was the keeper of a terrible secret, so terrible that it was like a huge stone that was dragging him to the bottom.

The world was moving toward war. It was obvious, it was in the nature of things. No one could contain Hitler's Germany. He had lived there, he had known that proud and stubborn country. The Germans had been humiliated by the victors of a war that had not been won on the battlefields.

Hitler was the man that country needed. He understood that when he was there. But since no lunch is free, someone had to pay to have a leader like the Führer, and that would be the Jews. Then it would be the turn of the Czechoslovakians, the Poles and the French. The war could be like the last great war, but with the bombs he had in mind it could be much worse.

Where did the energy released by the bomb end up? The fission products, the enormous quantity of neutrons released, what consequences would they have had on the world. He had in mind the death of Marie Curie, no one had understood the origins of her aplastic anemia, but Ettore did: the long exposure to radiation emitted by the materials he worked with. If they had used atomic bombs that would have been the fate of humanity.

The sun was beginning to rise in the east, the light spreading across the gulf. It was time to return.

The urchins...... the eyes of the spies

"But what are you doing...look at the sea and us, like idiots..." said Pasquale, hiding behind the corner.

"Totonno said that we should "control" him," he made with an explicit gesture of his hand from top to bottom, "like two germans."

Pasquale looked at Antonio with an unconvinced expression. Then he saw that the man was walking back towards the city.

"Let's go, maybe this is the one who's going home...so we're going to take care of ourselves too."

They followed him to the hotel. Where Totonno was waiting for them.

"What did the professor do?" he asked the other two.

"But here, professor, it seems like a fool to me, come and walk around Naples at night and look at the sea..."

"What do you know, professor...he is an important guy..." Totonno replied in a know-it-all tone

He released the two accomplices and remained around, keeping watch on the entrance to the Bologna Hotel.

The relief would arrive in two hours and he would have to report to his masters.

Sabine

Now they were wondering where Ettore was. The problem was how to contact him.

Suddenly appearing in front of him was not a good idea, he would run away!

Leave him a letter at the hotel concierge... he would be alarmed, and then how to explain everything in a letter? There was also the risk that the concierge would warn someone from the competition and read the letter finding out everything... Unless you used a language that only she and Ettore could understand... physics!

She took a sheet of paper and wrote

An athlete after a sprint of 4 s with increasing speed, rapidly decelerates and stops in 2 s, then returns to the blocks with constant speed. The clock law with which he moves in the acceleration phase is s (t) = 1.2(t)^2; in the deceleration phase he has covered 9.6 m and when he returns to the starting blocks a total of 20.4 s have passed.

a) Find the time law s(t) that describes all three phases.
b) calculate the functions s'(t) and s''(t) and explain their physical meaning.
c) draw the three graphs on the same plane

The answer to a) is as follows:

s = s1 + s2 - s3

Where
s1 = 1/2 a1 t1^2
s2 = v2 t2 - 1/2 a2 t2^2
s3 = v3 t3

Furthermore

1/2 a1 = 1.2 from which a1 = 2.4 m/s^2
v2 = a1 t1 = 2.4*4 = 9.6 m/s and a2 = v1^2 / (2 s2) = 9.6^2 / (2*9.6)
= 4.8 m/s^2
v3 = s3/ t3 = (1.2*4^2 + 9.6) / (20.4 - 4 - 2) = 2 m/s

Therefore

s1 = 1/2 a1 t1^2 = 0.5*2.4*16 = 19.2 m
s2 = v1 t2 - 1/2 a2 t2^2 = 9.6*2 - 0.5*4.8*4 = 9.6 m
s3 = v3 t3 = 2* 14, 4 = 28.8 m

Indeed

s = 19.2 + 9.6 - 28.8 = 0

If you want to see me you must tell the person who brings you this letter where and when.
    He took an envelope and put the paper inside.
    Then he went out. He decided to walk, about 20 minutes, passing through via Chiaia, so also a nice walk.

He was at the door of the Swiss consular office when he noticed that something was wrong.

There was a black car parked alongside the curb opposite the consulate, a few meters back. Two people could be seen, they were smoking.

He decided to wait...an hour, if they were still there after an hour, it was clear that the consulate was under surveillance, and he would find a way to evict the two inconvenient people.

He returned to the small office where he shared a desk with his father, who that day had gone to the Portuguese consulate for an operational meeting with the team that was supposed to deal with Maiorana's exfiltration, and began writing a letter to the prefect of Naples.

In which he asked on behalf of the consul that any surveillance activity at the consulate by any local police force cease. He signed with the signature of the consul, which he knew very well how to imitate.... He would inform his father as soon as possible.

She got out, walked around the car and started walking along the sidewalk. When she got close to the window she stopped.

She knocked on the glass. The man inside whirled around. He had a thin, gaunt face, an olive complexion, and a thin mustache. Sabine gave him a broad smile and signaled him to roll down the window. The man looked halfway between pleased and knowing. "Good night," Sabine said, with a pronounced German accent.

"I am the secretary of the convent, I asked me to deliver this letter to you for the Prefect..."

and threw the envelope into his lap.

The man was speechless and was turning the paper wrapper over in his hands, not knowing what to do.

"They know it is true that the surveillance of diplomatic institutions by intelligence agents is not permitted by the Treaty of Lausanne of 15 July 1920...she bluffed.

The mustachioed one turned to his colleague, who was wearing an expression just as surprised as his.

Sabine decided to take advantage of her opponent's disorientation: "By the way, I think that Zua Excelenza Bocchini would not appreciate your lack of caution in letting the consul, whose office is right behind the window in front of which you stopped, notice you." She bluffed again.

They started the engine and drove off.

Stupid cops are also scary, they were lucky, they were probably just informants, a professional wouldn't have been fooled like that! Now he had to make the most of the time. Before another car arrived with someone a little less naive on board.

Near the consulate there were some public cars parked...but they couldn't be trusted, perhaps the OVRA was less stupid than it seemed.

He returned to the consulate. Westerahaupt had left precise instructions on how to communicate: no telephone, no official channels. They had to call a certain Aniello Spavone and ask him to send a messenger to deliver three crates of anchovies in oil, he would take care of everything.

Sabine dialed the number. A hoarse voice answered: "Good morning: General Port Company," said the voice.

"Good morning, I'm Mrs. Capello, you should deliver three boxes of anchovies in oil to our priory..."

There was a second of silence, then the hoarse voice continued: "What order of chivalry are you?"

"Order of Malta," Sabine replied.

"Let's get to it right away, it will take an hour and have a good day..." The hoarse voice concluded.

Anyone expecting a fish delivery to the Order of Malta on Via del Priorato would have had to wait a long time.

Sabine opened her work bag and began to leaf through her notes. When she left Rome they had been working on a very interesting find: a Byzantine-style mosaic found by chance during excavation work for a new building near San Giovanni fuori le mura.

The telephone rang, it was the concierge: "There is a delivery boy with a package for you" the concierge's Swiss German was croaking like a flock of crows.

"Ankunft Sie es sitzen, ihn zu holen" (*let him sit down, I'll come and get him)*

The boy looked alert and wore a sort of uniform that looked rather worn, though clean and fit him as if it had belonged to his older brother, and a peaked cap that was also rather large. He had a lively look, but he imposed a respectful attitude on himself.

Sabine took the box and handed him an envelope, then whispered the destination address in his ear.

"And also tell the caretaker that you have to wait for the interested party's response. In fact, do one thing: tell him that you are waiting there for him to respond: personally and in writing... And be careful with the doorman... you never know"

The boy took off his hat and bowed briefly: "Thank you, madam."

"Then come back here and tell me...go ahead."

The boy bowed profusely again and disappeared.

The boy started running, he knew that place was controlled by the cops, and he had to carefully avoid them intercepting him. They were in the car, somewhere, he was sure that they were taking care of the Swiss consulate, if they had identified him there would have been trouble...

Inspector Masera, from the Ovra, was smoking a SOVEREIGN cigarette. He smoked thirty or forty a day, at that moment he was very nervous, because he was smoking the last one of the pack just as the delivery boy was leaving the consulate. He was on his way to the tobacconist when he saw him, the sense of duty, and more than anything the fear that someone else was checking that he was doing his job properly, had pushed him after the boy, who was running across the ploughshare, and he ran after him, but the thousands of cigarettes that had stratified his lungs with tar, took his breath away.

He saw him slow down, "luckily" - he thought, he felt his lungs burning, the fatigue was overwhelming him, the child was now walking almost slowly, along a road, suddenly he disappeared... Masera wondered if he was delirious. He made a last effort and lengthened his stride to the point where it seemed the boy had disappeared. He looked around, nothing, there was a door. He entered, there was no one, he advanced into the courtyard. There was a man sitting on a chair, in front of the stairs, he had a peaked cap on his head and he seemed to be sleeping. Breathlessly Masera said: "Hey you...". The man seemed not to hear: "Hey, raise your voice, can you hear me, wake up, police"

The man raised his head. "You don't understand," Masera said, almost out of breath, and took out the card. And the man moved his hands with pistol fingers, a rotating motion, pointing to his ears.

He opened his mouth and said, "soodoo... muooo."

Damn he was deaf and dumb. Nice find, A deaf and dumb doorman, that couldn't even give information to Jesus Christ, thought Masera. He turned and walked away.

"What the fuck do I do now?" he thought...then he decided to look for a tobacconist, he would think about the relationship this evening.

What you don't expect

The enterprising urchin

Totonno walked through the tunnels. He knew them by heart, one by one, since he was born he had wandered through those caves that pierced Naples under the surface, and went a bit everywhere. There was another city under the city, a place that, despite the darkness and the legends about the little monk, for Totonno was much more reassuring than the one outside.

It took him a while to get to the cellars of the Hotel, under Via DePretis. He had no intention of going through the reception, where there was a stinking doorman, a police spy.

He knew in which room the scientist was, Agent Viggiano, infiltrated by the Stephensons at the Naples police headquarters, had done his duty well.

Totonno went up a passage that was inside the walls of the palace and emerged into a linen room.

He approached the door and peeked, there was no one in the corridor.

He ventured in silently. Maiorana's room, fortunately, was on the same floor.

There was silence, Totonno knocked.

Ettore was doing some calculations. He had figured out more or less how the bomb would work. It was a matter of finding a sufficient quantity of uranium, enough to trigger a self-sustaining chain reaction, to produce the enormous amount of energy that all scientists had now understood would be produced. But the necessary critical mass had to be small enough in terms of size, to be able to fit into a device that could be transported on an airplane, for example.

Now the problem was how much enriched uranium to produce, the less enriched the uranium was the greater the mass had to be. But obviously the enrichment process was complex and expensive and therefore a compromise had to be found between the level of enrichment and the critical mass. Perhaps there was a solution, however, using an implosion of the mass and neutron reflectors. He was not far from a solution, he was checking, but probably, with a uranium enriched to 85%, a mass of 50 kilos of uranium would have been enough, small enough to fit in a medium-sized bomb.

He heard a knock at the door. It was a light knock, almost soft, as if someone was trying not to be heard, so much so that he wasn't immediately sure that it was a knock. He turned toward the door and listened. He didn't want any trouble. He turned around and went back to his calculations. But again that sound came to disturb him: knock, knock. Two knocks. Close together, but this time more decisive. He went to the door:

"Who is...?"

"messenger" he said in a low voice. What the hell could a messenger want.

"But are you sure it's for me...'" He asked, not knowing how to avoid that annoyance.

"Absolutely sure...sir," replied the little voice.

Maiorana opened. In front of him was a little boy, with a suit a little too large, and a delivery boy's cap.

"Are you Professor Maiorana...?" asked the urchin

"Yes it's me"

"So this is what you want...sorry but I have to wait for the answer...and – he looked around – it would be urgent"

Maioran sighed, looked at the envelope, it was headed: "Swiss Consulate"

The doubts increased. He looked, that handwriting seemed familiar to him...

He started reading. Who the fuck would send him that stupid... well not exactly stupid no.

But a mathematical puzzle....There was only one person who could have such an idea.

He felt a shiver, the turmoil he had felt in Rome, in front of

those perfect breasts. He could still feel their firm softness rubbing against his arm.

He could almost smell the light scent, Chanel No. 5, she had told him, "just a sprayed".

The boy looked at him from below: "Sir, what have I say to the lady "

"Tell her tomorrow morning, at 10 at the cloister of Santa Chiara...."

"All right sir."

Venus and the Spy

Mademoiselle Docteur had dressed as a woman, and she looked very well in that way, she thought to herself.

She had a suit designed by Elsa Schiapparelli. An Italian dressmaker who worked in Paris, Coco Schanel's main competitor. She didn't like Chanel's clothes. Too rigorous and too unfeminine and when she decided to be feminine she wanted to be. So to the rigour

The black suit was accompanied by decorations in deep pink, vaguely shaped like hearts or lips, or, if desired, a woman's genitals, placed on the lapels and at the bottom of the profile of the short jacket.

A skirt of the same black color, long to just below the knee, had two trimmings on the sides of the short slit that opened in the front. The whole thing was completed by a tricorne hat with a veil in front.

Dressed like this, she went to the painting of a painter whose talent was not particularly exciting, but who had important friendships, which was opening that day at a gallery in Chiaia.

At that same event she had found a way to get the American girl invited. There she was counting on finding a way to get in touch with her and this excited her a lot.

Chinthya received an envelope from a delivery boy wearing a strange livery. He thought it was the brilliant idea of one of the many "ciccisbei" (dandy) of Naples who had been trying in every way to insinuate themselves into her life for some time, risking four slaps and perhaps even a buttonhole in the belly from his ardent and hot-headed captain of the air force.

On the contrary, it seemed that the trap set for the enigmatic German spy was not working... Perhaps Stephenson had overestimated the emotions of the dangerous woman.

The envelope had a curious and intense scent of ginger and lemon. The paper was headed with a ducal crown and a rather complicated coat of arms carefully illuminated, a very expensive paper. The inviter was the Duchess of Paiano, an ancient Neapolitan nobility, her husband's, since the countess's maiden name was Marthe, MartheVon Heykenstein....

A small light went on in Cinthya's mind, maybe it was the noise of a trap being set in, the problem was understanding who would fall into it.

Mario read the invitation, written in ink the color of a cappuccino frock. A fluent handwriting of a scribe, in stark contrast to the kind of exhibition Cinthya was being invited to. A show of living paintings by the futurist painter Carlo Minetti, a complete unknown, in cahoots with a Neapolitan hierarch.

He looked at his companion: "I think we're there, now how do we move?"

"I would leave it to them...let's use the Judo technique..." Cinthya said slyly

"What would that be...._ he said with a foolish look. Mario"

Cinthya looked at him in turn, questioningly.

"Yes..I say this Judo..."

The woman smiled: "a form of oriental wrestling, which consists in using the physical effort of the opponent to one's advantage..."

"And have you ever practiced this fight...._ Mario asked, still astonished?"

"never materially...always psychologically..."

Mario was struck by a thought: "With me too...."

She looked at him, with those spectacular eyes, filled with a green light like a valley of paradise:

"When you love someone, there is no need for tricks and fighting. You run towards each other, as if you were driven by a powerful and irresistible force. I have always looked for you, as you have looked for me. I will never lose you no matter what happens, I will never lose you..."

Mario looked at her and felt as if an invisible hand had lifted him up to touch the sky.

The first living tableau consisted of two actors dressed in tights with geometric designs, who emitted onomatopoeic sounds; then another, where an actress recited poems by Marinetti and so on.

Mademoiselle docteur saw her in front of the third, two women making rumbling sounds aboard a red car.

She was dressed in a white suit with fox fur trim and two foxes around her neck. On her head was a black cloche hat.

She was talking to the landlady, in English. The spy passed by, as if by chance, and made an imperceptible sign of understanding to her friend.

Who interrupted himself, "Oh Countess Von Testory, what a good wind" he said in Italian

She replied as if she had been surprised: "Oh Marthe, how are you..."

Marthe said a series of banalities then, pretending to be completely taken aback, asked: "Oh, sorry Elsbeth, may I introduce you to Miss Stephenson, the daughter of the United States military attaché?"

Von Testory raised her veil and looked straight into Cinthya's green eyes, and shook hands.

Cinthya did the same and at the same time felt a kind of shiver, the same one she had felt a long time ago on her first day at Vassar University when she had met Caireen.

Those black eyes, burning like burning coals, seemed to penetrate her like a knife through butter.

She managed not to show either his confusion or his certain satisfaction with the meeting, and it seemed that the trap was finally being set in.

Von Testory looked at Cinthya with obvious admiration and was about to open his mouth when she heard a voice behind him. She felt like he was falling back in time, many years, it was the voice of Carlo della Torre, he was saying: "good morning sir, are you also at this ... um, exhibition?"

She turned, in front of her was Captain Mario Viallante, in his uniform, a pair of black gloves in his hand and his cap under his left arm.

A new wave of emotions hit Elsbeth Von Testory, she looked the officer straight in the eyes and smiled at him, he responded with a polite smile and gave the woman a perfect hand kiss.

"Well," exclaimed the hostess, "we want to visit the exhibition. I'll be your guide and cicerone."

They went all the way around. Mario and Cinthya chatted amiably with Von Testory and the landlady. They had both diligently studied a script and all the author's works.

The tour of the exhibition ended amid frivolous chatter and laughter. The group seemed to have blended well together. It almost seemed that a spontaneous sympathy had arisen between them that rarely emerges from groups, but the time had come to separate.

Mario was the first to point it out.

"I apologize, but unfortunately duty calls me, His Excellency Balbo asked me to assist him in a technical meeting. It was truly a pleasure to meet you." He said bowing to kiss Von Testory's hand.

The women remained.

Mademoiselle Docteur felt a fierce drive inside her, the desire for that woman and the will to complete her mission were like two powerful fuels that drove the engine of her instincts.

He had to see her again...alone.

"Well, madam, I really appreciated our cheerful chat," he smiled ironically, "even if I fear I have destroyed the patience of our heroic pilot..."

Cinthya smiled kindly in return.

"Mario is very patient... and he always has some commitment that takes him away from "situations" that aren't exactly to his taste."

"Well," added von Testory, "we could meet up for tea. Maybe at my house..." she spoke, trying to control her anxiety that the American would give a positive answer.

"Why not," Cinthya exclaimed cheerfully. "So we can gossip peacefully about all the black nobility or otherwise…"

Relief fell upon Mademoiselle Docteur's heart like a balm.

"What do you think about tomorrow?"

"Why not?" the others answered in chorus.

"I live in Via Degli Ombrellari, at number 59.

Cynthia

The house was low, probably had a garden inside. Cinthya got out of the car that had accompanied her and told the driver that she would return to the embassy alone.

She rang the bell. A few seconds passed and she heard the sound of the latch opening, the door opened. The maid was wearing a uniform, she had a rather stern look, but she was very young. Cinthya remembered Mario's story about her uncle's adventure. They walked along a short path that went through a small garden. The house was two stories, very well kept and recently restored.

She entered the antechamber. There was a strange smell, which immediately alarmed her. It was barely perceptible but very distinct. Someone had tried to cover it with another perfume, perhaps incense. But she knew it well, it was a pungent, spicy smell with a background of ammonia. She had smelled that smell too many times in the smokehouses of New York, she had miraculously escaped it, she did not intend to fall into it again.

Mademoiselle

She had to smoke. She was no longer the woman she once was. She was tense as a spring, she couldn't control that feeling of physical attraction she felt for the American. That way she would end up making some mistakes. She had to control her nervous tension and so she smoked a little opium, a small dose. She burned a little incense to cover the smell. Now she felt calm, ready for the first meeting with her beloved enemy.

Cynthia

Von Testory came towards her. She was smiling and seemed completely relaxed, but her pupils were dilated, you could see clearly, even though the room was dimly lit. Mademoiselle Docteur must have been on drugs, which meant she had bad intentions.

She smiled and went towards her and kissed her lightly on the cheeks, as was the custom in that strange country that was Rome. He had a very intense perfume, used perhaps in a slightly higher dose than necessary to cover the other smell, which however Cinthya's sensitive nose perceived.

"Can I offer you some tea?" There was something imperceptibly uninhibited in her attitude. Cinthya was sure that the woman meant to lure her, this was the trap they had been waiting for so long.

The waitress served the tea, Cinthya smelled it, it was normal darjeling, good.

"Don't tell me that Marthe is late as usual..." Cinthya asked in a nonchalant tone.

Von Testory smiled: "That's right... she had a setback, I thought maybe we could stay together for dinner and have her meet us at the restaurant..."

"What a wonderful idea.." Cinthya chirped.

Mademoiselle

The American seemed relaxed, she had accepted the proposal without hesitation: too easy? The spy part of the woman's brain seemed to want to put her on alert. But for once she preferred to believe in her luck and the reputation of a cheerful goose that the gossip attributed to the girl.

Cinthya's joke about Marthe took off and she started talking about her strange habits. A nice girl, but rather absent-minded... etc. etc.

The American was the very prototype of the Ivy League girl. Her perfect East Coast accent, her way of gesticulating, her "aug..", "bleah..", these Americans were just not very intelligent.

Cynthia

She had struck a pose, the kind her friends at the Joke Club used to strike when they wanted to pick up some rich scion of the East Coast's rich fauna.

She had one leg crossed over the other and made some cute little hand gestures, using all the sexy-but-dumb-girl skills she'd learned while attending Vassar.

She looked at her interlocutor languidly, trying to give, with her very bright emerald eyes, the most ambiguous messages possible. She smiled mischievously, as if she were talking about some erotic subject, while instead they were talking about the boring habits of the fascist nobility of Rome.

Ms. Doctor

She was shocked, no, more than that, she was shocked. This woman was courting her. This was beyond her wildest dreams.

She had not met her many times, but she had never noticed this sexy side. Probably in the presence of her Italian "Supermachos" she contained certain tendencies of hers that were certainly not appreciated in the fascist military environment.

But a distant voice alarmed her. It was a feeling of uneasiness that she knew. Every time she had the opportunity to seduce a woman this feeling emerged, as if of alarm, she had followed it often, she did not know if she had done well, but with the job she did she could not overlook anything.

But instead his wild inner voice was screaming at him to take advantage of this opportunity, because seducing that woman would be very, very useful to her.

She stood up and approached her, who looked down at him with a spectacular, simultaneously naive and seductive smile.

He took her chin, the woman did not resist and gave her a kiss. She did not answer, she seemed slightly embarrassed and, at that moment, the bell rang. It was Marthe, arriving at an inopportune moment, but Mlle Docteur had not foreseen such a rapid evolution and therefore had only asked her to delay her arrival a little.

"Devil, just now," said Mademoiselle docteur somewhat banally.

She walked away from Cinthya, pointed a finger at her and said: "We two need to meet again..."

"Without a doubt," the American replied.

The Impatience of Achilles

He had been waiting for a few minutes in an office of the Portuguese consulate in Naples. Stephenson had let him know that he needed to meet him through their secret communication system. Two rings of the phone, a break, two more rings.

Mario had breathed a sigh of relief, he could no longer stand wandering around the city dragging along the OVRA policemen who were watching him day and night. He had seen practically all the monuments, the characteristic places, those mentioned in Neapolitan songs. He had taken the little girl for a walk, always accompanied by a nanny, so as not to arouse the suspicions of her watchful companions.

He wondered why he was there. It was not possible that they wanted to use one of the best officers in the Italian Air Force just to throw off the political police, it seemed almost an insult to him, and he wanted to talk to Stephenson about it. When the call came he was determined to move first.

While he was thinking of these things, with a rather grim expression on his face, the office door opened and his father-in-law, Colonel William Stephenson, entered.

"Good morning Mario," he said in Italian with his strange accent, "what a dark face..."

"I... - the Italian said a little embarrassed - well, it's just that, well, I feel like I'm here acting like a pretty little statue"

Stephenson half-smiled: "No, you're here for another reason... have a seat..."

The Canadian said, pointing to an armchair.

He looked a little embarrassed. He took a bronze cigarette case from inside his jacket, opened it, and took out one of his Senior Service cigarettes. He lit it and expelled the smoke with a slightly odd expression, as if he were struggling.

"So Mario, your time will come soon, the mission we entrusted you with is not very pleasant...."

Mario resumed his frowning expression: "Another diversionary action?"

"No the main action.....You will have to kill the leader of the Nazi team.. Countess Von Testory"

Mario remained suspended for a second, as if he had misunderstood.

Then he sighed: "You see, Colonel...... - Stephenson offered him a cigarette - Mario took it, lit it", then he continued:

"After all, I am a soldier, so killing is also part of my job... But one thing is to pull the trigger of a machine gun, or to operate the lever to release a bomb, another is to kill...

"Directly and in cold blood," Stephenson preceded him.

" Exactly..."

"You know who Von Testory is... right.."

"My father's killer they say...."

"Exactly....But he is also a German agent who operated in Holland, eliminating many English agents, often in a ferocious manner.

Now there is an unwritten rule among spies, which is that nobody kills anybody. We are not highwaymen, we do a job, so we are all professionals, all equal...and one day the oddities of international relations may lead us to the same side of the fence.

So: it doesn't go beyond a few punches...

But not her, she has to humiliate her opponent, she has to do bizarre things to him, she is depraved, both in a psychological and professional sense.

"I understand, but it makes little difference. Someone broke the rules, fine. But it seems to me that the executioner you chose for the situation is a kind of scapegoat in reverse, someone who has nothing to do with it and who will do the dirty work for you."

"It's not like that. You've been in that game since you were born. Your family has an ancient history, dating back to the time of the Templars. A sort of large network present throughout Europe, closely linked by relationships of friendship, loyalty, mutual support, in which members of many intelligence services are included. A brotherhood with severe laws, aimed at ensuring that vulgar violence does not prevail within international relations.... De facto family relationships.

Mademoiselle Docteur behaved like a parvenu. A vulgar cutthroat in a gentleman's world, where women who entered did so on precise terms of equality... in every sense. She is a whore and nothing else, a murderous whore"

Mario felt a shiver, Stephenson sensed the disturbance: "What's the matter, Mario, does it seem so strange to you..."

"No... I'm thinking that Cinthya is on the front line, yes, in first person with her...."

"I think so too, and that's why I don't think it's a bad idea to withdraw this subject from the market. Besides, Cinthya is doing part of the work, which you will have to complete. Because in a certain sense it is your right and your duty, to avenge your father and the brotherhood."

Mario was quite upset. The idea of avenging his father had faded over time. And murder horrified him, as it does any civilized person.

Stephenson continued, almost as if he had read Mario's mind.

"It is not a murder, it is an act of war and in a certain sense, as I explained to you, an act of justice"

Mario looked straight into Stephenson's eyes, who responded with his calm, tension-free gaze.

"How no one told me these family stories?"

"Your grandfather was supposed to do it, he died before he could do it...and he was the only one who could do it."

"Meeting Cinthya wasn't entirely by chance...right?"

"...It was, she saw you in Budapest..eh..eh, well, she decided she would have a child with you...Cinthya is my daughter only by registry office. Her character is that of her father..a man to whom no one has ever been able to give orders!"

Mario shifted his gaze. He looked around the office they were in as if he were looking for something hanging on the walls, perhaps an inspiration.

"I feel like I have no other way out than to do this thing. It disgusts me but I'll do it anyway. More than anything to prevent the lady from hurting Cinthya and my daughter.

What are the instructions?"

A strange smile appeared on Stephenson's face. Between bitter and ironic.

"I knew I could count on you, young man... I have no specific instructions for now. We still have to perfect Majorana's exfiltration plan. Once we have a definitive plan, we will think about the phase of it that concerns you.

For now, continue with the diversionary actions.....And prepare yourselves physically and psychologically. The lady is not an easy pill to swallow."

A dangerous proposition

The player was looking at the sea. He was on top of the Posillipo hill, he had ventured there to get away from everything and everyone, to think about Spavone's proposal. Which then had little to think about: either eat this soup or jump out the window. A window that could be very high, the damned man had won one hundred thousand lire from him, an amount out of this world, a trap into which he had fallen like an idiot. But the offer that had been made to him was almost like a jump out the window... even if perhaps that window was a little less high, at least in that case he could count on himself, he could take his time, cheat a little. Spavone had told him that they would enable him to do it, he had believed it. What else could he do? He looked around, a skinny young man with a tacky but expensive suit and a borsalino was looking at him. He was absentmindedly cutting slices from an apple he was holding in his hand and putting them in his mouth, nonchalantly and with almost no expression on his face.

They kept an eye on him, he decided he would eat that soup, however indigestible it might be.

Castor and Pollux

The SS officer had slept badly. He was not happy with the way things were going. He had found a way to have Maiorana exfiltrated. But there was a disagreement within the operational team. Wirth wanted to make it a propaganda operation, the whole world, in his opinion, had to know that the great scientist had chosen the Thousand-Year Reich. He did not agree at all, the operation had to be done in secret, the enemy must not know that Germany had in its hands the best expert of what seemed to be the weapon of the future.

If they had known, considering that they had much more resources than Germany, they would have accelerated the development of the weapon to the maximum. If Diebner was right, the device manufactured using the processes of splitting Uranium atoms would have been of such power that whoever had it at his disposal first could have turned the outcome of any conflict to his advantage, even with a single attack. So Germany had to buy time. Luderitz was an SS man, but he wasn't a fanatic. He understood very well that in the event of war, Germany, if by chance the United States entered the game, would have had no hope, not if the confrontation had been on the level of conventional weapons. With the bomb, however, everything would have been very different. With what seemed to be Maiorana's discoveries, the theoretical part was taken care of, but there was a practical aspect, of industrial engineering to be perfected and of the resources necessary to build the device.

But that wasn't enough. According to Diebner, Germany would have had to exploit the conquered nations: the uranium of Czechoslovakia first of all, but also the financial and industrial resources of the countries it would have to conquer. In short, a massive effort that would have required five or six years, if everything had gone well.

Evidently America, in what would surely have been a deadly clash between Germany and France-England, would have sided with the English and would have invested all its potential in the project.

The calculation was easy to make. The American gross domestic product, according to Abwher data, was around ninety billion dollars, the English one about twenty-eight, the French one seventeen.

Total one hundred and thirty five billion dollars. Germany had about fifty.

If it had succeeded in conquering the Soviet Union, it could perhaps count on thirteen billion or so, considering that it would have had to practically destroy it, and it could not take possession of all its wealth.

The Allies had practically double what, with great optimism, Germany could have. In addition, the United States was across the Atlantic and England and France could count on their respective empires. Winning was very difficult, but in any case if the Allies had immediately committed themselves to the development of the weapon they would have had at least double the German resources at their disposal, again, to be optimistic. The Reich had to arrive at the bomb well in advance and already as it was the challenge seemed rather complicated. No, Wirth's idea was to be discarded. He too was to be discarded, even if... Even if that story of his double kept him awake at night.

After being in Santa Lucia that time he had no more time to deal with it.

But he was left with that unpleasant feeling that the idiot had, by pure chance, hit upon something that made sense.

His nature would normally have led him to resolve the matter in the quickest way possible...only this time there was no quick way, and that annoyed him.

How could he find out if his brother, Captain Walter Westerhaupt, was in Naples, dressed in civilian clothes and attending church.

He didn't know how to find out, unless he suspected that Walter was there for reasons that were against Germany's interests. An absurd idea. Walter was a naval officer after all, he could be in Naples for the most normal reasons: training Italians to use a U-boat? Getting in touch with the Navy, but that didn't seem sensible. Naples was a merchant port, it couldn't have anything to do with the Kriegsmarine, even if it wasn't a given that there wasn't some project in the works between the Germans and the Italians. It could have been a simple coincidence, in fact it certainly was.

He thought about confronting him, no! It was a great deal of nonsense. He would have found out he was there and become suspicious. Walter was certainly loyal to Germany, but his sympathies for the party were rather lukewarm.

Yet for some strange reason he felt that there was something in this story that he didn't know and that he should have known.

He could inquire at his command, but from whom? General Wolf himself was the only one who could answer him, but he had no reason to do so and, in fact, it might have put him in a bad light.

He thought of the myth of Castor and Pollux, the so-called Dioscuri. They were the sons of the King of Sparta Tyndareus and brothers of the mythical Helen, cause of the Trojan War.

The story of the two brothers reminded him a lot of his and Walter's story; because while Pollux was the son of Zeus and therefore immortal, Castor was the son of Tyndareus and mortal.

It was one of the many legends in which the gods, with their characteristic lack of control over their sexual appetites, had interfered in human affairs, creating enormous disasters.

He and Walter, unlike the Dioscuri, had the same father, not the same mother, but, in a certain sense, one could say that Walter was the immortal, the famous son of a heroic naval officer who fell in the great war. He was just a son of a bitch, so certainly not an immortal.

Yes, if this story of Walter in Naples had anything to do with some high-level story... who of the two would have run more risks: the immortal or the other?

The scientist in love

Hector

It had been a long time since he realized he was thinking about anything other than his physics.

Instead, he had been sleeping and dreaming of making love with Sabine for several nights, especially of touching her breasts. Those two firm and soft globes, the nipples that hardened every time he began to caress them. And then the smile of the young

Swiss girl that made him rise to the sky, that smile gave him the sensation of flying.

He woke up drenched in sweat, with an erection that almost hurt. It was the memory of that last night when he had accepted Sabine's plan.

They had met as agreed at the monastery of Santa Chiara. She was dressed like any Italian woman, her hair was dyed, so she was not blonde and, at first glance, she did not seem particularly attractive.

In fact, he hadn't realized right away that it was her. He was waiting for her in the cloister. There were few people. He had sat down on one of the seats decorated with majolica tiles. It was cold and the ceramic was like an ice pack whose chill penetrated Ettore's heavy clothes. But he was so focused on waiting to see her again that he almost didn't notice. He was smoking nervously and looking around. A woman passed in front of him and continued toward the church, taking one of the paths decorated with pillars, also covered with majolica.

Sabine

She saw him, the Saracen had not changed. He was sitting on one of the seats, a little stiff from the cold and was smoking nervously. He did not see her, she continued towards the church. She had scattered the guardian angels of the Ovra around Naples and she was not sure that somehow they had not managed to find her tracks.

Hector

He looked at his watch. Strange, Sabine was very punctual like every Swiss, but she still hadn't shown up. Unless that woman who had passed by. Possible, it didn't look like her... maybe.

He turned and saw that the woman had stopped in the porch as if waiting for someone.

He decided to go and see.

Sabine

Finally he understood, waited for him to get closer and went towards a door that led into the church. She entered and pretended to look around to see the wonderful baroque ornamentation of what was the royal church of the city, where the monarchs celebrated their solemn moments and where they were buried.

Now he had come in too.

She walked toward the exit trying not to be too "communicative" towards others who were watching them. She didn't turn around and hoped that Ettore had understood.

She went towards the external door and emerged in Piazza del Gesù Nuovo. He turned left, passing in front of the massive parallelepiped of the church bell tower, and headed towards Piazza San Domenico Maggiore .....

Hector

She walked slowly, looking around. Yes, it was her. She was well disguised, probably afraid of being recognized. Ettore understood that he had to follow her and he did so, cautiously without losing sight of her. He saw her come out of the main door. He hurried out, a doubt came to him, he looked around. He saw a street urchin that he hadn't noticed before. The boy was badly pretending to be indifferent. "Hey" he said, trying to be heard but not to raise his voice too much.

But he continued to pretend nothing had happened. He raised his voice a little, someone in the church turned around. The boy pointed to himself as if to say "you want me".

Yes, Hector nodded.

The street urchin approached, he had a slightly cocky expression, but he kept his voice low, after all he was in church.

"What do you want, sir?"

"If you leave I'll give you a cigarette"

The boy's expression changed and he looked around.

"make me ten"

"Let's make it five, I don't have any more..."

"Five cigarettes and ten cents..."

Ettore was fed up with the negotiation. He handed over the package he had in his pocket and ten cents.

The boy looked satisfied.

"Hey," added Hector, "tell your clients something credible..."

The boy smiled: "Trust me..."

Sabine

Ettore didn't come out. He went back, and saw him appear around the corner of the bell tower.

He went back, but looked around, that maneuver could arouse the suspicion of potential tailers.

Finally Hector entered the street and she started walking.

He arrived in the square and went into Scaturchio, the pastry shop.

He approached the counter and ordered a coffee and a diplomatica.

She waited for them to serve her

Hector

He saw her walking along the road that led to Piazza San Domenico Maggiore. He followed her at a distance.

He saw that he was entering Scaturchio.

He waited for him to succeed but he didn't show up.....

Evidently that was where she wanted to meet him.

He opened the door of the place and saw her. She was at the counter eating a diplomatica.

He also pretended not to see her and approached the cash register, asked for a coffee and paid for it and headed towards the counter.

"Professor..." he heard. He turned around and there she was: beautiful as always even if a little different because of the disguise, the freckles had not disappeared and the eyes were still that deep gray-blue

Two minds one soul

"They told me you were here in Naples," he said in a mock surprised tone.

"Dr. Trinkwasser...... how long" Maiorana replied, acting rather badly.

They started talking about this and that, then Sabine looked at her watch, put a hand to her temple and said, "Oh God, I have to go... Do you often come to this pastry shop?" Maiorana looked around himself , the clerk was looking at him with an indecipherable expression.

"Well not really, I just went for a walk in Santa Chiara and ended up here...."

"So maybe at university-...?"

"Here maybe there..."

Ettore felt a little confused, all that fuss to exchange a few words with Scaturchio?

Then Sabine reached out her gloved hand and, shaking his hand, passed him a note.

"Goodbye professor..." and he left

The note read: "in one hour, Molosiglio gardens, in front of the Lions fountain, make sure you are not being followed".

He saw her come out smiling.

Ettore went out, there was no one there, he set off on foot. He had time and he took a long detour to avoid being followed. But no one followed him, probably the urchin he had paid had done his job well.

Sabine was sitting on the edge of the fountain. She stood up when she saw him coming.

Ettore felt his heart beating in his throat. Sabine always had that effect on him, it was a feeling of warmth, a kind of happiness, a sense of freedom and security, an uncontrollable desire to hug her.

He stopped in front of her, speechless.

Sabine was smiling, the dimples in her cheeks more attractive than ever and her eyes were laughing, full of bright sparkles.

"So Hector, we'll see each other again...as I promised you"

Ettore remembered at that moment that day when they had seen each other for the last time. He was about to leave for Germany, and she was looking at him seriously. Ettore had said to him: "I think we will never see each other again..." and she had replied: "You're wrong - we will see each other again, professor" and she had kissed him in a way that he had not forgotten.

"Why did you come looking for me... Don't tell me you couldn't live without me," he said in a sad tone.

"No, as you see I live without you... you can't imagine why I looked for you..."

"I'm afraid so, it concerns my calculations on nuclear power, right?"

"I'm afraid so..."

"But what do you have to do with those things..."

"I work with my father, who, although he is Swiss, works with the English..."

Ettore felt a sense of disappointment growing inside him.

"What do you want ....."

"You can imagine, all physicists have understood that the energy of the splitting of the atom can be used to build a bomb.

Bohr found a notebook of yours with calculations that prove that you know how to build the bomb..."

"Not only do I know it, but it is something that has been tormenting me for a long time and is destroying my life. But I tell you right away that I will not work for the English....."

"You know very well that even the Nazis are looking for you, do you intend to work for them?"

"Not even. My calculations show that the device based on the splitting of the atom would have a power inconceivable up to now. It would generate a frightening number of deaths and, what's more, it would also have consequences for the future... it would make the place of the explosion a hell, but it would also bring death in time, as happened to poor Marie Curie.

It would be a disgrace for humanity, whoever possesses it will be able to hold the entire world in check..."

"It's one more reason why it shouldn't fall into the hands of the Nazis...."

"It's a reason why it shouldn't fall into anyone's hands, at least not through my fault."

Sabine made the expression she always made when she knew she was right but didn't want to do violence to Hector's reasons.

He had lowered his gaze, fixed his eyes on the ground and remained silent.

Sabina took his chin in one hand and gently turned his face toward her.

Hector had tears in his eyes.

"Saraceno, you know very well that if it's not you, someone else will finish this thing. Your calculation skills would only benefit one of the parties. It would be better if the good guys got there first...no?"

"Do you still believe that good people exist? Do you really believe that? Of course the Nazis did some very big things (he said surprisingly in Sicilian dialect, which he never used). But the English in the empire did even worse. And the Americans, with the American Indians and the Russians, the revolution cost a lot of blood.

You see, I have been racking my brains over this problem for years now. Producing that monster will be something of such industrial complexity that only an economy of gigantic dimensions could do it.

Germany, however powerful, cannot do it. The only ones who can do it today are the Americans, and even with some difficulty.

If I agreed to work for the English I would certainly end up in America, in a gigantic mincer of brains and human resources, something that would certainly be directed by the military, I don't know how to work with others, I would go mad...

"So you prefer the Germans...?"

"It's the same, I don't want to just produce this thing, I don't want to work on it, I don't want to work on a monstrous future of the world."

"So what do you want to do?"

"I would like to disappear...."

"You know that if you don't put yourself under one of the two hats they will kill you to prevent you from working for love or force with the opponents."

"I understood this too and I don't know what to do."

He had a sad and lost expression. Those dark Middle Eastern eyes were shiny like coal, red and full of tears. The expression was that of a lost and desperate child.

Sabine looked at him and felt infinite tenderness.

She had to find a way to help that man towards whom she felt a rebirth of a feeling of attraction made of tenderness, passion, and an almost telepathic understanding of his often confused, but radically good, soul.

"Okay Ettore, we'll find a solution... I'll talk to my father and our boss, we'll find a way."

Then she went up to him and kissed him.

It seemed to Hector that the gates of paradise had opened.

THE PLAN

Walter walked through the alleys of the Spanish Quarter, towards Via Medina and the Portuguese consulate.

He had met with "O maestro" who had explained his plan to him.

A brilliant idea. The problem was then the exfiltration of the scientist. The solution was up to him and he walked thinking of a solution.

But he needed to talk to the group because in any case everyone's collaboration was necessary.

Then there was the question of how to organize the disengagement and the disengagement of the opponents after and if Spavone's plan had succeeded.

There was the problem of his brother. He could become dangerous for his future.

He was an SS man and this guaranteed his fanaticism and determination. If he had recognized him and managed to confirm his identification, the entire anti-Nazi chain within the Abwehr would have been at risk, with Admiral Canaris at the head. If he had recognized him, Walter could do nothing but kill his brother, something that simply horrified him. Should he entrust the task to someone from the team? Their team tended not to use violence, there was the old "sporting" rule of the secret services.

So he absolutely had to avoid Horst.

He arrived at the consulate and entered as quickly as possible. The others also arrived one by one.

Cinthya was dressed modestly and had aged herself with makeup.

Mario had dressed up as a Portuguese colonist in Africa, in sight in Naples. He was accompanied by a black servant (who knows where the fuck he found him?).

The two Rinkweisers looked more Swiss than ever.

They found themselves in the usual office where Stephenson arrived shortly after. Normally dressed. He had remained a guest of their friend the consul. He looked around with his usual ironic smile:

"First of all, I would like to announce that we are almost done with the disguises. Tell the truth, you have had fun so far," he smiled. "Now that's enough, damn it, we are here to work."

Everyone present burst out laughing.

"Now let's get down to business. We have a plan to take Majorana away, Walter will tell us the general scheme shortly.

Inside it, everyone will have their own mission. That the others will not know, except to the extent that it is necessary. It is not a question of distrust. The opponents are very determined and to use a euphemism "bad" "

If they had to use strong methods and capture one of you and make him talk, everything would be ruined.

You know very well that no one resists torture and the lady who leads the Nazi team is very skilled in sadistic practices....

I assure you that you will be protected twenty-four hours a day, trust me, but we cannot afford to take risks. However, if you should fall into the hands of the adversaries, resist twenty-four hours before telling everything you know. I do not want heroes, and I hope they are not needed."

Stephenson finished, then turned to Walter: "Well now it's your turn...."

Walter stood up and began to tell, it took him quite a while, the plan was simple, very dangerous, but not even that hard to accept. He counted a lot on the psychology and the urgency of the enemy to bring home a result, sure there were big risks, but it could work.

Stephenson looked around: "You are all intelligent people. You know very well that this game is a game of shadows, mirages and feints. There are two things essential to success.

The first is that you scrupulously follow the instructions. Deviate only if your life or that of your colleagues is at risk, you are soldiers in a certain sense so prioritize the life of your colleagues and the result, rather than your life, as much as you can.

The second thing is that you will have to trust each other and me completely. Whatever you see and whatever happens, trust.

None of us will betray the others, you have been chosen because I know you personally one by one and because I know that you would never be late, so: T R U S T.

I'm done, now I'll meet you individually."

Sabine

The first were Rinkweiser and Sabine. The girl reported.

"I talked to Ettore at length. But I couldn't convince him to collaborate with us, at least not completely." She paused and Stephenson intervened:

"You know what our orders are, right?"

"Yes, and if it were to fall into enemy hands I would be the one to eliminate it.......

"Does he know?"

"No, but he told me that if someone had to send him to the other world, he would prefer it to be me. He is actually under a terrible amount of stress. He has been mulling over the bomb for years.

We won't be able to convince him to work in America. I know him well, he's as stubborn as a mule."

"So......?" Stephenson said softly.

"Then it will provide us with all the calculations we need...."

"These are complex calculations, they might not be enough by themselves. .....

"if there is a need to interpret them I will do it......"

Stephenson looked at her with a raised eyebrow. "You...? We're sure."

Rinkweiser smiled. "Absolutely sure, Intrepid...Absolutely sure."

"Ettore is already making the copies, he is working day and night and it will be ready soon"

Stephenson looked at the calendar, it was March 15, 1938, three days before the Nazi troops had triumphantly penetrated Austria putting a very heavy mortgage on what would soon be the plebiscite for the unification of Germany and Austria. Another gift given to the Ogre in the hope of saving peace, appeasing his formidable expansionist appetite. But perhaps also to stop the communist advance in Europe. An advance that in fact did not exist, but that equally disturbed the dreams of the entire establishment of the allied nations.

"I would say the operation could take place on March 25th, do you think you will be ready…"

"Yes, by that day he will have run out of copies…" Sabine said thoughtfully.

"Two copies…true?" Stephenson said with an expressive voice.

"It's obvious…" Sabine replied with a smile that reached her eyes.

Cynthia

She couldn't stomach it, no, she just couldn't stomach it, that woman somehow attracted her. She was a person totally different from everyone else, and she too, had always felt different from everyone else. She was in conflict, she felt feelings towards her that until that moment she had only felt for Mario. It was possible to love two people at the same time. Why not, where was it written that it couldn't be. Conventions said that it shouldn't be… but if she felt that sensation it had to be possible. The problem was another: she was the enemy, and you just can't love the enemy, not if he's on an opposing team against whom you're fighting a battle to the death

With Cairen it had been fun, with Mario a dream, and that dream was now disturbed by the apparently impenetrable face, surmounted by two eyes that burned with an internal flame that seemed inextinguishable.

Along with that ardor in the gaze of Elsbett, as the German spy was really called, there was a kind of infinite melancholy. It was a melancholy that she had seen in the eyes of other lesbians and homosexuals. It was the feeling of being different and rejected even by those who were like them, and there were many, perhaps most people, but who did not have the courage to face their true nature, and to feel less guilty they openly despised their fellow men. She had felt that feeling too in the days of Vassar, when she was irresistibly attracted to Caireen. Sabine had saved her.

They said Elsbett was sadistic, to her it seemed that she was just desperate. That she was cruel, to her it seemed only desolately, disconsolately, deeply disappointed. They said she was implacable, and to her it seemed that she was just tired.

But perhaps she was just the most formidable actress she had ever met.

She was going to the appointment, the fateful one. She had put on some red and black underwear, which she had given her. She had looked at herself in the mirror before putting on a very serious black dress with lace trim, perhaps a little funereal. The image that the mirror had sent back to her was frankly that of a whore. That's what she had asked him to look like. The problem was that Cinthya at that moment really felt like a whore. She had frequented Spanish brothels, for "work", but she had always managed to stay "above", but this time she was in it up to her ears, and it didn't seem like she felt so bad.

Men were convinced that all women were whores. But it was something that masked their hypocrisy, and their fundamental fear of the opposite sex, exorcised with a moral judgment as superficial as a pimple. But what she felt at that moment was the desire to give herself totally to another person, without hypocrisy and without moral restraints, a total liberation from inhibitions.

Von Testory's car arrived, a long black Hispano Suiza with shiny chrome. Vatican license plates, a driver who looked like Von Stroheim in one of his roles as a sadistic German officer.

She was in the back seat, Cinthya got in. M.lle Docteur's eyes were burning brighter than ever.

Cinthya sat down and nonchalantly showed us her legs, which were wrapped in sheer black stockings with a line.

The countess did not resist, she lifted the partition that separated her from the driver, looked her straight in the eyes, approached her and put her tongue in her mouth. The kiss was very long and exhausting.

When they broke apart, Ma.lle Docteur was visibly excited.

"I want you, I told her, I want you right away, let's go to my house..."

Cinthya felt strange excited and embarrassed, deeply upset. Then as often happened in those situations she suddenly felt calm and relaxed. Her mind was clear doubts were gone, she knew what to do she had made a decision.

ON THE OTHER SIDE OF THE FRONT

Mamoiselle Docteur had said she had the situation in hand. She was sure that she would soon learn what the English plan was, and consequently they would act, if necessary even with force. But she was sure she could get by with cunning and by manipulating the young American agent who she claimed to have "converted...". Walter knew well what kind of religion the lady practiced. But that was it, after all it was her business. Homosexuality in the Nazi party was almost the rule. Until the night of the long knives, Hitler had calmly tolerated and almost indulged Rhoem, the head of the SA.

The Führer himself had a... well, difficult relationship with women, perhaps a consequence of the mustard gas poisoning he had suffered during the war.

The woman had organized everything for the escape, at least the initial step.

They would have taken him by car to Abruzzo, to a convent where old friends from the Vatican, Von Testory alias Madmoiselle Docteur had arranged hospitality for a few days.

From then on it was up to him to organize the transport to Germany.

He would have transported him to Trieste on a large fishing boat, a disguised vessel of the Kreigsmarine that cruised off the coast of Yugoslavia to support the German submarines that landed saboteurs and agents there.

From Trieste they would have reached Innsbruck by car and from there by plane to Berlin.

He had checked and rechecked three times the routes to Abruzzo and then from Tireste to Innsbruck. Along the way in Italy they would be protected by OVRA men.

Once he got on the car of the German consulate in Naples Maiorana would be safe and his brain in theyr's hands... Luderitz already asked himself, in whose hands? It seemed to him that behind the apparent monolithic nature of the German party and government there were mysterious and unknown forces moving.

The escape plan from Naples was set for the end of March.

They would have constructed a cover story with letters from Maiorana to Carelli, his director and friend, and to his family, in which the scientist feared suicide.

They would have left contradictory but well-constructed traces around, such a mess that in the end everyone would have believed the story they preferred about Ettore Maiorana and no one would have gone to stick their nose where they shouldn't have.

What would have been the final destination of the Italian scientist?

Luderitz had an idea. Diebner had told him about it one evening.

There was a salt mine in Pribrans in Czechoslovakia, near a uranium mine. There would be a research center where the Italian would find all the facilities and support necessary for his work.

Wirth hadn't been seen for a few days, who knows what he was up to, the character was worrying like all idiots, but he had had the ability to put a worm in his brain.

Before closing this matter or maybe once it was closed, he had to solve that problem.

The SS officer said to himself.

Then he went to the embassy radio room and wrote on a piece of paper: "Black sun, eclipse expected on March 25th"

He took the paper and handed it to the technician in charge of the ENIGMA machine, who looked at it for a second and said, "Awaiting a response...?" Luderitz was lost in thought.

The technician, a boy with thick blond hair and large, very clear eyes, looked at him with an embarrassed expression... "Excuse me, Mr Luderitz, are you waiting for an answer?"

The officer recovered. "Of course, of course..." and muttered to himself: "More than one..."

AN IMPOSSIBLE LOVE

They were in Mlle Docteur's bedroom, she had covered her hands all over, they had kissed each other passionately, and touched each other greedily.

Then the German woman ordered her to undress, slowly.

Cinthya had done it with all the technique she had learned in the Spanish clubs, watching Elsbeth masturbating wildly.

When Cinthya was completely naked, m-lle Docteur accelerated the pace of masturbation and had an orgasm.

He stood up and said: "Wait for me, I have a surprise....."

He disappeared behind a booth. He fumbled around behind it for a few seconds and then reappeared, wearing a black, transparent dressing gown trimmed with ostrich. Garters of the same color and very high-heeled boots. From the center of his legs protruded a pink object of considerable size. Cinthya looked at him and a half smile spontaneously came to him.

"What is that...." He asked, laughing.

"Don't you see," replied the German woman, "the only thing about men in which we are not superior, assuming that the instrument of their power serves to be so...."

Ciinthya had seen others of these fake rubber contraptions around for a while now, but she had never liked them.

"Listen Elsbet, she said, I like you...a lot but for what you are. I want to touch you, caress you, feel your clitoris but that is not you, it is a fake appendage, you and I who want not a "rubber cock" he said in Italian..."

Elsbeth's expression changed. "Thank you, my love, thank you for what you said to me. It's such a beautiful thing, no one had ever told me that... God, it's true, we women have everything we need to love each other, love and pleasure are in the brain, not in an appendix..."

They made love for a long time, both of them reaching orgasm several times.

Elsbeth, exhausted, took a cigarette holder and stuck a cigarette in it. She hadn't smoked opium or taken morphine in days and yet she felt fine. She thought it was a bad time to ask Cinfhya about Maiorana. She told her the truth, without shame, in a calm and relaxed voice.

She told her that it was really her and why she was there and said: "Now you will despise me, you will think that I made love to you to make you betray your father and your colleagues..."

Cinthya remained silent. Then she spoke. She feigned surprise very well and even hinted at a certain indignation.

Then Elsbet told her that she was a patriot and Cinthya was American after all, so she had nothing to do with Europe.

She told her that Germany had suffered an injustice with the Peace of Versailles, she told her frankly that she did not have a great admiration for the Nazis, but they were the only solution to reborn Germany.

Cinthya resisted a little more.

Elsbeth then changed expression: "Listen Cinthya, I am a lost woman. I did this horrible, disgusting job because of the disappointment that life had given me. I was only sixteen when I fell in love for the first time. He was Italian, an attaché at the Italian embassy in Paris. I would have given him everything, I would have even crossed over to the enemy. But he made fun of me. His people even killed my adoptive brother. Of course we worked for the Nacrhichten Bureau, but I was so lost behind that Italian officer that I would have dropped everything for him. But he left me tied up in a room and sent the French police after me. The Fliks also made fun of me with heavy phrases and handshakes.

Well this operation on Maiorana is my revenge, I beg you not to take it away from me.

Cinthya looked her straight in the eye and said, "Okay, I won't take it away from you."

ACHILLES AND THE FANATIC

Mario thought that German was a fascinating language, even if a little complicated and often unlistenable. It also depended on who spoke it, for example the German of the German-speaking Swiss was terrifying.

But the man on the stage, even though he spoke perfect German, was having a hypnotic effect on the pilot, in the sense that he was making him feel irresistibly sleepy.

He was a "professor" who had come to Naples as part of a conference tour on the contamination of the Aryan race.

It was part of the program that Mussolini had put in place in preparation for the racial laws. Mario was sure of it and so was Balbo. The Duce felt isolated, his attempts to get closer to the English had not yielded the desired results. By now Italy was moving towards a close alliance with Germany. This was understood from large and small signs among which there was also the Ovra's involvement in the "black sun" operation on the side of the Germans.

The conferences on race were instead the cultural side. Mario thought that there was no people more mongrelized than the Italians. Truly everything had passed through this beautiful country over the centuries. Not to mention the open-minded policy of ancient Rome that recruited anyone who could be useful, regardless of their color or what language they spoke, since they also spoke Latin anyway.

Racism was an infamous product of the previous century, with illustrious and sordid precedents in medieval anti-Semitism, a boil produced by a disease called imperialism and nationalism. Of course Mario loved his country, but from there to despising those who were not Italian there was a long way to go.

He had married a black woman, no one knew that Cinthya belonged to that ethnicity, but he did and she was so beautiful and so... fascinating and so everything, that Mario had ended up thinking that the mixed chromosomes of his daughter's mother were a wonderful gift from America's troubled history, a rare example of good in all the evil that slavery had brought.

Stephenson had sent him on reconnaissance.

The speaker, a certain Eugen Fisher, spoke of the deleterious effects of the mixing of whites and blacks produced by the use of colored troops by colonial countries.

He looked around, there was everything, then in the front row he noticed a familiar face.

Damn, he thought, that's Wirth.

He decided that fate was sending him a signal to seize and exploit.

He waited for the demented eugenicist doctor to finish his ravings and then stood up, still keeping an eye on Wirth.

The German consulate had decided to accompany the conference with a rich buffet; they knew well that in Italy accompanying culture to the eating always worked well.

Wirth was sitting alone at a table and was drinking Traminer and eating sausages, Mario approached the table.

" May I....?"

The man looked at him with a questioning and slightly annoyed expression.

"Ja," said Mario, "Ich sage, erlaube mir an seinen tisch zu sitzen (yes, I say, he allows me to sit at his table)

"Oh," the German exclaimed slightly in disgust, "ja, ja!"

setz dich"

"You know," Mario continued in German, "among all these Neapolitan bourgeois of who knows what mixed origins, I prefer to sit with an authentic Aryan..."

Wirth lit up. "Oh sure, you're welcome...you're right, this city has always been a port. Dozens of African sailors and Jewish merchants must have passed through here. With all the brothels there, the population must be as infected as a lazaretto (cemetery for people died of epidemic dideas)." Then he felt like he had exaggerated. "Excuse me, you know, but...."

"No, no," Mario continued, "I completely agree with you. Imagine, I come from Piedmont (he lied) in the nineteenth century we sent troops to tame these subversive savages.

Interesting conference, isn't it..."

It seemed that the German had been invited to the wedding. He began a long rant about the contamination brought to Europe by the colonial soldiers of the English and French armies and continued with a vast anti-Semitic repertoire singing the praises of the Fhurer who was restoring racial order in Europe.

Mario patiently let him finish, it took a good twenty minutes, without interruption, except to gulp down some Traminer.

"And so fortunately the Lord's anointed has arrived...the Fhürer Adolf Hitler, sig heil "

Mario smiled broadly.

"Ah finally someone who speaks clearly...you know," he said, lowering his voice, "they say that soon the German armies will march across Europe and crush the democratic plutocracies. Naturally Italy will be at their side and I can't wait to march alongside them...or better yet fly alongside them. They say that the Me 109 and the Stukas are extraordinary machines...

You see Mr. ....-Mario said

"Wirth, Professor Wirth," said the other, assuming a proud expression...

"of course professor, I can't wait, in fact I think we should already do something..."

He showed the ribbon of the Spanish campaign, I have already fought alongside the German comrades

I was above Guernica "

Wirth looked at him a little suspiciously: "But there were no Italian planes over Guernica...."

"But I was a guest on one of your Henkels, I was a very good friend of a German pilot, a certain Molder" he shamelessly lied.

"He was a fighter pilot if I'm not mistaken..."

"Of course Mario continued with the most granite-faced brazenness, but he had friends among the bombers and on Guernica they hosted us aboard a Henkel"

Wirth was in a swoon and asked him to tell him how things had happened, but Mario was hesitant.

"You know, professor, these are somewhat secret things. Strategic bombing is the key instrument of the war that will soon come... I'll just tell you, God forgive the Luftwaffe and protect the inhabitants of London, Paris and Moscow... well, even if He doesn't protect them, they deserve what they're going to get."

Wirth burst into hysterical laughter, attracting the attention of a good portion of the audience.

"Comrade, this is just what we need for the new Europe that we are going to build and eee...- He lowered his voice,-perhaps you could already do something for Germany..."

"don't tell me...really?"

Wirth looked around suspiciously, lowered his voice.

"You see, Captain, I am working on behalf of the Anenherbe on a very important project for the Reich. I won't explain to you what it is, you know," he said almost with an air of revenge, "it's a secret. However, I suspect that a member of the group, in reality it is a female, is betraying Germany and is passing information to the enemy...."

"What a shame," said Mario, who was beginning to hope for the unexpected.

"You know, she is protected from above, perhaps by some traitor from old Germany, but if I could prove her betrayal....

"and how can I help you..."

"Following her, photographing her as she meets with enemy agents, and telling me everything she does..."

I'll give you a very powerful Zeiss and keep you informed about her mouvments, so you can keep an eye on her.

"Dear professor, it seems like a magnificent idea to me...when do we begin?"

"Come with me".

They left the room and went upstairs where Wirth had an office set up for himself. The professor opened the door and let Mario in.

He sat him down in an armchair in front of the desk. He opened a drawer and took out a Zeiss Ikon, one of those that opened like an accordion. He took out five rolls of film and handed them to him. And then he explained to him in detail what he would have to do.

Mario nodded and memorized.

Wirth concluded: "Every time you leave the consulate I will let you know. You should be under the consulate at nine o'clock. I will give you a signal from the window overlooking the street.

"Okay, every day at 9...if I have to be busy with work...?"

Wirth took out his business card with the Anenherbe logo and wrote down a telephone number. He looked at it proudly. "It won't go through the switchboard, I'll answer directly."

"Good, everything is in order... Mario concluded with a broad smile"

He came out of the German consulate whistling, he had what he wanted in his hand, he could control Cinthya and M.lle Docteur.

He was in a bad mood for a moment, maybe he was going to have to see something he wouldn't like... but never mind, you can't have everything.

A BRILLIANT LOVE

They had parted with the agreement to meet again. Ettore had strong doubts, but he also knew that if he went with the Germans he would have no hope, while Sabine had assured him that it would be enough for the English if he did not work for the Germans.

He finished writing the copy of the notes, they had asked him to do something strange, but he had not argued and had done it. Now they were ready

There were a few days left, and that evening they had agreed to meet to work out the final details of his escape. He had written a letter that could seem like a farewell, because the idea was to simulate a suicide, but it left doubts because the more people's imaginations were excited, the more everyone competed to invent lies, and the more the truth was hidden.

He looked out the window, waiting for Sabine like a child waiting for Santa Claus. In reality, he had always had a somewhat complicated relationship with women. They liked him, but he was too introverted to be able to start a relationship.

Only with Sabine had he succeeded, because she had practically done everything. Then he had continued, because he found in that woman something that he had not found in anyone else; the feeling that she understood his tormented soul, full of doubts, sometimes arrogant because what he could understand, no one could understand, but also desperately alone because he felt like a being different from the rest of humanity. When he turned around in the classroom and saw the astonished faces of the students, he felt a sensation of emptiness inside him, as if he were an alien among primitive creatures. But he also knew that those people were not ignorant beasts, they were not savages from the Amazon, but students of physics and mathematics, therefore people with good intellectual gifts, and this made him curse nature that had endowed him with an extraordinary ability that was his cross, even if when he did his calculations he had the sensation of flying. He felt like a great composer who wrote on the staff the notes of a music that was the same voice of creation. A symphony made of galaxies, suns, planets, elements, energies and forces, that only he could describe.

Well Sabine was the only one who felt that music like him. The only one who knew those numbers were the magnificent grammar of the world, and who spoke his same language.

He heard a knock at the door. He approached cautiously and asked softly: "Who is it?"

"It's Sabine, open up..."

And he found her before him: a dazzling star, with eyes like two diamonds behind tortoiseshell glasses, freckles on her perfect nose like a sprinkle of gold and a dazzling smile in a mouth like a Greek statue.

He had never told anyone but it slipped out: "Holy virgin, how beautiful you are...!"

Her smile widened even more. "Yes, but let me in, if someone as fictitious as the Madonna of the Seven Sorrows comes along..."

Hector stepped back, and she came in like a spring wind. He stood there watching her, frozen like a cod.

She took off her coat, went over to him and hugged him. "Hi Sarracino...how are your accounts going?"

She whispered in his ear.

He remained silent, he didn't want her to stop hugging him.

Sabine walked away and smiled at him again: "well...you don't answer"

"I just didn't want you to keep hugging me," and she did.

Then they broke apart and Hector said, "I finished that job you asked me to do...but"

She put her hand over his mouth and caressed him. Then she began to undress.

When she was completely naked she looked at him, while he assumed an expression of ever greater amazement and happiness, and said to him: "Now what do you say we play doctor a little?"

It was a long, sweet exchange, a deep embrace between two souls. It seemed as if time had stopped, as if they had ended up in the quantum dimension of two soul mates.

They reached orgasm at the same time.

Ettore was still, his eyes turned to the ceiling, enjoying that wonderful feeling of completeness, they remained still next to each other for a time that seemed to never end, then

Sabine touched his face. "Saracino, you and I need to talk...."

"I know," he said, "tell me."

"First of all, I confirm that my superiors have accepted your proposal. You will go to a very distant place, where no one will recognize you. However, I must warn you that you will be watched."

"How long will they watch me..."

"Forever...I fear"

"And you?" asked Hector.

She smiled a little sadly: "I'm afraid I won't be able to reach you. That's why I wanted to make love to you, I wanted something deep to remain between us, something that distance won't be able to destroy...."

He looked at her: "Do you also feel the same way I do..."

"The feeling of experiencing your own emotions, your own sensations, the idea of mathematics playing like a symphony explaining the universe...?"

Ettore was amazed, it seemed as if she had read his mind.

"Yes, that's exactly what I was referring to..."

"The answer is yes...but unfortunately this will not serve to keep us together. It is part of the conditions for your salvation. I will interpret your calculations..."

"So you will build the weapon...'"

"You know very well that this is not something that one person can do alone, your calculations will speed up the process...that's all. But either I go with them or you go and it seems to me that the second option is not practicable."

"How do I escape....."

"This is a little secret, but you will still be boarding a ferry to Palermo on the 25th.

Have you prepared the letter I asked you to write to your family and to Carelli?

"Yes, certainly...."

"Well, on the morning of Friday the 25th you will go to the university and hand over your notes to the person we will indicate to you, then you will withdraw all the cash you have from the bank so.........................."

Hector listened with great concentration.

"At this point, everyone will believe that you threw yourself off the ferry.....instead.....

THE GRAND FINALE....IS ABOUT TO BEGIN

PORTUGAL

Fleming had come back late, as usual. After playing a bit at the casino he had gone to see some friends. They had chatted and drank until late. There were some ladies, who played whistle and some sons of rich colonial owners, in the mother country to study. Jan frequented that environment that guaranteed him a quiet life far from curiosity and risks.

There was a sealed envelope addressed to him on the table in the room, where breakfast was usually served. He checked that the seal had not been tampered with, then opened it. There was a typewritten note informing him that a telegram would arrive for him from Germany that morning. He looked at his Patek Philippe. It was 11:00, he would not be able to go to bed and rest. He went out and went to the post office, where the usual old man dressed in black with the classic Portuguese cap was waiting for him. He handed him a small, square yellow envelope.

Jan opened it was in code.

He returned to the hotel, took the Bible and opened it. Inside was the decoding grid.

The text ordered him to meet Agent Baccara, two days later.

He went to the usual private airport in Estoril, where a Dehavilad Dragon took him and three other people to Bordeaux, France.

Here he boarded a German plane that took him to Berlin. The long complicated journey was the consequence of the Spanish civil war that was not yet over and made the direct route to Berlin impracticable.

He followed the usual procedure, but this time Baccarat did not meet him in his offices at the chancellery.

Carl Wolf was in civilian clothes and Baccara was also wearing civilian clothes, the house was in a suburb of Berlin.

Baccara had a thoughtful look and at the arrival of Bindung / Fleming, he seemed to wake up from a hypnotic sleep. He made the Englishman sit in an armchair in the living room. And he began.

"You must inform your superiors that our Führer has decided to expand German living space to the East. We have started with Austria, which will be occupied on March 12."

Fleming looked at him with his usual metallic gaze but couldn't hold back a little exclamation: "well..."

Baccarat waved him off.

"This is only the first step, the Führer is aiming much further east....he wants Russia, with all its raw materials and its spaces. By August 1939 we will occupy the Czechoslovak Republic and then Poland. We will do this by stipulating a partition agreement with Russia.

A brilliant trick of the Führer. Thanks to the unwillingness of the allies to collaborate with the Russians, Stalin will fall into the trap. "

Fleming was quite surprised. Why was Baccrà telling him these things. It is true that he was paid by the English and probably also by the Americans, but this was a real betrayal.

Baccarat had risen. He was tall and massive, and his figure obscured the large window of the room where they were.

"You tell your superiors that I am convinced that the attack on the Soviet Union by Germany alone is an unpardonable strategic error. It is necessary to have the support of the West, England, France and especially the United States. Without their support or their neutrality this operation will be a failure and the end of Germany........and the triumph of Bolshevism.

We must find an agreement for the division of Europe and obtain at least the neutrality of the capitalist powers...."

Wolf was impassive. Fleming was silent for a moment.

"Sir, this is a proposal that must pass through high-level diplomatic channels. I am merely a messenger."

"You will report to your superiors. They will take care of the rest."

In the black Mercedes taking Fleming/Bindung back to Tempelof Airport, Wolf was silent for a few minutes. Then he closed the divider between the back seats and where they and the driver were and began.

"Mr. Fleming, what do you think...?"

"I don't think, I'm just a messenger..."

"Well, I have some ideas. The English will never accept our friend's proposal. For about four hundred years they have been working to prevent a Russo-German alliance. No, I know what the English want, and the Americans too. A Germany reduced to what it was before the Peace of Westphalia. A mess of feudal microstates. I know what Churchill has in mind... I know exactly. Two thirds of Germany in his hands and in those of the French and Americans and the other thirds in the hands of the Russians."

The Englishman was perplexed. "Well, I would say that his ideas are anything but bizarre...but why do you tell me?"

"Because I need witnesses in my favor. You see, I know that we will lose the next war. Because there will be a war. I am sure that an attack on Poland will not please the English and French. A war will break out. A big one, European, indeed world war.

And we will lose her, as always, do you know why...?–

Fleming shook his head–

Because the Americans will enter the war. It is too good an opportunity to become definitive masters of Europe..."

"But you said that... a third will end up in the hands of the Russians...??

"Of course, the third one that doesn't count for anything: Poland, Hungary, Czechoslovakia, a few Balkan states.

Nations that were never nations. A mere mattress between Russia and us. Countries that have been divided since the time of Charlemagne."

"You didn't tell me why you are talking to me about this..."

"Of course. So, we will lose the war. As usual, there will be some psychopath who will want to make the Germans pay for this feat of wit. I could be an ideal victim. SS General, close to Himmler and Hitler. I will need reliable witnesses, like you, that I was not exactly on the wrong side...you understand. Besides, I would not like to end up in the Russian third of the new Germany. The Communists will not be gentle with us"

"Of course I understand."

"But what do you think will happen to Baccarat..."

"Too high up to let the Russians take him. Too high up to waste his contacts in Eastern Europe. They'll send him off to South America to live the good life. Cowmen, Whores and a few trips to strategic places..."

They had arrived in Tempelof. The usual Dehaviland Dragon was waiting.

"So you will return to Portugal. You will contact your superiors. Tell them what Baccara said. And remember what I told you..."

Fleming returned to Estoril. Damn this job was getting interesting. He had to inform Churchill, and someone else too: WB. He had received a letter from that strange character he had met at a strange party in Massachusetts together with Catherine Hepburn and Howard Hughes. Along with the letter had arrived a copy of FS Fitzgeral's "Tender Is the Night", which served as a coding grid. WB was always very imaginative and refined in his things.

MARBLE HEAD

WB finished feeding the Chipmunches. He did it at the same time every day. They would come over and hang out in front of the house patio. He would come over and hand out nuts. Then he would go back in for breakfast.

The butler delivered a telegram. It had arrived at the telegraph station in the basement of the house. It was in code.

He took the book, identified the reference pages. He inserted a series of numbers into a coding machine and a series of other numbers came out, referring to words on those pages. A somewhat lengthy job, which he preferred to do alone.

He read the text.

He stood still, motionless for five minutes. Baccarat proposed an agreement, to avoid war.

But the price was too high. The Anglo-Saxon world could not accept it. This power bloc in Europe. Hitler dominating the East. Absolute madness.

We had to talk to the English. But to whom.

Lord Alifax was a limp. An elegant idiot, ready to compromise in any way to avoid a victory for Bolshevism. The Prime Minister, Neville Chamberlain was an absolute qverage man.

Winston Churchill, he was needed. But at the time he was out of government. However, it was to be expected that if the Germans had implemented the plan revealed by Baccara, he would have returned to prominence.

He personally telephoned the politician's secretary and set up an appointment with him, for three days later.

He called his friend Hughes and had a seaplane sent. With which he would reach Newfoundland, where he would meet with the English politician.

NEWFOUNDLAND

Churchill stood at a large window overlooking a bay. He held a Havana and a glass of cognac, and watched the clouds pass, forming patterns, obscuring the sun, then fading away.

WB came in: "Good morning Mr. Churchill"

The Englishman turned slowly: "Good morning Mr....

"WB, Mr Chirchill, WB"

"Ah, I guess you have a name too......"

"That you know well, ..."

"Of course," he gestured with his hand, "of course...and what are we doing here, Grand Master?"

"I have some news for you..." WB said nonchalantly.

"Important news, I suppose, to make me travel all this way, and come to this place with the horrible climate, especially for a weather-sensitive person like me..."

"You be the judge... but first take a seat...."

Churchill looked around, saw a leather armchair, which he indicated with his hand where the glass of brandy was... "You allow me to sit there..."

"of course," WB replied.

"So, Count of Blemheim, we both know that an interesting proposal has come from your agent Baccarat...."

Churchill puffed out smoke: "Already it seems that his puppet has freed himself from his bonds and wants to play on his own..."

"Of course, unfortunately it has escaped our control, but we continue to control many important Nazi leaders: But can I ask you for an opinion on the project?

"Soon date: NO, I will stop that Kraut pig before he gets to Russia...I will not let him dominate Europe."

"You are not in government.........at this moment"

"It's true, but I will find a way to stop that madman, but above all I will move heaven and earth to prevent the formation of a Russian-German blockade, it would be the end of England and the Empire"

"I agree with you. But I will tell you more. It would be a colossal obstacle to the project of my .....confraternity, that is, the control of the world by Anglo-Saxon capitalism."

Churchill made a strange expression.

"Mr Churchill, you know very well that the British Empire has no future. The Empire is too large, England too small to control it, soon you will no longer be able to keep Gandhi at bay in India, and when India falls, the rest of the empire will follow...."

"That miserable fakir..." the English politician muttered.

"Come on Mr Churchill, you know very well that it is not a question of Gandhi, a country of forty million inhabitants cannot control one that has five hundred million."

Churchill made the face of an angry child: "Well, well then," he exclaimed.

"Then we, Mr. Churchill, will help you take over the government. We will put pressure on you to take over from Mr. Chamberlain as soon as possible..."

"Do you think you can manipulate me...?"

"No, we think you will do what you want, which is to crush Hitler. We will help you convince the United States to enter the war on the side of England and France.

At the end of the war we will understand which direction the world is taking and you will be one of the leading men of this new world"

"At the end of the war, if there is one, the United States will be the masters of the world, and we will lose the empire..."

"Yes, but it would happen anyway, if you lose the war with Germany it will be a disaster for the world..."

"You could have thought about that before putting that puppet in charge of Germany."

"A mistake, but it happens, it has happened other times, the important thing is to fix it..."

"Even if it costs millions of deaths...?"

"The war will be a great opportunity to relaunch the American economy, this will also be good for Europe and England. The world is changing, we must ride the wave...."

"So you're telling me it doesn't matter how many people die?"

"I don't know how many will die, it depends on how the war goes and how long it lasts... but it is inevitable. What made it so were the serious errors of the English and French governments at Versailles.

"However, there is a way to make it last very little...."

"Come on, I'm English but my name isn't Merlin..."

"But you know he's trying to prevent the Germans from beating us to the wall in building that weapon...!"

"Oh, are you talking about Operation Black Sun?"

"Exactly, it must be concluded as soon as possible, it is only a part of the solution, but an important part...."

Winston Churchill fell silent. He took a drag on his cigar and looked intently at WB.

"It seems like it's almost over, let's hope everything goes well..."

"Let's keep our fingers crossed...in the meantime, what do you think about my proposal..."

Churchill smiled: "I see no other solution...unfortunately, I accept."

BERLIN

Obersturmführer Bindung greeted the guard at General Karl Wolf's door with an outstretched arm.

The SS man snapped to attention. Then he turned like an automaton and opened the office door.

General sat at his desk, his uniform as always impeccable, his expression impenetrable.

Fleming sat down and began to talk about a series of very general information on the financial situation of the SS Corps.

Meanwhile, he took a file of about fifteen pages from his leather bag.

Wolf took it and opened it. Inside was described what would happen from that moment on and what he should tell Agent Baccara.

Wolf read carefully. He made a strange expression, Fleming thought it was one of bitterness, but he had difficulty attributing similar feelings to his interlocutor.

Fleming knew that from that moment they would never see each other again. The Baccarat operation was closed. The accumulated money plus a substantial amount of pounds was transferred from the Portuguese bank where it was located to a bank in Montevideo.

The fate of Germany and Europe was sealed.

DIANA'S BETRAYAL?

Madamoiselle docteur's tongue darted between Cinthy's large lips, brushed her clitoris, causing shivers of pleasure in the young woman, who panted and felt her orgasm rising like a flood wave. She came like a river breaking its banks, grabbed Anne Lesser's face and kissed her passionately.

He let her kiss him and they stayed like that for twenty minutes, exchanging tongues.

Then they lay exhausted on top of each other.

The first to recover was the German one.

"We need to see each other more often, I don't want to miss this...."

"And what do you intend to do? Take me with you to Germany, perhaps you don't know, but I'm black..."

The woman froze, as if struck by lightning... "How black you are...?"

Cinthya explained the story of her family and herself, while the German spy listened.

"So my love it will be difficult for me to follow you, wherever you go...."

Anne's expression hardened: "It doesn't matter if you're black, no one will know and as for me, I have no prejudices..."

"But your bosses, they have some, right?"

"If we complete this operation, no one will dare to open their mouths. I will become very powerful, and then who will have the courage to investigate you?"

Cinthya looked unconvinced.

Anne tried to kiss her again, but she pulled away: "You are asking me to betray my country and come to live in a country that hates my race."

"No, I'm not offering you a privileged life in a country that will dominate the world. Those in charge can give a damn about coherence. In fact, that's the beauty of command: you can say what you want and do the opposite. No one dares contradict you."

Anne looked Cinthya directly in the eyes. "I have never felt with anyone what I feel with you, you will be my mistress" she said placing her head in the young American's lap.

Cinthya remained silent for a few minutes, then

"Okay, what do you want me to do...."

"I need to know when they will take him away and how they will do it..."

"But you know that he won't come to you by force, and if he does, he won't cooperate."

"We will give him everything he wants, all living things have a price, whatever his is, we will pay it."

"No, from what I've been told, he's not an easy person to convince, but I have the way..." Cinthya said

"And how will you do it?" M.lle Docteur interjected. "I know that...don't worry."

ACHILLES, DIANA AND THE CYCLOPS

The Cyclops has only one eye, but he sees like an eagle. Glass cut with Teutonic precision, and he has a memory of silver and celluloid, which remembers everything and sees two women exchanging cards: "click" makes the precise mechanism of his heart and the ray of light starts from the image and is engraved on the silver.

Achilles presses the button and that image becomes an indelible memory, a silent but clear testimony, perhaps of a betrayal, but who is the traitor?

Ms. Docteur seemed very tense: "I don't like this thing about a written contract, but here it is...."

Cinthya took the papers and put them in a bag she kept at her side.

"Is it signed by you...?" asked Cinthya

"Yes, for what it's worth, I can't commit myself to the Reich...."

"It's worth it for him, that's what he's asking for, to agree to meet you"

Cards are passed. Click, the cyclops records his celluloid heart records

Suddenly M.lle Docteur felt an urge to kiss Cinthya.

"I want to kiss you..." she said smiling

Cinthy blushed, looked inside, it seemed like there was no one there

He came closer and kissed her

Click goes the Cyclops, a scandalous kiss, for the heart of the Cyclops a memorable scene. But also for the heart of Achilles it is a stab. Achilles hopes that it is all a theater, but it could also not be so. It could be quite the opposite, it could be Cinthya who is about to betray who can say what they are saying. The camera does not have ears, Mario would like to have them. They say that men get excited watching their women have sex with another woman, but he fucking does not. He Cinthya really does it and this lesbian kiss does not excite him at all. But he must resist. But damn this is not his job, he wants to fly again. He wants to go back to the s79. Damn.

A few days pass. Cinthya arrives at the same place as the previous meeting.

Wait.

The Cyclops snaps.

A man arrives. He is thin and lanky, he looks like a Saracen. He wears a borsalino hat. He shakes her hand cautiously.

The Cyclops does not snap, maybe Cinthya is really betraying her family, but why. Maybe for love. Maybe her sexual perversion has overwhelmed her and she goes to the other side, to join that damned fiery-eyed whore, who arrives. She shakes hands with the Saracen. And they begin to talk. She speaks and he listens.

He took off his hat and turned it over in his hands.

The Cyclops doesn't shoot, but Mario's eyes do. He burns what he sees but he has to trust. It's the woman who gave him a daughter. She's black, she can't go over to the racists. She can't, you have to trust.

The German had a stony look. The man listened. He said: "You swear to me that the bomb will never be used..."

"You have my word. We will launch one in a desert area to demonstrate to the enemy that we have an invincible power..."

"How are we going to escape?" the man asked.

"The operation is scheduled for March 27th. Did he explain to you how we will do it, Cinthya?

"Yes, I will go to Palermo, I will stay there for a day and then I will return to Naples. I will disembark at the port and you will wait for me in a car outside the maritime station.

"We will take you to a convent in Calabria, where no one will look for you. From here, when we tell you, you will take a ship from Ancona."

The Saracen goes away. The women say goodbye. Cinthya passes a yellow envelope to Mlle Docteur.

The Cyclops snaps, sees an envelope pass from one gloved hand to another and records.

"There are two letters in the envelope," Cinthya says, "two farewell letters, one for my father and one for Mario... . I don't feel like giving them to him, you'll give them to him..."

"Certainly..." smiles M.lle Docteur triumphantly.

The Cyclops snaps, his celluloid heart records.

COVER-UPS AND SECRET CARDS

Carelli was preparing his lesson when there was a knock at the door.

He opened it and in front of him was a person he had never seen before.

He introduced himself: "Good morning, I'm Buttarelli from the Ministry of the Interior.

Carelli hesitated for a moment, those were the times when such visits were rather worrying. What did a policeman have to do with him?

The policeman, or supposed policeman, asked: "We should go into your office, it's a confidential matter.

Carelli made him sit down and sat behind his desk.

"Tell me Mr. Buttarelli"

The man took an envelope from his inside jacket pocket and handed it to Carelli.

"Open it," the man from the ministry told him, "it's for you."

There was a letter signed by the Minister of Education, the highest authority above Carelli, inviting him to follow the instructions of the person in front of him.

Carelli folded the letter and was about to return it.

"Keep it, it might come in handy someday..." he said with a slightly threatening tone and an inscrutable expression.

Carelli leaned slightly across the desk and the man began

"On the morning of March 25, Professor Maiorana will show up at this faculty with an envelope of documents that he will have to deliver to a person you will indicate to me.

This person will have to deliver these papers to you, who will keep them until I myself come to collect them.

You must not speak to anyone about this matter, you will tell the person who collects the papers that these are physics notes that Professor Maiorana was supposed to give you.

In the following days you will receive a letter and a telegram from Professor Maiorana himself. A few days later you will have to deliver them to the professor's family.

Whatever happens, you must strictly adhere to these instructions...."

"But," said Carelli, "it seems a bit strange to me... what is it about?"

The interior minister's expression became more severe: "This is a matter of national security. You must not reveal anything about this meeting and all documents from Maiorana that may arrive, except the notes I told you about, you will hand over to the professor's family."

He paused briefly and with a completely indifferent expression said: "If you were to reveal this conversation or the things that were said to you to anyone, not only would your career be at stake but also the lives of your son and...naturally, the lives of other people who are dear to you..."

He stood up, stretched out his hand and shook the one that the poor professor was offering.

"Good day professor..."

Mario exited the entrance to the physics faculty and headed towards Corso Umberto.

He didn't mind playing the part of the OVRA cop. He thought that poor Carelli must have literally shit himself.

He thought back to Wirt's expression when he looked at the photos.

A tyrannical face, and he exclaimed: "Damned lesbian, she's betraying the Reich with this American, it's clear she gave her some documents and the other one paid her.... Well, well the Reichfhürer won't be happy to discover that he's harboured a snake in his bosom..."

"Who?" asked Mario. Wirth's expression was even more triumphant. "But Himmelr, my dear friend, he himself..."

BERLIN

Wlather Wüst was the director of the Ahnenerbe, he had received a package from Naples via diplomatic mail. It was certainly Professor Wirth who was giving news of himself.

That package was for the supreme leader, for Heinrich, the master of the Nazi party.

Wüst was sorely tempted to open it, but he knew that the Reich Fhürer would not appreciate it, so he held back.

He picked up the telephone and dialed a number. An impersonal, male voice answered.

"I am Wüst, I need to meet the Reichsfhürer... tell him that it is the black sun"

There was a moment of silence. "Please hold the line a moment," said the impersonal voice.

There was a long silence, then the voice came back: "The Reichsfhürer will see you in an hour, come to the Gestapo headquarters." And he hung up without waiting any longer.

Himmler sat at his small desk. Completely devoid of any signs of work.

That chicken farmer's face, with its cold, expressionless eyes, always worried the professor.

The gaze passed through the glasses as if it were made of glass too.

He stared at Wüst with a questioning expression, as if the man had appeared out of nowhere, as if he didn't even know who he was.

"A letter from Naples, from Professor Wirth," said the head of the Anhenerbe softly.

His gaze remained empty, the Reichsführer ran a hand through his hair, which was pulled back and held in place with brilliantine.

He looked like he was falling out of the clouds. "Naples? What is it?" he asked with a dazed expression.

"I think it's Operation Black Sun, my Reichsfhürer...."

Finally the hierarch understood, his expression almost changed, as if he had become slightly more cheerful.

He opened the envelope. There was a long three-page letter and some photographs.

Himmler read, completely ignoring Würt. Then, without changing his impression, he looked at the photographs. He turned them over as if he could not understand what they were about.

He looked at his interlocutor again, as if he had never seen him before.

Then he exclaimed: "Damn, never trust women..."

The professor did not know what to say or do: "Certainly, my Reichsfürer....." he said cautiously.

"This M.lle Docteur......is a traitor, and I trusted her blindly....."

There was a hint of roaring anger in his voice.

He took a sheet of paper and wrote a concise, very short, ruthless order:" beseitigen!" , delete.

He handed the paper to Wüst. He remained frozen like a piece of stockfish.

Himmler stood up, went to the bookseller and took a book. He began to read.

The director of the Ahnenerbe looked at him: "So," asked the Reich Fhürer, "...what are you waiting for, carry out the orders."

Wüst felt a kind of anger growing inside him, but he thought it best to control himself: "But I'm not a murderer, I don't have the slightest idea how it's done... what should I do?"

Himmler looked at him again as if he had seen him for the first time in his life.

"Mmmhh, that's true... Tell Wirth to sort it out himself... but... get rid of that viper" he shouted.

THE FANATIC AND THE AMAZON

Karl Wolf

The Reich Fhürer did not often summon him, but he did visit him periodically. The SS tyrant was a touchy little guy and liked his collaborators to pay him frequent homage. Wolf decided that that morning was a good time for the periodic visit. He notified the secretariat and asked for an audience. It was granted to him at eleven.

In the bathroom near the office he checked that his uniform was as usual impeccable, Himmler was very keen that uniforms were ironed and sparkling. Wolf had opted for the black uniform. It wasn't exactly the gala one, but it was more formal than the gray-green one, he wanted to make his boss think that he paid him special deference.

He left the bathroom, and from the office, took a thin sheaf of papers with some unimportant information to use as an excuse for the visit and put them in a leather folder. Then he left the office and walked towards the realm of the Reich Fhürer.

When he was near the large door that separated the chief's area from the rest of the headquarters, he saw Walther Wüst come out, holding a sheet of paper in his hand and looking slightly annoyed.

"Heil Hitler, Professor," exclaimed the general. The professor responded with a somewhat limp salute.

"Sigh heil my Gruppenfhürer. Are you going to the chief...?"

"Of course," replied the general.

"He's not in a good mood"

"Ah," Wolff replied with a questioning expression.

"Operation Black Sun... it seems the madam is cheating..."

Wolff heard a bell ring from the gun

"As if betraying..."

"Well, I don't know, it seems that Himmler had her checked and she's passing information to the enemy, and he gave me the order to eliminate her. I really don't know what to do, Wirth will be a burden..."

The general shuddered. If they eliminated Mlle Docteur, the operation would certainly fail.

And then Elsbette Muller cheating seemed so out of this world to him.

Wüst had meanwhile decided to go, he gave the lazy salute again and walked away.

The general's mind was in turmoil. He had to go to Himmler now, but there wasn't much time to waste. Luderitz had to be warned to do something. But what?

He went into the Reichsfhürer's house and after the usual pleasantries listened to him for two hours. He raved about living spaces and the great Reich of the future and how many marks all this would bring him, and how great Germany would be and how much better the world would be without Jews. Meanwhile Whürt sent the executive order to Wirth......

Wirth

He looked at the paper in front of him. It had arrived with diplomatic mail, strictly reserved for him, from the secretariat of the Ahnenerbe and there was an executive order, handwritten and signed by none other than Reichfürer Himmler.

Wirth looked at it over and over again, it was what he had been waiting for weeks, he could finally free the Reich from that infamous traitorous lesbian. Of course he would have liked her to be tried and shamed in front of all of Germany, but sometimes you couldn't have everything, the idea of seeing her die was enough for him. Of course he would take control of the operation.

He took his Luger, a souvenir from the war when he had been an officer on the Eastern Front, from the safe. The weapon was always perfectly oiled, the magazine inserted, with its eight pyramid-shaped bullets, shining like gold.

He touched the knurled-cheeked stock. He gripped it and pointed it at the wall. Yes, he could finally use that marvel of

German technique again. See the knee joint rise and the case come out. Feel the recoil in his hand. It was an almost orgasmic feeling.

And he knew when he would try it. The next morning the lesbian would go out at 9, dressed as a man to go and see her slut, he would follow her and kill her in the alleys of that rotten city.

Gallione

Inspector Gallione looked his five agents in the face: "Men, tomorrow morning we were going to raid the hideout of Gaetano the stinky rat , you know he holds the heart of a Lyon, he's a stinky guy who always carries two knives and a gun...so don't make me excuse him, as soon as he makes any gestures shoot him...and be careful not to shoot each other...Please!".

All five nodded.

Gallione was worried. Gaetano the mouse, despite his name was a ferocious beast, he killed like drinking a glass of water, in particular he hated the policemen, since one of them had the bad idea of shooting him and crippling him for the rest of his life.

They had received a tip, he was hiding in a basement in Vico Conte di Mola. The informant had said that he was inside the basement all day and came out at night. But he didn't want to take any risks. They would have watched the basement all day, they were just waiting for the signal from the informant to reach the alley. He already knew where to put the men. Of course it was a nightmare operation, they had to wait for night and break into a hole in the wall where bullets bounced everywhere, where "the rat" would satisfy his bloodthirsty desires by killing a couple of officers, before getting killed, assuming he didn't have an escape route hidden in some wall.

Mario

Wirth had let him know that he would not be needed that morning: which meant. Evidently his work as a photographer had worked!

In those days he had avoided talking to Cynthia about the things he was doing, even though a worry was gnawing inside him, was what he was doing with M.lle Docteur really a diversionary maneuver? Something told him yes, and a malicious and remote voice told him no, but malicious and remote voices were the enemies of teams of agents, but sometimes the friends of the success of spies. So he decided to go out that morning too and follow the madame. He still had to carry out the orders he had received: M.lle Docteur had to die, how? ...Yes, he hoped to avoid being the murderous hand.

Wirth

He didn't go to the office that morning. He posted himself not far from the German consulate and waited for his victim to come out. He clutched the butt of his Luger in his right hand and waited.

He saw her, she was dressed up, as she often did. This time she had chosen the character of the accountant, with a fake beard and a bowler hat on her head. She was shaking her hips slightly as she walked... as usual.

Wirth left him a few meters and then set off in pursuit....

Luderitz.

He entered the consulate, a bearded man of short stature was just coming out of the door. Luderitz didn't notice him and continued on. His contact in Naples had asked him for a fairly large sum in marks to help him on his mission. He needed to withdraw cash from the till.

He entered the office and saw an envelope on the table. It was a dispatch from Berlin, from General Wolf. He decided that it took priority over everything. He opened it.

Damn! He ran to M.lle Docteur's office. Empty! Shit!

He had to stop Wirth before it was too late. He went to the Ahnenerbe man's office. He knocked on the door...no answer. The door was locked. He called. Nothing evidently the madman was already outside.

Suddenly he remembered the man he had passed at the exit. It was her. He ran down the stairs into the street. Too late, there was no sign...Damn where the hell could she have gone.

Gallione

The Shelter of the rata, was located in front of the exit of the "Trinità degli Spagnoli" hill. Right at the beginning of the hill there was another shelter and above it a small apartment with a balcony overlooking the alley. Further on another alley where men could hide was called "Vico d'affitto".

In front of the Basso in Trinità degli Spagnoli sat an elderly woman.

Gallione had put on a commoner's suit. In those parts everyone knew each other and someone dressed even just decently was immediately identified: either he was a thug or he was a cop.

He walked past the shelter and decided to poke his nose in.

He turned to the woman. "Would you please offer me a glass of water?"

The lady sighed and shouted: "Luciaaa...Luciaaa bring this boy a glass of water!!"

The curtain blocking the entrance to the house was drawn aside and Gallione glimpsed a room where there were at least three children and a young woman, barefoot and wearing a shabby dress, who brought him a glass of water.

Gallione drank calmly and in the meantime looked around. He excluded any possibility of basing himself in the basement and hoped that the door would close at night, he thanked and returned the glass, continuing up the hill to Via Trinità degli Spagnoli, where he slipped in and continued to Via Toledo. He went to the police station and decided to return to the alley and do a reconnaissance with his men.

Great confusion

The man walked quickly, he was not very tall, he was dressed in dark clothes, a color between black and brown, the tie was black, the beard that framed that pale face was dark like the suit.

The woman was sitting in front of her vase and watched him approach....

Wirth

She, disguised as a man, walked quickly, had been following her for half an hour, had not noticed anything. Wirth was waiting for the right moment, convulsively gripping the butt of his Luger

The alley was wide enough, a little further ahead you could see the mouth of another alley on the right. He decided he had to strike now, there was a chance she might turn, he had to strike now, even if there were more people than he had expected, he would take better advantage of the confusion, he quickened his pace. Had he cocked his gun? Damn, no! He took it out, pulled the bolt lever with force, lengthened his pace further and saw the back of his target's head in front of his sights...

Gallione

He was walking down Salita Trinità degli Spagnoli, his people were following him at a distance, each on his own, their eyes open. He saw the old woman and passed in front of her, along Vico Conte di Mola a strange little man was coming, he saw someone approaching the little man. A tall man with a green raincoat and a floppy hat...

Damn he had a gun in his hand, a Luger....

Mario

he had been following him for a while and saw him moving through the alley, dodging people passing by, following that strange guy with a beard and a bowler hat.

Then he saw him accelerate, take out a gun, cock it and fire two shots at close range into the back of the little man's neck.

Wirth

the gun roared twice, the skull of the little man in front of him seemed to explode the bomb hat went flying. The man collapsed

Gallione

The woman sitting in front of the basemente entry began to scream: "Madonna they are killing each other".

His hand ran to the holster, grabbed the Beretta 32 and cocked it, shouting: "Stop, Police!"

From the basement in front of the Trinità degli Spaniards climb, Gaetano the rat, came out, with two Glisenti in his hand and began to shoot wildly.

Mario

He saw a man in a T-shirt and underwear come out of a basement with two pistols in his hand, who without aiming fired wildly. Wirth was holding the Luger which seemed to be jammed. The first two bullets from the man in underwear's pistol hit him squarely and knocked him down.

Gallione

He heard two bullets whizzing by a few centimetres away from him, splinters of the wall he had hit him, he aimed his Beretta and fired, missing the target – "Oh my God, he's going to kill me now" he thought.

Gaetano looked at him with a ferocious face, pointed one of his Glisentis at Gallione, but a flower of blood exploded on his forehead. Gallione turned and saw agent Pasquale, with his Beretta in his hand, still smoking.

Mario

The alley had turned into hell, people were screaming, there were three people on the ground. The little man, Wirth and that guy in his underwear.

He turned and walked away, he had no intention of being found in those parts. The little man was M.lle Docteur in disguise. Her red hair smeared with blood was scattered on the pavement. His mission was accomplished, even if he hadn't exactly been the one to accomplish it.

Luderitz

The phone rang. He answered. It was a guy from the police station, one of the OVRA men.

He said, "There's a mess here. There are two dead Germans in an alley. One is a woman disguised as a man..."

Luderitz let out a heavy exclamation. The transvestite was certainly M.lle Docteur, but the other one. Almost certainly it was that idiot Wirth, who had carried out Himmler's orders.

"Hello..." said the voice on the phone. "Can you give us some explanations...?"

"yes but you come to the German consulate..."

"Okay..." came the voice on the other end of the phone.

THE ESCAPE

Hector March 24, 1938

He walked slowly along Via DePretis, in the direction of the University. He carried a leather bag, worn and full of papers. Some were simple physics notes from the last lectures. Then there was a yellow envelope, that one had to remain closed, there were the calculations needed to build the bomb, starting from the production of enriched uranium, up to the configuration of the critical mass, those had to be passed on to Sabine, in exchange there was the guarantee of escape and freedom.

The agreement was that he would deliver the papers to a student in the physics course, a girl from Salerno: Gilda Senatore.

As usual, there were only a few students. Majorana leaned inside, saw the Senatore, and he waved at her and called out, "Miss Senatore...". The girl was thinking about something else, she saw him and remembered what Professor Carelli had told her. "Majorana will bring you some notes, give them to me as soon as you can...and...please don't talk about it with anyone...with anyone".

The girl came out, Majorana looked strange, more than usual, he seemed worried. She handed him the papers and said: "Then we'll talk about it......".

She watched him walk away, elusive as usual, mysterious and shy like a wild animal.

Ettore March 25, 1938, approximately 5:00 p.m.

He looked around. The letters to h family were on the dresser. He looked at his purse. Inside was the second copy of his notes, the second copy the one with some changes....

He had been to the bank and to the University secretary's office where he had withdrawn his last salary and all the cash he had. He had put it in a suitcase. He left the room, went down to the concierge's office, paid for his stay at the reception.

Then he went out and headed for the port. The ferry to Palermo was waiting for him. They had told him to walk so they could see him walking toward the port.

March 26, 1938

The concierge at the Grand Hotel del Sole was busy checking the guest register. He didn't notice the man who had approached the counter.

He heard a cough. He looked up. In front of him was a guy with an olive complexion, very dark eyes and a melancholic expression, he looked like an oriental, a Saracen.

"Good morning," said the oriental, "I am Professor Majorana, I have booked a room..."

The doorman looked in his diary and saw the reservation.

"Room 32, Professor." He handed over the keys.

March 27, 1938

The doorman saw him enter, walked quickly past the reception desk and nodded.

"Good morning," the foreman replied hastily.

"But had he gone out...?", the doorman wondered.

Then he went back to his papers, those damn reports for the police station were a real pain.

March 27, 1938 late evening.

The professor appeared suddenly as usual in front of the doorman.

"Good evening, I would like to settle the bill..." the doorman looked at him, who knows why he was surprised by that departure, he felt like asking stupidly: "Are you leaving, professor...?"

The young man looked at him with a curious and questioning expression: "Yes. Excuse me if you ask me for the bill..." the doorman continued.

He quickly wrote out the invoice and handed it to the professor.

"Have a good trip..."

The professor took off his hat and waved. Then he disappeared, turning into the street.

Night between March 27 and 28, 1938

Strazzeri was busy, he didn't really feel like going to Naples that evening, but he had a commitment at the university. The man entered the cabin of the ferryboat from palermo to Naples, and looked around a bit. He greeted those present. The professor was reading and barely noticed the man. He saw him put his suitcase in the compartment and leave the cabin again.

The other one who was in the cabin was sleeping and was English. He introduced himself as Carlo Price. He spoke a slightly southern Italian without an accent. He was also rather stocky. He didn't have much English. But he declared himself English.

As soon as the newcomer came out the Englishman got up and quickly put on his coat and went out, as if he were in a hell of a hurry.

March 28, 1938, 10 am.

The ferry entered the port of Naples and reached the maritime station. Luderitz was waiting just outside the gates.

There weren't many people, he immediately saw his man, thin, dark skin, a borsalino hat, a slightly worried expression on his face.

He walked calmly, looking around.

Luderitz let him get a little closer then walked towards him.

"Professor Majorana," he asked. The other seemed surprised: "Ah, yes, of course," he said in a low voice.

"Shall we go?" asked the German.

"Certainly," the professor replied...

Luderitz looked around, no suspicious faces, a man in a coat, stocky and robust, who had arrived by ferry, passed by him. He seemed lost in thought. He headed towards the city......first he stopped for a moment, took a cigarette, lit it and took a couple of puffs

The car was waiting for them. The professor hesitated for a moment before getting in, then looked around as if it were the first time he had seen Naples, or perhaps because it was the last.

The car set off, heading towards the Camaldoli convent.

The professor had with him a bag full of papers. He held it tight like a castaway holds a life preserver,

Luderitz asked him, "Does it contain your notes, Professor...?"

The professor looked at him a little strangely... Luderitz repeated "they are your notes?" – pointing to the bag – "

"Ah...yes certainly..." he replied.

They arrived at the convent. The friars were waiting for them. They entered through the driveway. They were shown to a seat.

The professor seemed quite strange, you could tell after all he was taking a rather important step in his life.

The father who had received them accompanied them to the refectory.

"We can offer you our humble breakfast"

The scientist nodded. "Thank you very much, I'm rather hungry..."

The German also accepted.

They brought two cups of milk and coffee, some fresh bread and cheese.

Luderitz ate rather quickly, he had to reach Diebner who was waiting for him at the consulate.

"Professor, Professor Diebner would be very pleased to meet you, this afternoon is fine for you...?" asked the German.

The professor had his mouth full, and he nodded, swallowed and said: "Of course, of course, gladly..."

Diebner was in his office, waiting and drinking coffee, he had gotten up later than usual. He had worked all night on a problem, he hoped the professor would help him solve it.

The events of the last few days had shocked him. The deaths of M.lle Docteur and Wirth had fallen on their group like a thunderbolt, incomprehensible to a scientist like him who was concerned with the world of atoms and understood nothing of politics and espionage.

Luderitz had taken matters into his own hands. He was very glad of it.

Now he was waiting to meet Majorana. He had never met him personally, but

Heisembreg said that the man had an exceptional mind, he was convinced that if anyone could transform the many theoretical ideas circulating on the separation of the nucleus of uranium atoms into a bomb, it was Majorana.

He heard a knock and said, "Come in..." with a slight anxiety in his voice.

Luderitz came in. He had his usual impenetrable expression. They spoke briefly, then went out. It was 5:00 p.m., it was still light and a little less cold. It occurred to Diebner that March was a strange month. The first month of spring, but he remembered that it was precisely in March that he had caught the worst colds.

They arrived at the convent, the professor was waiting for them in a cell.

Diebnere approached him and shook his hand and then left in a small greeting of welcome among the German scientists.

The professor nodded with a quiet thank you. Diebner was a little surprised. The professor didn't seem very enthusiastic.

"Allow me, professor, to submit to you a problem we are working on. I wasted some time on it last night but I wasn't able to get very far.

"Um," said the professor, "I actually have a bit of a headache, you know my ailments...."

Diebnere couldn't hide a certain disappointment, but he made his move.

"Of course...we'll have time to discuss these things...maybe tomorrow.."

"Yes, indeed," the professor said with an almost enthusiastic tone, "tomorrow."

Luderitz's expression had changed imperceptibly.

"Now excuse me," said the professor, "I would like to try to get some sleep. You know, I suffer a little from seasickness and last night I didn't have a good night."

"Aaahh sure, sure.." said Diebner.

They left the cell.

Luderitz's expression had changed again slightly, he seemed annoyed.

The German professor interjected: "Colonel... everything is fine"

Luderitz was silent for a moment. Then he sighed. "But, I wouldn't shoot something doesn't add up."

"What do you mean?" Diebner asked anxiously.

"This professor seems a little... dazed...."

"Well, he said it, the seasickness, and maybe also the emotion of an event like an escape. I can understand that he is a little down..."

Luderitz looked at Diebner, spread his arms and said: "Well, I don't know, maybe you're right..."

Horst Luderitz did not sleep all night. It did not happen often, but that night it happened. A kind of obsession had taken hold of him. There was something wrong with the professor. There was something wrong with the whole affair.

They returned early in the morning. The professor was in the refectory having breakfast. He said goodbye and continued calmly eating.

Diebner waited patiently. He held the bag with his notes as if it were a child,

Finally the professor finished.

He suggested going to the cell that had been reserved for him. Diebnere followed him. Luderitz decided to stay outside. He went into the cloister to smoke a cigarette.

Professor Diebner explained the problem. The other waited until he had finished. Diebner waited a few seconds then asked: "What do you think, could......" and went into a long mathematical lucubration on the possible solutions, the other waited watching him attentively.

Diebner finished, looked at the other who gave a slightly goofy smile and said: "I haven't the slightest idea...."

Luderitz saw Diebner emerge from one of the arches leading into the cloister.

She had a shocked face and was shaking her head while still clutching her bag.

He approached the SS man and shook his head again. "Well?" Luderitz asked.

"They made fun of us. This man is not Majorana, he is a lookalike and has no idea what physics is...."

How could they have been fooled like that, how the hell could they have passed off a loser, a Closhard, as the professor, and above all him, who should have recognized him, how could he have made such a huge mistake? He took out his wallet and looked at Majorana's photo, then looked at the man, damn him, two peas in a pod! He had fallen for it like an idiot, he should have checked, the scientist had been in Germany, he must have spoken German, the fact was that they hadn't expected a joke like that, but above all there was now a huge problem for him; in Germany they would have massacred him. He had to find a solution, immediately.

Mario looked at the little girl sleeping in the cradle, she was becoming more and more beautiful, the strange thing was that she had something of her grandfather, Count Carlo and this made him laugh an irresistible laugh, seeing the expressions on the face of that little girl and imagining them on the austere face of the old engineer made him die of laughter. Cinthya entered at that moment, she saw him laughing out loud and looked at him, with an expression somewhere between amused and amazed. "Why are you laughing so much?" she asked him, he explained, and she smiled in turn, she didn't know Grandpa Carlo and therefore couldn't grasp the hilarity of that resemblance, but she saw that Mario was happy to recognize in his daughter the familiar traits of the people he loved.

THE END...FOR THE MOMENT

THE EXCHANGE

Diebner had the expression of a child who has found no presents under the Christmas tree. Luderitz for the first time in his life felt an unpleasant sensation, an expectation that did not promise anything good, the feeling that the future had dark shades, he was afraid. What would they tell their superiors. Their "prisoner" was sitting on an uncomfortable chair in a corner, looking at the tips of his fingers, with an interest worthy of a better cause. His expression seemed resigned. Luderitz looked at him, and suddenly the fear disappeared, he felt relaxed and strangely serene. Yes, the man in front of them could help them get out of that quagmire. In the meantime, they could ask him how he had gotten there, he certainly knew the details of that deception, or at least some of them. He felt like giving him a good beating, before starting to question him, just to "put him at ease", then the phrase put him at ease echoed in his head.... sure, put him at ease. Those who had sent him there had not done him a favor, so it would be easy to get him to this side of the barricade, without effort and without blood, which by the way would certainly have been Diebner's preference. He signaled the scientist to come closer and murmured his plan in his ear, he also told him to pretend to disapprove, then to feign disappointment, then to give the man a sympathetic look. This would put the hostage in a state of terror, at which point Luderitz would assume a friendly attitude, explain to him that they would not hurt him...if he did his part. This would make him relax and give in immediately, thanking his God, if he had one, that he had gotten away with it, at least for the moment and by the skin of his teeth.

Luderitz approached him, he had a slightly threatening look, sat down in front of him and began to stare at him. The man stopped looking at his nails, which otherwise appeared well-groomed, his hands were typical of someone who used them as a work tool, but a job of the kind that does not cause calluses, that instead requires agile hands, capable of dexterity: a cheat perhaps.

The German opened his jacket and took out a Luger P08, he gently pulled the kneecap which, moving the bolt back, loaded a 9mm Parabellum bullet. He placed the gun in front of him, looked the man in the eyes, being returned with a neutral look, by a resigned expression. "Tell me dear friend: why shouldn't I shoot you in the forehead... now?"

The man grimaced slightly, he didn't seem scared. He began: "You see, sir, I don't have a why, because I am philosophy, and in these circumstances, philosophy seems out of place. But I can give you some good reasons...".

Luderitz looked at him with a condescending expression, waved his hand pointedly and said: "Okay, tell me these good reasons."

"The first is that we are in a convent, and explaining to the fathers the presence of a corpse with a hole in its head would be a complicated thing.

The second is that killing me and making a body disappear in a country like Italy where the police don't want trouble, would cause some difficulties... the third, and I think it's the best reason, is that I could help you understand why I'm here... and not whoever I think should be here..."

Luderiz took the gun and emptied it, then put it back in the holster. The man in front of him could not have been just any man, he was certainly a player, and he had considerable self-control, it was worth listening to him; "well - he said - let's start from the last part".

"My name is Tommaso, Tommaso Lipari, I am from Mazara del Vallo, Sicily...."

He told of his misadventures with the game and how he found himself in Naples and one day met "O Maestro" and how he had trapped him, forcing him to do something that he really didn't want to do, but which he couldn't do without, at the cost of his life.

FLASHBACK

The professor walked close to the walls, in the alley, it was morning, very early, the streets were silent, deserted, not even cats were walking around at that hour. He was carrying a heavy bag, which seemed to bend his back. From the way Sabine had put it, everything was perfectly organized, but he still feared that someone was waiting for him, kidnapping him, stopping his dream of freedom forever. He would finally disappear, forever for anyone, he would go where no one knew anything about him and where he would stop dreaming of those frightening destructive clouds, which arose like demons from his scientific discoveries. Totonno and three of the Maestro's thugs followed him at a distance, they had been paid to protect him from possible attacks from the competition, even if the blow they had pulled off by simultaneously eliminating madamoiselle docteur and Wirth, must have put their opponents out of the game.

Tommaso was already on the ferry, they had put him in a crew cabin, in the locker there were sailor clothes, rather heavy, that the man he was supposed to replace would wear, there was also a life jacket, yellow, rather bulky, with a small lamp hanging from the lapel. He then wondered what he would do. They had promised to help him escape after he had been captured by the Nazis, but he wasn't at all sure they would succeed. They had put him in a situation from which there was no escape: either eat this soup or jump out the window. But he was a player and he already had a solution in mind, probability of success, he thought for a moment... maybe forty percent, not a lot, but not a little either. The ferry started moving, left the dock and crossed the Gulf of Naples headed for Palermo.

Westerhaupt was at the chart table, he had boarded Uboot 254 at 21 hours. The submarine had headed south at low speed and submerged, it had reached point 39. 13.700 14. 24.096. off the coast of Italy in the Southern Tyrrhenian Sea, more or less halfway along the route of the Naples-Palermo ferry. They were waiting for the ferry that had left Naples at 22 hours, it couldn't have been far away, Westerhaupt ordered the surface, they couldn't stay long in that spot, a busy area, where a turret would have raised a lot of suspicion; he climbed up into the turret, it was quite cool, and he had put on a sailor's jacket, with the powerful binoculars he scanned the dark horizon, towards Naples, slowly, about seven degrees aft of the submarine, some superstructure lights appeared, it must have been the ferry. The officer ordered the men to prepare.

Tommaso heard a knock on the cabin door, he opened it, the man in front of him was almost a photostatic copy of himself, he felt like he was looking into a mirror, the other man was also looking at him in surprise.

He entered the cabin, Tommaso told him: "let's hurry up, we don't have much time", Maiorana quickly put on the clothes that were in the locker, took the jacket, while the other one put on his clothes, all of them, including the underwear, this disturbed the scientist a little, Tommaso noticed: "professor, this is not the time to be picky, let's hurry. When they were ready they went out and went in two different directions, they had to hurry before the ship's guards changed. They found themselves outside along the edge of the ferry aft of the funnel, there was no one there, luckily, they looked out to sea, it was pitch black, then they saw a small bright light in the night, which flashed three times. Tommaso took a torch that he had with him and answered, from the other vessel came first two flashes, a pause, then two more. Maiorana had put on the jacket; Tommaso looked at him, he had climbed over the parapet but was hesitating: "come on, throw yourself in... - I'm scared, give me a hand - replied the other, Tommaso grabbed the jacket and literally lifted the man who was inside, who flew towards the sea.

Marjoram

He felt a hollow in his stomach, he was falling, he tried to stay as stiff as possible, so as not to hurt himself when he hit the surface of the sea, suddenly the impact, the cold of the still winter sea, his clothes immediately got soaked, the blow had slightly stunned him, but the cold water made him wake up, he turned on the lamp attached to the life jacket, which began to flash, the ferry was moving away rapidly. He was cold, he felt he was going to drown, but he resisted his desire to let go, his life jacket kept him afloat, the waves, not very high but of a certain force, tossed him around and made him swallow salt water.

Westerhaupt

He saw the lamp flashing on the surface of the sea, appearing and disappearing among the waves, he ordered the sailors to row with all their strength, the dinghy was not the best in those conditions, but thanks to the strength of the four sailors he managed to reach the shipwrecked man. While the other three tried to hold the dinghy still, the fourth grabbed Westerhaupt by the legs, while he leaned over the edge of the dinghy and grabbed the life jacket of the man overboard.

Marjorana

He was sure, he would be dead, he would sink and goodbye, then a powerful hand grabbed the life jacket, another grabbed another point of the life jacket and pulled it towards him, he realized he was hitting the almost soft wall of a dinghy, powerful hands hoisted him on board, he fainted.

Tommaso turned to check that no one had seen him, the sailors were arriving for the change, but no one had seen anything, they had been very quick, he was leaning against the bulkhead and was finishing, a sailor passed between him and the rail and greeted him politely, he responded trying to appear cheerful.

<u>The fission.</u>

On December 10, 1938, Fermi received the Nobel Prize in Physics "for having demonstrated the existence of new radioactive elements generated by neutron irradiation, and for the discovery, linked to the previous one, of nuclear reactions provoked by slow neutrons". In his acceptance speech for the Nobel, Fermi mentioned the alleged discovery of new elements with an atomic number higher than that of uranium, "which in Rome ... are usually called respectively ausonium and hesperium" (the alleged discovery dates back to 34-35; at the time, the proposal to name one of the new elements "littorio" was dismissed by Corbino with a joke: the average life of the substances was too short to associate them with the regime). In reality, no new element had been discovered by the Via Panisperna group: Fermi, "the Pope" was wrong, and had also chosen the wrong moment to make his supposition public. In the autumn of that same year [1938], in fact, Otto Hahan and Fritz Strassmann, in Berlin, had undertaken a very accurate radiochemical analysis of the elements produced by irradiating uranium with neutrons: among these elements they identified barium and lanthanum, both with atomic numbers much lower than that of uranium.

The result of Hahan and Strassmann (which Fermi learned in January 1939, when he was at Columbia University) seemed truly surprising. Yet the explanation was extremely simple, as Lise Meitner (a Viennese Jew who took refuge in Stockholm to escape Nazi racial persecution - a great figure, too often forgotten, of

20th century physics) and her nephew Otto Frisch (who took refuge in Copenhagen) almost immediately realized: the nucleus of the uranium atom, absorbing a neutron, splits into two nuclei with approximately equal atomic weight, between 38 and 58.

Niels Bohr - one of the fathers of quantum mechanics - was also convinced of the correctness of this interpretation and, in collaboration with Frisch himself, published a letter in *Nature* (February 11, 1939), in which the term "fission" was used for the first time. Lise Meitner had the idea of fission during a walk in the woods of Southern Sweden, discussing it with her nephew Otto Frisch, a young nuclear physicist exiled from Vienna and active in Niels Bohr's Institute in Copenhagen: the two fragments (nuclei) resulting from the fission have a lower mass than the original uranium nucleus. With this difference in mass, Lise Meitner, using Einstein's well-known formula from the theory of relativity $E=mc^2$, calculated the energy released during the fission. The result she obtained was about 200 million electron volts for each fissioned nucleus. With this decisive calculation, Lise Meitner laid the foundation for the experimental development of nuclear fission, for its future military use (nuclear weapons) and for its peaceful use (nuclear energy). A few days after the discovery, Otto Frisch returned to Copenhagen and told Niels Bohr about the discovery, who was leaving for a conference in the United States, who reacted by exclaiming enthusiastically: "What idiots we all were! This is fantastic! It must be so!"

Berlin 1948

Westerahaupt (the SS brother) helps the Americans for the Berlin Bridge, through Gehlen (see the book Service Secret. Through Ghelen he is fished out in East Germany to organize the network of the SD and the Abwehr to act as a signal of the movements of the Russian forces during the Berlin Airlift (Rusty organization)

Budapest, March 2011

Loengrin left the hotel with a great desire to smoke his Tuscan newspaper, and while Sara, his wife, had been announcing for fifteen minutes that she was practically ready, and his son, Alessandro, immersed in his new Nintendo 3ds, seemed to have now fallen into another dimension from which he could no longer be extracted, he had been seized by one of those attacks of "now I have to do it" as his wife called them, he had said goodbye and left.

Having descended the stairs of the Hotel Central Basilica, sliding his hand over the black iron railing in nineteenth-century style and emerging into the small reception area, which looked pleasantly new and tidy, he responded, with a smile and a nod, to the polite greeting of the doorman, who was standing behind the counter, and slipped out into the street.

Having set foot on the cobblestones of Hercegprimás utca, he stopped, took out his briar-root case with his half-stacked Garibaldi Toscanos, took one out, took out his Zippo and after the usual three empty shots, managed to light the tobacco butt. The strong smell of the cigar, together with the gasoline smell of the Zippo, penetrated his nostrils, giving him a pleasant sensation. He knew very well that gasoline and a Toscano cigar shouldn't have gone together, but he loved the dry, ammonia-like scent of spoiled Kentucky tobacco of the typical Italian cigar, what non-smokers called stink, mixed with the back-of-the-shop-of-an-old-garage fragrance of the Zippo, because they gave him a feeling of happiness, like a pleasant memory of a happy past.

It was pretty cold even though it was March, or maybe because of that. March is a silly month, they call it the first month of spring, but according to Loengrin it was just the last month of winter. He still remembered a time when, relying on this bullshit spring, he had risked being stuck with his department in a dump in Bosnia, where enough snow had fallen to make a polar bear shiver.

The one who pulled them out was a bulldozer from the Hungarian engineer battalion attached to the multinational force.

It was morning, around eight o'clock, the square in front of the cathedral of Santo Stefano was filled with a variety of people: groups of tourists accompanied by guides, who were waving unlikely objects used to be spotted by any undisciplined or distracted trippers or those who had not kept up with the group; people who were probably going to work; kids going to school, some "artists" intent on reaching their station from where they could pay homage to one or another muse and ask for a few euros in exchange... even accepting Fiorini.

Loengrin felt good, it was the first time he had taken a real vacation since he left the Army two years earlier to work for a large consulting firm that did security and defense research. The company had its headquarters in the United States, an office in London and one in Geneva, where he worked. Loengrin coordinated an office that did geopolitical and strategic analysis for various governments, some United Nations organizations and the Swiss government.

They had gone to Hungary to accompany the boy who played in a handball team in the Swiss city where the family lived, namely Loengrin Sara, Alessandro and three other children, two boys, Simone and Valter and a girl Susanna. The latter had remained at home with their maternal grandparents.

He was almost finished with his Tuscan, and he felt that feeling of impatience growing inside him that took hold of him when things didn't go as fast and as well as he would have preferred.

A kind of comic fury, which provoked in him an irresistible impulse to launch into interminable tirades, which then ended as they had begun, without any consequences, like a balloon that inflates, only to suddenly empty and collapse.

He was about to set off with his spear in hand, when the door of the Hotel opened and Sara came out, smiling and bright as usual, and Alessandro with his comic book character look, chasing his center of gravity, also with the same smile as his mother.

The attack of gruffness was nipped in the bud, the two smiles had the effect of a jet of water on a red-hot sheet of steel, suddenly cooled. The impetus with which Loengrin was starting towards the hotel door was blocked, making him almost lose his balance, his pissed off face, distorted into a comical expression, and the last puff of smoke that he was about to violently expel, went down the wrong way, making him cough and spit. Sara looked at him, with her transparent and cheerful eyes, waited for the involuntary consequences of the small repressed anger to pass, ran a hand over his hair, and with an attitude that would have made her slap him, she said: "here we are... honey, are you okay? Shall we go?", that let's go sounded almost like a reproach, almost as if he had been the one wasting all that time.

Loengrin recovered from his cough, sighed, and smiled too... storm over!

"Where are we going, Dad?" asked Matthew.

"We go towards Buda to see the castle, then we come back down, we go to see the parliament square, then we take Andrassy Hut to the park, then..." and he continued describing a long route, which would take them towards the evening to the restaurant "Alàbardos", on the Buda hill.

Sara looked worried, but said nothing, she was used to her husband's forced marches, after all a paratrooper was always a paratrooper, who seemed to regularly forget that the person accompanying him might not have served in some commando unit. Alessandro looked at him, opened his eyes wide and stopping in the middle of the road exclaimed: "Dad, I play handball, I'm not a marathon runner..."Well... – replied Loengrin – a little physical exercise won't hurt you and seeing this city will be useful, because, you don't know it, but our family history is very tied to Budapest... when I was just born I spent several months there, and your grandparents were also tied to this city, Alessandro changed his expression: "What grandparents, I don't have Hungarian grandparents!" "They weren't Hungarian... my parents... the ones you didn't know. Today I'm going to tell you a story that started a long time ago right here, I think it's right that you know where you come from..." he turned to his wife, "right Sara?" She looked at him seriously, thought for a moment and then said, convinced: "Yes, I think so, absolutely".

379

THE END... FOR THE MOMENT